Penguin Books
Mackenzie

Andrea Newman <!-- obscured --> brought up in Shropshire and Cheshire. In 1960 she graduated from London University, where she married while still a student, and then worked as a civil servant and a teacher before becoming a full-time writer.

Her publications include *A Share of the World* (1964), *Mirage* (1965), *The Cage* (1966), *Three Into Two Won't Go* (1967), *Alexa* (1968) and *An Evil Streak* (1977). *A Bouquet of Barbed Wire* (1969) was dramatized by her for London Weekend Television and *Another Bouquet* ... followed in early 1977. Her most recent novel, *Mackenzie*, was originally written for the BBC television series screened in autumn 1980. She has also contributed to other television series such as *Tales of Unease*, *The Frighteners*, *Love Story*, *Seven Faces of Woman*, *Intimate Strangers* and *Helen, a Woman of Today*.

Andrea Newman is divorced and lives in London.

Andrea Newman

Mackenzie

Penguin Books

Penguin Books Ltd, Harmondsworth,
Middlesex, England
Penguin Books, 625 Madison Avenue,
New York, New York 10022, U.S.A.
Penguin Books Australia Ltd, Ringwood,
Victoria, Australia
Penguin Books Canada Ltd, 2801 John Street,
Markham, Ontario, Canada L3R 1B4
Penguin Books (N.Z.) Ltd, 182–190 Wairau Road,
Auckland 10, New Zealand

First published 1980

Typeset, printed and bound in Great Britain by
Hazell Watson & Viney Ltd, Aylesbury, Bucks
Set in Linotype Times

Dedicated to Charles Price, property consultant, who generously provided all the business detail for the television serial, and to Colin Tucker (episodes 1–4) and Kerry Crabbe (episodes 5–13) who proved to be invaluable script editors.

Author's Note

This book contains both more and less material than the
television serial on which it is based, because it is written
from three viewpoints.

1955

Jean

Afterwards, she dated everything from meeting David and Ruth. They made him think of London and big money every time he looked at them. She had lived with the spectre of London for so long that she fancied she might control it. But now it was here, in tangible form, no longer a ghost she could exorcise.

She liked David and Ruth. She admired David's patient gentleness; she envied Ruth's vitality. She liked them separately and as a couple. Liking them made it worse. She would have preferred to dislike and avoid them because she could see, even then, that they were going to be an innocent source of trouble.

The evening that the question of moving came up began harmlessly enough. David had arrived from London for the weekend as usual, paid his customary visit to the hospital and been cheered to find his father much improved. 'He really seems to have turned the corner at last,' he said with relief.

Jean said, 'It must be hard, not being able to visit him more often.'

'Oh, I think he'd rather know I'm keeping the office running smoothly. So long as he sees Ruth every day, he's quite happy. I see his point.' He and Ruth exchanged affectionate smiles.

Robbie asked, 'Do the rest of the family get up to see him at all?'

'Oh yes,' Ruth said, 'they're very good. They've all been up.'

'For a day at a time.' David looked far from satisfied. 'Then they scuttle back home and leave Ruth to hold the fort.'

'I don't mind,' Ruth said. 'I'm fond of him.'

Jean believed her. She had first met Ruth at the hospital and had been amazed to discover that Ruth was actually renting a flat in Glasgow in order to visit her father-in-law every day. She had never heard of such a devoted family.

'She gets on with him better than I do,' David said, 'though I hate to admit it.'

Robbie laughed. 'Just like Jean and my mother.'

'Don't exaggerate, Robbie.'

'Well, you get on better with her than your own mother, don't you, hen?'

'Oh, families,' Ruth said, 'they're all the same. It's this dreadful business of loving people you don't like.'

'And then feeling guilty about it.' David was obviously talking about himself.

'Not me,' Ruth said. 'Guilt is counter-productive. I gave it up years ago.'

'It's all right for you.' David turned to Jean and Robbie. 'Her parents are in Israel. That's a good safe distance away.'

Jean envied her. 'I wish I could give up feeling guilty. My mother's such a hypochondriac I lose all patience with her. Then I think, What if one day she gets really ill and I won't believe her because she's cried wolf so often?'

'Oh, she'll go on for ever, more's the pity,' Robbie said. 'She's the original creaking gate. Did they say at the hospital how soon your father can go home, David?'

'Not really. They're being very vague.'

Ruth poured more wine. 'I can't wait to get back to London. Oh – no offence, you two, Glasgow has a charm all its own, especially when you make friends, but after a few weeks anywhere, even on holiday, I just get terribly homesick.'

'I know what you mean. I'm exactly the same,' Jean said. 'But it's a very good hospital. If they're being a bit vague, it's only because it's hard to tell with a stroke.'

David said, 'I suppose he's been lucky really. His speech isn't affected. And he's getting some movement back already in his arm and leg.'

The door of the dining-room opened slowly. Lisa Isaacs,

all of five years old and wearing a long nightdress, wandered in.

'Darling, why aren't you asleep?' Ruth pretended severity.

'I'm thirsty.'

'Oh yes?'

They all gazed fondly at Lisa and she stared back at them, a tiny replica of her parents: big dark eyes and glossy dark hair. Jean had always thought David and Ruth looked more like brother and sister than husband and wife, but that often happened with married couples.

'Can I have a drink of water?' Lisa asked, enjoying the attention.

Ruth smiled. 'Not very original, sweetheart, but yes, of course you can.' She poured water into David's almost empty wine glass.

'Ooh, it's pink.'

They all laughed. Lisa drank the water slowly, making it last, watching them all over the rim of the glass.

'Right,' Ruth said eventually. 'Back to bed.'

'Daddy take me.'

'No, Daddy's tired. You'll have to make do with me.' She scooped Lisa up.

Jean offered to clear the table.

'No, leave it.'

'It's no trouble.'

Ruth was pleased. 'Well, if you're *looking* for work, who am I to talk you out of it?'

She disappeared with Lisa and Jean started stacking plates. The men began to talk shop. As she went into the kitchen she heard Robbie asking David, 'D'you do much commercial property at your office, David, or is it mainly residential?'

Jean was starting to wash up when Ruth came in. She said, 'Hey, don't you bother with that.'

'It's the least I can do. That was a lovely meal.'

'But there's no need. David'll help me later.'

Jean was fascinated by this whole new angle on married

life. 'Will he really?' But she went on washing up out of habit.

'Oh yes.' Ruth seemed to take it for granted. 'He's very good like that. Isn't Robert?'

Jean laughed. 'If I had a temperature of 103 and both arms' in a sling and it happened to be my birthday, well, maybe then he would, but only as a special treat. Anyway, doing *your* washing-up's not like doing my own – it doesn't feel like work.'

'Well, it's very sweet of you.' Ruth put the kettle on for coffee and began to dry plates.

Jean said, 'Lisa's awfully pretty, isn't she?'

'Yes, I am rather proud of her.' Ruth looked gratified. 'I only hope we don't ruin her character, making too much fuss. It's always a risk with an only one – or so they say. I'm not sure myself. I think a bit of spoiling's a good thing for everyone.'

'I'm an only child too.'

'Well, you're certainly not spoilt. Just look at you now, doing my washing-up.'

The atmosphere was suddenly warmer, closer. Jean felt able to ask, 'Aren't you going to have any more children?'

'Only wish I could. I lost two before I had Lisa and then something got mucked up. I'm not sure what they said because I didn't want to believe it. You feel such a fraud – not like a proper woman at all.' She looked at Jean for agreement. 'Anyway, it's very unlikely I can have any more and of course we'd have liked a son as well.'

Jean said, 'That's a shame.' She felt inadequate: she had uncovered more than she had intended. 'I'm sorry.'

'Oh, you get used to it.' Ruth ground coffee briskly.

The terrible hunger welled up in Jean, uncontrollable. She knew she ought to be sympathizing with Ruth, but instead she merely envied her. 'I'd love to have a little girl.'

'Why not? Third time lucky. What's to stop you?'

'Robbie.' To her surprise she had actually admitted it. 'He's not very good at the baby stage and he's really had

12

enough.' She tried to make it sound reasonable. 'If they could all be born aged three, he'd be fine.'

Ruth said, 'But it's not really his decision.'

'Oh yes it is.' She wondered if she sounded as bitter as she felt.

'Well, it shouldn't be. Can't you just ... cheat?'

Jean thought about it. Ruth made it sound so easy. 'I'm afraid not.' What very different marriages they must have.

'Don't worry. I'm sure you'll find a way to persuade him.'

When they went back to the dining-room with coffee Robbie was saying, 'You know I started with nothing and now I've got a little – frankly, for the amount of money you get down there and the amount of work I put in up here, I've been seriously thinking of moving to London.'

Jean's stomach lurched at the sound of this old threat. 'You might have mentioned that to me.'

Instead of looking guilty, he smiled at her as if they were agreed on the subject. 'Och, we've often discussed moving.'

'Not lately – and you said it wouldn't be for years yet.'

'No, I think that's what *you* said.' He turned back to David. 'If a deal comes up, we'll go. It wouldn't make sense not to. And it could happen soon. I've only got these houses to finish, I'll be through in a few months. There's only one not pre-sold and I've got people buzzing round for that already. All I need is a small building site to make a start on – even outside London would do.'

'Well, I could certainly find you one,' David said. 'If you're serious.'

Ruth was pouring coffee and handing it round. 'But Jean doesn't want to go.'

'She'll come round – won't you, hen?' Again the heart-melting smile that had always won her over in the early days, making her feel she was the one person in the world who mattered to him.

'I'd rather we talked about it on our own,' she said.

'What's the difference? We're among friends.'

David said, 'What sort of price did you have in mind?'

Ruth turned on him. 'David, you're not to encourage him.'

'Darling, this is business. If Robert wants to buy a site, I can hardly refuse to sell him one. That won't stop him moving to London, it'll simply make him go to another agent.'

Jean felt suddenly weary. 'You're quite right, David. If he really wants to go, no one can stop him, least of all me.'

'You'll like it fine once you get there,' Robbie told her.

David said gently, 'Is it just London you don't like, or the idea of moving anywhere?'

'I don't know anyone in London.'

'You know us.'

Ruth said, 'Two swallows hardly make a summer. Honestly, you men, the way you assume your poor wretched wives have to follow you anywhere like sheep.'

'But surely ...' David teased her, 'you'd come with me to the ends of the earth, wouldn't you?'

'Yes, of course. Within a three mile radius of St John's Wood.'

They all laughed, grateful for even a small joke to ease the tension. Jean tried to explain.

'It's just that ... I grew up here. All my friends are here. My family, and your family ...'

'Well,' Robbie said, 'it's the same for me.'

'No, it isn't, because you don't depend on them as much as I do, you've got the business to think about twenty-four hours a day.'

'Exactly,' Ruth said, as if that settled the matter. 'David's just the same. That's why women should choose where to live, because they really care about the home, and men don't.'

David smiled. 'I think,' he said to Robbie, 'we should change the subject before we get hammered into the ground.'

'All right,' Robbie said instantly. 'I bought a shop today. Alexander's. Sweets and tobacco.' He sounded smug.

Jean said, 'What on earth for?'

'Because I think I've got a buyer for it. I know someone looking for a shop as an investment. I can do it up, sell it to him and make a quick profit.'

14

'Ah,' David said, 'you fancy yourself as an estate agent as well, do you?'

'Why not?'

'There *is* a little more to it than that, actually.'

'Well,' Robbie said with total confidence, 'I can learn.'

On their way home in the van Jean tried not to think about London. Instead she thought about David and Ruth, their tolerance and good humour, the atmosphere of warmth they created around them, and the beauty of Lisa. It was good to make new friends.

She said, 'They're nice. I'm going to miss them.'

'Not necessarily. If we go to London, we'll be seeing a lot more of them.'

How quick he was to turn everything to his own advantage. 'Don't rush me, Robbie, there's so much to think about.' It seemed more certain each time he mentioned it.

'There's nothing to think about, once we get the right deal. We just sell the house, pack up and go.'

The house. Did he not even realize how much the house meant to her? He went on talking about site offices and rented flats and how easy it would all be. She found herself becoming very angry and at the same time she wanted desperately to make love. The two feelings confused her.

When they got home, the babysitter left and Robbie went straight to bed. Jean lingered in the boys' room, ostensibly to tuck them in but really to comfort herself by looking at them. She knew she was reducing her chances of making love, for Robbie might well fall instantly asleep, but she needed to see her children: Duncan so vulnerable still and Jamie already so tough. She saw herself and Robbie mirrored, as if in opposition. Or was she reading too much into the childish faces?

When she went to bed the room was in darkness, so she undressed without putting on the light.

'Are they all right?' Robbie's voice startled her.

'Fine. I thought you were asleep.'

'Nearly.'

15

She couldn't resist touching obliquely on the dangerous subject. 'We're lucky to have Sandra, you know. They really like her. They're always good when she's here. Or your mother, of course. And that's about it.'

He said easily, 'Don't worry, they have babysitters in London too.'

She got into bed beside him. 'Don't go on about it, Robbie. I can't stand it. Not tonight.'

'All right. Not another word.'

Silence. She knew, of course, she was being unfair. It was all right for her to mention it but not for him. Still, he had been unfair earlier on, discussing it in front of David and Ruth.

'I love this house,' she said, unable to leave well alone.

'I'll build you another one.'

'You won't have time. You'll be too busy building them for other people.'

'Eventually, I mean.'

She said bitterly, 'Aye, that's what I'm afraid of. Eventually.'

'It hasn't happened yet.'

'Oh, I know you. And the boys are so happy at school, too.'

'There are other schools.'

His calm enraged her. He was so sure of getting his own way, because he always had. 'Don't we count for anything?' she burst out. 'I mean, don't our wishes count at all?' She really wanted to understand how he could ride roughshod over people and not even feel guilty about it.

He said, 'I'm doing it for you – all of you. Don't you know that?'

She almost laughed. 'That's a lie. You're doing it for yourself.'

He was unperturbed. 'I'd be a fool if I let a good chance slip.'

Suddenly all her anger evaporated and she felt only sad resignation. 'We've had enough good chances, Robbie, and we've grabbed them all. We don't need any more. We're doing well enough.'

16

'There's no such thing.'

She said helplessly, 'I can't answer that,' and turned towards him, expecting only a goodnight kiss but wanting more. He put his arms round her; the smell and the feel of him worked their usual magic. She was surprised as well as grateful when he started to make love to her. She always imagined that she wanted him more than he wanted her, not through any rejection of his, but because she simply could not believe that anyone else in the world felt as strongly as she did.

'I thought you were tired,' she said, teasing, loving him. He kissed her, not answering. She took a chance. 'Oh, Robbie – can't we have another baby – please –'

He said tenderly, 'Not this time.'

It was always a treat to see Robbie's mother. It made her angry about mother-in-law jokes, for the more her own mother rejected her, the closer she felt to Robbie's. She was sure he didn't appreciate her fully, having always taken her for granted. Being used to a mother who was warm and cosy and tolerant, he had no idea what it was like to grow up with a cold, narrow and bigoted one. Their marriage, she felt, had changed nothing for Robbie, whereas she had lost her own mother and gained his.

She even loved the messy, shabby interior of the flat, knowing how her mother would despise it. A real home, she thought, with no appearances kept up for the neighbours. Jamie and Duncan clung to Marie, Robbie's youngest sister, as she came out of the kitchen: they virtually hung from each side of her. She gave Robbie an insolent grin. 'Well, if it's not the great tycoon himself,' and he pretended to punch her. The children dodged away and Marie ducked behind Jean. 'How are you then?'

'Not bad, Marie. That's a pretty dress you're wearing.' She liked Marie too: she envied her confidence.

'Aye, d'you like it? I just made it.' She twirled round, pleased with herself. Another source of envy: Jean could not sew. She had tried, time and again, but it only made her bad-tempered. For Marie, it was easy.

Robbie said to his mother, 'All right if I use the phone?'

'That's why you had it put in, no doubt. It wasna for my benefit.'

He made an interminable call about the shop to his lawyer, Bill Campbell. Jean chatted with his mother and Marie played with the children. Finally he put down the phone. 'Now then,' he said, as if they had kept him waiting, 'where's that food you promised us?'

After lunch Marie took the children out. Jean had looked forward to that: she wanted to relax. But she also dreaded it: Robbie used these visits to check up on the family. Now, predictably, he said, 'Is Marie still going with that Lavery fellow?'

'Aye.' His mother looked innocent.

'Can't you have a word with her?'

'About what?'

'About getting rid.'

Jean, silent, felt guilty. Out there Marie was entertaining her children; in here she was being attacked.

'They like each other,' Robbie's mother said calmly, so calmly as to be almost provocative, Jean thought.

'Are you encouraging them?'

'I don't see why not. He's a nice lad.'

Robbie glowered. 'He's not good enough for her, that's why not.'

'I dare say this lassie's parents said much the same about you' – she looked at Jean fondly – 'and you've not done so bad.'

Jean said, 'Oh, come on, Robbie, you know Marie's in love with him.'

His mother looked gratified. 'And they've been going together a long time.'

Robbie said severely, 'She could do better for herself, that's all. Anyway, she's too young.'

'She's eighteen. Not much younger than you two were and I don't see you regretting it.'

Robbie took refuge in the newspaper. His mother and

Jean discussed his sister Ella, who was expecting another baby.

'She's always been lucky,' Jean said wistfully.

'Aye, that's true. She gets her own way all right. And why not?' She glanced at Robbie and caught him yawning. 'You look tired, Rob. Are you working too hard?'

'No more than usual.'

'I was thinking maybe you and Jean could have a wee holiday. You know I'd be glad to look after Jamie and Duncan.'

He brightened at once. 'That's a good offer. How about a weekend in London?' He turned to Jean. 'You enjoyed the last one.'

'I didn't know the real reason for it then.' She paused, trying to work out a strategy. 'No, I'm thinking maybe it's not you that's doing too much, it's me that's doing too little. Now the boys are both at school, I've got a fair bit of free time. I could go back to nursing.'

She kept a poker-face, but it was hard going. He looked so amazed and horrified she wanted to burst out laughing.

'Part-time, of course,' she added.

His mother caught on fast. 'Aye, the lassie's right. They're crying out for good nurses.'

Robbie said, 'I'd rather we talked about this at home.'

Revenge at last. Jean wondered why it was not as sweet as she had imagined. 'What's the difference? We're among friends, aren't we?'

He turned at once away from her, back to his mother. 'Mam, did I hear you say our Ella's having another one?'

'Aye, that's right.'

'She must have more money than sense. What's Jack thinking of, letting her wear herself out?'

His mother said defensively, 'They're both very pleased.'

'Well, I saw what it did to you, having four of us, don't forget, and I wouldn't wish that on Ella. She's not that strong.'

Jean was at once enchanted and furious at his protective tone.

'Och, she's as strong as an ox,' his mother said. 'It was

wartime that got me down, and losing your father. Ella's got a good man – she doesna want for anything. And she always fancied a large family, you must remember that.'

'She was always pig-headed, if that's what you mean.' He looked away.

'Aye,' his mother said drily, 'you have a lot in common.'

Jean felt it was time to change the subject. 'How's Margaret enjoying Aberdeen?'

Robbie's mother looked relieved. 'Och, it made all the difference changing hospitals. I canna say for sure, she hasna written a word about it, but reading between the lines, I think she's met somebody there. She's awfully happy all of a sudden and she can't quite decide when to come home; they keep changing her shift, she says.'

Jean laughed, more from lessening tension than the tiny joke. 'Yes, I know that one.' She would always be grateful to Margaret for introducing her to Robbie, when they were nursing together. 'What's she on now?'

'Men's Surgical.'

'Oh, she'll be having a fine old time.'

Robbie's mother looked doubtful. 'I don't want her fetching up with some cripple. I was hoping it might be a nice young doctor.'

Jean said soothingly, 'It probably is. But the patients on Men's Surgical do get better, you know, most of them. That's the whole idea.' She felt herself hurrying; she was aware of Robbie's impatience. The domestic conversation had lasted long enough for him.

Impervious to atmosphere, his mother went on: 'Well, I hope she has better luck than poor Princess Margaret, that's all I can say. That's who she was named for, you know. Margaret Rose. Och, I think it's a shame, they should let her marry whoever she likes. What's the good of being a princess if you canna please yourself what you do?'

Jean could practically hear Robbie's silent screaming boredom next to her, yet she wanted to be fair to Princess Margaret, and even more to Robbie's mother. 'I know it's hard, but there's no getting round it – he *has* been divorced.

20

In the eyes of the Church he's still married, so she's doing the right thing not to marry him. I admire her a lot.'

Too late she realized that she sounded merely as if she were sticking up for her own religion. But before she could work out how to put this right, the front door suddenly slammed. They were all startled.

'It must be Andy,' Robbie's mother said anxiously.

A man's voice called, 'Annie?'

'We're all in here.'

Andy came in, a big man, still in his work clothes. Jean was torn between feeling genuinely glad to see him and thinking no greater calamity could have befallen the afternoon. She could feel Robbie's tension beside her like a physical presence.

'You're early, Andy,' Robbie's mother said. She sounded worried. 'There's nothing wrong, is there?'

'No, I took a slice out of my hand, that's all.'

Too late Jean noticed the bandage. 'Let me see.'

'There's no need.' Andy looked cheerful as always. 'They fixed me up fine. How are you, lassie?'

'Not bad. It's nice to see you.'

He turned to Robbie. The pause seemed endless. 'And you, Robert?'

'I'm well.'

The hostility between them was almost tangible. Andy turned away. 'Is there any tea left in that pot?'

Robbie's mother jumped up. 'I'll make some fresh.'

'It'll do fine as it is.' Andy was always glad to be obliging.

'I'll go.' Jean went into the kitchen and put the kettle on. She heard Andy asking after the children and Annie telling him they were out with Marie. Andy said he'd like to see them.

Robbie said, 'Why?'

'I'm fond of them. You know that.'

'But they're mine.' Robbie made it sound as if Andy might contaminate them.

'If you two start all that again,' Annie said, 'I swear to God I'll knock your heads together.'

21

Jean went cold. They were going to have a row.

'Mam, I've been thinking,' Robbie said. 'There's a chance Jean and I might go to London to live. Nothing definite, mind, but the way things are going, it just might happen. You know I've always had it at the back of my head for one day. Well, if we do, you could have our house.'

Andy said, 'What for?'

'To live in.'

'But we like it here.'

'In this place?' Robbie's voice was full of contempt. 'But it's rented. It'll never belong to you. Don't you want a house of your own?'

'I can look after my own wife without any help from you.'

'And I've got a right to take care of my mother.'

Trembling, Jean made the tea. Robbie's mother suddenly shrieked, 'Will ye both shut up? I'm perfectly happy where I am. This is our home and there's nothing wrong with it.'

Jean went in with the tea. 'Whatever's all this?'

Robbie gave her a bland smile, as if his behaviour were perfectly in order. 'I thought it was time my mother had somewhere decent to live.' He turned back to Andy. 'It wouldna cost ye any more. I've only got a small mortgage and you could take it over. It'd be the same as the rent you pay here. You wouldna feel the difference, I promise you.'

Andy said, 'We'd feel it in our pride.'

'You speak for yourself.'

Robbie's mother said sharply, 'He's speaking for me too.'

'Oh God, Robbie, not today.' Jean felt helpless. 'It's supposed to be a happy day. I've got your present in the van. I forgot to bring it in.' She looked round anxiously at them all, wondering if it was safe to leave them. 'I'll not be a minute.'

On her way to the van, actually running, she almost collided with Marie returning with the children. They went back together, Jean clutching the parcel, and Marie sensed the atmosphere at once. 'Have we missed something? Dad, what's up with your hand?'

'It's nothing, hen.'

Mercifully the children were there now to distract and show off their ice-creams.

'Grandad, look what Marie bought us. I've had two.'

'Well, you're a wee pig, aren't you?'

Jean looked at Duncan. 'I hope *he* hasn't had two.'

Marie laughed. 'No, I thought better not, after that last time.'

Duncan said proudly, 'I was sick all over the van.'

'Yes, you certainly were.' Jean remembered it well.

Marie said, 'I got him a bar of chocolate to make it even.' She handed it to Jean. 'You can give it to him later.'

'Much later. Thanks, Marie.'

Duncan tried to grab. 'I want it now.'

'You'll have to wait. You're no a good traveller.' She put it away safely and held out the parcel to Robbie's mother. 'Mam, this comes from both of us with lots of love – happy anniversary, you and Andy, and many more.'

Everyone was very embarrassed.

'What's that?' Jamie asked.

Marie said, 'Wait and see.'

Robbie's mother unwrapped it slowly. 'This is very good of you, Jean.'

Jean couldn't look at Robbie or his step-father. 'We chose it together,' she lied. 'I didn't know what to get . . . I hope you like it . . .'

An electric blanket emerged from the wrapping. Robbie's mother seemed genuinely delighted, much to Jean's relief. 'Oh Jean, that's a lovely present, hen.'

Jamie said urgently, in case he might be missing something. 'Why are they getting a present? It's no their birthday, either of them.'

Andy said, 'Thanks a lot, Jean.' Neither he nor his wife looked at Robbie and Robbie didn't speak.

Marie told Jamie, 'It's for being married ten years.'

Jamie said, 'You mean like a sort of prize?'

They left soon afterwards.

The boys scrambled into the van. Jean and Robbie stood on either side of it and talked across it, as if they needed protection from each other.

'I was ashamed of you in there,' she said.

23

'Were you now?' He sounded so belligerent she knew he must be feeling guilty.

'He's a good man and she's happy with him. That's all that matters, not the past and not your pride.'

'You don't understand the first thing about it.'

'I understand what's important.'

He dropped the keys on the roof of the van. 'Lucky you can drive.'

'Why?'

'I'm going to see Bill.'

'Will you be back for supper?'

'I'm not sure. Don't wait, all right?'

She gave the children their tea and ate with them; she had learned from experience it was pointless to wait for Robbie on these occasions. She regretted the ruined day, but there was nothing she could do about it now. She got the children to bed quite easily for once; they were tired from their outing. Then she settled down to the ironing and the radio. It was a peaceful, mindless evening: she managed not to think about London, or rather she managed, each time the thought returned, to push it away.

Eventually he came in, depressed and aggressive and slightly drunk. 'Why aren't you in bed?'

'Is it that late?' She was surprised. 'Did you see Bill?'

'No. I walked a bit and I had a few drinks. I thought about phoning you but I didna get round to it.'

'Have you eaten?'

'More or less. I'm sorry. Did I ruin supper? I told you not to wait.'

'It doesn't matter.'

'Oh, Jeannie.' He suddenly put his arms round her and she hugged him tight, longing to be able to comfort him as if he were one of the children.

'It's all right,' she said. 'It's all right.' She felt more than ever in love with him, more even than when they were first married. 'If you could just stop hating him, you know. It's not good for you.'

24

'He wasna meant to be there today.' His voice was muffled against her neck.

'I know.'

'We timed it so carefully.'

'He couldn't help injuring his hand.'

'Pity it wasna his head.'

The hatred in his voice shocked her. It wasn't an idle joke: he really meant it.

She said, 'It's surely not because of him you want to go to London?'

'If it is, I've taken my time about it. No, I wouldna let him have that much effect on me. But if we do go, I'd like to see my mother all right first.'

'You couldn't expect him to accept charity, though – especially from you. And can we really afford to go around giving houses away? She's happy as she is, she said so.' It still rankled that he could offer to dispose of their house, *her* house, without even asking her first.

'It's a bloody slum.'

'Oh, come on, it's not as bad as that. You had to get out, of course, but it's still home to her.'

'Aye, she's made it pretty clear she doesna want any help from me.'

'Were you really trying to help her – or just make him feel small?'

There was a long silence. Robbie said finally, slowly, 'After my father was killed ... I did all I could for her ... but it was never enough.'

Jean was sure he was being unfair, but the pain in his voice made it difficult to argue. She hugged him instead.

'You were only a child,' she said presently. 'She had to have a man of her own again.'

When it happened, after all the agonizing, it happened suddenly. He came home during the day and began to pack. David had come up with a site in Ruislip. Jean took over the packing, too shocked by the suddenness to feel very much. He was going to catch the sleeper.

'I don't need all that, hen, it's only a day trip. I can make do with a briefcase.'

'You might decide to stay over – there could be more than one site – and then you'd be in a dirty shirt.' The more she resented the trip and its purpose, the more she felt obliged to behave like a good wife.

'Or I might get run over and not have clean underwear.'

She didn't smile; his cheerfulness annoyed her. He was already looking forward to this trip too much. 'Best to be on the safe side.'

'I wish you'd come with me.'

She knew he meant it, but her resolution hardened. He'd made the decision, she felt, before he'd even seen Ruislip. He'd always wanted to go to London and this was a mere excuse: he would make her agree, no matter how much she hated the idea, even though she was convinced (at some obscure level she dared not express to him) that it would somehow endanger their happiness. It was asking for trouble and she knew it; he didn't.

'I've told you – how can I? The kids are back at school tomorrow, I've got to be here.'

'Mam would see to them for you.'

'She's got enough on. Besides, they get nervous after a break.'

'I thought you said they're happy at that school.'

'So they are – but they still need me to hold their hands.' How much did he resent that she wouldn't go with him?

'And I don't.'

She made an effort. 'You're bigger – well, just a wee bit.'

To her relief, he laughed and they kissed. She hung on to him: suddenly she was very afraid of his going.

'Good luck anyway,' she said.

'D'you mean that?'

Afterwards, when he had gone, she felt guilty because he had been so nice about it. She went to see his mother, wanting to talk it over with someone she knew could be on both sides at once.

26

His mother was ironing. Jean sat and watched her, investing her with all kinds of wisdom.

'The thing is, if I really dig my heels in – what will happen? I've never gone against Robbie yet – not over anything important.' And she was not at all sure she could do so now.

'Are you really that set on not going?'

'It would mean taking a rented flat again and using the living-room as an office, to begin with. All the things we hated – all the things we tried so hard to get away from. And new schools for the kids, and not knowing anyone. It's just like a big step backwards.' She heard herself sounding emphatic: did Robbie's mother believe she actually had a choice? 'It's as if we'd be cancelling out everything we've worked for and starting again from scratch. It's such an upheaval.'

Robbie's mother ironed placidly, not looking up. 'I know – but it could be exciting as well. Like at the pictures. Those pioneers in the covered wagon, going west in search of gold.'

'And getting scalped by the Indians instead. Serve them right for not staying at home.'

'Some of them got through – and they got rich.'

'But we're rich already – I mean we've got enough. I don't understand why Robbie wants more.'

'He always has.'

'But why can't he be satisfied with what he's got?'

'It's not in his nature – just as you're not satisfied with two children.'

Jean said resentfully, 'You're on his side still – in spite of everything.'

'No, I'm on your side. But I didna ken you and he were on different sides – I thought you were married.'

'You make it sound easy,' Jean said, 'and it's not.'

'I know it's not, but sometimes you have to pretend. Look, lassie, if you disagree about this, he'll either stay here and blame you for it, or he'll go without you and then where will you be?'

Panic. 'D'you really think he'd do that?'

'Och, I don't mean to walk out on you, no. But he might

27

just go down there Monday to Friday and come home at weekends . . . and sooner or later he'd miss a weekend.' There was a pause while they both considered the implications. 'Whereas if you make a big fuss now about hating the whole idea of moving – and then you give in gracefully and go – he'll be so grateful . . . he might give you anything you want.'

Jean watched the clothes being folded. 'It doesn't seem quite right somehow. I mean I can see it makes sense, but it's not quite honest.'

'All's fair in love and war, don't you think?' Robbie's mother said briskly. 'Especially marriage. Haven't your parents come round at all?'

'My father would but my mother won't let him.' She felt a great surge of bitterness. 'She's never been in our house once. I'm so ashamed. I take the kids to see her once a month, but sometimes I think maybe I shouldn't. She's so against Robbie – just like he's against Andy.'

Out came another tea towel. 'Aye, what with one thing and another, maybe you'd be better off in London.'

A sudden sharp pang of loss. How could she say it so calmly? 'Won't you miss us?'

'Of course I'll miss you, hen, but I'm thinking of your own good. All this feuding, it's no healthy.'

So now they had both admitted it was settled. Jean changed the subject. 'Why do they still hate each other so much?'

'I suppose it's because of the fight.'

Jean was startled. 'Fight?'

'Ah, he didna tell you about that.'

'No.'

'Maybe he's embarrassed. It was a terrible mess. I didn't know what to do – go for the police or let them get on with it. I was running around like a scalded cat, screaming at them to stop. It was just before the wedding, too.'

Jean sensed a touch of pride amid the horror. 'What happened in the end?'

'Andy's a big man but Rob's very strong. And he had twenty years on his side.' She paused importantly. 'He broke Andy's arm.'

28

There was a silence while Jean imagined the scene. 'What did you do?'

'I sent for the doctor.'

'No, I didn't mean that.'

The words came reluctantly now, sounding ashamed. 'I ordered Rob out of the house and he went. And he never came back till he met you.'

So I gave you back your son, Jean thought. She wanted to have sympathy for Andy and Robbie's mother, but all she could feel was Robbie's pain as if it were her own. 'So you chose between them.'

'I had no choice. You canna blame me. It broke my heart, but I had to do it. If it comes to it, you have to choose your man, not your kids, or you'll not have a life of your own.'

Jean waited at the school gates with the other mothers, chatting idly. She had grown up with some of them: they were like an extended family. But there would be no more of that in London.

She spotted her two as soon as they came out: both short and sturdy like their parents, Duncan with her own reddish curls, Jamie brown-haired, the image of Robbie. As always, Jamie was leading, Duncan hanging back just a little. She collected them and bundled them into the van, answering their questions absently. Her mind was with Robbie in London. She wanted so much to believe it wasn't a risk.

She woke early. Something had fallen on the bed. She opened her eyes. Something else fell on the bed, a parcel in shiny wrapping paper with a big rosette of ribbon. She looked up and smiled. Two more parcels thudded beside her. Bribery, she thought, but she was past caring. She had already made the sacrifice in her head.

She said, 'Tell me about it.'

Robbie landed on the bed. They made love as if they had been apart for a long, long time.

Next day, after seeing his lawyer, he was triumphant. 'We've made an extra thousand on the last house and that shop. I knew that bloody shop was cheap in spite of the short lease. An extra thousand. D'you realize what that means?'

She was hanging out washing and would not look round. 'It means we're going to London.'

'It's just that extra we needed.' He marched up and down the garden in delight. 'Don't you see, it's like a sign.'

She smelt the clean clothes. 'It's nothing of the sort. You were always set on going and now you've got the perfect excuse.'

He stood beside her. 'And you still hate the whole idea.'

All the elation of the morning had vanished. She had never had a choice. They were going to live in London and build houses in Ruislip, come what may, because that was what he wanted. And her own house, so beloved, her only real home, would belong to strangers.

'Well, I was going to put up new paper in the lounge,' she said, 'but I won't bother. The new owners might like to choose their own.'

She went to see her parents. She was not sure what she was expecting; they had to be told, and perhaps the shock would have some effect. She could feel herself hoping for something.

But it was all just the same. She was made to sit in the parlour like a visitor while her father went upstairs. The room was cold from disuse; he had put on a one-bar electric fire. She looked around while she waited: it was still the tidiest room she had ever seen. There were three photographs: her parents' wedding, herself as a child and Jamie and Duncan as babies. A clock ticked loudly in the silence. She shivered.

Her father came back, a small, meek, grey man. She could not remember him ever being young. Everything about him was the antithesis of Robbie's youth and vigour. She felt a spasm of pity for him: poor Dad. What must it have been like, all those years with her mother?

'It's no good,' he said. 'She won't have anything.'

'Should I go up?'

He shook his head. 'She says she'd rather be alone to rest. She may be down later.'

'What's the matter with her?'

'It's one of her headaches.'

'Oh, is that all?'

Her father looked mildly reproving. 'They get pretty bad, you know. You haven't seen her lately.'

Jean resented the injustice. 'I saw her last month and she was right as ninepence, just off to play bridge. Is it a migraine?'

'I don't know.'

'Hasn't she seen the doctor?' How quickly the old exasperation mounted.

'No, she won't. She says there's nothing he can do.'

'She's afraid he might cure it, and then what would she do? She might have to behave like a normal person.'

Her father sank into the chair opposite her. 'You mustn't speak of your mother like that, Jean.'

There was a long, tense silence. Jean wondered what would happen if she screamed.

'I'll make some tea,' her father said eventually.

'I don't really want any, thanks all the same. Look, Dad, I came specially to see you *both*. I want to tell you something.' She waited, but he didn't answer. She stared at the one red electric bar and felt colder than ever.

'Your mother said why haven't you brought the children.'

Jean nearly exploded. 'She means if I don't bring them, I might as well not bother coming myself.'

As always he shrank from anger. 'No, no, but she likes to see them, that's all. You know that.'

'Not enough to come to our house. Not ever. Not once.'

'You know your mother. She's got very fixed principles.'

Instead of the indignation she wanted, she sensed a certain relief. He felt safe with her mother's principles. They gave him boundaries in which he could function. For some reason this enraged her.

'You mean she might get contaminated in Robbie's house. It probably brings on one of her headaches just to think I'm married to him. I'm surprised she even likes the children, knowing they're half his. How can she tell which half to love?'

Why wasn't he upset? Instead he folded his hands in front of him and avoided her eyes.

'You can't expect her to visit you, Jean. She wouldn't feel comfortable. You can't expect it. She's never got over you marrying outside the Church.'

If only he'd speak for himself for a change. Instead he acted as a kind of interpreter.

'But I didn't. That's the whole point. Robbie went through with all that specially to please me and you and *her*.'

'He's still a Protestant.'

'Oh, you mean she'd like him to turn as well. Would that make it all right?' He had got her doing it too, pretending he didn't exist. She attacked her mother and he defended her and that allowed him to be a cypher.

'Well, it would help. You know it would.'

'It would probably help if he was an architect, too, or a brain surgeon.'

'Don't make it difficult for me, Jean. I have to live with your mother.'

And what must that be like? But the sympathy turned to contempt. It had all gone on far too long. Why didn't you stand up to her, then, so we could both respect you?

She said, 'I suppose she's never forgiven me for getting pregnant when I did and that's it. She puts all the blame on Robbie and wraps it up in the name of religion.'

'Ssh.' Her father was listening. For a second she had a quick comic vision of him as a guard dog with his ears at the correct angle.

There were slow footsteps on the stairs. Jean's mother came in, a short, plump woman with an air of self-righteousness. Jean recognized her own red hair going grey. But the dressing-gown and the martyred expression ... she prayed swiftly she would never come to that.

Her mother said, 'So you're still here,' and turned to her father. 'I thought there might be a cup of tea going.'

'But you said you didn't want one.'

'I think it might help. Just a little.' She stretched herself languidly on the couch.

Jean's father got up. 'I'll put the kettle on.' He went out of the room – relieved, Jean assumed, to leave her alone with her mother. They listened to the ticking clock.

When she could bear it no longer she asked, 'How's your head?'

'The same. I try not to complain.'

Another silence. Jean was nearly choking with fury: envying her mother's power and despising her father for tolerating it.

'How are Jamie and Duncan?' her mother said eventually.

'Very well.' Jean paused. 'Robbie's well too.'

No reply. She gazed at her mother, willing her to speak. You made love, got pregnant, gave birth to me. You didn't hate me till I married Robbie but now you treat me like a stranger. All right, it was never perfect, but it wasn't as bad as this. We used to get along well enough. It was tolerable. Aren't you *ever* going to forgive me?

Her father returned. Jean said, 'Look, now you're both here, I only came to tell you Robbie and I are moving to London. It's a great opportunity for him. He's done very well up here and he'll do even better down there and I'm proud of him. We'll be going in a few weeks' time and we're very excited about it.'

She was surprised, almost convinced, by the enthusiasm in her own voice. She sounded like somebody else. Her father looked at her mother. Jean looked at them both. She longed for him to speak first, to be dominant for once, to win.

Her mother said, 'You'll bring Jamie and Duncan to see me before you go.'

Jean said, 'Are they all you care about?' No one answered. 'And what if I don't? Will you come to the house? Or will you let us go without a good-bye or a good wish?' She couldn't believe she would ever treat her own children like this, no matter what they had done, even murder.

Her mother closed her eyes and put a hand to her head. Her father said, 'Jean, you mustn't upset your mother. She's not well.'

Jean stood up. She addressed her mother. 'I don't know how you square it with your conscience. Don't you remember what Our Lord said about turning the other cheek and forgiveness and charity?' She was close to tears of rage. 'I don't know how you dare preach religion to anyone. I don't know how you have the gall to go to Mass and look God in the face and not be ashamed.' She saw their mounting horror and astonishment; she searched for the most telling word she could think of. 'You're a hypocrite.'

The kettle screamed.

They lay like spoons, curled into the curves of each other's bodies, fitting exactly. She felt safe and warm and anaesthetized. He said, 'So we're agreed. You'll come to London.'

'Yes.'

'Willingly – or dragging your feet?'

'Willingly.'

He turned her face so he could kiss her. 'I love you.'

1956

Jean

They rented a flat in Ealing. Jean thought she had never seen anywhere so depressing in her life. Everything they had brought from Glasgow was the wrong size and shape, and some of it had to be stored since they had only three rooms now. Packing-cases stood in the hall and seemed likely to stand there for ever because there were not enough cupboards for their contents. There was no garden and the flat looked out on to a main road, so that they were never free from the noise of traffic. But it was only temporary and it was cheap, or so Robbie kept telling her. To Jean it seemed wildly expensive because the very idea of paying rent after owning a house was an outrage. She had to make a considerable effort to remind herself that it was presumably her job to remain cheerful and tolerant at home while Robbie got on with the Ruislip site.

He put an advertisement for labour in the local paper and the phone started ringing at half past eight. Breakfast was totally disrupted as Robbie kept getting up to take calls and make appointments. Jamie was fascinated by his first brush with the working world.

'Who are they, Dad?'

'Workmen for the new site.'

'Will there be a lot?'

'No. But we want to get the best ones, don't we?'

Jean noticed Duncan was pushing his food around his plate. 'Duncan, what's up with you?'

The phone rang again and Robbie went out of the room. Duncan said reluctantly, 'I'm not hungry,' making her feel she was dragging words out of him.

Jamie said, 'He's got a pain.'

'Where?'

'In his stomach.'

'He can speak for himself, can't he?' She turned to Duncan. 'Have you got a pain?'

He wouldn't look at her. 'I'm just not hungry.'

Robbie came back from the phone and went on with his breakfast. 'That was a brickie. He'll be here at six.'

She tried to take an interest. 'How many of them are you expecting?'

'How should I know? You put in an advert and take pot luck. Bloody hard to understand what they say, some of them.'

'I suppose they're Cockneys.'

'Cockneys or Irish, aye. They can't understand me either. It's a joke.'

'Couldn't you get them from the Labour Exchange? You did back home.'

'I knew everyone there, it was different. Besides, this way I can cream off the best before they're out of work. It's worth a try, anyhow.'

She said abruptly, 'Duncan's not eating,' annoyed that he hadn't noticed.

'Why's that?'

'He's got a pain in his stomach.'

'Oh yes?' He seemed unperturbed. 'Maybe a don't-want-to-go-to-school pain?'

Jean stroked Duncan's hair. 'Can't you manage a wee bit – just to please me?'

Duncan shook his head. Robbie said irritably, 'Don't molly-coddle him, Jean. It won't hurt him not to eat for once.' The phone rang again and he got up to answer it.

She called after him, 'I must try not giving you breakfast some time if that's how you feel. I could save a fortune.' She turned back to Duncan and went on coaxing him. 'How about some bacon? Or a bit of sausage, hm? You like that.'

Jamie was wiping his own plate with bread. 'I'll have it if he doesn't want it.'

'Bread and honey?' Jean said desperately. But Duncan only went on shaking his head and staring at his plate in a maddening repetitive way. Anxiety turned to rage and she lost patience with him. 'All right, then, don't eat. Please yourself.' She got up from the table and marched into the next room where Robbie was on the phone. Anything to put an end to the problem. Maybe she could even get him to help her if she was tactful.

He was saying, 'Right, then, I'll see you at six thirty,' and putting down the phone. She forgot about being tactful and transferred her irritation to him. 'Can't they come during the day?'

'They're at work. Besides, I won't be here.'

'What?' She was so shocked, all thought of Duncan went out of her head.

'I've got to see the bank manager and the solicitor and all the builders' merchants. You know that.'

'How long will that take?'

'I don't know. Maybe all day.'

She said bitterly, 'Aye, very likely.'

'Look, Jean, they're all new people, I've got to take time getting to know them. You know what it's like.'

'So I'm stuck here all day answering the phone.' There was nowhere she particularly wanted to go, but she hated the flat so much that the thought of being obliged to stay in it all day seemed like a jail sentence.

'It would be a great help, hen. Just make appointments every half-hour and get their names and their trades.' She stared at him. He added, as if it were a big favour, 'I'll take the kids to school for you.'

'Thanks a lot.'

'And I'll be here tomorrow to see the overspill if you can't fit them all in tonight.'

'Great.' But the irony was wasted on him. He was already turning away, back into the hall, calling the children. She followed him but she knew from the look on his face, the cheerful, shut-down concentration, that mentally he was at his first meeting, out in his exterior day. She had shrunk to the person who answers the phone. She looked at Duncan, lagging behind Jamie, and felt a pang of guilt for losing her temper. He was so small. What if he really wasn't well?

'Maybe he shouldn't go,' she said doubtfully.

'What?' Robbie was impatient to be gone.

'He does look a bit pale.'

'Och, they'll soon send him home if there's anything wrong.' He patted Duncan's head. 'But he's all right – aren't you, my laddie?'

She spent the day answering the phone. In between she re-arranged the furniture, but there was no way it could please her. She took down the curtains and hung others but they fell short, looking undignified and ludicrous, leaving her with a three-inch gap of window pane. She thought of Robbie going from one appointment to another, meeting people, talking, doing a job, and she thought again about nursing. In Glasgow she had hardly missed it after the children came because there had been friends and relatives to see. Here she knew nobody. There was literally no one she could telephone. Except Ruth.

She wondered if it would be a good idea to phone Ruth. She stood at the window and looked at the traffic and the people in the street. She ached for Glasgow. She thought of Bearsden and the house and the FOR SALE notice and she felt herself almost starting to cry. She couldn't phone Ruth if she was going to cry. It was awful to be a burden to someone you hardly knew. She went briskly to the kitchen and sorted rubbish into sacks, dragged them to the front door. The important thing was to keep busy, not to brood. She knew that. As she opened the door the woman opposite opened hers to take in her milk. She was in dressing-gown and curlers and didn't look particularly nice, but she was about Jean's age and, most important of all, she was there.

Jean didn't stop to think. She simply said, 'D'you fancy a cup of tea?'

The woman looked surprised and somehow outraged as well, as if Jean had hit her. 'What?'

'A cup of tea.' Jean spoke more slowly and tried to modify her accent. 'Would you like one? I'm new here and I've got to stay in to answer the phone.'

'Oh.' The woman looked trapped; Jean could see her casting about for an excuse. 'No. Thanks all the same. I've got to go shopping.' She managed to smile but it was a false smile and she shut the door abruptly. Jean turned away, confused by her own mixed emotions: rage, disappointment, amusement. They wouldn't have got on; it was all for the best, she told herself.

Inside the flat the phone began to ring again.

The interviews took all evening. When the last workman had gone, Jean came back into the living-room and flopped on the sofa beside Robbie. He said, 'You did great with all the tea and sandwiches.'

'Think nothing of it. I'll do it all again tomorrow. I could do it in my sleep. In fact I nearly did.'

He put his arm round her and they both went on sitting there with their eyes shut. It was lovely and peaceful for the first time that day, but presently she had to get up to pour whisky.

'How d'you get on today?' she said, remembering his appointments.

'Not bad. But not good. They were all a bit sticky.' He didn't look worried, though. 'But they'll all come round. It's only a matter of time – and going back – and turning on the charm.'

As always, she found his self-confidence both exciting and exasperating. 'Well, you're good at that – when you can be bothered.'

'You're getting cheeky.' He replaced his arm round her.

'The curtains don't fit.'

'They nearly do.'

'That's what I mean.'

'Can't you put a fringe on them?' Another minute and he'd be bored.

'Oh, aye. I could start a new fashion. Fringed curtains. The Ealing look. Put Christian Dior out of business in no time.'

He laughed. She snuggled up to him, leaning her head on his shoulder. The familiar smell of him made her want him, no matter how tired she was. 'Will you help me move furniture tomorrow?'

'I thought you already had.'

'The bits I can't manage.'

'Of course. But it looks all right the way it is.'

'It'll never look all right. Everything's either too big or too small, too long or too short.'

'Sounds like a sex problem.'

She punched him. 'And we're never going to get rid of those packing-cases in the hall.'

'Why ever not?'

'Because we've nowhere to put the stuff that's in them.'

'Maybe we could chuck it.'

'It's essential.' She wondered why she had this urge to keep on at him when she was really, temporarily, quite content.

'Jean, I can't think about that tonight.'

'I know. But we're one room short, whichever way you look at it.'

'It's only for a few months. Till we get on our feet.'

There was a long silence. She wanted to make it up to him, compensate him for her complaints, make love perhaps. Instead she found herself returning to her deepest worry.

'Duncan was awful quiet when he came back from school.' There was no reply. She looked at him anxiously. 'Robbie?' He was sound asleep.

Pretty soon she began to feel disconnected from real life. Once work on the site began, Robbie was completely absorbed in it. She could see that it hardly mattered to him whether he was in Glasgow or London: if she had woken him suddenly in the night to ask him, he might not even have known where he was. All that mattered was the site and the work. Whereas she, once the children were at school, had six empty hours a day. It did not take very long to keep three overcrowded rooms clean and tidy. Not compared to a house where you were continually interrupted by neighbours, friends and family. She remembered with a kind of sick amusement that she had once actually complained of being too busy, knowing too many people, not having enough time to herself.

She was lonely. She had never been lonely in her life before and it seemed such a shaming condition that she kept it to herself. There must be something she could do about it; she felt it reflected badly on her if she could not make new friends. She had always thought of herself as an outgoing, gregarious person. She tried smiling at people in shops and launderettes, but they did not smile back. Perhaps they could see that she was nervous and desperate, not her true self. Like dogs, they could smell her fear.

She went out. It was absurd, she reminded herself, to be in one of the great cities of the world and not explore it. She took buses and tubes, lost her way and found it again. She became a tourist, looking at buildings, museums, parks. It was interesting, even enjoyable, but it made her feel lonelier than ever to the point of schizophrenia, because by day she was a tourist and by night a resident. She didn't know how to handle the dual role of housewife and holiday-maker: they seemed in permanent intrinsic conflict. She had never been sightseeing in Glasgow because she had always lived there.

At the same time she felt that because Robbie's life had not changed at all, she must behave as if hers too were still the same. He would be expecting all the usual responses from her. She played with the idea of pouring out her troubles to him, but when she thought about it, what troubles did she really have? Only a sense of disorientation. Not illness, or poverty, or heartbreak. Just simple homesick, lonely misery. Nothing he could change.

One day in the National Gallery she was so worn out with walking and looking that she sat down on a seat in front of one of the larger pictures and shut her eyes. The warm, dark emptiness was beautiful, and the weight off her feet. She would have liked to put them above her head, but she felt that would be taking eccentricity too far. Then she wondered swiftly if she were going mad, for such a thought even to occur to her. Sometimes she did feel a little mad, spending

43

so many hours alone, and her throat constricted and ached without speech.

An American voice, young, said, 'Yeah, it looks better that way, doesn't it?'

She opened her eyes and saw a young man in jeans and jersey, blue-eyed and crew-cut, blond and tanned, smiling at her. She made an effort and smiled back. However much you longed for someone to speak to you, when they actually did, it was quite a shock.

'They should lend you a spare set of feet when you come in here,' she said.

'That's a real cute accent you've got.'

'So's yours.' She was amazed to hear herself sounding so assured. 'American or Canadian?'

'American. From Norfolk, Nebraska. Tom Franklin.'

'I'm Jean Mackenzie. From Scotland.'

He held out his hand. 'Glad to know you, Jean. The folks who invented whisky can't be all bad. I'm hoping to see Edinburgh just as soon as I'm through with London.' He paused at the look on her face. 'Have I said the wrong thing?'

She said without thinking, 'Edinburgh's all right, if you can spare the time. But it's Glasgow you really ought to see.'

He took her out. She meant to refuse but somehow she could not. 'Convince me over a cup of coffee,' he said, and suddenly he looked as lost as she felt. They were two foreigners together. She felt nervous and wicked: she was having an adventure, like a real tourist. They went to a coffee bar and with very little coaxing she found herself talking about Glasgow, a great torrent of words, all the feeling she had dammed up. '. . . After a while you won't notice if it's dirty or raining, the people are so friendly, and you've only got to drive twenty minutes and you're out in real country, with mountains and lochs like you've read about, and if you go the other way it's less than an hour to the sea, I mean you can have whatever you fancy, it's all there.'

He was staring at her but he smiled sympathetically. 'I guess you're pretty homesick.'

'Yes.' She tried to lighten the atmosphere: she had exhausted herself. 'I *guess* I am.'

He beckoned the waitress. 'Say, Miss, two more coffees.'

'No, really. I must be going.'

'Why?'

'I've got to pick up my kids from school.'

'You don't look old enough to have kids.'

She said proudly, 'Jamie's eight and Duncan's six.'

'And how do they feel about London?'

'Oh, Jamie's fine, he'd get along anywhere. I'm not sure about Duncan. He's not very happy at his new school.' Funny how easy it was to tell a stranger.

'What does your husband have to say about that?'

'Oh, he's worried too, of course – but he's very busy just now . . .'

Their coffees arrived. There was a pause and she felt Robbie's presence like a shadow across the table.

Tom said urgently, 'Meet me tomorrow.'

'What?'

'We could explore London together. We're both tourists after all. It might be more fun for you than going it alone. Well, it would make my vacation, anyway.'

She waited until after supper, when the boys were in bed. Robbie was doing accounts at the dining-table. There was just room enough between the sofa and the dining-table for her to put up the ironing-board.

She said, 'I got picked up today.'

'Things will be a bit tight till we've sold the house and paid off the bridging loan. But don't worry. It won't take long.'

She didn't know whether to laugh or scream. 'I said I got picked up today.' He finally looked up from the accounts. 'By a young American tourist. He wanted us to see London together.'

There was a slight pause. 'What did you say?'

'I'm meeting him tomorrow.'

'Great.'

But it was no good; she couldn't keep it up. 'I said no, of course.'

'Why? You could do with a guide.'

'Oh aye? The blind leading the blind.' She eyed him curiously, disappointed. 'Would you really not have minded?'

'Why should I? You might have enjoyed it.' He waited a moment, teasing her. 'Of course I'd have minded. I'd have been jealous as hell.'

'Would you really?'

'Of course I would.'

But it was too late: she didn't believe him. She felt he was play-acting specially to please her, as if she were a child.

'He was very nice.'

'I should hope so. Can't have my wife getting picked up by just anybody.'

She put down the iron with a crash. 'Robbie. I've been thinking. I can't just spend my time sightseeing. It's all very fine, but we can do that together at weekends with the kids. I really ought to get a job. We need the money and I'd be happier.'

He frowned. 'It was all right you working when I was doing my National Service and you were living with your parents. It won't do now.'

'You mean I've got to hang around all day just to get breakfast and supper?'

'And fetch the kids from school.'

'You could do that. You're not tied to that bloody site, are you? You're the boss, as you've often told me.'

He said, with amazing obtuseness, 'Are you upset about something?'

'Robbie, let's be practical. You don't want another baby, you've made that pretty clear. We couldn't have one here anyway. If I don't have another baby I might as well work. It's very lonely here. Nobody speaks to you. If you say hullo to anyone on the stairs, they look at you as if you're mad. I can't spend my whole life on a sightseeing tour of London, getting picked up by American tourists.'

'Jean, we've only been here a few weeks.'

All her resentments boiled up, just and unjust. 'Oh, you

mean if I persevere I might get picked up by tourists of other nationalities? Great. Or of course I could just stay at home and move the furniture and sew fringes on the curtains and persuade Duncan he really loves that school.'

'I'm sorry, I know it's rough but it's not for long. I can't help it.'

'Of course you can.'

'I know you didn't want to come here, hen, but it's done. I'll make it up to you, I promise.'

As always the sudden unexpected gentleness melted her heart. Besides, it was painful to be angry with him for too long. She squeezed round the end of the ironing-board to reach the dining-table and he gave her a big hug. 'I'm sorry,' she said, as if it were all her fault. 'I'm being a cow.'

'I've got a weakness for cows.' He kissed her. She was home again, safe. She held on to him, tight, for a long moment, feeling everything become bright and balanced once more. She began to make plans.

'Why don't we ring David and Ruth?'

'Whatever for?' He sounded startled.

'We could ask them round.'

'What, here?'

That could only mean he was equally ashamed of the flat. 'Well, they're the only people we know in London.'

He was silent, thinking it over. She longed for him to say yes; it would give her something to look forward to. It would be like normal life, having people to supper again.

He said, 'I don't need them yet.'

All next day she thought about it. She kept very busy, shopping and cleaning and cooking; she even wrote cheerful letters to both sets of parents. But all the time she could feel her brain churning away. She hardly knew Ruth; they had only met half a dozen times. She couldn't afford to take her out and Robbie had rejected the dinner party idea. Was it acceptable to phone someone you hardly knew, just for a chat? Ruth had said, 'Do ring us if you come to London', but that could be mere politeness.

She took a large swig of whisky and picked up the phone.

The restaurant was tiny, dimly lit and wildly expensive, but Ruth seemed at home in it and it was clear from the fuss the waiters made of her that she went there often. Jean felt out of her depth and yet thrilled to be there. For once she could enjoy feeling out of her depth: Ruth wouldn't let her sink. And she had gone against Robbie and done what she wanted for once and he didn't even know.

'You should have rung me before,' Ruth said.

'Yes, I should. I meant to. I don't know what stopped me.' She was still taking in Ruth's clothes, hair and make-up. They all made her feel very provincial indeed in a way that they hadn't in Glasgow because there Ruth had been the outsider and Jean on her home ground. But it didn't matter: Ruth seemed genuinely pleased to see her.

'How's Lisa?' Jean asked.

'Oh, she's fine.'

'And David?'

'Trying to persuade his father to retire.' She searched Jean's face with a look of concern. 'Is London getting you down?'

Jean remembered all the childhood lectures from her mother about her give-away face, and how she must learn to hide her feelings so as not to upset other people. She said, 'I try not to moan because it's dreary for Robbie if I do, he's got enough on his mind.'

Ruth said gently, 'You can moan to me.'

'She was ever so nice.' Jean watched Robbie eating his supper. She was too full of excitement and exotic lunch to eat much herself. 'She really cheered me up.'

'Yes, I can see that.' But he didn't sound pleased: more surprised and amused and ever so slightly annoyed. Or was she imagining things?

'She might be able to help with a job too. She's got all sorts of hospital connections. She does good works in her spare time.'

'Really?' He was concentrating on his plate, not looking at her.

'Yes. It does seem a bit out of character, doesn't it?'

'Does it?'

'Well, she always seemed so carefree. But today she said a funny thing.' She recalled it carefully to make sure she quoted correctly. 'About doing voluntary work as a sort of bribe to the gods to let her go on being lucky. Like an insurance policy. Wasn't that odd?' She had been amazed that Ruth, of all people, could have premonitions of disaster, like herself.

'Aye.' Robbie looked up. 'But I don't think we need her help. I've got the perfect job for you.'

'What?' She was intrigued. It was the first time he had shown any interest in her working.

'Well, you're used to being on your feet at the hospital and you're good at getting picked up in the street and you're fond of being on your back with me – I mean it's obvious – part-time, tax free, night shift, no problem with the kids – you should go on the game.'

She laughed. 'I'll think about it. On my back indeed. On my knees more like.'

'They want all sorts. You could make a special feature of virtuosity. "Miss X. All positions catered for. Exotic preferences a speciality." I'm sure you'd be a great success. And I could be your ponce. Or pimp. Whichever it is. I'd make a fortune.'

She threw something at him, pretending indignation, but she was flattered and he knew it and she forgot about Ruth.

When she looked back on their time in the Ealing flat, her happiest memories were of football. The England–Scotland final came in the middle of April, during the school holidays. Duncan was a different child, his old self, cheerful and lively, yet she had never got him to admit he hated school. 'It's all right', was all she could get him or Jamie to say, but that could not be true and she promised herself a word with the teachers if the small appetites and dismal faces went on next term.

Robbie and the boys sat together, close to the radio. Jean stayed in the kitchen, washing up and making a cake; she did not much care for football, though they begged her to join them. It was sufficient for her to hear their shouts and groans through the dining-hatch and to know that for once they were all together, contented and safe. She felt powerful then, in control of her family.

When she went in with tea for them all, they clamoured for her attention. 'Jean, you're missing it all.'

'Come on, Mam. It's great.'

She smiled. 'It's all right. I can tell from the noise you're making we're going to win.'

Robbie said, 'Sit down for God's sake, there's only a minute to go. Christ, they're bloody good!'

She put down the tray and listened for a moment, intrigued in spite of herself. Somebody scored a goal and great howls of agony went up from the sofa. She turned to see them all slumped together as if suddenly injured. Obviously that must have been the equalizer. She left the tea for the children and gave Robbie some whisky. The match was over.

Duncan said with absolute horror, 'Dad, we've lost.'

Robbie pounded the sofa with his fist. 'Jesus Christ. That bloody Haynes.' He gulped the whisky. 'God almighty, I could murder that bastard.'

Jean said, 'It's a draw. I'm sorry.'

'Good God, woman. Is that all you can say? We've lost, that's all. We've bloody lost.'

'But it's one-all, isn't it? That's a draw. How can we have lost if it's a draw?'

Jamie said, 'Mam, it's obvious.'

Robbie said, 'God give me strength,' and Jean poured him more whisky. 'The others scored three points each, right?'

'What others?'

'Oh, Mam. Wales and Northern Ireland, of course.'

'Oh. Yes, of course.' She was bewildered. 'How did they do that?'

'They all played each other and – oh, never mind.'

'No, I want to understand. How did we lose if it's a draw?'

Jamie said, 'On points of course,' as if she were an idiot. Robbie leaned back with his eyes shut and she refilled his glass. He said, 'Right. Four teams. They all play each other, so that's three matches each.'

Jean hesitated. 'Yes.'

'And it's nought if you lose, one if you draw and two if you win.'

Duncan said triumphantly, 'It's easy,' delighted there was something he could understand and she couldn't.

'Ye – es.'

'Points,' said Robbie.

'Yes, of course.' She thought it over. 'That seems fair.'

'So everybody lost, drew and won, so everybody got three points.'

'So it's a draw.' Jean couldn't understand why they were suddenly back where they had started. 'Why were you so upset?'

'Only because we were winning.'

'How could we be winning if everyone got three points?'

'Come on.' Jamie had given up on her. Duncan followed him out and they started playing with their cars in the hall. But she had enjoyed their sense of superiority.

Robbie said, 'Oh, Jean, give it up, please.'

'No, I really do want to understand.' It had all slipped off like a piece of knitting.

There was a long pause. 'Before this match started – and this was the final, right? – Wales and Northern Ireland had three points each, Scotland and England had two points each.'

'So we were losing.'

'I'll ignore that. If we'd scored and England hadn't, we'd have got two more points, making four points in all and we'd have won. But England *did* score, so we got one point each, making three.'

'So it's a draw.'

'As you keep saying.'

She thought it over. It did make sense at last, but only just, like a theorem or a quadratic equation at school, and like them it was not worth the effort. 'I'm sorry,' she said. 'I see it now.'

Robbie sighed. 'Half a bloody minute to go.'

She still thought of the football and their united male superiority as her happiest time in Ealing.

Ruth didn't seem to mind not being asked to the flat. She invited Jean and the boys to her house instead and they played in the garden with Lisa while Jean and Ruth relaxed after lunch. Jean loved the house. It was large and warm and expensively furnished – in slightly more than good taste, she suspected, but she did not care. If it was overdone, it was in the nicest possible way, like Ruth herself. It made Jean feel cushioned from the outside world. Nothing bad could happen in Ruth's house. And the sight of the children so happily occupied out of doors was infinitely soothing.

Ruth was saying, 'Oh, why not take the summer off and start work in September? You can always come and sit in my garden –' when the phone suddenly rang. She picked it up saying, 'Sorry, just a minute, hullo?' and her manner changed. 'Oh – it's you – yes – well, I .... Jean's here, a friend of mine, so I can't really – yes, I see – yes, it would – of course – no, but if it's an emergency ... look, if I can't I'll ring you back, but expect me in half an hour. Bye, love.' She turned to Jean, slightly flustered but rapidly collecting herself. 'Jean. You're going to think me awfully rude, but there's a bit of a crisis on.'

Jean said automatically, 'What? Is there anything I can do?' but she was puzzled by a sort of suppressed excitement in Ruth that she sensed but could not understand.

'Well – yes, there is, actually, it's awful to ask you, but this friend of mine is ill and I really ought to dash over and minister. You know.'

Jean said, 'Of course. What's the matter with her? Maybe I could help.'

She got the impression Ruth had forgotten she was a nurse. Ruth frowned slightly and said, 'Oh, that's sweet of you, but I don't think it's nursing that's needed exactly, more

52

just having me there.' She paused. 'I mean it's more of an emotional crisis.'

'Well, of course you must go.' Jean didn't actually mind, but she had the feeling it would have been all the same if she did.

'I'm terribly sorry, it means leaving you with the children and spoiling our afternoon. I feel so dreadful.'

'Don't be silly, these things happen. I'll be perfectly happy holding the fort.' She looked around appreciatively. 'It's a very nice fort.'

'Oh, you're an angel.' Ruth nearly hugged her, but at the last moment she turned away and examined her dress critically. 'Maybe I should change.'

'Surely your friend won't care what you're wearing when she's ill.'

'No – except I always think it's important to look your best in a sick-room – it sort of raises morale.' Ruth looked in the mirror. 'No, of course you're right. I'm just wasting time.' She glanced at the children, still happy and busy in the garden. 'Better not disturb them. Bye, love, thanks a million.'

The french doors were open and the draught made the front door slam after Ruth. Lisa looked up from the game. 'Where's Mummy gone?'

It was a shock to see David strolling across the terrace towards her. She had expected Ruth to be back long since, but one hour had stretched into two and there was still no sign of her.

Lisa ran to David and he gave her a big hug. Jean felt like an intruder: she was embarrassed to be found in sole charge of his house and child, but he smiled and said it was nice to see her, seeming to mean it.

'Ruth's not here, I'm afraid,' she said, as if it were somehow her fault.

'No, I gathered that.' He stroked Lisa's hair as she clung to his legs.

'She's gone to see a friend. Somebody rang up and they're not well and Ruth's gone to look after them.'

'Oh yes? Well, that's not unusual. She's very good at that.' David turned away as Lisa rejoined the boys. 'Would you like a drink?'

Jean would in fact have loved a drink, but the longing to escape was stronger. David's words were affable enough, but she sensed a terrible anger towards Ruth and she did not want to be near it. She looked at her watch. 'It's very nice of you but I really ought to be getting home. We've had a lovely day – I mean Ruth made lunch and the children played in the garden – it's really been a treat.' She felt she was pleading Ruth's case. 'But Robbie will be home soon and we've got quite a journey.'

'Just one drink.' David had never been so firm before. 'I'm sure the children don't want to leave yet. What would you like?'

She gave in. 'Whisky, please.' Perhaps she could do Ruth more good by staying. For she felt certain Ruth was in some kind of trouble.

'A woman after my own heart.' He went back into the sitting-room and she followed him. 'Anything in it?'

'A little water, please.'

'Look the other way, won't you, if I have some ice.'

They chatted like old friends about work and Robbie, London and the flat and the Ruislip site. Then they ran out of things to say. Jean was just about to insist on going home when David said heavily, I'm glad you and Ruth got together.'

'So am I.' More special pleading. 'She's been marvellous.'

'Yes, she is.' Everything he said seemed loaded with irony. 'Did she say what time she'd be back?'

'No, she didn't. I'm sorry.'

'No – well – these sick friends – they take a lot of time.'

'Do they?' She began to pray for Ruth's return; it was clear there could be no going home till then.

'I mean she can't predict how long she'll be away.'

'No.' She longed to know why he was so angry, and so busy pretending not to be, but more than that she longed to escape. She was infinitely relieved when she heard the front door open at last.

Ruth called out some apology to Jean as she crossed the hall. She sounded happy; her voice was light and innocent. But she stopped in mid-sentence when she saw David. 'You're early.'

'Am I?' He sounded grim.

'I got stuck in traffic.'

'Funny, I just missed it.'

'Do I get a drink?'

He poured her one. 'How's your sick friend?'

'Better.'

'Who was it?'

'Diana.'

'Yes, I thought it might be Diana.'

'Why?'

'She's sick quite often, isn't she?'

'No.'

Jean said firmly, 'I really must be going.'

All the way home on the tube she tried to puzzle it out. Who was this Diana person and why did David resent her so much? Or was it possible Ruth was lying? Jean didn't want to think that; she had always regarded them as happily married. She couldn't imagine lying to Robbie, so why should Ruth lie to David? But if Ruth *had* lied to David, did that also mean she had lied to Jean? It was alarming, as if the ground were shifting under her feet. It gave a new, uncomfortable dimension to the whole relationship with Ruth.

When she got home she described to Robbie what had happened without expressing any suspicion, hoping he would interpret for her. He listened but all he said when she had finished was, 'Maybe he doesn't like her friend.' A few days later David invited him to the office, and he came back with the news that as a special favour to David he had agreed to supervise the conversion of a house belonging to someone called Diana Crawley.

It started like any other day. They all had breakfast together, Robbie left for Ruislip and she took the boys to school. She did some shopping, washing and ironing, cleaned the flat, wrote to Ella and Margaret, put a stew in the oven for supper and went to collect the children.

Jamie had a black eye. She was so shocked she hardly glanced at Duncan, pale and quiet behind him.

'Jamie – oh, Jamie . . .'

He wriggled away from her. 'It's all right, Mam.'

'It's not all right. Whatever happened?'

'I got in a fight.' He had Robbie's sulky look that appeared if too many questions were asked: a certain way of setting his mouth that meant 'shut up and leave me alone'.

'I can see that,' she said. 'I'm not daft.'

'It's okay. I won.'

'Yes, I'm sure you did. But what was it about?'

He shrugged. 'Just a fight.'

They confronted him, she and Robbie, when Duncan was in bed.

'All right, Jamie, now tell us about it.'

'I got in a fight and I won. It's okay.'

'It's not okay. We want to know what happened.'

'I told you.'

'Don't speak to your Mam like that.'

'Robbie. Just a minute.' Jean knelt in front of Jamie. 'Now, Jamie. I want you to tell me why you were fighting.'

'I got in a fight.' He looked round at Robbie for help. 'Dad, *you* know.'

'Yes, I know. But you don't fight without reason. I never did.'

There was a long silence. 'I dinna like telling tales.'

Jean said, 'Jamie, it's not telling tales if you tell your parents, only if you tell other people.' She could feel Robbie growing impatient.

'Come on, Jamie lad, you've got to tell us or we canna help you.'

'You canna help me anyway.' He stared at them defiantly. 'They were picking on him. They've been doing it ever since we got here. They can tell he's scared. He canna help it, he's

56

too wee to look after himself. It's up to me to take care of him. And now you've made me tell you and I promised I wouldn't.'

Jean said, 'Who made you promise?'

'Duncan, of course.'

'But why? Why ever didn't you come to us the minute it started happening?'

'Oh – you might have gone to the teachers. That'd only make it worse.'

'It's the only way to stop it.'

'You don't understand.' He turned away.

'The laddie's right, Jean. If the other kids found out we've been to the teachers, they'll only pick on him more.'

'But the teachers can stop it.'

'They can't, Mam.'

'Of course they can't. How can they watch one child every minute of the day?'

She turned on him in a fury. 'So you're willing to let your son go on being bullied and do nothing about it.'

'Jamie, what do they actually do, these kids?'

'Oh, they hang around and make fun of the way he talks. They kind of get round in a circle and imitate him. They push him around and trip him up and take his pencils off him. That kind of thing.'

The mixture of matter-of-factness and compassion in Jamie's tone made Jean want to cry. She didn't trust herself to speak.

'They don't actually hit him?' Robbie went on.

'Not when I'm there.'

'Are these the kids in his class – the same age?'

'Aye.'

'What about the ones in your class?'

'Oh, they're okay.'

'They don't bully you?'

'They did at first but they don't any more.'

Jean felt lost. Jamie and Robbie were talking some private language.

'So it's the kids in Duncan's class you're fighting.'

'It is now. I dinna like hitting younger kids but I've got to – till they leave him alone. Of course they dinna think it's fair, so they set on me two at a time.'

Jean said, 'Oh, my God.'

Jamie looked surprised. 'It's okay, Mam, they're not very big and they haven't a clue how to fight.'

'No,' she said, looking at his black eye, 'I can see that.'

'Och, that's nothing. I got a bit careless.'

'But why didn't the teachers stop it?'

'They didna see, it was in the playground. There was a whole gang standing around. It didna take long.'

Robbie said, 'It's a pity Duncan canna fight his own battles.'

Jamie shook his head. 'He's too wee.'

Jean felt excluded. They seemed to have reached some kind of understanding without her, based on common experience she knew nothing about.

Robbie said gently, 'All right, Jamie, off to bed now. You've done well.'

'You won't tell on me?'

'No.'

'Robbie –'

'Ssh.'

'Promise?'

'Promise.'

Jamie gave a deep sigh of relief. 'Night.'

When they were alone Jean poured whisky for them both. She was so angry and so alarmed, she didn't know where to begin.

'How can he fight his own battles? He's only six.'

'It's something you have to do at any age.'

'But he can't.'

'Obviously.'

She felt herself and Duncan jointly attacked. They were weak and the other two were strong. 'What d'you mean?'

'He's hiding behind his brother.'

'What else can he do?'

'Stand up and fight. If he beat them just once they'd leave him alone.'

58

Jean was sickened. 'How can he beat a whole gang?'

'They'd take him on one at a time.'

'Oh yes? The way they do Jamie.'

'That's only because he's older. That's fair.'

'My God.' She was shocked. 'You're actually on their side.'

'Jean, I'm simply trying to explain to you how it is.'

'But if the teachers knew, they could stop it.'

'No. Jamie was right. Those kids would only pick on Duncan more if they knew he'd been telling tales.'

He sounded so positive that Jean asked, 'How do you know?'

'Oh – it happened at my school.'

'Were you one of the bullies?'

'Thanks a lot. I wasna bully nor victim.'

'No, I didn't imagine you'd be a victim.'

'Jean, it was someone else, in another class. I just knew about it.'

'And you didn't try to stop it?'

He looked exasperated. 'I couldna stop it. Anyway, it wasna my business.'

'God, it's barbaric. Well, I'm going to stop it, I'm going to the school.'

'No, you're not. We promised Jamie.'

'That doesn't count.'

'Oh, doesn't it? So you make things ten times worse for Duncan, and Jamie learns never to trust us again. Is that what you want?'

'Robbie, this is an emergency. Don't you even care?'

'Of course I do, what d'you think I am? I'm bloody sorry for Duncan, poor little bugger.'

'Yes, I can see how sorry you are. So sorry you won't lift a finger to help.'

Suddenly, unexpectedly, he softened, beguiling her. 'Jean, listen to me, hen. I'd like to take those kids apart. But what would that prove? Just that I'm bigger than they are. That's all Jamie's proving now.'

Only one fact got through to her. 'You mean they'll give up?'

'Eventually, yes.'

'Thank God. That's all I care about.'

'You're missing the point.' He poured fresh drinks for them both and she half resented he could think of such a thing at that moment, and yet she was also grateful. 'If Duncan doesn't learn to fight his own battles now, one day Jamie won't be there to save him and then what will happen?'

She was alarmed. 'You're talking as if he's going to spend his whole life in a jungle.'

'Jean, in the long run, it's no good depending on anyone but yourself. That's a fact and the sooner he learns it, the better.'

The words seemed to mark such a deep division between their attitudes that she wondered how it could ever be bridged. She said feebly, 'Couldn't we ... try another school?'

'We may be moving again in the autumn. It's hardly worth changing schools now.'

At last she found herself starting to cry. 'But he must be so scared.' She felt Duncan's terror as if it were her own. 'And Jamie ... it's not right encouraging him.' In a way this was the worst thing of all. She could hardly say it. 'I think he's half enjoying it all.'

Robbie put his arms round her.

In June Ruth gave a party. It was mainly business disguised as pleasure and Jean didn't want to go. She only liked small parties where everyone knew everyone else and was genuinely friendly. She also didn't want to observe any more friction between David and Ruth, though she tried to tell herself that what she had seen on the day of the phone call might be just an isolated incident.

It was a fine summer evening and the drawing-room was crowded and warm. The party spilled over onto the terrace; Jean had to admit that Ruth's house, like Ruth, was ideally suited to party-giving. They were both glossy, expensive and extrovert.

Inevitably Robbie drifted away to talk shop and Jean wandered around by herself, glass in hand, trying to pretend she was perfectly happy and looking for someone. Odd snatches of conversation reached her from different people, making no sense at all. It was all taking place in another world.

'... The only problem is, Fred wants to be chairman or he won't agree to the terms.'

'... Don't talk to me about the Press.'

'... So they're both paying her double and she's still living with him.'

'... If there's a tenant below the market rent, he's living on the backs of the shareholders.'

'... It's quite absurd. *He* was rusticated but *she* was sent down.'

'... Ah well, it was a privately promoted scheme, wasn't it?'

'... She's asking for so much money, he simply can't afford to get rid of her.'

'... What else can you expect if you don't have sole right to negotiate?'

'... Well, yes, he was successful all right, but he spent every penny he earned.'

She was lost in a dream of these separate people, trying to imagine what lives they led that could possibly make such remarks part of their everyday existence. It was all rather impressive and at the same time ludicrous. Her earlier pretence became true: she was actually, suddenly, quite happily contemplating those around her. She didn't even see Ruth until she collided with her.

'Jean – I've been looking for you everywhere. Come and meet some people.'

Too late. 'No, really, I'm okay. I never know what to say to them and I hate seeing their eyes glaze over when they don't know what to say to me.'

Ruth looked sympathetic. 'Yes, it's bloody awful, isn't it?'

'Surely it doesn't happen to you.' Jean was surprised and disbelieving.

'Well, on this occasion,' Ruth said wryly, 'most of them know I'm the hostess, but that's the only advantage I have. How are things? It's nice to have a chance to talk to you.'

'Everything's fine. The bullying's stopped.' Even as she spoke she could hardly believe it: her own words sounded like a lie, a piece of wishful thinking.

'That's marvellous.'

'Yes, *I* think so. Robbie doesn't though, because Jamie stopped it, not Duncan.'

'What's the difference so long as it's stopped?'

Jean warmed to Ruth all over again. They were two mothers together – against the world if need be, the world in which husbands and fathers and other men pursued their strange priorities. She glanced across the room and said with a touch of asperity, 'Robbie seems to be getting on well.' She could see him deep in conversation, but smiling and joking, using the charm he seldom bothered to display at home.

Ruth said, 'Yes, doesn't he?'

'Funny, it's not like him. He usually hates parties.'

As if she had been reading Jean's thoughts, Ruth said, 'But he's meeting some useful people.' She paused for a moment, almost, Jean felt, on the verge of a confidence, but changing her mind she merely added, 'All ambitious men are the same.'

In August she went back to Glasgow for a month with the children and Robbie joined them for two weeks. It was strange to be home again, although she had looked forward to it, longed for it, ever since she left. It was not the same. People expected her to have changed in some subtle way, so she was obliged to prove she had not. She had trouble adjusting her vision because proportions had altered. London was so big that Glasgow, which had seemed normal, now appeared small. She was also busy being careful not to love it too much since she would not be allowed to stay there.

Then in the autumn everything seemed to happen at once: they moved to a better flat, the children changed schools again and she got a job. Only a part-time job, of course, but nevertheless a job. She was excited about it. From having very little to do, she was suddenly busy. Robbie took little interest in it, beyond vague approval; he seemed preoccupied with the Northolt site. But Ruth made as much fuss as if the job were her own, meeting Jean outside the hospital on her first day so that they could celebrate together.

'Well – how did it go?' she said eagerly.

'Oh, not bad.' Jean got into the car with a feeling of relief and exhaustion. 'It's very odd being a new girl again but lovely to be working.'

'I've booked a table at our usual place.'

Jean looked doubtfully at her uniform. 'Can I go there dressed like this?'

'Why not? On you it looks good.'

They laughed, comfortable together.

'I really meant to go shopping for curtain material,' Jean said, thinking of the new flat.

'Tomorrow. Today we're celebrating. It's not every day you start a new job – in my case, never. So relax. Enjoy – as David's father would say. Drives David into a frenzy.'

'Why? It sounds nice.'

'Ah, you haven't heard the threatening way he says it.'

Robbie took her out to dinner. She wanted to talk about the hospital, but he was full of a warehouse he had seen near the Northolt site. The sums he mentioned terrified her: forty thousand to buy it, ten or fifteen to do it up.

'It's an awful lot of money, Robbie. To borrow, I mean.'

He was unperturbed. 'Aye, but it's good value.'

'What does David think?'

'Oh, he's agin the whole idea, of course.'

'Why "of course"?'

He looked scornful. 'Well, he's so bloody timid.'

'Maybe he's just prudent.' Because she agreed with David, she felt criticism of him was also directed at her.

'Thank you for that vote of confidence.'

'Robbie, I'm sorry, but it does sound a lot to take on, on top of the house. You know about houses, but a warehouse – you've never . . .'

'I didn't know about shops but I made a profit on that shop back home.'

She could see he was set on the idea. 'Only because you sold it so quickly.'

'I'd sell this quickly too.'

'Maybe.' She tried to find another angle. 'What did the bank manager say?'

'Oh, he won't look at it. But there must be someone with the money, prepared to put it into this kind of deal. There must be. I've just got to find them.'

Useless to argue. 'You're not eating.'

'What? Oh, sorry. It's very good.'

'It's supposed to be my treat. To celebrate my first pay packet.'

'But you haven't got it yet.'

'Very nearly. I've got a bridging loan from the house-keeping.'

He smiled. 'If I'd known that, I'd have ordered steak.'

'I mean it.'

'I can't let you pay.'

'Why not?'

'Well ... I can't.'

'Not even if I pass you the money under the table?'

They laughed, remembering earlier days when she had actually earned more than he did.

'You know,' she said, 'we really must have David and Ruth to dinner soon. I'd like them to see the new flat.'

'Why bother? They never saw the old one – thank God.'

'Ruth's been awfully kind.'

He looked sullen. 'I wish I could say the same for David.'

'He's all right, isn't he? He found you the Northolt site.'

'It'd be more to the point if he'd find me someone to finance the warehouse. Spencer thinks we're going to do a deal.'

She was appalled at how far it had gone. 'On his terms?'

'Oh, I can beat him down a bit, I think. But I need finance.'

'I'll try to come up with a bright idea while I'm doing the bed-pans.'

He looked faintly indignant. 'Are they still giving you all the dirty jobs?'

'Someone has to do them.'

By the time David and Ruth did come to dinner it was early November and admiration of the new flat somehow slid into a violent argument about Hungary. Afterwards Jean couldn't remember how it began. They all had too much to drink, presumably, but it was more than that: as if Hungary lay like a firework under the table and a careless match ignited it. Suddenly they were all shouting, Ruth most of all, as if she had some special interest in the subject. Jean wondered if she had relatives there.

'We should have done something, that's all,' Ruth shouted, 'before it was too late.'

Robbie looked sceptical. 'Didn't we have enough on our hands with Suez?'

'But that's the whole point.' David was supporting Ruth. 'The Russians simply used that as a smokescreen.'

'How could we take on the Russians?' Jean longed to pacify everyone – she could see the dinner party disintegrating before her eyes – but how could she be on all sides at once? 'I know it's terrible about Hungary but...'

'It's a moral duty, that's all.' Ruth looked round the table as if challenging them to disagree with her. 'They asked for help and we didn't give it. How would you feel if that happened to us?'

'It's not very likely,' Robbie said.

'Because we're an island?' David looked scornful. 'Don't be too sure. It damned nearly happened in the last war. We weren't too keen to take on the Germans, were we? But in the end we had to.'

'And we beat them,' Robbie said, as if he'd done it personally.

'Only just,' Ruth said. 'By which time it was a bit late for Poland – not to mention six million Jews.'

Robbie said, 'I might have known we'd get to that,' and Jean's heart sank. She wondered if he did it on purpose.

Ruth snapped, 'What's that supposed to mean?' and Jean said wearily, 'Oh, Robbie, don't.'

David said, 'It's supposed to mean,' looking at Robbie,

'there are more important things in life than saving your own skin, believe it or not.'

'Sorry.' Robbie was unrepentant. 'I can't accept that. It'd be fine to help Hungary but it's a luxury we simply can't afford.'

Ruth said, 'Luxury?'

'Aye, luxury. Of course they deserve help, but we simply can't give it on our own. There's no way of stopping Russia without provoking a third world war. Is that what you want?'

'We could stop them,' David said, 'if the Yanks backed us up.'

'Aye, well, if they're as quick off the mark as they were last time, I'd rather not hang around waiting for them.'

Ruth said, 'Is that all that matters to you – being on the winning side?'

Robbie looked at her with genuine surprise. 'Well, we wouldn't be much help to the poor bloody Hungarians if we lost. There's no point in starting any fight you can't win – I mean that's just basic common sense.'

'So it doesn't matter,' David said, 'that thousands of people are shot in the streets and mown down by tanks? We just sit here saying "Sorry about that and what a bit of luck it's not us."'

Jean said tentatively, 'Maybe if we'd tried to do something, other people would have followed – if we'd given a lead ...'

Robbie interrupted her. 'The way we're going on in Suez, we're in no position to give anyone a lead.'

'For Christ's sake,' Ruth shouted, 'shut up about Suez. I'm talking about Hungary.'

There was an awful silence. When Jean could bear it no longer she got up and went into the kitchen to make coffee. Her hands shook as she handled the cups; she strained her ears for sounds of conversation next door. Surely someone would start talking again soon – calmly, normally? But no one did. When she went back with the coffee there was still the same awful silence in which she was obliged to say inane hostessy things like 'Help yourselves to milk and sugar', and

'Would anyone like some brandy? Or whisky?' No one answered.

Suddenly, as if nothing had happened, Robbie said in a perfectly normal conversational tone, 'Talking about Hungarians, I met one the other day. George Kovacs. D'you know him?'

David and Ruth, who had been staring at the tablecloth, both looked up. David said, 'Yes,' but guardedly, and Jean felt the atmosphere change, although not necessarily for the better. Instead of outright war there was a wary, ominous calm.

'Well, can you tell me anything about him?' Robbie said impatiently.

David looked blank as if on purpose. 'Where did you meet him?'

'At Diana Crawley's house.'

Jean was surprised. 'I thought you'd finished work on that ages ago.'

'I had to go back and do the snagging list. I told you.'

'I don't remember.' In fact she was sure he hadn't.

Ruth said, 'What do you want to know about him?'

'I thought he might be useful.'

'How?'

'About the warehouse.'

David said, 'Oh, you're not still on about that.'

'I'll get it, sooner or later.' He looked around, as if to challenge them. 'Miss Crawley said he's a very important banker.'

Ruth said, 'Yes, he is.'

'I rather got the impression they might be having it away.'

David said, 'I hardly think so.'

'Oh, why not?' Nobody answered. Robbie went on, 'Well, d'you know anything about his history?'

'You'd better ask my father.'

'I don't know your father.'

Ruth said, 'David's father is a friend of George Kovacs, that's all. We don't really know much about him.'

'Well, is he good for financing a warehouse?'

David sipped his coffee. 'No more or less than any other

merchant banker. If you give him a good deal, he'll take it, and if you don't, he won't.'

'So there's nothing special about him?'

Ruth said, 'How d'you mean, special?'

'Well, isn't it rather unusual for an immigrant to get that far in the city?'

'I suppose so.' David sounded reluctant to admit it.

'Well, how did he do it? What's his background?'

Jean was embarrassed. David and Ruth obviously didn't want to discuss Kovacs, for whatever reason, and Robbie kept pressing the subject. 'Why are you so interested?' she said.

'I thought he might help me, that's all. As one self-made man to another.'

'What makes you think he's self-made?' David sounded quite aggressive. 'Perhaps he had a rich family.'

'Like you, you mean?'

'Why not?'

'That's what I'm trying to find out.' Robbie paused but no one added anything. 'So you don't know anything about him?'

Ruth said smoothly, 'Nothing that would help you.'

David said, 'Robert, there are dozens of merchant bankers. Sooner or later you'll find one to finance a warehouse, if you're really set on it.'

'But you'd rather I didn't choose George Kovacs.'

'It's hardly a matter of your choosing him,' Ruth said.

'Put it this way – he's the first merchant banker I've met.'

Jean said, 'I shouldn't think now's a very good time to approach him. He must be awfully upset about Hungary.'

'He can always send a cheque.' David, out of nowhere, suddenly sharp.

All the time Jean had the feeling they were talking about something else.

The letter came as a shock. She had kept a wary eye on the children, of course, for signs of trouble, but both insisted the new school was 'all right'. Perhaps, she thought later, she did not watch as carefully as she might have done because of her mornings at the hospital. The job did not improve. Gradually the novelty wore off and her optimism faded: it was clear that part-time nurses were regarded and treated as a useful but inferior breed, not to be integrated with the rest of the staff. They were given all the nastiest and the dreariest jobs, without any responsibility, and were even expected to sit apart, fraternizing only with each other, during tea or coffee breaks. Jean had not expected such segregation in a hospital. She was even more surprised to find that not all the part-timers resented it as much as she did. Some actually seemed to collude with the hospital's attitude by treating the work as merely a job with convenient hours, doing everything as slowly as possible, and watching the clock for the moment when they could stop and go home. She supposed, charitably, that it was a vicious circle: they were treated as inferior so they behaved accordingly, which led to even lower expectations and so on, endlessly. It depressed her very much, but she was determined not to give in.

She tried several times to discuss it with Robbie but she could tell he scarcely listened. He was obsessed with the warehouse: there seemed room for nothing else in his head. He eventually got to see Kovacs to ask for a loan, which was refused, on the day that the letter came, so all through dinner Jean had to listen to a detailed account of the interview when all she wanted to talk about was Duncan.

'Oh, he was nice enough,' Robbie said finally, 'but the fact remains, he's not going to help me.'

'I'm sorry.'

'It's very galling because I'm sure I'm right. I can't prove it but I know this is a great opportunity. It's quite absurd to have to let it go because I can't raise the cash.'

She could bear it no longer. 'Robbie, we've got other problems.'

'What?'

'This came today.' She took the letter from her pocket and gave it to him. He read it quickly and looked angry.

'Why the hell didn't you tell me before?'

'Oh – you were tired and depressed – and you wanted to talk about the warehouse.'

'God almighty, this is more important than any warehouse.' He glanced at his watch. 'Why did you wait till they're in bed? We could have had it out tonight.'

'I know, that's why I waited. We had it out last time and where did that get us?'

'So what do you suggest?'

She said patiently, 'Read the letter again. She wants to see us.'

The teacher was older than they were and made them feel rather like naughty children themselves.

'So this has happened before,' she said, as if it were somehow their fault.

'At his last school, yes.'

'How long was he there?'

'Only a term and a half.'

'I see.' She looked disapproving. 'It's very unsettling, of course, for a child of his age to keep moving around.'

'We're not doing it for fun,' Robbie said.

'No, I'm sure you're not. Tell me, what exactly happened at his previous school?'

'He was bullied,' Jean said. She found the words painful. 'And Jamie got into fights sticking up for him.'

Robbie said, 'In other words he hid behind his brother. Is that what he's doing here?'

'In the playground, yes. In the classroom, of course, he can't.'

'But then you're here.'

'Yes, but I don't have eyes in the back of my head. I only wish I did. Children can be very cruel and they have surprisingly subtle ways of doing it.' She sighed. 'Duncan is such a nice little boy, and very bright, but he's physically timid and of course they pick on that.'

'Isn't there anything we can do?' Jean looked at the teacher, willing her to come up with a solution.

'Well, in the long run the child will sort it out himself.'

'Aye, by fighting back,' Robbie said. 'It's about time he learned to do that.'

The teacher looked at him with faint distaste. 'Well, I actually meant by making friends. And that *is* something you can do – encourage him. Invite other little boys to tea. It's not that he's unpopular, you see. There are several children who'd quite like to be friends with him. But they're timid too, and they're afraid to make the first move. Before Duncan came *they* were the ones getting teased and picked on, and now he's the scapegoat and they've been let off. So it's difficult for them to stick up for him.'

'Fine friends they'd make,' Robbie said, 'by the sound of them.'

'It's not quite as bad as it sounds, Mr Mackenzie. These are very young children, remember. There's bound to be some kind of pecking order while they sort themselves out.' She glanced at Jean as if for support. 'I just wanted to be sure you understand the situation, so you can do your best to help and also make allowances for Duncan if he seems a bit subdued at home. Being bullied can make children very withdrawn. They're often afraid to tell their parents what's happening in case the parents make it worse by complaining.'

Jean sighed. 'Yes. That's more or less what Jamie said.'

'Well, he's right up to a point. But he's probably thinking you'd simply make a fuss at school. There are more positive things that parents can do.'

'Like what?' Robbie's tone was aggressive – defensive: Jean could tell he had taken a thorough dislike to the teacher.

'Like making sure you give Duncan every encouragement. Lots of praise whenever he does something well. He's very good at drawing, for instance –' she pointed to some of the drawings on the classroom wall.

'Yes,' Jean said, pleased. 'I've got several pinned up in the kitchen.'

'Lovely.' The teacher beamed her approval at her. 'That's just what I mean. Make him feel important.'

There was a moment's silence. 'That's all very fine,' Robbie said, 'but a few good drawings hardly make up for being a coward.'

71

'Robbie –' Jean recognized what he had said as a cry of pain and shame, but she knew it would sound quite different to the teacher.

'It's true. He's never going to get on in life till he learns to stick up for himself, and no amount of messing about with paint will change that.'

From the way the teacher looked at Robbie, Jean realized the dislike was mutual. 'Mr Mackenzie, d'you think it's possible Duncan feels a lot of pressure at home – as if it's not a place to relax but a place to compete with his brother and you?' She paused, placing the final dart with care. 'That would be a very heavy burden for a little boy, don't you think?'

Outside the school Robbie fumed as they waited for the children. Jean watched him pacing up and down and prayed they would not have a row in such a public place.

'Bloody woman. She as good as said it was all my fault.'

'Robbie, she didn't.'

'As near as dammit.'

'She was only trying to help. She's really concerned about Duncan.'

'Meaning I'm not?' He seemed determined to misunderstand.

'No, of course not. She was just tackling it from a different angle.'

'Well, as far as I'm concerned there's only one angle and as soon as they come out I'm going to ... ah, there they are.'

The children were emerging, Jamie and Duncan close together. They looked so vulnerable Jean panicked. 'No, Robbie, don't say anything.' She grabbed his arm. 'Not yet. Not till you've had a chance to calm down.'

'What the hell d'you mean?'

The children were getting nearer and she had made matters worse. 'You can't talk to Duncan in this mood – I won't let you.'

'Right. Have it your own way.' He walked towards the car.

'Where are you going?'

'Back to the site, of course. Where d'you think I'm going?'

She talked to Jamie instead and he told her the school was not as bad as the last one, he thought he could handle it, and Duncan was managing. The teacher was making a fuss, he said. Any guilt Jean felt at leaning on him was soon dispelled by his answers: he seemed so much older than eight. He would probably have the answer to her hospital problems too if she asked him.

Robbie came home in an even worse mood that evening, so she couldn't talk to him about anything. Instead of giving up on the warehouse he began answering advertisements for warehouses, as if he had one for sale. Then he advertised it himself. Jean was embarrassed and scared: it seemed both dishonest and dangerous. Worse still, it didn't work. But Robbie said it was only a matter of time. The longer it went on, the less downcast he seemed, which she found amazing and admirable. She wished she could copy him.

'I thought it would get better,' she said one night in bed, 'but it hasn't.'

'If they're not treating you right, you can always leave, you know.'

'Oh, it's not the dirty jobs, I don't mind that. It's not being given any responsibility that gets me down. You get a feeling that part-time means second-rate. And we just don't mix with the others. D'you know, we even have our coffee at different tables. They give us all the bed-making and the teas and bed-pans, all the fetching and carrying, and then they don't even talk to us.'

He put his arm round her. 'I don't know how you stick it.'

'I don't like to be beaten.' Perhaps they were not so different after all. 'I keep thinking it's bound to improve, but it's nearly two months now and it's just the same. We're like a lot of skivvies. I wouldn't mind if I hadn't had all the training and experience, but it's such a waste, it's not like proper nursing at all.' If she thought about it too long or too often, she wanted to cry like a child with disappointment; the only defence was to become angry.

'You're wishing I'd never brought you down here.'

'Well, Duncan and I don't seem to be doing too well, but you and Jamie are all right.'

'It's not like that at all.' He cuddled her.

'That's how it feels sometimes.'

'I'll talk to Duncan. Don't you worry, I'll be careful. Just have a wee chat with him. Make sure he knows we're on his side, like that teacher said. Maybe she was right. And if it's not better after Christmas, we can always move them again.'

It was unlike him to be so humble; she wished she could agree with him. But she had had too long to think about it. 'I'm not sure that's the answer.'

'Why not? That's what you wanted last time.'

'Aye, but if it goes on happening he's no better off. He might as well stay put till he makes some friends.'

'Don't think about it now,' he said soothingly. 'It's nearly the holidays.'

She sometimes thought that was the one thing that had kept her sane recently. 'Can we really go home for a whole week?'

'We may as well. We've got to be there for Marie's wedding and you want to stay on for Hogmanay.'

'Don't you?'

'Aye.'

'You don't sound very sure.'

'I'd like to be further on, that's all.'

She teased him gently. 'Have more to boast about, you mean.'

'I thought by now I'd have found somebody for the warehouse.'

'Oh, Robbie, you've answered every advert that ever was and you don't even own the place. You can't keep stringing Spencer along like this.'

'No, I can't – only as long as David will let me. And he's putting on the pressure.' But he didn't sound resentful, merely matter-of-fact. 'The minute he finds another purchaser, I've had it.'

'Why can't you let it go?'

It was as if he hadn't heard her. 'I think I'll try advertising it again. It just might work.'

'Oh, you can't.'

'It's perfectly safe under a box number.'

'It may be safe but it's not honest. How can you advertise something for sale if it doesn't belong to you?'

'Very easily.' He didn't sound worried at all. 'And the minute I find a purchaser, I'll buy that warehouse so fast Spencer's feet won't touch the ground.'

'I wish you'd leave it alone.'

'No, you don't. When I make a fat profit on the deal, you'll be pleased as punch.'

'I shan't be pleased at all,' she said firmly. 'I don't like the way you're doing it.'

'Not even if it means we can have a house?'

Silence. 'That's not fair.'

'You'd like that, wouldn't you?' He kissed her. 'I thought you would.' He kissed her again. 'Is there anything else you might like?'

Making love, she forgot the warehouse, the school, the hospital – forgot even how long it had been since the last time.

Suddenly, when she at least had given up hope, it all came right. Robbie found a purchaser for the warehouse and Kovacs said a loan was quite likely. It happened just before Christmas and was the best present she could have imagined. They went back to Glasgow in a state of euphoria. At midnight Mass with the children she gave thanks to God from the bottom of her heart: she felt they had been delivered from some terrible danger. On Boxing Day she even found the courage to drive past the Bearsden house with Jamie. He got very excited and made her stop.

'Look, that's where we used to live.'

'Yes, I know.' She stared at the house, willing herself not to cry. There was so much to remember.

'Who lives there now?'

'I don't know. Just other people.'

'Shall we go and say hullo to them?'

She smiled at his tough, friendly indifference. 'No, I don't think so.' But it was something done; she had seen it again. It was over.

She started the car.

Marie's wedding was brief and simple, in a registry office. The baby didn't show yet. Only Robbie had doubts about the marriage; everyone else was delighted. Jean couldn't stop thinking about her own wedding and how much had happened since then.

They were staying in a cheap hotel because they couldn't stay with her parents and Robbie wouldn't stay with his mother and Andy. Jean spent a lot of time visiting both families and Robbie spent a lot of time in the pub, proving to everyone he used to know that he hadn't changed. Jamie and Duncan played with neighbourhood children again and showed off about London: Jean had a strange feeling that in some way, despite all the problems, they actually liked it, or at least that it made them feel superior. All the time they were so busy enjoying themselves in various obligatory ways, they managed not to talk about the fact that Robbie was still waiting for a decision from Kovacs.

Two days before Hogmanay. Jean had hoped to sleep late: too many drinks and late nights had caught up with her and she felt sure Robbie must feel the same. But she woke to an empty bed. A moment later Robbie came in, brisk as if he'd been awake for hours, tossing a newspaper onto the bed.

'We've got a warehouse,' he chanted round the bed, 'we've got a warehouse.'

She was dazed with sleep. 'I'd sooner have a cup of tea.'

'The deal is on.'

'What's the time?'

'Half past nine.'

'And you've rung him already?'

'Why not? He was there.'

He looked so triumphant that somehow she couldn't share the moment: it was as if he had a monopoly of elation. She sat up and started reading the paper, in self-defence.

'We've got a warehouse,' he said again.

'That's wonderful.' The paper was full of a story about a Hungarian teenager, an interview with pictures. She read it while he went on talking about his plans for the warehouse and how soon he could start work on it; she didn't take in the words. At some deeper level she suddenly felt the warehouse meant trouble and she wished he hadn't got it.

'There's a girl here had a baby at fourteen,' she said.

'What?'

'She's a Hungarian refugee. She says: "I can't think why people look on me as a young mother. I was working at eleven, courting my husband at twelve, married at thirteen." Isn't that interesting?'

'Jean, I think I better go back to London today.'

She looked up, shocked. She had been vaguely aware that the story would bore him, as the warehouse bored her, and she'd read it by way of reprisal, but she hadn't expected this. 'But what about Hogmanay?' she said, feeling stupid and rejected.

'Oh, you stay on and see everyone.' He made it sound like a favour.

'But it won't be the same without you. Surely a couple of days can't make that much difference.'

He turned away, looking out of the window. 'I don't know – they might. I've just got a feeling, the sooner I get back down there the better.'

And nothing else mattered: her feelings, the children, the holiday. She said bitterly, 'Suit yourself. No doubt you will anyway.'

Diana

I met him at one of Ruth's summer parties. I noticed him at once because I was just coming out of my tall thin blond phase back into my short dark hairy phase, and he was it. A sort of zing went through me, which is always reliable, but I pretended to ignore it because he was much too far away to deserve to be noticed.

Peter and I were just on the steps between Ruth's sitting-room and terrace, so I waved to her and we went over. He was even better when I got close to him, just like a gorilla, only a sort of benign, sexy gorilla, who might have a nice nature (which, of course, we are always told they have, only it's hard to believe from looking at them).

Ruth said, 'Hullo, love,' and we kissed on the cheek. She was wearing Mitsouko and her favourite red dress: she looked rather stunning actually.

I said, 'Sorry we're late. Peter couldn't get the car to start.' I didn't look at Peter but I could feel him practically squirming with embarrassment beside me, which was fun.

He said feebly, 'Oh, Diana, really,' and I remember thinking, Yes, Peter will definitely have to go. All in good time, though.

I said, 'Well, what do you want me to say?'

Ruth was doing her hostess bit. 'Can I introduce Robert Mackenzie? Diana Crawley, Peter Langton.'

I looked at him as if for the first time. 'Hullo.'

'We've met.' Peter sounded grumpy.

Ruth said, 'Oh yes, of course. How stupid of me, I wasn't thinking.'

I said, 'So you're converting my house for me.' I was both pleased and upset: I hadn't expected a mere builder to look like this, but I also hadn't expected to be interested in a mere builder. 'I hope you're doing it well.'

He stared insolently back at me. 'I always do.' He had brown hair and brown eyes and a sort of brown aura. He was about my height, five eight, so in heels I was taller than he was. I wondered if he minded.

'Will you excuse me?' Ruth sort of faded away. She was good at that. I'm better at entrances than exits myself.

'I could do it better still,' he said, 'if I had a free hand.'

'Really?' This was fun. We'd only just met and already we were playing games.

Of course Peter had to interrupt and spoil it. 'Then it wouldn't be what Diana wanted.' Somehow he managed to use my name in a very proprietary way, yet without putting any emphasis on it.

'We had a slight argument about the plans,' my brown gorilla said.

'Did you?' I noticed how chunky he was, a nice solid rectangular man for a change, with hands that looked as if they'd done a lot of work but had started recovering from it.

'Mr Mackenzie wasn't too keen on my design, darling.' Peter, stirring it again.

'So you're an architect, too, are you, Mr Mackenzie?'

'No. But I know how to make the best use of a good building.' The Scottish accent was very sexy.

'Yes, it is a good building, isn't it? Only they were my plans. Peter was just kind enough to draw them for me.'

'Maybe I can still persuade you?' He was definitely interested; I could see it in his eyes. But he was wary, too, perhaps because I was the client. 'Will you be at the site meeting next week?'

'No, I'll be working.' I was sorry in a way, but there was no point in seeing him again with Peter.

'Really? What d'you do?'

'Guess.' I amused myself trying to imagine what his cock was like.

'I can't imagine.'

'Diana's a model,' Peter said.

'Of course.'

Short and thick, I decided. 'So you and Peter will have to manage without me. But I'm sure you'll be able to agree. Just keep remembering it's my house.'

I left them to it and wriggled through the crowd to Ruth. We were both getting fresh drinks.

'What d'you think?' She looked pleased with herself. 'He's quite something, isn't he?'

'Yes, but bloody aggressive.'

'So are you.' She smiled at me. 'Talented though.'

'That too?' I was cross I hadn't realized before. She must have discovered him in Glasgow, those three months when she was so bored and missing my father.

'Mm. Very.'

'Rough trade...' I said doubtfully. I wanted her to convince me otherwise.

'Rather more than that.'

'And up for grabs?'

'That's his wife over there, talking to David.'

I looked, and there was this woman, about my age, with red curly hair cut short, listening to David with an alert, kind, interested expression, as if he wasn't a bore. 'She looks nice,' I said. She really did.

Ruth said simply, 'She is.'

I looked back through the french doors at my new gorilla.

Then in July it bloody pissed with rain and Peter got clingy and I was working hard, and the weather made my hair go straight when it was meant to be curly, and curly when it was meant to be straight, and I nearly went out of my mind. I was so busy and so tired and I couldn't decide what to do about the gorilla. As time passed I kept forgetting details: I remembered the nice suit and shirt and tie (probably all his best gear) but I couldn't remember if I'd noticed hair on his wrists, which would probably indicate hair on his body. I remembered the brown hair and eyes but not the expression; I remembered the chunky shape but not the smile. It all got very confusing, like one of those dreams you've half forgotten when you wake up, so I didn't know what I wanted to do. Did he have nice teeth? I couldn't remember seeing his teeth, but I must have done.

Reconnaissance, I thought. So one Friday I told Peter I was with my parents and I bought some champagne and changed into jeans and a jersey and my oilskins. Piers had taken some pictures of me like that, so I knew I looked good, and Peter had told me the gorilla was always there on Friday afternoons paying the workmen. I hung about opposite, getting my hair wet (I'd been surprised how good I looked in the photographs with wet hair) and watching them all leave. I thought it would do the gorilla good to see me looking totally different from Ruth's party where I'd had my hair up and the usual black dress, and anyway it would be fun to surprise him while I made up my mind. I really wasn't sure at all at this stage: I'd forgotten most of the details by now.

When I'd counted all the departing workmen and I knew he was alone, I went in. As soon as I slammed the door he called out, 'Is that you, Bill? Have you forgotten something?' and that accent went through me just the way I'd hoped it would. At the same time I made a mental note that the foreman (presumably) had a key and I must get the locks changed when I moved in.

I went up the stairs and when I was nearly at the top I said, 'No, I don't think so.' He spun round: he was really startled to see me, though he tried to conceal it. 'Well,' I said, ever so surprised, 'fancy you being here.'

He recovered quickly and his eyes went blank. 'I'm always here on Fridays to do the wages.'

He was still brown and chunky but he looked awful in his working clothes. 'Really?' I said, very cool. 'That must be why I haven't run into you before; I usually go away weekends.'

'You've been taking an interest then...' He sounded surprised (pleased, relieved?). 'I thought maybe you were leaving it all to your friend.'

It was my turn to look blank. 'What friend?'

'Peter.'

'Peter who?'

'Peter Langton, your architect friend.'

What was this? Surely nothing as basic as jealousy. I didn't bother to pick it up. 'Oh, goodness no. I never leave things to other people. I've been here every week.' I started wandering round inspecting things, removing my oilskins. I could feel him watching me.

'You're very wet,' he said finally.

'Yes, I am rather.' I could have hugged him. It was all right: we were playing games again. The ugly clothes didn't matter; he'd been dressing up at the party. Now I was dressing up, whereas then I'd been real. I went on inspecting; I was so excited suddenly I couldn't trust myself to speak.

'Well, what d'you think?' He sounded impatient for the first time.

I turned round. 'I think we're making progress. Don't you?'

'I hope so.'

'In fact I think you've worked quite fast.'

'Oh, I can work very fast when I get the chance.'

'All things being equal.'

'Aye.'

I'd been keeping a score-card: it was deuce, more or less. I felt so elated, I made an interim decision. 'Shall we christen it? The house. There's a bottle of champagne downstairs.' I'd left it there in case I decided I didn't fancy him after all.

There was a pause, not long but intense. He said, 'Shall I get it?'

'That would be very kind of you.'

He went downstairs. I stood at the window, watching the rain, and I could feel what Piers called my pussycat smile ('Come on, darling, cat with the cream, that's it, terrific') spreading all over my face.

He came back. He started struggling with the cork. I wondered how many bottles he'd opened in his life.

I said, 'D'you like champagne?'

'It's all right.'

I watched his hands. His hands were a big turn-on. 'But you prefer whisky.'

'Aye. Were you going to drink all this yourself?'

He sounded so shocked (the first hint of Calvin?) I nearly laughed. 'Well, how was I to know you'd be here?' It was lovely to sound so innocent. And then the cork popped. 'Oh, well done. And not a drop spilled. That's the right way to do it.'

'Yes, I do know that.'

Had I offended him? Did I sound patronizing? 'I hate waste, don't you?'

He didn't look at me, just held out the bottle. 'Here's to your house.'

I took a swig and wiped the top of the bottle. 'I'm afraid I didn't bring any glasses – you don't mind, do you? I'm quite healthy.' I watched him drink. He had straight, thick eyelashes that concealed his eyes. 'How soon can I move in?'

He handed me back the bottle. 'Next month, I hope.'

'As soon as that.' This time I drank without wiping the top. 'Oh, that would be splendid.' I gave him the bottle again.

'It would suit me too.' He drank immediately. 'I'm supposed to be off on holiday. My wife and kids have already gone.'

Now why had he told me that? I accepted the bottle again and took a long, long draught. 'Really?'

I moved in three weeks later. I could hardly believe it because builders nearly always lie or miscalculate about when things will be finished. He'd done it beautifully too, including all the things he'd argued about, like the spiral staircases. I had all the carpets laid, but I didn't buy any furniture because I thought it might be fun to camp there for a bit while I decided what I really wanted. I felt excited like a child; I couldn't remember feeling like that about anything for ages.

I brought wine and whisky and some glasses from the flat

83

and bought some delicious food from the delicatessen and arranged it all on a cloth on the floor. It looked pretty splendid – casually splendid. So did I, actually, in my nicest kaftan and bare feet and my hair hanging loose. Quite different from the drowned waif of last month.

I picked up the phone and dialled. When he answered he sounded ever so slightly sleepy and offhand: I imagined him watching television with a drink in his hand and maybe expecting a call from his wife. An idle sort of evening – perfect. I made up a story about something having gone wrong in the flat and he offered to come over and fix it, with only the merest hesitation that could mean eagerness or reluctance or just a sense of duty. I wasn't sure which, and that made me feel more childish and excited than ever. Definitely in a mood to celebrate.

I left the front door open, so that when he rang the bell (punctually in half an hour as promised) I could shout down the stairs, 'Come on up.' I wanted him to discover me sitting on the floor with my picnic spread before me, and he did. 'Wine or whisky?' I said, looking up at him. He looked rather smart – dressed casually but nicely in a good jersey and corduroy trousers.

'Don't you think I should get the work done first?' He sounded all brisk and purposeful, the way workmen should but seldom do.

I said airily, 'Oh, I fixed it. I tried to ring you back but you'd already left. I'm terribly sorry.' I couldn't tell if he believed me: he'd have made a good poker player.

'That's all right,' he said. 'I didn't know you were so resourceful.'

'Sometimes I surprise myself. I just fiddled about with it and suddenly it came.' I was really having trouble keeping my face straight. 'Do have some pâté – it's the least I can do after dragging you all this way.'

He sat down on the floor opposite me. 'The carpet makes quite a difference.'

'Yes, it's nice, isn't it? I like it so much it seems a pity to put furniture on top of it, but I suppose I'll have to. One or two bits and pieces anyway. D'you know, this is the first time I've been able to do everything in the right order – conversion, decoration, carpets, furniture. I can't believe it.'

He looked at me as if he were seeing me for the first time. 'You're really pleased.'

'When I like something I really like it.' Let him think that one over. 'Have some olives.'

'Thank you.'

Now – be careful. 'When are you going on holiday?'

'Next week probably.'

'Where to?'

'Back to Scotland to see everyone.'

'That'll be nice. I'm off to the sun but I'm not sure where yet. Greece probably.' I pointed at the salami. 'That's good, too, you should try it.'

'I will.' He took some, but gingerly, as if he wasn't used to it. 'So you don't plan very far ahead.'

'Not often. I think it spoils the fun.' Time to risk something? 'I'll come back very brown, of course.'

'Yes.' He looked up; we'd both been concentrating on the food. 'That will suit you.'

'It's always a big improvement.'

'I wouldn't have said there was very much room for improvement.'

I was so amazed I said, 'Oh, that was nice of you,' as if no one had ever paid me a compliment before, because that was how it felt.

'I mean it. You know that.'

'It makes all the difference if people mean things. So many people don't.'

Now we were really looking at each other.

He said, 'I've only met you three times but you're never the same.'

It occurred to me that although he'd undoubtedly been attracted from the start, he hadn't actually liked me before. Not that it was essential for us to like each other, but it would be a welcome bonus. And he obviously liked the new childish enthusiastic unspoilt me better than the old sophisticated blasé games-playing rich bitch.

85

I said, 'I don't believe I've ever really thanked you properly for making my home look so beautiful.'

'I enjoyed doing it.'

'Did you?'

'More than I thought I would.'

Well, it was now or never. I took a large bite of pâté. 'Would you like to make love?'

He looked so stunned I nearly laughed, but I knew that would ruin everything and probably choke me as well. 'What?'

I pointed at my mouth and swallowed. 'Sorry. Nanny always said I shouldn't talk with my mouth full. I said would you like to make love?'

He swallowed too. 'I heard you.'

'With me, I mean.'

'Now?'

'Well, I thought we could finish this first.'

I suppose the day will come when my method doesn't work and then I'll know I'm getting old.

I didn't see him again till October. Apart from that week, I mean. We met three times in three days, without arrangement: he just turned up and I was there. We were at it like knives; I don't remember much conversation, apart from jokes. We really turned each other on: it was incredible. We liked all the same things – sucking, fucking, stroking – and even more important he was very warm and cuddly, so I felt it was safe to be silly and childish with him. He made me come such a lot, we were both very proud of ourselves. We wanted to devour each other, drown in each other, all the usual crazy feelings. No – it wasn't usual, it was special. Even then. I think I had premonitions and that's why I ran away. Besides, I had to go first, I had to be the one to leave. I couldn't have him desert me to join his wife in Glasgow, so I left for Greece two days early. I didn't say I was going, I just went. Oh, I was very cool in those days, when I put my mind to it.

'Why did you disappear?' he asked when we finally surfaced for air in October after all that coming together again.

'I told you I was going to Greece.' I was impressed by how casual I sounded.

'For two months?'

'Why not? Besides, we got a bit carried away.'

The 'we' was deliberate: I simply couldn't resist it. I was delighted when he picked it up.

'Who's we?'

'Piers and I.'

'And who's Piers?'

Better and better. 'My brother, of course.' I hadn't told even Piers much about him, except that I'd had a fling with my builder and wasn't it a joke? But of course, being Piers, he knew it was more than that.

'Of course. While I had two weeks in Glasgow. That just about says it all.'

I laughed. Then the bell went off and he was really startled, as if someone had shot him.

'What the hell's that?'

'The kitchen-timer. I set it for an hour in case we went to sleep.'

'Don't use it on anyone with a weak heart or a nervous disposition.' He still sounded a bit shaken.

'I don't know anyone like that.' I stroked the fur on his chest, wondering if he'd appreciate knowing I'd labelled him my brown gorilla. I decided he probably would but I preferred to keep it to myself. 'Who told you I was away for two months?'

'I came round.'

Pretty constantly, too, to be sure I wasn't back in September. I was gratified. 'To see me?'

'No, to do the snagging list.'

'That's a good word for it.' I traced his blunt profile with my finger. 'You'd never have made the first move back in August, would you?'

'Well, you were the client.'

'Quite.' Just thinking about it made me laugh. 'Oh, what a game it all is. I was taking a chance – you might have turned me down.'

'Not very likely.' He bit the end of my finger gently.

'No one ever has – but it's always possible.'

'Is that your usual approach?'

'Why, don't you like it?' I detected a sudden slight tetchiness. 'Oh, you're not going to be all stuffy about the others, are you? All boo-hoo and sulky-poo?'

'All *what*?' He was intrigued; I had succeeded in diverting him.

'When I was little and I stuck out my bottom lip and stamped my foot and started to cry with temper – I did that a lot –'

'I can imagine.'

'– Mummy used to say I was "all boo-hoo and sulky-poo," just to annoy me.'

He laughed. 'I should think it would, too. It sounds revolting.'

'Yes, Mummy is pretty revolting.'

'What about Daddy?'

'Oh, *he's* all right.' Dangerous ground. I changed the subject fast. 'Hey – what am I going to call you?' For so far we hadn't used names at all.

'I thought you called me God just now.' He looked smug.

'Oh – that was below the belt.'

'Where else?'

I kissed him. It was years since I had felt so comfortable with anyone and yet so stimulated. 'What does your wife call you?'

'Robbie.'

'Oh, like Robbie Burns. Isn't that sweet. And your mother?'

'Rob.' He began to look faintly embarrassed. I was delighted.

'Like Rob Roy. It gets better and better.'

'We're not living in the Middle Ages, you know.'

'Don't be silly, that was the eighteenth century.' Poor darling, he probably didn't know the difference, not having had much education. 'What does David call you?'

'Robert.'

'Yes, he would.' Suddenly it came to me. 'I think I'll call

you Mack. Would you like that? It sounds like a newspaper editor with a green eyeshade in a "B" picture.' I put on my best American accent. ' "Say, Mack, hold the front page." I think it suits you. Now all we have to do is sign the Rule Book.' Actually I was impressed that he had come back: I wasn't so conceited as to think I couldn't be forgotten in two months. I suppose I'd done it on purpose to look as if I was rejecting him. I certainly wouldn't have chased after him again. But here he was.

'What d'you mean?'

'Like joining a Trade Union.'

'Not me, I'm self-employed.'

I laughed. 'Not here you're not. You're a happily married man and I'm your bit on the side.'

'I wouldn't put it quite like that.' He cuddled me.

'Well, I would. You *are* happily married, aren't you? I hope.'

'Aye.' He sounded uneasy.

'So you don't want me ringing up your wife and making trouble.' As if I would.

'No, I certainly don't.'

'Right, that makes me a bit on the side. So we sign the Rule Book. I promise not to rock the marital boat.'

'And what do I promise?'

'To let me paddle my own canoe.' I was rather pleased with my extended metaphor, having only just stumbled across it. 'No jealous scenes about other lovers, if any. I don't tell and you don't ask. We go on as long as it lasts and no one gets hurt. Okay?'

'Okay.' After a long silence.

'Cross your heart and hope to die.'

'If you like.' He sounded indulgent.

'No, you must say it. I'm serious.'

'Cross my heart and hope to die.' Now I detected something else in his voice – amusement mixed with alarm. He kissed me. 'Do we have time for an encore? Just to seal the bargain.'

'We can always shake hands. Besides, you're due back on site.'

'I am on site. This is a site meeting.'

We rolled about in bed, laughing, and started to make love again. Those were the days, those wonderful early days when everything could be solved by making love. But even then, he had to spoil it with one sentence. I should have been warned; I should have taken notice.

'D'you really have a brother called Piers?'

I told my father all about him. He was amused and indulgent as always, wanting only for me to be happy. It's like a drug, having someone like that in your life: you get high on it and you get addicted.

I wanted them to meet, so I asked my father to tea one afternoon when I was expecting Mack. I warned my father, of course, but I didn't warn Mack, and it was really very amusing: when he found I wasn't alone you could positively see him leaping to all kinds of ridiculous conclusions, suspicion all over his face for a moment and then swiftly concealed, like someone putting on a mask. 'Fancy seeing you,' I said, as if he wasn't expected, and then to my father, 'This is the builder who converted me. Robert Mackenzie – George Kovacs.'

They shook hands and said how do you do and all that, and then there was silence.

I said, as something seemed to be required of me, 'Mr Kovacs is an old friend of my parents.' It was all I could do not to laugh.

Mack said at once, 'I only called to do the snagging list.'

'Really?'

My father said, 'You are very conscientious, Mr Mackenzie.'

Mack shrugged. 'It's all part of the job.'

'And a very good job you have done. I am most impressed.'

'I enjoyed doing it. I found it very stimulating.'

I wondered how they saw each other: Mack, my brown gorilla, and my father a bit like Orson Welles. Did they see glamour or merely competition? It occurred to me suddenly, for the first time, that they were somehow alike, not in size or colouring, but in some curious way in texture: they were made of the same material. I was excited by the thought.

'We're having lemon tea,' I said. 'Will you join us?'

'No, thank you. I promised my wife I'd be home early.'

I turned to my father. 'Mr Mackenzie has a wife and two little boys.'

'You are a fortunate man, Mr Mackenzie.'

'Aye.' Mack, looking vaguely uncomfortable, got out pencil and paper and started roaming about making notes. 'Now that window catch isn't fitting right – there's a shrinkage crack by the left hand wall – and they've chipped the paint on the stairs. I told you it'd chip easy and it has, but you would have a spiral staircase.'

'That was what I wanted.'

'And you always have what you want?'

'Usually. Or else I stop wanting it.'

'It's just not very practical.'

'No. But it's beautiful and it's fun.'

My father said nothing throughout this tennis match, and his face revealed nothing, but I knew he was enjoying our performance.

'I'll get the plumber to come,' Mack went on in fine form, 'and adjust your hot water supply so it doesn't bubble. You need a new valve.'

'Thank you.'

'And those missing tiles from the bathroom can be fitted next week. Now you said there were some cupboards need easing – and a squeaking floorboard we should nail down – which room was that in?'

How blank and innocent his expression was. 'My bedroom.'

'Is that the lot then?'

'I hope so.'

He put away the paper and pencil. 'Wouldn't you like me to have another look round?'

I signalled appreciation with my eyes. 'No, I think you've been extremely thorough.'

My father finished his tea and stood up. 'I must go, Kisleanyom.'

Mack said defensively, 'Mr Kovacs, I've nearly finished.'

My father smiled. 'I have an appointment.' He patted my cheek. 'The tea was delicious as always.'

'I'll see you out, Apukam.' I turned to Mack. 'I won't be a minute.'

They shook hands. My father said, 'Goodbye, Mr Mackenzie. You are to be congratulated,' and Mack said, 'Thank you,' a shade tight-lipped. I don't know how I kept my face straight.

Downstairs on the front step my father hugged me and we kissed on both cheeks. 'I like him,' he said. 'He rose to the occasion like a man.'

I was thrilled. I watched him out of sight and waved and dashed back upstairs to Mack. 'Oh, you were lovely.' I gave him a big hug and kissed him hard. 'You were so amusing. I was proud of you. Have some lemon tea.'

'No thanks.' He didn't hug me back; in fact he looked a trifle grim.

'Have some Scotch.'

'Who is he?'

'I told you.'

'I mean really.'

'I told you.' Teasing him was irresistible: he took the bait so beautifully. 'You've forgotten the Rule Book.'

'So he's a lover.'

I started to laugh. 'No.'

'That old man –'

'He's not old, he's only fifty.' I was proud of my father's appearance.

'He seemed very much at home.'

'He's my godfather.'

He stared at me. 'Why didn't you say so?'

'Does it matter? I didn't know you were religious.' I poured myself a drink while he walked up and down, looking broody.

'What did he call you?'

'Kisleanyom.' I resented sharing it with him. 'It's a sort of pet name.'

'And you called him something odd.'

'Apukam. Yes.' In spite of myself, I giggled. He was still glowering at me, jealous as hell.

'What's so funny?'

'It's Hungarian, that's all. Actually I wanted you to meet him.'

'Oh aye?'

'Yes. Don't be so boring and stuffy – he could be useful to you.'

'Useful?'

'He's a merchant banker. And they always come in handy, sooner or later.' Suddenly I was sorry for teasing him, he looked so hurt, but I couldn't bring myself to tell him the truth just yet, I didn't dare risk it. I went across to him and put one hand behind his head and the other between his legs. I felt full of tenderness towards him. 'You're not really in a hurry, are you?' I said.

Then I didn't see him for about ten days. I had to go to Paris on a modelling job and while I was there the whole Hungary thing broke. I could hardly wait to get home. I nearly forgot about Mack; all I could think of was my father. I dropped my luggage at the house and went straight on to the flat. I'd been hoping Ruth might be with him, but I suppose she was tied up with David; anyway, my father was all alone. I let myself in with my key and there he was, watching newsreel of Hungary, tears running silently down his face. I didn't know what to do. I sat down beside him on the sofa and we watched the film together. It was ghastly, horrifying. People were just being murdered in the streets, shot or run over by tanks. The Russians were slaughtering everyone in their way. But it wasn't just that. I held my father's hand and I couldn't speak. I've never before or since felt so involved in someone else's pain. I would have done anything, made any sacrifice, endured any ordeal, to ease it. In a way it was as if I were the parent and he were the child.

Mack and I were meeting about twice a week, but what with my being away, and Hungary, and him being busy, it didn't always work out. Anyway, he didn't understand about

Hungary, or why I was so upset, and I couldn't explain. We always met by arrangement, too, so when the entry phone went one afternoon just as I'd finished washing my hair, I was both amazed and furious.

'It's me,' he said.

'I wasn't expecting you.'

'Can I come in?'

'I suppose so.' I pushed the button and went downstairs into the drawing-room clutching my hair drier and wrapping a towel around my head. He came bounding up the stairs in his usual way, which normally charmed me, it was so energetic, but didn't tonight: I had too much on my mind, to dry my hair and change and get to the party where there might be some useful people. It didn't alter my feelings for him at all; it was just inconvenient.

'God,' he said, looking round, 'what a bloody awful day.'

I said, 'It was all right till just now. What's the matter with you?' Because there are times, no matter how keen I am on someone, when I simply don't want to see them.

He said, 'Can I have a drink?'

'Help yourself.' I plugged in my hair drier, determined to minimize the interruption as far as possible.

He said, 'Oh, d'you have to do that now? I want to talk to you.'

He seemed so disappointed that I switched it off. 'What?'

'Can't we talk?'

'You mean can't I listen while you talk.'

'Maybe I do – does it matter?'

He was doing his little-boy-lost act, but I didn't want to be drawn. 'Why didn't you phone?'

'I don't know. I didn't think. I just wanted to get here.'

'It's in the Rule Book – always phone first.'

He said, 'Oh, stuff your bloody Rule Book.' That was enough for me: I switched on the hair drier again. He promptly pulled the plug out of the wall.

'I'm all attention,' I said, heavily sarcastic. I could feel my heart pounding with shock at this new outrage: it made me very calm in my head.

94

'My kid's being bullied at school,' he said, as if I were interested.

'Which kid?'

'Duncan, of course.'

'Well, how am I to tell them apart? I've never met either of them. Is he the younger one?'

'Aye.'

'What's the matter with him?'

'He's very timid.' He paced up and down my drawing-room. 'I wish to God I knew how to put some backbone into him.'

'Why don't you move him?'

'Move him? Christ, you women, you're all alike, all you want to do is run away.'

I was furious but I controlled myself. 'Move him to a decent school, I meant. Or can't you afford one?'

That got him. 'What did you have in mind, Eton? Don't tell me no one ever got bullied there.'

'I was thinking of somewhere like Dean's Academy. My brother went there.'

'Piers?'

The suspicion made me even angrier. 'I've only got one brother. It's in Scotland, too, so it ought to suit you. Is he artistic, this timid son of yours?'

'So they tell me.' He sounded cross, as if he should have noticed for himself.

'And rotten at games?'

'Aye.'

'The usual pattern. Piers was a misfit too.'

Predictably he sprang at once to the wretched child's defence. 'I wouldn't say Duncan —'

'Oh, for God's sake. D'you want help or not? Dean's Academy is a very special place, you get small classes, lots of attention, all the usual academic stuff plus a lot of outdoor stuff —'

He was determined not to be impressed. 'What's so special about that? It sounds like any other public school.'

'Oh, do shut up and listen. They do a special two-way

95

responsibility thing. A sort of training. All your time there, except your last year, you have somebody one year older looking after you, and apart from your first year, you also look after someone else one year younger. Piers said it was fantastic – it really worked. Now may I dry my hair?'

He looked at me lovingly. It was a total, abrupt change, although in fact I'd merely been knocking myself out doing a PR job. 'You're tremendous. I thought you were going to be bored but –'

I interrupted him. 'I was bored.'

To my surprise he smiled. 'Come to bed. You won't be bored there.'

Typical male arrogance. 'I'm not in the mood.'

'I want you. I want to make love. Now.'

'Could you plug in the drier on your way out?'

'I'm not leaving yet.'

'Oh yes you are.' It was our first row. I think now, looking back, that our row potential was one of the big mutual attractions. 'Look, Mack, you didn't ring, you didn't have an appointment. You broke the rules. It wasn't convenient at all, but I listened and I told you what to do. Now will you please have the courtesy to leave me alone. I have to go out and I'd like to go with dry hair.'

'Where are you going?'

'That's my affair.'

He came towards me. 'Is it that Kovacs? He turned me down, you know. I tried to get a loan and he turned me down.' I shrugged. 'Did you tell him to do that? Did you?'

I was furious. I got up, plugged in the hair drier and switched it on; I started drying my hair. To my astonishment he seized the drier and smashed it. I must have looked at him with my mouth open. He grabbed me by the shoulders and shook me. 'Is he your lover? Did he buy you this house? Did he?'

I didn't stop to think: I caught him in the balls with my knee. It was almost a reflex action but not quite. He let go of me at once and doubled up. I was so angry I could hardly speak: my throat was tight with rage.

'Yes, he did buy me this house, he's my father. And you can piss off for good because we're through.'

I thought he'd phone but he didn't, and of course neither did I. I had dreams about him instead, dreams in which he was being nice to me and I woke up coming and then started to cry. I was amazed and furious at how much I missed him: calling me lassie in that sexy accent, telling me jokes about his childhood, which sounded frightfully primitive, sending me up for being posh and privileged. I remembered the solid, chunky feel of him when I hugged him, the way it felt dangerous yet reassuring to have him around, the delicious touch of slumming that I'd felt and kept to myself. I relived his making me come with his tongue, his fingers, his cock; or the way he'd lain back like a sultan with a self-satisfied expression on his face while I did everything I could think of to him to prove I was irreplaceable. I even missed his anecdotes about the building site, which were so remote from my world that they seemed like real life. In short I behaved like an idiot and made myself thoroughly miserable, which served me right.

I told Ruth about it eventually, but not properly, more obliquely, the way I always tell things. We were sitting in the square watching Lisa on the swing: she was standing up and wobbling all over the place but terribly proud of herself. 'Mummy, watch me,' she kept yelling. 'I can do it standing up.'

I smiled in spite of my mood. 'She's got a great future.'

'Yes, sweetheart,' Ruth called to her. 'I see you. Be careful.' In an undertone she added to me, 'If she falls on her head – God forbid – David'll murder me.'

'She won't and he won't.'

She said in the same concerned tone, 'I can't believe it's really over. It was going so well.'

'Oh, I'm well out of it.'

'But what happened?'

I pulled my coat closer round me. Lisa didn't feel the cold, so Ruth and I were obliged to sit here wrapped in fur while she got on with her swinging. 'Did he ever lose his temper with you?'

'Not exactly. He got a bit . . . put out once or twice.'

'He was like a maniac. All over nothing. I mean it's absurd. Nobody could put up with it.'

'No.'

Strange how implausible the truth sounded. 'And he's so possessive. God. Great jealous scenes. Well, you know how I feel about that.'

'Yes.'

'Mummy, look.' Lisa had climbed down to sit on the swing again and swivel round and round.

'I see you, darling, that's lovely. How many times can you do it?' Ruth turned back to me. 'Well, it might hold her for a bit.'

'Pity you can't tether her to a post like a goat.'

'Yes, I've often thought that.'

'Actually she's being very good.'

'That swing's a godsend.'

I could feel her waiting for me to go on. 'I mean, he wanted me to listen to some great tale of woe about his bloody children and give him advice and then he wasn't even grateful, just furious I wouldn't go to bed with my hair wet.'

'Ridiculous.'

'He didn't even phone, just turned up and put me through all that, smashed my hair drier and made a fool of himself about my father.'

'You didn't *tell* him?' She sounded alarmed.

'Yes, I did. I lost my temper and it slipped out.' But it was more than that : I had been boasting.

'I hope he keeps it to himself.'

'He probably will. Anyway, it's done now.'

She sighed. 'It sounds awfully serious.'

'I told you – it's over. Thank God.'

'No, I mean as if *he* was . . . awfully serious.'

I was hopeful, furious, terrified. What had I thrown away?

'I told you, he's mad. I've had a lucky escape.' I got up

from the seat and called to Lisa, 'Lisa, shall I give you a push?'

'Yes, please.' She was always grateful, not expecting attention, amazingly unspoilt for a child of such adoring parents. She must simply have had a nice nature. And I didn't even like children.

I walked over to the swing. I could feel Ruth watching me as I went: worrying, sympathizing. I was appreciative but I was also glad to escape.

It's funny to think that Ruth was a sort of stepmother as well as a friend. I often forget. She only met my father after her marriage to David because my father and David's father do so many property deals together, and I gather it was a *coup de foudre* for them both. But Ruth was already pregnant with Lisa, so it was a while before they really got going.

I suppose Ruth was more of an elder sister than a stepmother. I approved of her, anyway, and I was relieved my father had stopped having affairs with girls younger than I was. I'd always found that faintly embarrassing. Ruth and I were never sure if David knew or not: Ruth said he didn't want to know and that was the main thing. Besides she loved him, too, only not in the same way. I used to feel sorry for David at first and then I forgot about him.

My father and I had our usual Christmas Eve date. I was really looking forward to it: I hadn't seen him for a while and it took the edge off the gruesomeness of the festive season. Piers was coming too, so I was feeling quite good, as if they'd both anaesthetized me from the pain of losing Mack.

My father was early. I ran down to welcome him and there he was like a big, grey-maned lion, making my heart turn over. He said, 'Kisleanyom,' and hugged me, and I said, 'Oh, it's good to see you,' feeling suddenly close to tears and feverishly excited.

He held me away from him for a moment and looked at me searchingly. 'How are you? A little tired? A little unhappy?'

I said, 'You've been talking to Ruth.'

'No, she has been talking to me. I didn't say a word.'

I laughed. 'He's gone. It's a good thing.'

'Is it?'

'I've got some Tokay – will you open it for me?' I took the bottle from the fridge. 'And it's not too cold – just cold enough. I was very careful.'

My father began opening the bottle. I watched his hands.

'You are all I have left,' he said. 'No one is allowed to hurt you.'

'It's all right,' I said. 'Nothing's broken.'

He poured Tokay and gave me my glass. 'Happy Christmas,' I said.

'Happy Christmas, my love.'

We kissed, touched glasses and drank. I was struck once again by the strangeness of it all, how for the first ten years of my life I had not known that this man was my father. I was still angry when I remembered the shamefaced way my mother had told me, as if she wanted to wipe out the time when she had been so reckless, and wipe me out with it.

'Are you going to the country?' my father asked. It was as close as he could get to asking about my mother and stepfather.

'I'll have to, yes. Piers is coming too, otherwise I couldn't bear it. He's arriving tonight, thank God.'

'That's good. He's a nice boy.'

'And you and I have a date for New Year's Eve, don't forget.'

'Yes, I'm looking forward to it.'

'D'you want your present now?' I had got him a lovely chess set and a silk dressing-gown.

'No. Let's save them for next week.'

'All right.' I suddenly hugged him, overcome with panic at the thought of Christmas with Mummy and Daddy. 'Oh, Apukam, it's so lovely to have you here. I hate Christmas without you. What will you do?' It was awful to think of him all alone.

'I shall indulge myself. Eat, drink, sleep . . .'

I had a sudden vision of him enjoying teenage girls again, with Ruth and me safely away. 'I'm going to miss you.'

'This Mackenzie . . .' he said.

'Yes?'

'He wants a loan from the bank to buy a warehouse.' I shrugged. 'Is it a good deal?'

'Yes.'

'Then you must help him.'

'I won't do it if you don't want.'

'I don't mind, why should I?'

He looked at me closely. 'Tell me the truth. Has he hurt you?'

'If he deserves a loan, he should have it.' Thank God the buzzer went at that moment. It was Piers; I pushed the button. 'No, really, Apukam, it's business. Nothing to do with my nonsense.'

Piers bounded up the stairs looking more than ever like Rupert Brooke, only sharper; I flung my arms round him and he swung me off the floor. 'Oh, Piers, you're really here.'

'Hullo, rabbit.' He kissed me and turned to my father. 'George – good to see you again.' They shook hands, then kissed on both cheeks.

'Welcome home,' my father said. 'You look well.'

'I'm in training for the rigours of a family Christmas.'

'Where's your luggage?' I said suspiciously, as if he might run off.

'Downstairs, full of presents.' He looked round. 'Well, this is rather swish.'

'Glad you approve.' I poured Tokay for him, feeling dizzy. Having them both there at once was quite something.

'You're not going to fancy a loft in Greenwich Village after this,' Piers said, but I knew he was really proud of it.

'Course I am. Are you sharing it with anyone yet?'

'Only a few cockroaches. They're quite friendly.' He sipped his wine. 'Well – where's my dark-room then?' he explained to my father. 'All the time we were in Greece last summer she kept promising me a dark-room in her new house, but I could tell she was only after my traveller's cheques.'

I said smoothly, 'It's on the top floor, next to the guest room.'

'You meant it.' He was so thrilled he looked like a child again: I got a sort of double image of Piers past and present. He hugged me and I sat there between him and my father, holding hands with both of them and thinking about Mack.

'Now you're both here,' I said, 'it's really Christmas.' And I started to cry.

It wasn't too bad, I suppose, once we got there. Mostly a matter of accepting a different way of life. We only went for three days and Piers was wonderful, full of jokes about New York and photography to keep Mummy and Daddy amused and take the weight off me. He wouldn't let me go hunting though, because since being away he'd got the idea it was cruel. I'd never thought about it; it was simply something one did. But we went for lovely long rides on the downs instead, anything to get out of the house and that atmosphere. It always seemed worse at Christmas because of all the stress on *family*; maybe it was my imagination, but I always felt Mummy was chalking up another year of dissatisfaction with Daddy because he wasn't as rich as my father. I could practically see her thinking she'd married the wrong man. I felt specially fond of Daddy at Christmas and I thought Mummy ought to be more grateful to him (after all, it had looked like a good marriage at the time and had got her out of a nasty mess) but I suppose twenty-five years is a long time to go on being grateful.

He came back two days before New Year's Eve. I'd been talking to Piers about him and suddenly there he was, as if I'd conjured him up. I got a terrible shock and my stomach really lurched when I saw him. Sometimes people are less attractive when you see them again, because you've built them up in your mind, but he was more so, even though he was wearing a terrible old overcoat. I wouldn't let him in, so we had to stand on the doorstep. It was freezing and I only had on a kaftan.

He said, 'I brought you a present,' and gave me this parcel.

'I don't know if it's for Christmas or New Year, but it comes with all the right wishes. Seasonal greetings.'

I said faintly, 'Thank you.'

'Aren't you going to open it?' He sounded disappointed, like a child.

'If you like.' The truth was I didn't want to because I was afraid my hands would shake and he'd notice, but then I thought that could just mean I was cold, so I unwrapped it and it was a hair-drier. 'Just what I need,' I said. 'Somebody broke mine.'

'I hope it's the right sort.'

'Oh yes, it's a very superior sort.'

Then we couldn't think of anything else to say. We just stood there, him warm and snug in the awful coat and me shivering in my kaftan, and neither of us making a move.

'Did you have a good Christmas?' he said finally.

'Yes. Did you?'

'Yes.'

Well, that didn't get us very far. We were like some frightful old car jerking forward with the handbrake still on.

'May I come in?' he said suddenly. 'Please.'

'No – I'm sorry – I've got someone here.' I hadn't planned to say that at all, but out it came.

'Oh, yes, of course.' He stared at me longingly. 'Are you busy for New Year's Eve?'

'Yes, I am.'

'Well, I really only called to give you that and say thank you.'

'Whatever for?' I was so faint from gazing at his mouth and wanting to touch him that I could hardly take in what he said.

'Your father's loan came through. I thought you might block it but you didn't.'

'Why should I?'

'I just thought you might.'

'I wouldn't be so petty.'

'No, of course not.'

Another ghastly silence. I was so desperate to ask him in and so determined not to, I began to feel sick. And that made me feel hysterical, thinking how frightful it would be if I suddenly threw up right there on the steps in front of him. What a thing to remember about someone.

'Well,' he said eventually, 'Happy New Year.'

'Happy New Year. Enjoy your warehouse.'

'Yes, I will.'

He began to turn away; I was frantic to keep him.

'Oh, Mack –'

He turned back eagerly, oh, so eagerly. 'Yes?'

'If you could keep quiet about my father being my father. I don't care but my mother and stepfather would be grateful.'

'I wouldn't dream of mentioning it.'

'No. I didn't think you would.' And I'd meant to say something quite different. 'Well, goodnight.'

'Goodnight.'

The pain was quite bad now and I shut the front door quickly, even rudely, so I wouldn't have to see him go. I groped my way back up the stairs, which all had blurred edges.

Piers looked up from the television and said, 'Rabbit. Whatever's the matter?'

I dumped the hair drier on the sofa. 'Christmas present. Belated.'

'He came back?'

'Only to say thank you. He's so glad to have my father's money.' I sat down and cried.

Piers got up and poured me a drink. 'Di, you *are* a fool. Why didn't you ask him in?'

'I said I had someone here.'

'What, me?'

'Why not? You're here, aren't you?'

'Not like that.'

'I wish you were.' I took a large gulp of the mercifully strong drink. 'It might solve a lot of problems. At least we understand each other.'

'Di, you should have made it up with him.'

'Couldn't.' I sobbed a bit more and Piers held my hand. 'God, I wish we could fancy each other, it would be so easy.'

'No, it wouldn't.'

I felt trapped and hopeless, but terribly glad he was there all the same. I kept seeing Mack going away. 'Oh, Piers, why does sex screw everything up?'

Next day I felt better: all that crying and talking to Piers and seeing Mack (especially seeing Mack) had done me good. At least he had made the first move and that must have been difficult. Piers thought I was mad to care about things like that, but then Piers doesn't have any pride, which is lucky for him. I rang my father, who understood about pride, and he told me when Mack would be coming to his office to sign papers. I spent a lot of time getting my hair just right and changing my clothes; I was so excited I kept dropping things.

He was still with my father when I got to the bank, so I sat in reception and waited. They'd never seen me in such a good temper before: I kept smiling at them. When he came out, he was so amazed to see me he just stood and stared. Then a broad grin spread over his face.

'I thought we had something to celebrate,' I said.

All the way home in the taxi we just held each other and kissed and looked. He smelt the same; he tasted the same. It was wonderful. We didn't talk much. Back home in bed (Piers had gone out to be tactful) the feeling of all that skin contact made me want to cry. We were in the middle of making love when I suddenly said 'Don't ever leave me again.' I knew I was committed to him now and it was a terrifying thought.

'But you told me to go.'

'D'you have to do everything I say?'

1958

Jean

She came out of the hospital with Maggie, who was on her ward, and they discussed the day. Maggie came from Dunfermline and was turning into a friend; Jean would have liked to prolong the discussion, but as they reached the gates she saw her bus coming and had to run for it, since it was so rare. Maggie waved and she waved back.

Once on the bus, she felt depression set in. The end of work meant the beginning of worry. It had been like that for over a year now, so that she dreaded having leisure, dreaded even coming home because it meant there would be time to think. Even her pleasure in the new house was spoiled because she associated it with anxiety: it was the place in which she had begun to worry.

When she got home she changed out of her uniform and began preparing supper. Every time her fears surfaced she pushed them away till she was exhausted with the effort. Perhaps today would be different. Perhaps there was nothing to worry about. But she knew otherwise.

The phone rang. In theory it could have been anyone, but she knew it was Robbie and it was. He said he was spending the evening with Kovacs and not to wait supper.

'But I've done something special.'

'Won't it keep?'

Surely he hadn't forgotten the weekend as well. 'We're going away, aren't we?'

There was a pause. 'Look, I'll make it up to you,' he said, as if she were a child to be bribed with the promise of some distant treat, 'but this is really important.'

'Yes. I suppose it is.'

'See you later.'

'Yes.' She hung up before he could, and poured herself

a drink. Her heart was pounding. She abandoned the supper and went into the sitting-room, hoping to distract herself with television. But it was hopeless: she might as well have had her eyes shut. Presently she picked up the phone.

Ruth said, 'Jean? Hullo, love. How are you?'

'Oh, I'm fine. I was ringing about the weekend.'

'You *are* still coming?'

'Yes, of course. We're looking forward to it. What time d'you want us?'

'Oh – in time for lunch.'

'Right.' Now she couldn't think of any more to say. The acceptable bit was over.

Ruth said, 'Are you okay?'

'Yes, of course. I'm fine.'

'You just sounded a bit down.'

'Well – Robbie's working late again.'

'Oh, is he?'

'Yes. He's in a meeting with Kovacs and it might last all evening, so that's the end of dinner.'

'Oh, what a bore.' Ruth suddenly had a nervous edge to her voice.

'Yes.'

There was a pause. 'David's just the same,' Ruth said.

'Is he?'

'Oh yes, always working late, having dinner with people, drives me mad. I never know where I am.'

'No.' So Ruth knew. 'It'll be lovely to see you.'

'Yes, it's been ages. How's the job going?'

'Fine. It's much better being full-time. Quite different.'

'I thought it would be.' Another pause. She could feel Ruth making a decision. 'Look, if you're fed up, why not come on down here tonight? Robert can join you tomorrow.'

'Can't. He's got the car.'

'Oh. Yes, of course, he would have.' Ruth sounded quite cross.

'It doesn't matter.'

'Well, have a large drink instead.'

'I already have.'

110

'So have another – who's counting?'

They laughed nervously.

'Well,' Jean said, 'I better go. See you tomorrow.'

'Make it nice and early. Bye, love.'

Jean hung up and went on staring at the television screen. She wondered how long Ruth had known.

She went to bed early but she couldn't sleep. By the time she heard Robbie closing the front door and mounting the stairs, she wondered how late it was and whether she had dozed; she felt as if she had been turning over for hours. She listened to him in the bathroom and arranged herself to look convincingly asleep before he came in.

'Jean? Are you awake, hen?'

She did not answer. He undressed in the dark and got into bed beside her. She longed to touch him, hug him or hit him, beg him to tell her it wasn't as she feared, but she couldn't move. He was soon asleep, while she lay awake and listened to his breathing, with gratitude, as if he had come back from the grave.

Robbie said again, 'Well, I think you got a bargain,' and Jean said, 'Yes, it's lovely.'

Ruth looked gratified. Lunch was nearly over and the cottage had been thoroughly admired. 'It will be when it's finished. At least that's what I keep telling myself. The trouble is, only getting down here at weekends, there's no time to do very much.'

'You could get someone in,' David suggested.

'No, I want to do it myself.'

'Of course.' He pretended to disapprove while looking rather proud.

Lisa said suddenly, 'Mummy, where are Jamie and Duncan? Why aren't they here?'

'I told you, darling, they're at school.'

'At the weekend?'

'It's a boarding-school. In Scotland.'

'Can I go there?'

'No, sweetheart, it's for boys.' Ruth turned to Jean. 'How are they getting on?'

Robbie said proudly, 'They're doing fine.'

Jean said, 'Aye, they love it. I was all against them going, but I was wrong. They think it's great.'

'It costs a fortune,' Robbie said, 'but it's worth it.'

Lisa had already lost interest. 'Mummy, please may I get down?'

'Yes, darling, of course you can.'

They all watched indulgently as she ran into the garden and started splashing about in a tiny pool.

'That child,' Ruth said. 'She's only happy in water. She should have been a mermaid.'

'Can she swim yet?' Jean asked.

'Can she swim! Like a fish. She's much better than I am. I feel like some old walrus, puffing and blowing, while she zooms up and down the baths yelling "Come on, Mummy, hurry up." Makes me feel about a hundred. And she's only eight. It's going to get worse before it gets better.'

David asked Jean, 'How are things at the hospital?'

'Oh, fine. I'm a Junior Sister now.'

'Really? That's pretty good, isn't it?'

'It's not brilliant but it's progress.' She had the feeling he was overdoing his enthusiasm because he felt sorry for her. So David knew too.

'She's doing all right, aren't you, hen?'

'I suppose so – more or less.'

Ruth said, 'It's made a big difference going full-time, hasn't it?'

'Oh yes, staff are much more friendly and you feel part of a team. It sounds awful to say this, but I'm beginning to see why part-timers are treated the way they are – some of them are pretty slack. Well, it's true,' she added, when Ruth laughed.

'I'm sure it is. It's just funny to hear you say it.'

They went on talking idly about hospitals, shift work and the problem of the school holidays.

'We've got pretty good neighbours,' Robbie boasted. 'The boys can play next door.'

'Well, they can always come to us if you want to give the neighbours a break.'

'That's kind of you,' Jean said. 'It would be a pity to wear them out.' Again she had the feeling that everyone was being much too nice to her, out of pity.

It was a fine afternoon so they sat in the garden, discussing property and plants. Lisa got bored and wandered off to play with the little girl next door.

'Marianne has a pony,' Ruth explained, 'so she's rapidly become Lisa's best friend. Funny how materialistic they are at this age. I used to suck up to the little girl next door because she had a sandpit. It wasn't till I grew up I could admit I never even liked her.'

'In my case it was a kitten. My parents wouldn't let me have one and the kid next door had two. I used to borrow one and try to smuggle it into the house.' Jean remembered the warm, unprotesting fur of the creature hidden under her jersey. 'My mother always caught me.' Was that when they had begun to dislike each other?

Robbie, bored, looked at his watch. 'Well, come on, they're open.'

'Already?' David checked. 'Good Lord, so they are.'

Robbie got up. 'I'd like to talk to you about my land bank.' He turned to Jean and Ruth. 'We'll see you girls later, okay?'

Ruth said with heavy irony, 'Well, we're not going anywhere, apparently.'

David looked embarrassed. 'Won't be long, love.'

They watched the men leave. Jean's heart was thumping: she was alarmed by what she intended to do.

Ruth said, 'Typical. It never enters their heads we might like to go too.'

'Maybe they thought we'd rather be on our own.'

'If they thought at all.'

'I'm not very keen on pubs anyway, are you?'

'No, but it's the principle.' They laughed. 'They'll have to make do with steak and salad – *when* they show up. I'm not cooking another big meal.'

'No, don't. We all ate far too much at lunchtime.'

Ruth stretched lazily in her deck-chair. She reminded Jean of a cat – not the cooperative kitten of childhood but a sleek, complacent mother-cat. 'Would you like a drink?'

'In a minute. It's so peaceful just sitting here.' She sat savouring the moment before she had to start destroying it. 'You're really very lucky, aren't you?'

'Why?' Ruth sounded instantly alarmed.

'Well, you've got two lovely homes, for a start.'

'No point in marrying a dentist if you don't get your teeth fixed.' The tone was much too bright.

'And David's very attentive, isn't he? I mean, he didn't even want to go to the pub just now, you could tell. He only went to please Robbie.'

'Well, David doesn't drink much, but they wanted to talk shop.'

'And he doesn't really work late, does he?' She envied Ruth her devoted husband. 'I mean you only said that to cheer me up.'

'When?'

'On the phone yesterday. You were very kind.'

Ruth said briskly, 'Well, it's horrid being left on your own with dinner ruined. Men are so thoughtless.'

'It's a bit more than that though, isn't it?'

'What do you mean?'

'Oh, please don't pretend you don't know, I can't bear it.'

To her own horror she began to cry. Ruth had to take her indoors and give her a stiff drink.

'He's having an affair, isn't he?'

Ruth poured a drink for herself. 'I don't know. How could I?'

'Oh, Ruth, please. If I've noticed, you must have. They say the wife is always the last to know. You and David see so much of him, you must have noticed something. He's different, isn't he?' She wanted to hear the worst now: it would be a relief.

Ruth said reluctantly, 'He's working hard, he's under a lot of pressure . . .'

'He's not the same any more.' Another flood of tears, just when she thought she had finished.

Ruth said, 'Oh, love, I'm sorry.'

'I must talk about it. I'll go mad if I don't talk about it.'

'Yes. All right.'

Jean blew her nose. 'All these meetings with Kovacs – nobody could have that much business to do – but they're meeting all the time, two or three evenings a week – it can't be true – I've never set eyes on Kovacs – for all I know he doesn't even exist.'

'He does exist and he financed the warehouse deal for Robert. You know that. Come on, love. That's how you got your house.'

'I know, but what are they doing now? They're always meeting, but nothing happens.'

Ruth said soothingly, 'They're planning something. I'm sure they are. David's mentioned it, but I didn't listen properly.'

Jean clasped her arms round her knees and started to rock to and fro in her chair. 'Every time he says he's with Kovacs, he must be with *her*. God, he must think I'm stupid to go on believing him. Only, I was so frightened. I couldn't ask him.' She remembered the fear like a physical pain. 'I thought if I kept very quiet it might go away. But it hasn't.'

Ruth shifted uncomfortably. 'Look, you may be imagining the whole thing. Honestly.'

'No. He's much too nice to me – polite, considerate. Like a stranger. As if I was a child or an invalid. And in between he's with Kovacs.' She thought about it. 'But he hardly ever wants to make love any more. And when he does, I feel he's doing me a favour – and I'm so pathetically grateful I despise myself.'

She started to cry again. Ruth hugged her and poured fresh drinks. Jean tidied her hair and repaired her make-up. 'I don't know what to do,' she said.

'Nothing. Believe me. When in doubt, do nothing.'

She took the drink gratefully. 'But I'm not in doubt. I know he's got someone.'

'You don't, love. You only think he has.'

Jean tried to believe Ruth, but she couldn't. 'No, I'm sure. I can feel it. He's not really with me any more. There's always part of his mind somewhere else.' She couldn't describe the agony and she didn't believe Ruth had experienced it.

'Look,' Ruth said, 'let's try and be logical. If you ask him he'll only deny it – you still won't be sure – and if he's innocent he'll be furious.'

'Maybe he won't deny it.'

'Of course he will.'

'Why?'

'Either because it's not true or because he doesn't want you to know.'

'Perhaps he does.'

'If he did, he'd tell you.'

'Maybe he's waiting for me to ask him.'

There was a pause. She felt sorry for Ruth, to be trying so hard to no avail.

'How long have you been married now?' Ruth said at last. 'About the same as us, isn't it?'

'Ten and a half years. Jamie's ten next month. I was three months pregnant.'

'But you would have got married anyway.'

'Oh yes, we did it on purpose. It was the only way to get my parents to agree, they were so agin Robbie and I was under age.' She remembered the terrifying thrill of defying them, facing their wrath, and her own certainty that nothing could ever go wrong.

'And you've been happy all this time, haven't you?'

'Everything was fine in Glasgow. I never had any doubts about Robbie there.' She stared at Ruth without really seeing her, collecting her memories, and Ruth looked away. 'I'd have sworn he just wasn't the type – it was all work and me and the children, I'd stake my life on that. But since we came to London ... it's funny, I had a feeling it'd be unlucky, that's why I didn't want to move, it wasn't just leaving home. He's changed since we came here. I'm not sure when it started but he's not just ambitious now, he's greedy. It's as if we don't fit into his plans any more ... packing the boys off to boarding-school and letting me get a full-time job when he used to hate me working even a few hours ... it's as if he was clearing the decks for something.'

'But you like your job. And the boys are happy at school.'

'Oh, yes.'

'So he's really done the right thing for all of you.'

'Yes,' Jean said bitterly, 'it's fallen into place.'

'And he's bought you a house. He wouldn't do that if there was anything wrong.'

'Conscience money.' Jean felt she was punishing Ruth as a substitute for Robbie by being so stubbornly depressed, but she could not stop.

'Look,' Ruth said at last, 'whether he's guilty or not, surely what really matters is you love each other and you're going to stay together.'

'But I can't assume that.'

'Yes, you can. That's the whole point.'

'Not if he's having an affair.'

'But people can have affairs for years without wanting to leave home.' Ruth seemed to have become rather agitated. 'It may mean they're selfish and greedy but it doesn't mean the end of a marriage. In fact it can even make it better.'

'I don't believe that.'

'It's true. I *know* it is.'

Jean stared at her in amazement. Ruth sounded so positive. 'You can't be talking about David.'

'No, I'm not.'

The front door opened while Jean was still taking in what Ruth meant. Lisa burst in ahead of David and Robbie and the whole atmosphere changed instantly.

'Mummy, Mummy, I rode Pegasus round and round the field and over the jumps and I didn't fall off once.'

'Good for you, darling, aren't you a clever girl. Poor bloody Pegasus must be worn out.'

'No, he's not, he likes jumping, and you shouldn't swear, you're naughty.' Lisa leaned on Ruth and looked sideways at Jean, delighted to be the centre of attention.

'That's right, and I'm too old to change.'

'You won't let me swear.'

'You're only a little girl.'

'No, I'm not, I'm a big girl.'

'Well, whatever size you are, you can't swear and I can,

117

so there.' Ruth detached Lisa and stood up. Jean thought she looked both relieved and exhausted. The men came in.

'Marianne fell off Pegasus,' Lisa said with satisfaction. 'She fell off twice.'

'I'm not surprised. She hardly gets any practice with you around.'

'Come on, young lady.' David ruffled Lisa's hair. 'Bedtime.'

'Oh, Daddy, not yet.'

'Right now,' Ruth said. 'You're late already.' David offered to put Lisa to bed but Ruth refused. 'I rather thought I'd put her to bed and you might do supper.'

'Whatever you like.'

Jean got up. She suddenly needed to be alone, to recuperate; too much had been said. She couldn't look at Robbie. 'I'll start on the salad, shall I?' She went quickly into the kitchen and then, to her horror, found herself listening at the door.

'Well, aren't you all helpful,' Ruth said. 'What are you going to do, Robert?'

'Suppose I pour everyone a drink – and make sure the television's working.' How normal he sounded, as if there was nothing to conceal.

'Don't tell me. There are more of those chaps who keep kicking something and hugging each other and getting mud on their jerseys.'

'Well, now that you mention it ...'

She heard him go out of the room.

David said to Ruth in a low voice, 'Are you okay? You're being terribly bright,' and Jean, ashamed of herself and afraid of being caught, opened the door of the fridge and became very busy.

But she couldn't leave the subject alone. Next day, on a country walk, she said to Ruth, 'How long?'

'Seven years.' Ruth actually seemed smug rather than guilty.

'And he doesn't know?'

118

'I'm not sure. I keep changing my mind about that. But we've never had it out. We just go on as if it wasn't happening.'

'But how can you?'

'What else can I do?' Ruth's tone suggested this was the civilized way to behave. 'I love them both.'

'I don't understand.'

'I'm sorry, I'm not explaining very well. It's not something I expected to happen – until it did, I wouldn't have understood it either. But I can't let go of either of them, I really can't. I'd go to pieces. I just think I'm very lucky they both put up with me.'

Jean thought about it. She felt as if she had carelessly opened a window and found herself on a different planet. 'Is he married too?'

'No.'

'Doesn't he want you to marry him?'

'No, he's used to living alone. He's older than me and he works very hard. He couldn't cope with Lisa.' Was there a shade of resentment in Ruth's voice? 'Besides, I couldn't take her away from David, what's he done to deserve that? Anyway, I love him. I love them both.'

Jean said, 'I can't imagine loving two people.'

'But you love Robbie and the boys.'

'That's different.'

'Oh, you mean sex,' Ruth said easily.

'Yes. Isn't it a problem?'

'Well ... no. They're so different ... and I still want them both.'

'But don't you feel guilty?' She couldn't imagine the kind of life Ruth was describing.

'Not so long as I'm making them both happy, no. I'm sorry, I've upset you.'

'I must be very old-fashioned.'

'No, no, it's just another point of view. Look, I live in terror the whole thing will collapse, but all I want is to go on as I am.'

Jean suddenly felt very bitter. 'Yes, but you're a winner. You've got two people in love with you.'

'Well, not exactly. Two people tolerating me.'

'But I only want Robbie. And I'm so afraid I'm going to lose him.'

Ruth squeezed her hand. 'That's why I told you about me. There's no reason why you should lose him.'

'I'm an all-or-nothing person.'

'But why? When I started this affair of mine, it was just sex, and then it got serious.'

'I don't understand.' Jean began to feel cross and excluded. 'I don't know what you mean by just sex.'

'Well, I was terrifically excited by him.'

'But you see – I've only ever had Robbie. And he's all I want.'

'Well, it wasn't till later I realized I need them both – I mean really *need* them. The same thing might happen to you.'

Jean's control snapped. 'Oh, I see. If I can manage to find a lover, it might be all right.'

'Please don't be angry. It's not easy for any of us.'

They walked for a while in silence, but the mood was broken. Presently Ruth looked at her watch. 'We must go back, it's time for lunch.'

'You know who she is, don't you?'

'Why do you say that?' Ruth sounded startled.

'You're so close to it all. Besides, you look guilty.'

'Oh, God.'

'I'm sorry.' She felt she was hounding Ruth into a corner, but it had to be done. 'You just look as if you're carrying a nasty secret around with you and you wish you could put it down somewhere.'

Ruth said with feeling, 'I wish we'd never started this conversation,' and after a pause : 'They met at one of my parties two years ago. I can't tell you her name, that wouldn't be fair, she's a friend of mine. That's why I feel so ghastly about the whole thing. You're both friends of mine.'

'So you've known all this time. Cosy.'

'Don't, Jean, please.'

A sudden flash of intuition. 'Was she a client?'

120

'Why d'you say that?'
'Robbie has so little spare time.'

They drove home on Sunday evening. Ruth and David were hospitable to the last, but she sensed their relief at the prospect of being alone again and she envied them. She was terrified of being alone with Robbie. With her worst fears confirmed, every minute alone with him meant a conscious decision not to say or do anything provocative. She listened to their voices – his so normal, hers so artificial, she felt – as they chatted about the cottage and the weekend. It all sounded so unreal, as if they were playing charades.

When they got home, to her infinite surprise he made love to her, and while she responded with amazement and delight her mind ran a cynical commentary. She wondered if David had warned him and he was being nice to her to avoid a scene. Afterwards, she started to cry uncontrollably and he cuddled and soothed her, but without asking what was the matter. It was like a confession.

Next day, after he had gone to work, she went through his files, cold-blooded and efficient like a spy. It was an easy task: she had done so much book-keeping for him. And he had had only one woman client: Diana Crawley. There she was, the name and the address. Jean stared at it for a long time.

In her lunch hour she took a cab, not caring about the expense, and walked round the garden square till she came to the house. It was very beautiful, tall and narrow, shining with white paint like the others, but in her imagination it stood out. She stood there for a while just looking at it, not knowing what she intended to do, then suddenly panicked and walked away. Once safely across the road she glanced back for a final look and saw with horrified fascination a tall, slim woman coming out of the house and locking the door. Jean hid instinctively behind a bush and watched her. She had long blonde hair and the sort of beauty that looked as if it had come easily to her. Jean's heart hammered with terror and jealousy. A taxi drove questingly round the square; the woman hailed it and got in. But Jean stayed behind the bush for a long time till she was calm enough to return to work. She did not even notice it had started to rain.

When she got home that evening Robbie was already there, doing accounts and looking cheerful. He got up to pour her a drink and the unexpected courtesy made her furious and distressed.

'Don't say a word, we're celebrating.' He put the glass in her hand.

'What?'

'Mackenzie Industrial, of course. I've agreed the deal with Kovacs. We're going to be partners.'

He looked so pleased with himself she wanted to hit him. 'Are you? Well done.'

'And you and I are going out to dinner.'

She sat down. 'Sorry. I'm too tired.'

Never one to be overly tactful, he said matter-of-factly, 'Yes, you do look a bit rough. Had a bad day?'

'You could say that.'

'What happened?'

How to describe this day of all days? 'Oh, staff were off sick, so we all had to work twice as hard. The doctors were in a foul mood. One of the patients couldn't have his operation because of vomiting and that put all the theatre staff out, they had to rearrange the list. That sort of day.'

'Don't know how you stand it.'

'Neither do I sometimes.'

He refilled his glass. 'Never mind, forget the whole lot of them, you can give it up if you want, we're going to be rich.'

'I thought we already were.'

'This is just a beginning.'

'Is it?' The words sounded like a mockery.

'You sit down. Have another drink. If you can't face going out, I'll get supper.'

'You?'

122

'I can do my bacon, egg and sausage special.'

'Oh yes. So you can.' She accepted a fresh drink. Perhaps it could yet be all right. 'Maybe we can eat out tomorrow.'

'Sorry, hen, I've got to see Kovacs tomorrow.'

'Of course. Silly of me.'

'Well, we have to finalize all the details.'

'No doubt.' How blank and innocent he looked. 'Do I get to meet him?'

'Yes, of course, if you want.'

'Now you're going to be partners.'

'Any time you like.'

'But not tomorrow.'

'No, tomorrow wouldn't work. You'd be bored.' He hesitated, reached into his pocket. 'Look, I got you something.' He gave her a small box. 'I thought we could add a bit every time I do a deal.'

She unwrapped a charm bracelet. 'Very nice.'

'Don't you like it?'

It was the final humiliating bribe and she lost control. 'Why don't you give it to Diana Crawley?' She felt sick as she said the name and she saw his mouth open in self-defence. 'Don't bother to lie to me, I'm sick of your lies. I can't go on pretending, Robbie. You pretend it's not happening and I pretend to believe you. It's making me ill. I went to her house today. Oh, don't worry, I didn't *do* anything.' His look of concern made her frantic. 'But I saw her come out. She's very beautiful.' She heard herself screaming, 'I'd like to kill her. I'd like to kill both of you.'

He put his arms round her. She lost all control and yelled, 'I hate you, I hate you,' bursting into howling, sobbing tears all over his jersey, making animal sounds. He comforted her and they talked until she started to cry again and he took her to bed where they made despairing love as if they might never meet again. It left her hoping there could yet be a miracle. But then she felt empty and alone, drained of feeling. There was such a silence between them.

'D'you love her?' she said into this great void.

'I can't give her up.'

'Where does that leave me?'

'I still love you.'

Round and round. 'I wish I could believe that. I do so want to believe it.'

'It's true.'

'It doesn't feel true. If you love me, how can you do this to me? I couldn't do it to you.' He didn't answer. 'Well?'

'I don't know. I'm sorry.'

'For two years, Robbie. That's a long time. What did you think would happen? You must have known I'd find out sooner or later.'

'I suppose . . . I didn't think at all.'

It was awful to feel such love and such contempt at once. 'Well, try thinking now. What are we going to do?'

'I don't know.' He sighed.

'D'you want me to leave?'

'No, of course not.'

'Are you planning to leave?'

'No. Not unless you want me to.' He looked at her beseechingly. 'Can't we just . . . go on as we are?'

'For how long?'

'Well . . . as long as it lasts.'

'I see.' The suggestion took her breath away for a moment. 'Yes, I suppose that would suit you very well. I do all the work, run the house, do the washing, ironing, cooking, plus a full-time job, plus the boys in the holidays – and you go off with her whenever you feel like it. Great. Am I supposed to give you a big welcome each time you come back?'

He said humbly, 'I know it's not reasonable –'

'Reasonable! It's bloody insulting.'

There was a long, painful silence while they both considered what to say next.

'Look, I'm sorry.' He seemed to be dragging the words out. 'I love you, you're right and I'm wrong – what more can I say?'

'Is that supposed to make it all right?'

'No, of course not, nothing makes it all right, I know that. I feel very guilty, I never wanted to hurt you –'

She lost control again. 'Oh, shut up. You make me sick. Could you sleep in the spare room tonight?'

'If that's what you want.' He got out of bed like a sulking child and left the room. Jean turned over and began to cry. She was surprised there were any tears left.

She lay awake most of the night. It didn't seem possible they had reached this point. She was terrified, exhausted, incredulous. How could so many years of happiness dissolve like this? She turned over and over, worn out with thinking. What could they have said and done to avoid all this? What to do now? Her head ached and her eyelids were swollen. Birds in the garden started their squeaky song. Thin pale light began to filter through the curtains. Why had she sent him away, when she needed him to comfort her?

'I brought you a cup of tea.' He was standing beside the bed. Was it morning already?

'Thanks.'

'Did you sleep?'

'I'm not sure. I suppose I must have done but I don't feel as if I did. Did you?'

'Not much.'

She sipped her tea. He sat on the edge of the bed.

'It's a mess, isn't it?' she said.

'I'm sorry.'

'I know you are.'

There was a long silence. To her surprise she felt pity for him.

'Don't leave me,' he said at last.

'Why not?'

'I need you.'

She had the dreadful feeling they were both dead and talking nonsense. 'What about the boys?'

'I need them too.'

'No, I meant what shall we tell them?'

'Nothing. They don't have to know anything, surely?' He looked alarmed.

'They do if we split up.'

125

'But it hasn't come to that.'

'If I ask you to choose ... you said last night you can't give her up.' Out of everything he said, that stood out.

'No, I can't.'

'You really mean that.' How pale and tired he looked. Almost ill. But it was madness to feel sorry for him.

'I could lie to you ...'

'Oh, I see. You deserve extra points for telling the truth.'

He stood up. 'I'm not going to leave you. If you want to break up you'll have to leave me – or throw me out.'

She looked at him for a while before saying quite matter-of-factly, 'It's horrible seeing you like this – it's as if you've gone mad.' Then she thought of the outside world. 'What's the time?'

'Seven thirty.'

'God, I'll be late.'

'You can't go to work, you're not up to it. I'll ring up and say you're sick.'

She was suddenly very angry. 'Don't be stupid, we're short-staffed already. I'd like to get up now, would you go away please.'

When she came downstairs into the kitchen in her uniform he was making tea and toast as if he could atone by being domestically useful. She despised him for it, yet found it endearing. She was worn out by conflicting emotions. In her head she knew all was lost, but she had only to look at him to feel the tug of their shared past. And in some way he seemed to be suffering as acutely as she was. She wanted to comfort him but also to punish him for her own pain.

'I can't give you an answer now, Robbie,' she said. 'I'm too tired. I'll have to think about it.'

'What d'you mean?' He appeared surprised, alarmed.

'Well, I have got it right, haven't I? You want to go on living with me and visiting her and I'm supposed to put up with it.' There was no reply, but he looked embarrassed enough. 'Yes, I thought that was it. I wish you hadn't told me about her, Robbie, I really do.'

'But I didn't tell you – you found out.'

126

She wondered if he really believed that, when he had done everything but tell her in words. 'You could have lied,' she said.

She telephoned Ruth from the hospital, feeling she would go mad if she didn't talk to someone else. They met at lunchtime and walked in the hospital grounds. Ruth looked at her with concern.

'Let me take you home, you must be exhausted.'

'Yes, I look awful, I know.'

'I didn't mean that. At least have something to eat.'

A dreadful idea. 'No, I couldn't swallow, I feel sick. Besides, I haven't got time.'

'You shouldn't be working at all.'

'Are you afraid I'll poison someone? I'd rather work, it's helpful. There really are people worse off than me. If somebody said that, I'd hate them, but actually seeing it around you is different. I'm not old and I'm not ill. I must remember that.'

Ruth said gently, 'Don't do anything in a hurry. You're in a state of shock.'

'Not really, I've been expecting it. Only I feel so helpless. He's like a child, just waiting to be forgiven. He won't *do* anything, it's all up to me.' She paused, fighting temptation and giving in to it. 'What's she like? Not to look at, I've seen her; as a person, I mean.'

'Well ... she pretends to be tough but she's really very insecure. She had a peculiar childhood. Her mother was Caroline Venables, a great society beauty in her day, and she got pregnant by someone unsuitable when she was nineteen. The family was appalled and married her off to Tom Crawley, the M.P., who'd been in love with her for years. But they promised Diana's father that if he kept quiet about it they'd tell her the truth as soon as she was old enough, so she's virtually grown up with two fathers. It's created a lot of problems.'

'Don't – you'll have me in tears.' She was surprised how much it hurt to hear the actual name spoken aloud.

'Sorry, but you did ask.'

'Could he be in love with her? He won't say he is but he won't give her up, so it must be pretty strong.'

'I think...' Ruth hesitated, 'she might be more of a status symbol. I mean, he hasn't met anyone like her before. Honestly, if you can just hang on, I'm sure it won't last. He'll get over it. She's not at all keen on marriage, I can promise you.'

'Funny, he didn't mention that.' She looked at Ruth gratefully. 'I'm sorry I argued with you at the weekend. You were right. It's much more painful this way.'

When she got home she went straight into the kitchen to make tea. Robbie stood in the doorway, watching her, like a child waiting for permission to go out and play. She had to make a decision, as much for her own sake as for his: she could not bear the racking arguments in her head any longer.

'All right, we'll try it. I don't think it will work but we'll try.'

'You won't be sorry,' he said eagerly. 'I swear you won't.'

'I think I will. I think I'll be very sorry. I think I should get out now but I can't quite manage it, so there we are.'

He said with every appearance of conviction, 'I love you.'

'So you keep saying. Just do me one favour – don't ever mention her name.' She looked at her watch. 'Well – shouldn't you be getting changed?'

'Changed?'

'Yes – didn't you say you were having dinner with Kovacs?'

'Aye, that's right.' He went out, but slowly, as if not to appear insultingly eager, she thought.

She called after him, 'Oh, by the way – I'm on nights next week. That should suit you fine.'

She went to bed early, worn out, and couldn't sleep. She wondered if she would have to go to her doctor and ask for tablets, explain the reason. A further humiliation. She tried to convince herself she had made the right decision, and failed. She felt doomed. She had taken the only course open to her because she did not believe he was bluffing and she could not face being without him. But she felt she had only postponed the inevitable and she despised herself for not having more courage.

When he came in, about eleven, he hesitated on the landing, then came into the dark bedroom.

'Do I have to sleep in the spare room again?' he asked, like a child being unjustly punished for some offence he has forgotten.

She said, 'I don't care where you sleep,' and he undressed in the dark and got into bed beside her.

Diana

After that, we settled into some kind of pattern. I don't like the word settled and I doubt if I even noticed at the time, but looking back, that must be what we did. At first we met two or three times a week for lunch, then that got difficult because we were both working, so I started turning down work, but Mack noticed and my agent was furious. So Mack started making time to fit in with my schedule, which meant early evening, until that turned into dinner, using my father as an excuse. Of course, Mack really had to see my father during the day, so he had even less time to spend on the building site. It got rather complicated. We seemed to be forever rushing from one place to another, looking at our watches.

I stopped going to bed with other people. Now I see that as proof I had fallen in love, but at the time it just seemed the natural outcome. I was too exhausted to fit in more than work, Mack and my father. And I was happy. Really happy, as if for the first time. I didn't think about the future.

Once I let Mack come to a show. He'd been nagging me for months, but as soon as it started I wished I hadn't said yes. It went well enough, but knowing he was there made everything more effort: I was self-conscious, I felt he had invaded my territory. And those feelings seemed wrong, because I loved him.

He drove me home afterwards. 'You were great,' he said, sounding as if he meant it.

'Was I?'

'A real toffee-nosed bitch.'

I laughed, beginning to relax. 'Thanks. Just behaving naturally.'

He kissed me. 'Why didn't you let me watch before? I enjoyed it.'

'I knew I'd feel silly if you were there, and I did. I'm not letting you in again.'

'It's a job like any other.'

'It's bloody hard work actually. People think it's terribly glamorous but it's not.'

'Beats working on a building site.'

'Don't you believe it.'

It was so good to be home. I changed into a bath-robe and lay down while he made drinks for us both. 'God, I'm so tired,' I said.

'You don't look it.'

'Thank you for that enormous lie.'

He laughed. 'Why do it if you don't like it?'

'I never said I don't like it. Besides, I need the money.'

'Oh, come on.' He gave me my drink. It was nice to be waited on.

'Course I do. I've got to be independent. You can't live on pocket money at my age. Anyway it's quite fun. You get all keyed up like a race horse.' I thought about it. 'The only bit I really can't stand is changing my clothes with a lot of other women. No matter how clean they are – and one or two are actually rather grubby - there's always that funny smell. I hate the smell of women.'

He smiled. 'I'm very fond of it myself. Especially yours.'

'Oh, well, you approach it from a different angle.'

We laughed. He sat beside me. It was lovely to be relaxing, together, with no pressure to go out or make love or do anything. No clock-watching. Just being.

He said, 'What about photographic modelling? You love that, don't you?'

'Oh yes, that's super.'

'Because you can screw the photographer?'

'No, of course not. People always think that. Well, it does happen but only sometimes.' I saw his face. 'In the *past*, I mean, not now, don't look like that, darling.' How quickly one had to be reassuring. 'No, it's mostly work, on the level, honestly, but it's so intensive and personal it makes you feel really good. At least you've got some record of what you've done.'

He seemed mollified. He sat behind me and massaged my neck. I made a purring sound. 'Mm. That's terrific. You've got magic hands – along with a few other magic bits and pieces.' I loved to think of his hands touching me when they had done so much work I didn't understand. He kissed the top of my head. 'My father's coming round later – can you stay?'

'Why not? I'd like to see him.'

'What about Jean?'

'Oh, I'll ring her in a minute.'

I seldom thought about her except as a duty and a nuisance, never as a person, but suddenly I did. 'Better do it now and get it over. She might like to go out.' It seemed a shame for her to be sitting there, waiting for the phone to ring. I pictured her trundling off to the cinema instead.

He rang her when we were in bed. His voice was different when he spoke to her: more relaxed, yet managing to sound both conciliatory and bossy at the same time, the voice of someone on familiar ground, used to getting his own way. I lay there listening to the one-sided conversation and trying vaguely to imagine her end of it. I could, of course, have listened on the extension downstairs, the way I had as a child when Mummy was trying to get my father to come back to her, but I felt in this case it would be cheating.

Mack said, 'Look, I'm sorry, hen, but you better not wait supper for me. I'm still with Kovacs and it might take all evening.' Short pause. 'Won't it keep?' I imagined she was talking about food, the way wives do. 'Look, I'll make it up to you, but this is really important.' Pause. 'See you later.'

He turned back to me. I said, 'Did she believe you?'

'Why not?'

'If I was a wife I'd know. I'd smell a lie a mile off.' But of

132

course I had no intention of being a wife. Then we started to make love and I forgot about her.

When my father arrived I went down to welcome him while Mack was still dressing. 'You're early, Apukam, how lovely,' I said, hugging him.

He kissed me. 'Not too early, I hope.'

'No, of course not. Impossible.'

He held me away from him, checking my face to make sure I was happy, then saying as Mack came down the stairs, 'Well, how are you, my children?'

Mack said, 'Pretty good. How are you?'

'Oh, I'm surviving.' My father put on his world-weary face that always made me want to laugh, and they shook hands.

'I've been thinking over that idea of yours,' Mack said.

I interrupted quickly. 'Come on now, drinks before ideas. D'you both want your usual?'

They both said they did. It was fun to be waiting on them because it was a novelty.

'All right, carry on. I'll do the drinks while you shake the Empire. What's left of it.'

They were instantly absorbed. 'I should get planning for the last two acres of warehousing any day now.'

'Have you really got time to develop it with all the house building you are doing?'

'Oh aye, why not? I've got a good foreman.'

'Well, we have both done very nicely so far. There is no reason we cannot have another success.'

I served the drinks. They thanked me absent-mindedly.

'So the only question is whether we do it as Mackenzie Industrial.'

'What's that?' I was suddenly interested.

'Your father suggested I should form a company and his bank would have shares in it.'

'So you're going to be partners? Terrific.'

Mack said with his usual caution, 'Nothing's decided yet.'

'No, of course not, but that's the basic idea?'

My father smiled at my enthusiasm. 'Well, we would lend

money to the company and charge interest on it, but instead of a percentage net profit on each deal, we would have shares in the company.'

I thought it over. 'Same thing, really.'

'Yes, in a way, but we would be putting our name behind the company, which means we wouldn't let it get into trouble. It would be a lot of prestige for Mackenzie.' He turned to Mack. 'So – in principle you're interested, yes?'

'Aye – but it all depends how much it costs.'

Silence. I suddenly got the feeling they'd rather I wasn't there. 'I'm ravenous,' I said tactfully. 'Anyone fancy an omelette?' My father said he'd already eaten. 'You're afraid of my omelettes. Mack – what about you?'

'I'd be grateful for anything.'

I remembered he'd missed his home-cooked dinner, whereas I was used to not eating very much. 'That's the spirit that made Britain great. Plain or cheese?'

'Plain, I think.'

'A wise decision. The cheese has a beard.'

I went downstairs to the kitchen, leaving them to it and pausing in the hall to eavesdrop.

'She's not joking,' my father said. 'She really can't cook anything else.'

'I know.'

'Of course.'

I shouted up the stairs, 'I heard that. Nobody's good at everything, just you remember that. You're not so hot on a catwalk, either of you.'

They laughed, then my father said to Mack, 'We would want a twenty-five per cent share in the company.'

It was such an ordinary weekend: no hint of trouble to come. I caught up on sleep. I rang friends I hadn't seen for a while and had dinner with one, saw a film with another. I checked everything in my model bag ready for Monday, cleaned my hairpieces and set them on rollers, gave myself a really good facial and manicure. My hair had to wait till Sunday night because my father and I were lunching together and I insisted on going swimming first. He had bought a flat in a block with its own private swimming-pool, God knows why, since he hardly ever used it except with me. I suppose he liked to think it was there, just in case.

We fooled around for a bit, playing with the water and splashing each other like children, then we had a race. I won.

'You're too good for me,' he said when he got his breath back.

'Nonsense. You're out of condition, that's all.'

We got out and sat on the edge of the pool. It was really very pleasant: we had it all to ourselves.

'Success has gone to your stomach,' I said, punching him lightly.

'We cannot all be as thin as you, my love.'

'Actually, Ruth is putting on weight, have you noticed?'

He shrugged. 'She is lazy, that's all. What does it matter?'

'It's very unhealthy. We all went swimming the other week – I said I'd give Lisa some coaching because she's so keen – and Ruth could hardly manage two lengths.'

'It's not important.'

'Oh, I know she's perfect.' I jumped back into the pool. 'Come on, another race.'

'Is it compulsory?'

'It'll do you good.' I knew he secretly enjoyed being bullied – by me, at any rate.

'It is something you learn at your terrible English public schools, this mania for exercise and competition.'

'That's why we used to rule the world – long after the Austro-Hungarian Empire bit the dust.'

He plunged in after me and we did another two lengths. I still won, but this time he was closer behind me.

'See? You're improving,' I said proudly, as if I were responsible.

'Are you seeing Mackenzie tonight?'

'No, he's down at the cottage.'

'Do you miss him?'

The sudden change of subject, the seriousness, alarmed me. 'When I'm with you? Don't be silly.'

He hauled himself out and sat on the edge, while this time

I stayed in the water. 'I have never seen you so serious about anyone. You're not pregnant again?'

'No, of course I'm not.' I swam off, faintly cross, and did a racing turn at the end to show off, knowing he was watching. When I got back I said, 'You ought to be timing me,' and climbed out. 'You ought to be sitting there, stopwatch in hand, bursting with pride.'

He looked at me thoughtfully, refusing to be diverted. 'D'you want to marry him?'

'No, of course not. I don't want to marry anyone. You know that. I never have. It only leads to trouble.'

'What about his wife?'

'What about her? She's his problem not mine.' I dived back into the water.

Ruth came to see me. She'd had a bad weekend with David, Mack and Jean, and a bad morning with my father, whom she would have liked to be more dissatisfied by the permanence of her marriage, so she wasn't in a mood to be tactful. Neither was I, going out to lunch and liable to be late (something I never am) thanks to Ruth.

'She knows,' Ruth said, all dramatic. I shrugged. 'Don't you care?'

'Nothing to do with me.' I went on doing my face.

'That's just what your father said.'

'Well?'

'Look – I'm pig in the middle, don't you realize? I know everyone concerned in this mess – God help me, I introduced you two.'

She sounded really annoyed. I said, 'Are you jealous?'

'Don't be silly.'

'Sorry. Just a thought. You sound so ... put out. Maybe you wish you'd kept him for yourself.'

'I didn't want to keep him.'

'Well, then.' I couldn't understand what all the fuss was about. 'Does it matter who has him?'

'Jean's my friend.'

'That didn't stop you having him in Glasgow.'

'That was a long time ago. I hardly knew her then. And it was only a few weeks.'

I finally lost all patience. 'I see. That lets you out all shining white and I'm the one who gets God's thunderbolt. Thanks a lot.' A thought struck me. 'Does my father know about you and Mack?'

'No.'

I went on with my face, letting the silence develop. I felt a bit guilty because I was fond of Ruth really, but she did deserve it for being so tiresome.

'I'd rather he didn't,' she said eventually, to my satisfaction.

'Who would tell him? He'd only be upset.'

I was lucky and got a taxi straight away. Once I knew I wasn't going to be late (you have to be punctual in modelling and punctuality invades the rest of your life) I was able to relax and think about it more calmly. It was hard for Ruth: no wonder she was a bit edgy. Being married to David and having an affair with my father was quite some juggling act, whichever way you looked at it, and she'd been doing it now for a long time. The whole complicated structure depended upon nobody asking or answering too many questions, and I suppose she was afraid that if Mack and Jean stopped obeying the rules, David and my father might follow suit. Not logical, of course, just superstitious – a far stronger feeling.

I wondered if I should warn Mack. If Ruth was right and Jean really did know, perhaps Mack could avoid a scene if he was clever. Although in my experience if people want to make scenes they always do eventually and nothing can stop them. You may as well let them get on with it. Also, I really didn't feel it was my business. I wasn't being heartless, as Ruth seemed to imply, just detached. Once you start worrying about a married man's wife and children you are done for and it soon affects your relationship with the man.

By the time I got to the office I was feeling a bit down. But the minute I saw Mack I cheered up. That's how it was in those days: he could always make me feel better. He didn't have to do anything, or speak, although the accent was still magic: it was enough just to see him, all brown and wary and cuddly, waiting for me. At the time I thought it was something in him, nothing to do with me, that would last for ever. And I did so want something to be magic and last for ever.

This time he looked so cock-a-hoop, so pleased with himself, so jubilant, like a little boy who has just won a prize. I felt my heart turn over with love and pride, and that was what I needed, real live sensations that I could feel. He and my father had glasses in their hands. I said, 'Amanda's gone to lunch, so I sneaked in. Are we celebrating?'

'Mackenzie Industrial.'

'Really? Tremendous.'

My father gave me a drink and I looked at them both with such joy and satisfaction that I had brought them together. I felt so powerful. But for me, they would never have met.

I said, 'Now you can both take me to lunch.'

All the same, I managed to haul myself out of my euphoria by the end of the afternoon, in time to tell Mack, while he was getting dressed, what Ruth had said about Jean. He said David had warned him, too, and maybe he should buy her a present. I said fine but not to overdo it or she'd be suspicious. He kissed me goodbye and I think I was asleep almost before the front door closed. I was always tired in those days and needed all the sleep I could get. Working hard and having a big love affair took all my energy. But I had an editorial and two commercials the next day, so I had to get up later and wash my hair.

When he told me she'd accused him and he'd admitted everything, I was amazed and depressed. Amazed because I'd never really expected a confrontation and depressed because now everything would be different. Telling the whole truth is like granting a licence to make scenes, and the very thought of it made me feel tired. I said, 'Oh, darling, why didn't you lie? That was what she wanted.'

138

He looked as baffled as if I were speaking some strange foreign language. 'I couldn't. Not any more.'

'But the truth hurts. None of us can stand it. Anyway, it's an old rule – always lie unless you're caught in the act – and even then you can probably think of *something*. Nobody wants to believe the worst.'

He said, as if he had done the right thing, 'I think ... once she gets used to the idea – it'll be easier for us to meet.'

I couldn't see the logic of that. 'No, it'll be harder. Even when you're not with me, she'll think you are – and when she wants to be nice to you, she won't be able to, because of her pride.'

'So I've hurt her for nothing.' He sounded very sombre, as if he had tried his best and failed. I couldn't bear his misery; I also couldn't bear the image he had given me of the wretched woman all alone and in pain. It was so unnecessary.

'You can put it right,' I said. 'Just wait a few weeks, then tell her we've broken up. She'll be delighted, you can have a big reconciliation, and we can go on just the same. That way everyone'll be happy.' Anything rather than having myself landed with a crisis. All that responsibility. The very thought of it made me feel heavy. I peered at his face in the candlelight. 'Well, darling, that is the point, isn't it? For everyone to be happy?'

1960

Jean

She had lived through the two worst years of her life and somehow survived. Every day she prayed the affair would end, but it showed no sign of ending. She and Robbie became like two polite strangers or an amiably detached brother and sister, except for the times when they urgently made love, he to prove there was still affection, she to steal something from 'that woman', or simply for auld lang syne. The name Diana was never used between them; if Jean heard it from anyone else, even in a film, it caused her sharp physical pain.

When she was on days he slept at home, usually with her in their double bed, although he occasionally retreated to the spare room after a quarrel. All their quarrels were about Diana, but always expressed in other terms such as children, money and food. When she was on nights, she presumed he slept away from home, but she did not ask him and he did not tell her. In the holidays they both made huge efforts to convince the boys that nothing was wrong. Jean did not think these efforts were at all successful, but Robbie insisted that they were.

Business thrived. The house-building, Mackenzie Industrial, deals with Kovacs, deals without Kovacs. She hardly knew what he was doing any more, but he was always busy: in his office, on the telephone, on site, in meetings with his accountant, his lawyer, agents, runners. Jean knew logically that he must in fact have very little free time to spend with *her*, but that was not the way it felt. She had hoped that sexual jealousy might lessen with time, but instead it seemed to get worse, like an aching tooth left unattended. She watched him for signs of the other woman, marks or scent; she imagined them together, tortured herself with fantasies.

143

Most of the time she wanted him and was too proud to admit it, while he was too busy or exhausted to notice or to offer. She longed for him and she hated him: the two feelings left her worn out.

One evening he came home early when she was making up the spare room bed for Bill. She heard him calling her and something in his voice gave her an instant premonition of disaster. She kept very quiet, repressing an urge to hide, and went on with the bed-making.

'Why didn't you answer?' he said when he found her.

'It's not that big a house. You were bound to find me eventually.'

'I've got to talk to you. It's important.'

Her heart contracted with terror. 'Not now, Robbie, I'm busy.'

'I'm sorry, this won't keep.'

'If it's about *her*, I don't want to know.'

He hesitated, crossing to the window and looking down into the garden where Jamie and Duncan, home for Whit-sun and half-term, were idly kicking a football. 'Look, Jean –'

'Anyway, we don't have time for one of your cosy little chats right now. Have you forgotten Bill's coming?'

'Oh, my God.' He looked put out, yet also somehow relieved.

'*You* invited him.'

She liked Bill and had not meant to sound angry: it was just another excuse to quarrel. Bill was welcome, as anyone from Glasgow would have been, but particularly because he reminded her of the early days when he was Robbie's law-yer and they had no problems other than bank loans and house-building. It seemed a lifetime ago and was only five years.

Bill insisted on being shown all over the house and garden before settling down with them in the living-room for a drink.

'It's a fine place you've got here, Rob,' he said approv-ingly.

144

'Aye, it's not bad. Be better if I'd built it myself though.'

'No doubt.' They all laughed. 'I suppose you havena the time these days.'

'Well, I'm working flat out.'

'Aye, you've done all right.' He turned to Jean. 'You must be very proud of him.'

'Oh yes, I am.' She felt her face muscles stiffen as she smiled.

'And as for these two' – Bill looked at Jamie and Duncan – 'why, you were wee laddies when I saw you last. D'you remember me?'

Duncan shook his head.

Jamie said, 'No, sir.'

'Speak up, Duncan,' Robbie said.

'No, sir.'

'You don't have to call me sir,' Bill said fondly.

'Och, they even call me sir the first week of the holidays.'

'They're at Dean's Academy now, aren't they? My sister's lad went there. It's a good school. How are they liking it?'

'They like it fine,' Jean said. It was still a surprise to her that they did.

Bill turned back to the children. 'Is it all right, the big school?'

'Aye. We go mountaineering and all kinds of things. Duncan's better at it than me.'

'No, I'm not.'

'You are. You're better at Latin too. And you've got some of your pictures in the exhibition.' But Jamie did not sound envious, merely proud.

'And what are *you* good at?' Bill asked him.

'Oh – maths and football. That's about all.'

Robbie said, 'He knows what's important,' and a faint chill crept into the atmosphere.

Duncan said proudly, 'I have to look after a boy called Williams this term. He's Welsh and he talks in a funny way like singing, so nobody can understand him. But I've helped him quite a lot. He used to be homesick and he's not any more.'

Bill smiled. 'Aye, it's a good school. But you must miss them, lassie, when they're away.'

'Yes, I do. Only I'm full-time at the hospital so I'm really very busy.'

'Aye, you're looking a wee bit tired. Don't let her overdo it, Rob.'

'She likes it, don't you, hen?'

It was all suddenly too much. 'I must have a look at the dinner.' She got up and went out.

From the kitchen she heard Jamie ask Bill, 'How long are you staying with us?'

'Only the weekend.'

'Can't you stay longer?'

Bill laughed. 'How's that for diplomacy?'

'Aye, he'll go far.'

Duncan said hopefully, 'I'd like you to stay too.'

'Little Sir Echo,' said Robbie.

'What does that mean?' Duncan sounded hurt. Jean was trembling for him: the discrimination was hard to bear. She heard Bill making an effort.

'D'you ken I've known your father since he was your age?'

Jamie said eagerly, 'What was he like?'

'Oh – always too big for his boots.'

They all laughed and Jean seized her chance to return on a good note. 'Right. We can eat.'

Supper went easily and pleasantly, but Jean brooded: what had Robbie been about to say to her before Bill arrived? She was actually very frightened and wished now that she had not put off hearing it, whatever it was. After supper the two men went to the pub as usual. She knew Robbie wanted to discuss business with Bill, something about Bill buying an intermediate lease for Robbie in some deal she did not understand, but she convinced herself that Robbie might also be telling Bill his troubles. After the boys were in bed, the fantasy took over and she began to drink rather heavily. It did not take much to make her drunk these days, since she was always tired. She sat by herself watching television, refilling her glass and wondering what Robbie was going to tell her. When they returned at eleven she said, 'Welcome home,' in quite an aggressive tone.

'Aye, sorry, we are a bit late. Are the boys in bed?'

'Where d'you think they are?' She got up and turned off the television. 'I'm sorry, Bill, I'm a wee bit drunk.'

'It's all right, lassie.' He looked at her with such compassion that she was terrified: what had Robbie said to him?

'Did you have a good time?' she asked Robbie.

'Aye, Bill's going to act as nominee in the marriage value deal.'

'Oh, good. That's what you wanted. But then you always get what you want, don't you?' She finished her drink. 'Marriage value, that's a joke. How much value d'you put on our marriage, then, tell me that? No, don't bother, not very much. Well, why should you? It's not much of a marriage, is it, not any more. It used to be but it's not any more. All the value's gone out of it.' She saw their shocked faces and began to laugh.

Robbie said, 'Jean, stop it.'

'Why don't *you* stop it? Because I can't stand it any more. Did he tell you, Bill, he's got this woman and I'm supposed to put up with it? Did he tell you "man to man"? Well, I'm sick of pretending it's all right, I can't pretend any more, I'm bloody sick of it. It's not all right. It's bloody awful.'

Bill said, 'I know, lassie, I know.'

Surprise made her silent, then she started to cry.

'He's on your side,' Robbie said bitterly. 'Don't worry, he's on your side.'

When he told her he wanted a divorce, she screamed, 'No,' with all her strength.

They were standing on either side of the bed. 'Be quiet,' he said, as if she were being unreasonable. 'You'll wake the boys.'

'What's the difference? They'll have to know sooner or later.'

'Jean. Calm down and think for a minute. You said yourself you couldn't stand it any more. You said you were sick of it.'

She shouted, 'I'm not going to divorce you.'

'But why not? This is no good. You told me all along it wouldn't work and you were right. If we make a clean break now, it might be easier all round. Take the pressure off. We could meet when we feel like it. I'd take good care of you and the boys. You know that. You can have anything you want. I promise.'

She was astonished that he could have the gall to make divorce sound like some kind of treat. She screamed, 'No,' and ran round the bed to attack him. She wanted him to feel pain; she wanted to see him bleed. He held her off. As they struggled, the bedroom door opened slowly behind them.

Jamie said, 'Mam. Are you all right?'

They both looked round, shocked, at the small figure in the doorway, hitching up his pyjamas.

'Duncan woke up,' Jamie went on. 'He was frightened.'

'I'm all right, Jamie,' Jean said. 'Tell Duncan I'm all right. You can both go back to sleep.'

Robbie said, 'Come on, Jamie lad, I'll take you back to bed.'

'No, thanks.' Jamie's voice was very cold. 'Are you sure you're all right, Mam?'

'I'm sure. Off you go now. Night night.'

When he had gone there was a long, shocked silence between them. 'You see?' Jean said eventually. 'That's what it's going to be like. Is that what you want?'

'That's what I'm trying to prevent. *You* made that happen.'

So now they were both angry again. An idea came to Jean, a very simple one.

'Does she know I'm never going to divorce you?'

Next day, before she lost her nerve, she dressed and made up with care, rang the house twice but did not speak, and arrived in time to see Ruth leaving with a grey-haired man. As soon as the car was out of sight she went up to the front door and pressed the buzzer. A light, offhand, upper-class English voice said, 'Yes?'

Jean swallowed. 'This is Jean Mackenzie.'

'Oh, Christ,' said the voice.

'I want to speak to you.'

There was a short pause.

'Yes, well, all right. You better come up.'

The buzzer went and Jean, trembling, pushed the door open. She went into a hall off which opened kitchen, dining-room and cloakroom. There was nobody there.

'Up here,' said the voice.

Jean mounted a spiral staircase to an enormous drawing-room. There was a tea-tray on a low table and an amazing assortment of shoes, underwear, make-up, jewellery and wigs all over the floor. In the middle of it all stood a young woman with bare feet and long blonde hair, wearing jeans and a shirt and no make-up. 'Hullo,' she said, 'this is all frightfully embarrassing, don't you think?'

Jean couldn't answer. Her heart was pounding so much she didn't trust herself to speak.

'Would you like to sit down?' the other asked. When Jean refused, she went into a long speech about how nervous she felt and what a shock she'd had. Jean didn't believe a word of it. She had never seen anyone more arrogant in her life – actually making jokes about how she hoped she wouldn't get acid thrown in her face.

'I didn't think of that,' Jean said, though now she realized it would have given her acute pleasure.

'I bet you wish you had,' the other said with satisfaction, and offered her lemon tea.

Jean refused and looked round the room. 'So this is the home he made for you.'

'Well, the workmen did most of it, he only supervised it really, but it is jolly nice.' She picked up a wig. 'D'you mind if I get on with this? It might calm me down.'

Jean watched her putting rollers into the wig. It seemed an extraordinary occupation for a grown woman.

'What did you want to say to me?' she asked, looking up from the wig, as if Jean were an ordinary visitor.

'Now I'm actually here . . . it's not very easy.'

'I expect you hate me so much it nearly chokes you. Or is that just my guilty conscience?'

'No, that's about right.'

'I'd feel the same in your position. I must say, I think you've been awfully good about things all this time.'

Jean's control snapped. 'Don't be so bloody patronizing.'

The other said calmly, 'I meant I appreciate it, that's all.'

'I didn't have very much choice.' Jean tried to think why she'd come, what she'd meant to say. Terrible images of Robbie in bed with this woman were distracting her. 'I suppose there's no point in asking you to give him up.'

'Not really.' The other looked faintly surprised.

'Right, then you better get one thing clear. You won't hear it from him, so you might as well hear it from me. I'm never going to divorce him. Not ever. So no matter how many years you hang on with your claws in him, you'll never be his wife.' She wasn't sure what she expected, but she had shot her bolt and needed some reaction.

The other merely shrugged. 'I never expected to be.' She went on about being happy as they were and enjoying being a mistress, but Jean was hardly listening. What could she say next? The whole scheme had collapsed. It had simply never occurred to her that this person, having put her through so much, might not want to be married to Robbie. It made nonsense of all the suffering. What was it all for? She only came to again when she heard the words 'beginning to wish I'd just had an abortion the way I meant to and never told him about it. Would have been much simpler all round.'

Jean felt as if someone had hit her on the head. She sat down. Suddenly the whole dreadful mess made sense and she felt a fool not to have seen it before.

'Oh God,' the other said, 'how frightful,' and started pouring drinks. 'Didn't he tell you? Oh God.' She put a large drink in Jean's hand and Jean, ashamed, drank it because it was necessary. The voice went on but she didn't hear it. Everything had fallen into place. Of course. There could only be one reason why he wanted a divorce after all this time. She had been stupid. It was obvious, but she had never thought of such a thing because it was too painful. No wonder he had not dared to tell her. All the years she had longed for his third child and now this creature was going to have it. She struggled not to cry.

'Look, I *am* sorry,' said the other, actually leaning towards her.

Jean shouted, 'Get away from me,' and the other drew back. 'D'you ever stop to think how much misery women like you cause? Men are so weak. We were happy till you came along. I've got two boys at home who are going to lose their father because of you. Are you proud of yourself? You could have anyone and you pick my husband.'

The other said, 'Well, if it's any consolation at all, you've made me feel absolutely ghastly about it.'

Jean was at a loss for words. She had expected to hear something about love, about guilt; instead she had received what might have been an apology for failing to return a library book. Was this a flesh and blood woman? How could she be having a child? And why, oh why, was Robbie so besotted with her when she did not appear to have feelings at all? She was going on now about leaving things as they were, not caring about marriage or divorce, how they might all change their minds, as if all that mattered was what suited her, as if she were graciously giving Jean permission to stay married.

Jean stood up. 'I think I better go before I actually hit you.' She had never felt such a strong urge to do violence.

The other said calmly, 'Well, I can't say I'll give him up, but you didn't expect that, did you?'

Jean heard herself say what was in her heart. 'Right now, God forgive me, all I want in the world is for you and your baby to die.'

She rang Father Murphy and he offered to come and see her. He had known the situation for a long time now; sometimes she felt he was the only person left in the world that she could trust.

'Even if I don't divorce him,' she said, 'he's going to leave me. I can feel it. I thought all this time if I really tried and I prayed ... but it's no good, it doesn't work.' She was close to despair.

'You mustn't give up,' Father Murphy said. 'There's a long way to go yet. You're doing the right thing, you must find some comfort in that. I've seen this situation many times and you'd be surprised how often the husband comes back, if only the wife can be patient enough.'

'Really?' She had promised herself to be realistic, yet here she was, clutching at straws.

'Would I tell you a lie? Why should you divorce him when you don't believe in divorce? You can have a legal separation and get all the security and maintenance you need for yourself and your children – and just wait for this madness to pass. It often does.'

And if it never did? Jean thought about the bleak road ahead of her. 'People keep telling me I'll meet someone else. But I won't. And even if I do, what's the use? I can't ever get married again. I'm married to Robbie, whether he leaves me or not.'

'Ah well,' Father Murphy said tolerantly, 'if they're not Catholics, they probably don't understand that.'

'I'm sure he thinks I'm just being spiteful not divorcing him.' Jean tried to examine her conscience. 'Maybe I am. That's the terrible thing, I don't know any more. I hate that woman so much I want her to die. Father, I've never wished that before in my life. It's awful.'

'It's a very natural feeling, you know, but you must pray to Our Lord and his Blessed Mother to help you overcome it.'

'I know, but I can't. I can't pray any more and I can't go to Communion. I want to, but I can't. I'm too full of hatred.' She was sure it was mortal sin to feel as she did.

'That will pass. You must come to Mass and say your prayers as usual, even if you don't feel you can go to Holy Communion. It's a great help to practise your faith at times like this. Then when you feel you're ready I'll hear your Confession.'

If only she were ready for that. Ready to be sorry. Ready not to hate any more. 'I even want her baby to die. That's an innocent child. Oh, Father, I'm so ashamed of myself.'

152

And she longed to go to Communion but she knew she was not worthy.

'I know, I know.' Nothing she said seemed to shock Father Murphy; no doubt he had heard it all before. 'You mustn't forget God understands all these feelings. Would you like me to have a talk with your husband? D'you think that might help? I'd be very willing. We often find non-Catholics are surprisingly eager to talk to us in situations like this.'

If only that were possible. 'Thank you, Father, but I don't think so. Robbie really hates the Church; I mean it was a big concession he made getting married in the Church and letting me bring up the children as Catholics – I think he feels he's done more than enough already.' She gave way to self-pity as it were to a drug or a drink to bring blessed relief. 'I'm so alone, Father, all my friends are Robbie's friends too, and I can't talk to my parents, they'd only say I told you so –'

She heard the front door open and close. Robbie, home early. He came into the room. 'What are *you* doing here?'

Father Murphy looked up calmly. 'I called to see your wife.'

'I asked Father Murphy to call.'

'This is a very unhappy situation, Mr Mackenzie. If there's anything I can do to help –'

'I'd like you to leave now. That would help a lot.'

'Robbie, there's no need to be offensive.'

Father Murphy stood up. 'It's all right, Jean. I'll call again another time.'

'I don't think so,' Robbie said.

'It might be better if I came to the presbytery. I'll see you out, Father. I'm sorry.'

They chatted on the doorstep. When she got back to Robbie he was finishing a drink and pouring himself another.

'I'm ashamed of you,' she said.

'Oh aye? Well, that makes two of us. Look, I'm sorry, but I don't want him in my house again.'

Jean poured herself a drink. They were long past the stage of waiting on each other. 'Oh really? I don't think what goes

153

on in your house concerns you any more.' She took a large swig of whisky to boost her courage. Anger was already helpful. 'Why didn't you tell me she's pregnant?'

He was startled. 'Who told you?'

'She did. I went to see her.'

'You had no right to do that.' Not a word about her pain and shock.

'I can do whatever I like. You do. Why shouldn't I?' She finished her drink and poured a refill. Now she wanted desperately to hurt him as she had been hurt. 'I don't know what all the fuss is about. She doesn't want a divorce because she doesn't want to marry you. In fact she's not even sure she wants the baby.'

She saw from his face that the blow had gone deep. Why, then, did she not feel better? 'Go on, hit me, why don't you? It's about the only thing you haven't done.' The phone rang and she picked it up. 'Yes? Paul Davies for you.' She dimly remembered the name of the runner who had brought Robbie the marriage value deal; the unfortunate connotation had fixed it in her mind.

'Oh God, not now.' Robbie took the phone. 'Yes, Paul. Yes, it's all going well. No, I am not going to lose it. It's under control. Look, when I have any news I'll ring you and now will you get off my back? And don't bloody call me at home again.'

He hung up savagely. Jean said, 'Another satisfied customer.' Then Ruth arrived back with the boys. Jean did not really trust Ruth any more, although she still liked her, because she was trying to be on both sides at once; but she was useful for taking charge of the boys if the neighbours were away. Jamie and Duncan ran in and Jean, who did not feel like speaking, watched Ruth and Robbie in the garden. He seemed to be talking earnestly, Ruth shrugging and trying to get away. Then they both drove off in opposite directions.

It was late when he came back and he went straight upstairs, ignoring the light in the sitting-room. Jean turned off the television and followed him up. When she came into the bedroom she found he was packing a suitcase. She watched for a moment in numb silence. The end of the road. She had made every possible effort for the past two years and she might as well not have bothered. This was her reward. She should have thrown him out at the start, when she still had some pride. She wanted to cry like a child. ('It's not *fair*.')

Instead she asked, 'What are you going to say to the boys?'

'I'd rather you didn't wake them. You can tell them I've gone away on business and I'll go and see them when they're back at school.'

Why did he not look different? How could he be the same person she had known and loved for thirteen years, so calmly preparing to leave her? 'You make it sound so easy.'

'Jean, I don't want to quarrel with you, but we can't go on living together, you must see that. I'd like us to be friends.'

She couldn't believe he had actually said that word.

'I'd like us to remember the good times,' he went on with affectionate pity. 'You've been wonderful to me. Everything that's gone wrong is my fault.'

'Is that supposed to make me feel better?' What was the use of being blameless if you were still going to be punished?

'It's true, that's all.' He seemed to be saying that was all he could give her now: the truth.

'Don't leave me, please.' She lost her last shreds of dignity. 'I swore I wouldn't beg you, but I haven't any pride.' Tears came.

'I'm sorry, hen.'

'No . . .' The word stabbed her heart.

'I'm asking you to divorce me as a favour – I'll give you anything you want, your lawyer can have it all his own way – I'll come and see you and the boys whenever you want me to.'

She sensed that something even more terrible was coming. 'And if I don't?'

He closed the suitcase. He looked sad but inexorable, as if programmed by some exterior force. 'I'll still support you, of course, but I won't see you any more.'

The final unbelievable cruelty. There was no doubt he meant it. She felt stunned for a moment, then suddenly noticed he had gone from the room. She ran after him.

'Robbie.' She hardly noticed she was shouting with all her strength. 'Robbie.'

He was half-way down the stairs. Jamie and Duncan came out of their room.

Duncan called out, 'Dad, where are you going?'

'He's leaving us.' Jean was by now too upset to spare Duncan's feelings.

'No, Dad, don't go. Don't leave us, please.'

'It's no use, Duncan,' Jean said loudly for Robbie's benefit. 'I've tried that. It doesn't work.'

At the foot of the stairs Robbie hesitated, looking up at them all in what seemed to Jean's surprise to be a sudden agony of guilt and indecision. Jamie put his arms round her.

'It's all right, Mam, I'll look after you. We can manage without him.' There was new hatred in Jamie's voice that frightened her. She saw it reached Robbie too. For a moment father and son stared at each other. Then Robbie turned away and the front door slammed behind him.

Duncan burst into tears and ran downstairs after him. Jean and Jamie on the landing heard the car drive away.

She learned to live alone. It was strange and sad at first, but she felt a kind of pride when she began to master it. There was an element of relief in being able to eat, sleep and cry when she needed to; and the job helped. She was very busy and very tired. If she couldn't sleep, she took pills, which her doctor prescribed to mix well with the alcohol she took when she was depressed, which was often. She cut herself off from people because she had nothing to say to them and no energy to listen. She became a hermit. It was peaceful. Pointless but painless. She needed all the strength she could muster to cope with Robbie's weekly guilt-laden visits, for which she lived.

Ruth called. Jean made tea and produced cake. Ruth said it looked lovely and Jean said good. There was then an awkward silence for too long.

'It's so nice to see you,' Ruth said. 'I hope you didn't mind me dropping in.'

'Not at all.' Jean poured tea.

'Only you're either out or engaged.'

'Yes, well, I'm on nights and I sleep all morning, so I take the phone off the hook.'

'I was worried about you,' Ruth said.

'Why?'

'You *know* why.'

Jean cut the cake. 'There's no need to worry. I'm fine.'

'You don't look fine.'

'Thanks a lot.'

'No, I didn't mean that, you look marvellous, it's just – oh, you know what I mean.'

Jean felt perverse and unfair: she enjoyed seeing Ruth flounder. 'How's David?'

'All right.'

'And Lisa?'

'Yes. Jean, I can't stand this.'

'What?'

'Either throw me out or tell me we're still friends.' When there was no reply, she added, 'Bad as that, is it?'

There was nothing to lose now by being honest. 'You're making it very difficult for me, Ruth. I'd like us to stay friends – God knows I need all the friends I can get right now – but how can we when I know you're seeing her as well? How can I relax with you?'

'You mean I've got to choose.'

'I don't see how you can expect to have a foot in each camp.'

'I don't actually want to.' Ruth looked embarrassed. 'Only ... she's related to ... the man I told you about, so I can't not see her. I'm very angry with her, actually. I think she's behaved outrageously.'

Jean felt herself disarmed. 'She couldn't have done it without Robbie's cooperation.'

'I'm very angry with him too.'

'Oh, what's the point? We can't have been as happily married as I thought we were or it couldn't have happened.'

'I'm not so sure,' Ruth said, as if she knew better. 'I think sometimes people do mad things for no reason at all.'

Suddenly Jean felt immensely weary. 'Oh well, it's done now.'

'Are you divorcing him?'

'Yes. Not in time for the great event, that wasn't possible, but early next year.' She wondered if Ruth could possibly understand how she felt, how bleak her future seemed.

'It's very generous of you.'

'Not really. He said he wouldn't see me again if I didn't.'

There was a shocked silence, then Ruth said, 'And you still want to see him?'

'It's all I have to live for.' She tried to sound matter-of-fact so Ruth wouldn't think she was mad. 'I've spent thirteen years with Robbie. They were good years, most of them. You don't stop loving someone just because they leave you. Why shouldn't I still want to see him?'

'I know, it must be very difficult.' Ruth obviously didn't understand. 'But wouldn't a clean break be less painful in the long run?'

'I don't think so. There's no point in my meeting anyone else, you see.' Not that she even wanted to. 'In the eyes of God and the Church I'll always be married to Robbie.'

Ruth looked at her with amazement. 'And you really believe that?'

'Yes, I do. I can't change now just because things have gone wrong. Would you like some more tea?'

Ruth said faintly, 'Yes. Thank you.'

'He's being very good really.' The unaccustomed luxury of being able to talk about him began almost to cheer her up. 'He calls in to see me once a week. I think he feels guilty. He was always very nice to me once he'd got his own way. He's even offered me a house in Scotland – as well as this one, I mean – so I can see more of the boys, but I think it would be an awful waste of money, I can always stay with his mother.' She had thought it over carefully and decided he had already been too generous with money: she could not accept any more from him.

'I think,' Ruth said, 'if someone treated me the way Robert's treated you, I'd really hate them.'

Jean was surprised. 'Oh, no. I don't think you would.

You'd like to, of course – *I'd* like to – but when it comes to the point, it's not possible.'

'But it must be so bizarre – what on earth do you talk about?'

'Oh, the boys mostly. And a bit about work.' She could hardly remember: his presence obliterated the words. 'He doesn't stay long.'

'God, I couldn't stand it.'

She wanted Ruth to agree with her. 'The thing I've got to remember is not to get emotional. If I'm too pleased to see him or too upset when he goes – I mean if I *show* all that – then he'll be embarrassed and he may not come back. I've got to make it easy for him. I've got to be cheerful.'

'Bloody men,' Ruth said, not understanding at all, 'they have it all their own way.'

'Not really.' Jean made one last effort. 'If you left David and promised to see him every week – he'd behave like me, wouldn't he?'

Robbie arrived early for his next visit; she had only just finished doing her face. They stood awkwardly in the hall, smiling at each other, and she kept her hands behind her back so he wouldn't see them shake.

'Well . . . how are you?'

'I'm fine,' she said brightly. 'Shall I put the kettle on?'

'I'd rather have a drink.'

'Yes, of course.'

He followed her into the sitting-room and sat on the edge of the sofa like an uneasy guest. 'Have you thought any more about the Christmas holidays?'

'Yes, I'll be staying here.' She poured two drinks with great care. 'It's easier. So any time you want to call in and see the boys, you'll be very welcome.'

'Thank you. You still . . . don't want them to come to us?'

'I'd rather not.' How that word 'us' hurt: it gave her a pain in the chest so that she could hardly breathe.

'It's just that . . .' he looked apologetic ' . . . I'd like them to meet her before –'

'Yes, well, you can always take Duncan out somewhere, that's easy, but Jamie doesn't want to meet her.'

'He hasn't changed his mind, then?'

'No.' She was proud of Jamie's stubborn hostility.

'I suppose it's not surprising. He hardly wants to see me any more, does he?'

'I havena set him agin you, Robbie, if that's what you mean.'

'No, of course not, I know you haven't. But all that business back in the summer when he went out every time he knew I was coming round ... I mean, that's ridiculous.'

There was silence while they both remembered the events of the summer. He looked so despondent now that perversely she wanted to comfort him.

'As I'm not going home for Hogmanay,' she said eventually, 'I thought I'd go up and see everyone this weekend. I've got a few days off. I just thought I'd mention it in case you were going. We don't all want to bump into each other on your mother's doorstep.'

'No.'

'You don't mind me going to see her?'

'No, of course not. She'd be very hurt if you didn't.'

'I really am fond of her, apart from anything else ... and I'll have to see my parents ... so she's like the jam after the medicine.' And I can see you in her face, she thought.

'How are they taking it?'

'Oh, I've written them all, of course, several times, but they don't really understand. That's why I thought it might help if I went up. It's always easier to explain face to face, isn't it?' She longed to ask him for help. 'My father says my mother's ill, but that's nothing new.'

'Don't let them bully you.'

'Oh, this is their big moment, they can say "I told you so." I mustn't do them out of that.'

Silence. Panic. There seemed nothing more to say, except things that could not be said. Stay with me, come back, don't leave me again, I love you. It was always the same. She looked forward so immoderately to his visits and then they were over before she could even enjoy them.

160

'Well, I best be on my way,' he said, embarrassed.

'Yes, of course.'

They both stood up.

'Are you all right for money?'

'You know I am. You've been over-generous.'

'I don't think so.'

Sometimes she wondered if he found these visits even more of a strain than she did. 'Is everything going well?'

'Aye, fine.'

'That's good.' She led the way back into the hall as if he were a stranger. 'Well, nice to see you.' It was unbearable to look at him and know that he did not live with her any more.

'Take care of yourself, hen.' He hesitated for a moment, then kissed her on the cheek. She kept quite still, not daring to put her arms round him in case she broke down.

'You too,' she said lightly.

'See you soon. Good luck at the weekend.'

'Thanks. I'll need it.' But there was one last thing to be said, if she could get it out. 'Oh, I nearly forgot. My solicitor says the case comes up next month. So you should be clear by February.'

He knew what that had cost her; she could tell from his face. But he said only, 'Thank you,' and went out. She closed the door after him and leaned against it; when she started to cry, she turned round, wrapping her arms round herself.

On her way to Glasgow she tried to believe her parents would not be as she remembered them; she fantasized that they would rally round and comfort her. Outside their door she recognized the fantasy for what it was and nearly ran away. It took a real effort to ring the bell. Even the sight of the garden depressed her.

Her father opened the door. 'Ah, Jean, you're here at last.'

'I'm not late, am I?' Already she was on the defensive. She went in and dumped her suitcase in the hall. He looked her up and down with an air of dissatisfaction rather than sympathy.

'All these months,' he said, 'and you haven't been near us. We've been so worried.'

'I wrote to you,' Jean said. 'I telephoned.'

'It's not the same though, Jean, is it?'

She removed her coat. 'I even asked you to visit me.'

'But you know your mother's not fit to travel.'

'Well, I wasn't fit to travel either, as it happens.'

He looked faintly surprised. 'But you're young and strong and you've got your health.'

'I've been very depressed and that's just the same as being ill. Where's Mother?'

'In bed, of course.'

'At this hour?'

'She doesn't come down much these days.' He shook his head sadly. 'I'm afraid it's hit her very hard.'

'What?'

'Your troubles. She hasn't been the same since you told us.'

Jean fought to control her temper. 'Well, I could hardly not tell you, could I?'

'You could have broken it more gently.' Her father looked quite severe. 'You know how sensitive she is.'

'I'll go up,' Jean said.

'Would you like some tea?'

She mounted the stairs savagely. 'Yes, I would. If it's not too much trouble.'

The room was hot and dark, with the fire on and the curtains drawn. Her mother lay on her back with her eyes shut, looking rather like a corpse. Jean had trouble resisting the temptation to shout 'boo' to frighten her. 'Mother. Are you awake?'

For a moment there was no reaction; then the hooded eyes opened suddenly. 'There you are.'

'How are you feeling?'

A heavy sigh. 'I don't know what I've done to deserve this.'

'Is it one of your headaches?'

'Headaches? You don't know the meaning of the word. I

don't get a wink of sleep, day or night. Oh, I lie here and keep still so as not to disturb your father, but I don't sleep. I haven't closed my eyes for weeks.'

Jean sat on the edge of the bed. 'Have you seen the doctor?'

'He's a fool, and he's heartless into the bargain. He says there's nothing he can do.'

'You mean he can't find anything wrong with you.'

'I think he's afraid to tell me what it is. But I'd rather face it, no matter what.' She became confidential. 'D'you know, I've got no appetite left. Your father tries hard with his cooking, I must give him that, but I don't fancy anything.'

Jean's patience snapped. 'I'm not surprised if you stay in bed all day.'

Shock and indignation. 'I hope you treat your patients better than your family.'

'So do I, they're seriously ill.'

Her mother burst into tears. They were still a potent weapon.

'Oh, God. Don't cry, Mother, please don't cry. I'm sorry. Only I've been under a lot of strain too. It's been pretty grim lately without Robbie – and trying to keep the boys on an even keel – and I get very tired at work.'

Her mother sobbed, almost wailing, 'I can't bear it.'

'*You* can't bear it?'

'I always knew he'd make you unhappy, but I never dreamed he'd leave you.'

As if on cue, her father came in with the tea-tray. 'Jean, what have you done? How could you upset your mother?'

'Very easily, it seems.'

Her mother wiped her eyes and blew her nose. 'She's got to get an annulment, that's all there is to it.'

'Your mother's quite right, Jean.' Her father poured tea. 'I've had a word with Father Logan and there are plenty of grounds that might do, it's not just non-consummation; obviously that wouldn't do at all, but there are other things. In fact, now you're here I think you should go and see him.'

'Yes, you must ring up and make an appointment. You want to get started, it takes a long time, it has to go to Rome.'

163

Jean said, 'Am I hearing you correctly? That Catholic wedding you bludgeoned Robbie into thirteen years ago – you want me to pretend it never happened?'

Her father shook his head. 'It wasn't valid, Jean. That's the point. It can't have been or this wouldn't have happened.' He looked pleased with his own logic. 'Now it's just a matter of putting our finger on the reason.'

'You mean making one up.' She was outraged. 'Why don't we pretend you forced me into it? That would do nicely.'

Her mother sat up in bed, suddenly very lively, and shouted, 'You silly girl, we're trying to help you. D'you want to be alone for the rest of your life or living in sin?'

It brought back the image of the empty double bed. Going to sleep alone and waking up alone. For ever. She shouted back, 'For Christ's sake, what d'you think I want?' then started to cry and ran out of the room. She ran down the stairs and grabbed her coat and suitcase, which were still in the hall. She ran out of the front door, slamming it behind her; she ran down the path and got into the car. She was crying too much to notice if her father shouted after her or followed her; she felt as if she had been running away from her parents for years.

When she tried to start the car, she turned on the wind-screen wipers by mistake and for a moment thought they were not working properly because her vision was still blurred. Then she realized what was happening and drove off with a sense of panic and relief, as if she had escaped only just in time to save her life.

Robbie's mother's flat was such a haven, she wondered how she would ever leave it. She had tea and whisky and talked as much as she wished to a totally sympathetic and responsive audience. At the end of it all, Robbie's mother said, 'If you want my honest opinion, Jean, I shouldna go near them again.'

'I wish I didn't have to. But they're still my parents.'

'They're no good to you, lassie. Not while all this is going on. No more is my Rob any good to me. It's like he's lost his mind. I've not written or phoned and I don't want to see him.

Of course I still love him, he's my own flesh and blood, but I'm ashamed of him. If I saw him now we'd only quarrel.'

'I don't want to make trouble between you,' Jean said, and immediately wondered if that was true.

'You havena made it, hen, *he* has. I'm so ashamed I don't know where to put myself.'

Jean tried, belatedly, to be fair. 'Oh – there are faults on both sides.'

'That's all rubbish and you know it. That woman's turned his head and that's all there is to it. I never heard such nonsense, to leave you and his bairns for some fancy woman. He must have taken leave of his senses.'

She felt so soothed, having all her wounds bathed and dressed, that it was suddenly easy to be generous. 'She's very beautiful.'

'Handsome is as handsome does.'

'Mam – I know he wants you to meet her. Please don't feel because of me – I mean I don't want to get in the way of you and Robbie and her meeting – you might like her.' Terrible thought. Impossible, surely, please God. 'I'd just like to think I can still see you now and then, that's all, and bring the boys, of course.'

Robbie's mother saw she was about to cry, and hugged her. 'Jean, there's no question of me meeting her, I don't want to meet her, I think I'd hit her in the face.'

Two weeks later Ruth told her, very gently, that Robbie now had a daughter, born prematurely. The pain and envy made everything that had gone before seem trivial.

Diana

I couldn't believe it at first, we'd always been so careful. I checked my dates and told myself I was overtired (which God knows I was) or else it was too much travelling that had made me late. Then I tried not thinking about it on the watched kettle principle. Nothing. So I faced facts and had a test. Positive, of course.

The result came through on a day when I had two bookings, which was a relief: at least I could hide behind work for a little while longer. I did the editorial first and took off my hairpiece in the cab on my way to Jake's Studio, much to the amazement of two men in a car alongside. Jake and I were advertising ice-cream and we were supposed to create an atmosphere of 'seductive rapture', although I said astonished nausea would be nearer the mark. I was beginning to feel ominously queasy again.

'You don't have to lick it if you don't want to,' Jake said, 'as the bishop said to the actress.'

'No, but it looks better if I do.' I was holding this amazing ice-cream cornet. 'What's it made of, for God's sake?'

'Lard and icing sugar. It's built to last.'

'Oh well, makes a change.' The moment came abruptly. 'Jake, d'you mind if I throw up in your bathroom?'

'It's not *that* bad.'

I ran out. He called after me, 'It *is* that bad. Don't worry, I've got to reload anyway.'

Being sick was awful – I hate it so much I always fight it – but the moment it was over I felt tremendously better, as usual, as if it had never happened. When I went back Jake was on the phone, and I drank some water and fixed my make-up. I could feel him looking intently at me: he knew me so well and you couldn't hide much from him in any case.

'You're not in the club again, are you?' he said when he'd hung up.

''Fraid so.'

He looked so sympathetic I wondered how I'd ever let him go. And he suddenly reminded me of Mack – the same dark hairiness and stocky build, the regional accent (Cockney in his case). Had he perhaps been a dress rehearsal? Never mind, he was still my friend and that was important.

'You should've stuck with me, love,' he said. 'I was a boy Scout.'

'Don't worry,' I said, 'it's not for long.'

I rang up my father and we met in St James's Park. I was dying for some fresh air. He carried my model bag for me and I broke the news. I felt better as soon as I'd told him, although I also had the odd feeling that he already knew. Perhaps parents develop a kind of extrasensory perception about their children. Good parents, anyway.

He said, 'Have you told him yet?'

'No, of course not.'

'But you are sure?'

'Oh yes.'

'Then he must be told.'

I said, 'I don't see why. It's nothing to do with him really.'

'But he has a right to know.'

'I'm not going to have it, so what's the point of telling him?'

We walked for a while in silence and I began to feel afraid and confused, as if my right hand didn't know what my left hand was doing.

'Your mother told me,' my father said presently.

'And look what happened.'

'I wanted to marry her.'

'Well, they wouldn't let you, would they, and now they're sorry. Serve them all right.'

'You see what I mean.' He sounded oddly triumphant.

167

'No. It's different. He's married already, or hadn't you noticed?'

'These things can change.'

'Anyway, I never wanted to be married, don't you remember, and I don't even like children. I can hardly tolerate Lisa and she's ten, for God's sake.' I heard myself going on and on as if it would be dangerous to stop.

'It is different with your own.'

'I don't believe that.'

My father smiled. 'I used to say I could never be a politician because I cannot kiss babies, but when you were a baby I could have eaten you up.'

'Pity you didn't.' We sat on a seat and gazed at the ducks. 'Oh, I'm sorry I dragged you out when you're so busy, but I had to talk to someone and I just couldn't stay cooped up indoors a minute longer, I was suffocating.'

He held my hand. 'You shouldn't work so hard, especially now.'

'What does it matter? Anyway, it takes my mind off it. Apukam, don't look like that, I'm not going to tell him. And you mustn't, either. Promise.'

'Promise.'

'Cross your heart and hope to die.'

He repeated obediently, 'Cross my heart and hope to die.'

'I'm doing the right thing, I know I am. It would only make problems. Anyway, I don't want it.'

'But you love Mackenzie.'

'That's got nothing to do with it. He wouldn't want it either, he's bound to say get rid of it.' I paused, getting up my courage. 'I'm going to see Mummy.'

All the way down in the train I tried to work out what I really wanted: an abortion without telling Mack, an abortion with his knowledge and approval, or no abortion. But then what? I didn't know; I was really scared not to be in touch with myself. Had I done the right thing in telling my father? If I had such confidence in his wisdom and strength, why was I now going to see my mother? How many options did I need?

168

By the time I got there I had no idea what was true and what was false any longer. I took a taxi from the station and walked slowly up the drive: my model bag weighed a ton and I should have gone home first to dump it. But I felt if I'd done that I might never have gone to my mother at all.

She was in the conservatory, as I'd thought when I rang her and there was no reply. She didn't see me approaching; she was too absorbed. I tapped on the glass and she looked up, more exasperated than pleased to see me, but that was predictable. I walked round to the door and let myself in, feeling I was at the end of a long, weary journey. We looked at each other for a while till she said, 'They don't like draughts, you know,' and I closed the door and dumped my bag. She eyed me critically for another moment and I remembered she was still a beautiful woman and I was glad I resembled her. My face would also last well into middle-age: her good bones and good skin would not let me down.

Now she looked away from me, back to the plants, giving them all her attention. 'You don't look well,' she said.

'No, I'm not.'

There was a pause while we both accepted what we were saying.

'When's it due?'

'In seven months.'

'Is it that builder person?'

'Yes.'

'My God, you're stupid. I really wonder sometimes how you can be my child.'

'You weren't always so clever.'

'At least I didn't make the same mistake three times.'

'Maybe you didn't get the chance.'

After tnat we rested: honour was satisfied. Eventually I said, 'Is Daddy about?'

'No, he's got an all-night sitting. Anyway, what d'you want *him* for? There's nothing he can do. You surely weren't planning to *tell* him, were you?'

I shrugged. She had always come between us and defeated me: jealous, I suppose, because I had two fathers and she had only one husband. 'No.'

We went indoors and had tea; we were both more relaxed now that there were only the practicalities to be discussed.

'Well, I suppose Mr Sinclair is still practising,' my mother said.

'If not, he can always recommend one of his bright young men.' I thought it was fascinating that neither of us would dream of admitting there could be any alternative. We liked our scenario as it was: we were on familiar ground.

'I should think he'll be very booked up himself. Still, you're not in a desperate hurry, are you?' My mother actually got her diary out of her bag and flicked the pages. 'I'm awfully busy next week anyway, I've got two committee meetings and three dinner parties, but the week after might be all right ... yes, two weeks today would do very nicely.' She closed the diary and put it away. 'If he can fit you in, I've got to be in town anyway to have lunch with –' She suddenly stopped and stared through the window. I simply couldn't believe it. Mack was getting out of his car and walking up the drive. 'Oh really,' she said in her crossest tones, 'now who's that?'

I couldn't stop a big stupid grin from spreading all over my face. I felt like Guinevere about to go to the stake when Lancelot turned up. 'Mummy, this is your lucky day. You're about to meet my builder person.'

'Diana, this is too bad of you. Why did you invite *him* down here?'

'I didn't.'

'You know how busy I am. It's bad enough your turning up without telephoning.'

'I rang, but you didn't answer.'

'Of course I didn't, I can't hear the telephone in the conservatory. You know that. That's the whole point of gardening.'

I couldn't bear it any longer. I ran out of the house to meet Mack and we hugged each other desperately, as if we were meeting in a time of great danger, like war. 'You can't get rid of it,' he said. 'I won't let you. Why didn't you tell me?'

We kissed. I didn't know what to say. 'Come and meet Mummy.' I took him into the drawing-room. 'Mummy, this is Mack – otherwise known as Robert Mackenzie.'

'Pleased to meet you, Mrs Crawley.'

I saw my mother wince at the phrase. 'How do you do, Mr Mackenzie?' She extended her hand reluctantly. 'Well, it's no use pretending that we're meeting in very happy circumstances. Still, I suppose it's a point in your favour that you're prepared to meet me at all. Many young men in your position would be too ashamed.'

'Mummy, you're not to be beastly to Mack.'

'Mrs Crawley, there's no point in beating about the bush. I love Diana and I want to marry her.'

I was startled. I looked at my mother with a smug expression on my face. There wasn't a flicker of anything on hers.

'Wouldn't that make you a bigamist?' she asked Mack.

'I can always get a divorce.'

I said quickly, 'There's no need to go that far. If I don't have an abortion, I might as well have a bastard. After all, I *am* one.'

My mother sighed. 'Really, Diana, you can be very coarse at times. You don't have to abandon your wife, Mr Mackenzie. My daughter and I are perfectly capable of handling this situation without any help from you.'

'Aye, so I've heard from Mr Kovacs.'

I tried to sound indignant. 'He promised not to tell you.'

'Oh well,' my mother said, 'that explains everything.'

'Only I don't happen to like the way you're handling it. This is *my* child and I've got a say in what happens to it.'

My mother looked at Mack and said casually, 'How do you know it's your child?'

'What?'

'Even Diana's best friend – whoever that may be – couldn't pretend she has a spotless reputation. Not a thing one likes to say about one's own daughter, but there you are, one must face facts.' How she was enjoying herself.

'It *is* yours, Mack.'

'I know it is. And I don't want it killed. Please don't kill it.'

We looked at each other. I think we were more in love than at any time before or since.

'I'm afraid Diana is too unstable to be a mother, Mr Mackenzie. She's neurotic and irresponsible, as you will find out for yourself if this liaison continues. Would you like some tea?'

'No, thanks.'

'He'd like some whisky actually.'

'I don't believe we have any. I think your father finished it last night.'

Mack looked baffled; I knew what he was thinking. 'She means Daddy.'

'Will you excuse us, Mrs Crawley? Diana and I have a lot to talk about.'

My mother looked past him. 'Diana, d'you want me to telephone Mr Sinclair or not?'

I hesitated: I had never had options before. Mack said, 'No, she doesn't. Is he the abortionist?'

'We're not discussing anything sordid or illegal. My daughter's health is at stake.'

Mack and I stood up together, as if we were already of one mind. 'I'll ring you,' I said to Mummy.

Mack picked up my model bag. 'I never know how you manage to carry this thing around.'

'A curious profession to be called glamorous,' my mother said, 'when young girls develop one arm longer than the other.'

I said sharply, 'You wouldn't expect a plumber to turn up without his tools.'

We all went outside and stood around, not knowing how to separate. My mother picked up a shotgun which had been propped against the wall. Mack was so startled that I nearly laughed.

'Don't look so alarmed, Mr Mackenzie,' she said with satisfaction. 'I'm not as old-fashioned as that. We've been having trouble with the rooks this year.'

I hugged my mother. I could see Mack was surprised, but

after all she was the only mother I had. 'Thanks anyway,' I said, and she kissed the air beside my cheek.

Mack and I walked down the drive. As we reached the car we could hear my mother firing away at the poor bloody rooks.

When we drove off I said, 'Isn't she priceless? She absolutely loathed you, didn't she? That's a class thing, of course, she's a frightful snob.'

He didn't answer, just drove in silence for a bit, then said almost sternly, 'Why were you going to have an abortion without even telling me?'

'I assumed that was what you'd want me to do.'

'Why?'

'That's what people always want.' I'd been so afraid he'd be like all the others and I'd hate him for it. I didn't want to hate him.

'Maybe I'm different. And anyway, abortion's bloody dangerous. You can die from it.'

'In the Gorbals, maybe. Not in Harley Street.' It was lovely that he was so concerned about me.

'Don't be so sure. There are butchers everywhere. I'm not having you risk your life.'

It seemed only fair to warn him. 'I'm no good with children, Mack.'

'You've never had one of your own.'

I thought about it. 'Well, it would certainly be a new experience. I can't think how it's happened, though, we've always been so careful.'

'You have, you mean – I told you that thing wasn't reliable. You should have left it to me.'

'*Oh* no. Not those ghastly things you use with your wife. I had enough of those when I was seventeen. Ugh.'

'She can't use anything, she's a Catholic.' He sounded a touch defensive.

'So she leaves it to you. Isn't that cheating?'

'You don't understand. Anyway, we hardly ever do it nowadays.'

'Oh, but you must.' I was pleased, of course, but I still

thought how rotten it must be for her. 'You've got to keep her happy. We agreed you would. I'm not jealous. I mean, a wife isn't like another woman. What did you think of Mummy?'

'I thought she was a bitch.'

'She is but she can't help it. She's so furious my father turned out heaps richer than Daddy. When she gets sloshed she says to Granny and Grandpa, "Look what you made me do. I hope you're satisfied. I could have had my own bank by now." That's why Christmas is always so gruesome.' I wanted to go on talking about my family: it seemed safer than talking about the baby. Was I really going to have it? I was excited and terrified and I still didn't know what I really wanted.

'Why did you go to see her?' Mack asked.

'I don't know. She's just marvellously helpful when I'm pregnant.'

'You mean she's good at arranging abortions.'

'Well, yes. I seem to need her, even though I don't like her. She's like the witch the Little Mermaid went to see to get her tail turned into legs. I mean I'm sure she wishes she'd aborted me, so this is the next best thing.' But I didn't feel I was explaining adequately.

'God, it's revolting.'

'I wish you'd met Daddy, he's sweet. I always think Mummy was so lucky he was standing around willing to marry her.'

'How could he do it – knowing she was having another man's child?'

I smiled. 'Not something you'd do, is it? I don't know, he was at Oxford with my Uncle Rupert and they used to call him Creepy Crawley because of the way he hung around Mummy like a spaniel. It wasn't fair. He's not creepy, he's cuddly.' And he had never made me feel he loved Piers more than me, though he surely must have done.

There was a long silence. Very abruptly Mack pulled in to a lay-by and stopped the car. He held both my hands tight and stared at me. I had never seen him look so serious, as if

174

he were afraid of losing me. 'Diana. Promise me you'll have this child and we'll be together.'

Next time my father came to tea he brought Ruth, as if for protection. 'I ought to be very angry with you,' I said. 'How could you tell him when you gave me your word you wouldn't?' Had that been what I secretly wanted him to do? And, more important, was I really pleased now he'd done it?

'Don't you remember, when you were a little girl I told you never to trust anyone?'

'Not even my own father?'

'Not if he's Hungarian,' Ruth said and we all laughed rather too much. 'Are you really going to have it?'

'Oh, I don't know. I suppose so. He'd be frightfully cross if I got rid of it now.' It was a new role, subservient woman.

'But there *is* still time?' Ruth said.

'Just about.'

'No,' my father said, 'I think it is already too dangerous.'

Ruth was looking at me curiously. 'I can't imagine you with a child.'

'Neither can I. Maybe it'll be fun.'

'I don't think fun's quite the word I'd use,' she said severely. 'Not for the first year or two anyway.'

Then the phone rang and when I answered it, no one spoke. It was the second time that day.

'Jean's in a frightful state, you know,' Ruth went on. 'I feel dreadful, she's so upset.'

I said, 'Yes, I'm sorry about that.'

'Are you?'

'Of course I am. Don't look at me like that. It's not *my* fault Mack's gone berserk. I never mentioned divorce. It must be his Calvinist blood.'

'It's going to cause a lot of unhappiness.'

'My love,' said my father to Ruth, always a bad sign, 'you mustn't bully Diana.'

'God forbid.'

'Look,' I said, 'I never wanted her to know about me. I don't give a damn about marriage or divorce, and I've

175

offered to have an abortion. I don't see what more I can do.'

'You have behaved very well.' My father stroked my hand.

'We'd better be going.' Ruth stood up. 'I've got to be home by five.'

'Off for a quickie?' I said to annoy her because she'd been so tiresome.

When they'd gone I emptied my model bag on the drawing-room floor and started checking everything for repairs and renovation. It's always worth doing when you have a spare moment. The entry phone buzzer went and I said hullo absently. Then I got the shock of my life.

'This is Jean Mackenzie.'

'Oh, Christ.'

'I want to speak to you.'

I was so shattered I didn't know what to say. The habit of politeness prevailed. 'Yes, well, all right. You better come up.' I pushed the button. Then I looked at the mess on the floor, abandoned it, checked my face and hair in the mirror and abandoned that too. There was no time to do anything. Of course I would have to be in jeans and a shirt and wearing no make-up, and of course when she appeared at the top of the stairs she was all in her Sunday best. I hadn't seen her since that first time at the party and I'd managed to file her away as a wife. It was quite a shock to have a real human being in my drawing-room.

I said, 'Hullo. This is all frightfully embarrassing, don't you think?' but she didn't answer, just stood there looking at me with such hatred, I felt quite alarmed. 'Would you like to sit down?'

'No thanks.'

'Oh dear, I hope it's not pistols at twenty paces. I think *I* better sit down if you don't mind, I feel a bit wobbly.' It was awful, I heard myself rambling on and on, sounding terribly flippant, but I was so nervous I just couldn't stop. 'I mean, you knew you were coming here but I've had quite a shock. I hope you're not going to throw acid in my face or anything, that would be ghastly.'

She said quite seriously, 'I didn't think of that.'

'I bet you wish you had.' And I wished I hadn't mentioned it. 'Would you like some lemon tea?'

'No, thanks.' She looked round the room. 'So this is the home he made for you.'

She sounded so envious that I babbled on about the workmen doing most of it, and would she mind if I put rollers in a wig to calm myself down. There was another long silence and she went on staring at me till I asked her what she wanted to say to me.

'Now I'm actually here,' she said, 'it's not very easy.'

I said honestly, 'I expect you hate me so much it nearly chokes you. Or is that just my guilty conscience?'

'No,' she said matter-of-factly, 'that's about right.'

Her accent unnerved me; it was (of course) so like Mack's, but more than that there was an alarming stillness about her, like an animal waiting to pounce. 'I'd feel the same in your position,' I said, trying to be soothing. 'I must say, I think you've been awfully good about things all this time.' She was quite pretty and she'd done her face very carefully, but you could see that underneath she was all pale and tense and miserable.

'Don't be so bloody patronizing,' she said.

'I meant I appreciate it, that's all.'

'I didn't have very much choice.' She paused. 'I suppose there's no point in asking you to give him up.'

What could I say? 'Not really.' I was surprised she'd asked.

'Right, then, you better get one thing clear.' You could see her gathering herself to attack. 'You won't hear it from him so you might as well hear it from me. I'm never going to divorce him. Not ever. So no matter how many years you hang on with your claws in him, you'll never be his wife.'

Was that all? I was quite relieved; I'd been imagining she was going to say something terrible. I shrugged. 'I never expected to be. Look, honestly. I wish he hadn't mentioned the word divorce, it's obviously upset you, and we were all drifting on quite nicely without it. I hope you believe me, it wasn't my idea, I simply don't care about things like that one way or the other. I'm perfectly happy being a mistress, that's what I'm used to, and I hate all this drama.' I wondered how to convince her I meant what I said. 'In fact I'm really beginning to wish I'd just had the abortion the way I meant to, and never told him about it. Would have been much simpler all round.'

Then a dreadful thing happened. Her face crumpled up with shock – I don't know how else to describe it – and she sat down very suddenly as if her legs had given way. I said, 'Oh God. He didn't tell you.' I was really horrified. 'Oh my God, how frightful. You'd better have a drink.' I got up and poured us two enormous drinks. I thought she might throw it in my face, but she took it and drank quite a lot of it right away. So did I.

I said, 'I hope you don't think I said that on purpose. It never entered my head he hadn't told you.'

All the fight had gone out of her, poor thing. 'I've been very stupid,' she said. 'I couldn't think why he suddenly wanted a divorce after all this time. I should have known. Of course. That was the obvious reason.' She was almost talking to herself.

I said, 'Well, I'm frightfully sorry you had to find out like this. I can't understand why he didn't tell you himself.'

'I can,' she said. 'He was too embarrassed.'

I thought it an odd word to use. 'Well, these things happen.'

'I always wanted a third child. And he didn't.'

Well, that really finished me off. Then I noticed she was crying silently. I leaned towards her. 'Look, I *am* sorry –'

She let out a yell. 'Get away from me –' as if I were contagious.

'Yes, all right, all right.' I drew back at once.

And then she became savage. It was very staccato, like somebody firing a machine-gun. 'D'you ever stop to think how much misery women like you cause? Men are so weak. We were happy till you came along. I've got two boys at home who are going to lose their father because of you. Are you proud of yourself? You could have anyone and you pick on my husband.'

She made it sound as if Mack had no will of his own and it was all my fault. I suppose it was more acceptable that way. I said, 'Well, if it's any consolation at all, you've made me feel absolutely ghastly about it,' but she didn't look appeased at all. She had gone white with rage and all her freckles stood out: I must say I was glad not to have red hair. All I wanted was for her to go: she wasn't doing herself any good and I was worn out. 'Look,' I said, all conciliatory, 'you're quite right not to divorce him if you don't want to. You stick to your guns. I'm not at all sure about marriage anyway, it might not suit me. Why don't we just leave things the way they are? After all, you never know, he might go off me or I might go off him or you might meet someone else . . . I mean, anything can happen.'

She stood up. 'I think I better go before I actually hit you.'

It was not a moment to panic. 'Well, I can't say I'll give him up, but you didn't expect that, did you?'

She looked at me with such loathing that if I'd been superstitious I might have felt she was putting a curse on me. 'Right now, God forgive me, all I want in the world is for you and your baby to die.'

By the time Mack came to see me I was in bed. I'd had a couple of large drinks after she'd gone, to stop myself shaking, and they'd knocked me out.

'Are you all right?' he said anxiously.

'Of course I am. I just kept falling alseep so I thought I'd lie down.' Maybe it wasn't the drinks after all, but merely being pregnant.

He held my hand. 'What did she say to you?'

'Oh, I can't remember.' I was yawning my head off. 'She went on a bit. Still, she's entitled.'

'She had no right to come here and upset you,' he said sternly, like my father.

'Oh, why not? She might as well. It probably made her feel better to let off steam.' Now it was over, it seemed important to minimize it. 'I'm only surprised she didn't stick a knife in me. That actually happened to a friend of mine – Suzie, did you meet her? She was sitting quietly at the

179

theatre one night minding her own business, and her lover's wife sat behind her and actually stuck a knife in her back, I mean literally.'

But I could never distract him by chattering away. He was always obsessed by the main issue – the same in business, I suppose. 'Jean said you don't want to marry me.'

'Well, she kept on about not divorcing you, so what else could I say? I thought it might calm her down. Besides, we're all right as we are, aren't we?' I couldn't understand this endless harping on marriage. Wasn't it enough that I was still pregnant?

He said very seriously, 'I want us to be married before you have the baby.'

'Oh, darling, that's a long way off.'

'Not really. Only six months.'

'I hope I'm not going to keep falling asleep all that time.'

Again he wasn't listening. 'If I can persuade her to start proceedings now, we may just make it.'

'But I'll be enormous by then. I can't get married when I'm nine months gone, everybody'll laugh. It'll look as if you're doing me a favour.'

'What does it matter what it looks like?'

'Oh, darling, of course it matters.' Really, men were extraordinary. 'I'll be like an elephant, imagine the pictures in the papers. No, if I'm going to get married, I want to do it properly, very thin, long dress, the whole bit. It's all right for you, second time around, but I've never been married, I want to look my best.' I still wasn't sure I wanted to do it anyway, but there seemed plenty of time to decide. 'If we do get married, Mummy will be *so* cross.'

'I'll have to move out,' Mack said. 'The sooner the better.'

'Where will you go?' I was wearing my poker face, but he looked so anxious I broke up. It was always fun to tease him. 'Of course you can put your shoes under my bed. Any time. And your suits in my wardrobe. No, on second thoughts I think we're going to need an extra wardrobe.' I felt a great surge of love for him. 'Isn't this exciting? Would you believe I've never actually lived with anyone before?'

Now, looking back, I can hardly believe that I let it all happen so casually.

Before he moved in that night, he sat in the car for a long time and wept. I hesitated at the window, but in the end I did not go out to comfort him. I thought perhaps he needed to be alone just then.

It was a magic six months. He treated me as if I were the original precious vessel, waiting on me hand and foot, not letting me do a thing. It was lovely. I lay about on sofas, reading magazines and doing absolutely nothing. From being really quite busy, I became totally idle. I didn't know I could. I also got enormously fat, but I felt terribly well and my blood pressure was okay. It was odd to be fat: a completely new experience.

Living together seemed strangely natural. Not that we were actually together very much because he worked long hours: virtually a twelve-hour day. I slept a lot, went to the cinema, walked in the park, saw my friends. But when we were together, Mack and I, we were amazingly harmonious. I suppose it was the newness of everything. There's a sort of golden haze when I look back on it, like childhood summers.

He used to come home from work with cuddly toys for the baby. By the time I was eight months pregnant there were soft toys all over the place.

'Another one?' I said, as he threw the latest one onto the sofa beside me. But it was awfully sweet. 'Let's have it on our bed. The nursery's practically full as it is.'

He crossed the room and kissed me, then put his hand on the bulge. 'How are you, lassie?'

'Just a bit tired of being kicked.'

'She's a ballerina, what d'you expect?'

'*He* is a footballer.' We were forever having this argument and we both enjoyed it.

'Sorry, she's a girl and that's all there is to it.'

'But I don't like girls.'

'You will this one. Drink?'

'Please. I've been very good, haven't had one all day.' I watched him pouring the drinks; I smiled at the soft toy. It was lovely to be so happy – a chance to be soppy again like a child.

'How about Arabella?' Mack said.

'As in Stuart?'

'As in Mackenzie.'

'I prefer Robert George Istvan Thomas Mackenzie myself.'

'Wouldn't suit her.' He gave me my drink and sat beside me. 'Maybe we should call her after your mother.'

I was appalled. 'Caroline?'

'She might be so flattered she'd get off her broomstick.'

I laughed: it was such a gratifying image. 'Better try my grandparents, they've got the cash.' Mack looked inquiring. 'Nicholas and Edward.'

'No, you idiot, the women.'

'Annabel and Clarissa.'

He made a face. 'Maybe we can do without the cash.'

'Oh, quick.' The baby was getting really lively.

He put his hand on me again. 'I see what you mean about the football.'

'Yes. That's never Covent Garden, is it?'

'Are you sure it's not twins?'

'Mr Sinclair says not.'

'Well, he should know, I suppose.' There was an edge to his voice. 'I still can't get used to him doing abortions and delivering babies.'

'Set a thief to catch a thief.' I stroked his face. 'Don't look so worried. He won't be standing by ready to hit our son –'

'– daughter –'

'– on the head as he –'

'– she –'

'– comes out. This time he's been programmed for survival.' And to think I had once believed that was not what I wanted.

'You really want him to deliver you.' He sounded surprised; he still didn't understand.

'Of course I do. I trust him.' I started thinking about

names again. 'Maybe we should butter up *your* mother. What's *her* name?'

'Annie.'

'Oh well. Perhaps we can get round her some other way.' He held my hand. 'She'll love you when she meets you.'

'And we'll all be old and grey by then.'

'I'm still working on it.'

Such tenacity. I suppose he was like that in business too. I admired it in a way, but I could also see when to stop. 'Darling, why not give up? It's much easier and you're so busy. If she doesn't want two daughters-in-law, who can blame her? It's messy. I quite see her point. Why don't we just leave her in peace and send photographs of little Robert George Istvan Thomas at a later date?'

Piers arrived from New York during the week, a day early, while Mack was at work. It was wonderful to see him and have him all to my self. He came up the spiral staircase and stared at me in amazement.

'My God, Di, you're enormous.' We kissed across the bulge, the great divide. 'How on earth are you managing?'

'With great difficulty.' We hugged with arms only, no chance of body contact. 'I'm so glad you're here.'

'So am I.' He looked delighted, a real childhood glow that I remembered lovingly and well. 'D'you know, I never thought you'd go through with it.'

'Neither did I.' I noticed he was carrying a sort of gift-wrapped wicker basket.

'Can I put this down?'

'What is it?'

He deposited it with great care. 'Present for you. I thought you might need cheering up. But you can't open it till you've guessed what it is.'

I made a face. 'That's not fair.'

'New rule. Shall I get us a drink?'

'Please. I love being waited on.'

'Well,' he said, pouring drinks, 'I never thought I'd see you like this. What made you change your mind?'

'I don't know. Mack was so sweet about it – really keen

to have it – I suppose I was flattered. He's very special.' There was a faint squeaky sound at the edge of my consciousness. 'And – oh, I don't know, I just thought it might be exciting.' The sound went on.

'And is it?'

'Yes. It's absolutely weird having a –' But I couldn't ignore it any more. 'Piers, what *is* that noise?'

He looked absurdly pleased with himself. 'I was wondering when you'd notice.'

'Oh, Piers, I can't believe it.'

'Well, you always said you wanted one when you stopped work.'

'You're an angel.' I was so excited: I tore off the wrapping paper and found a black and orange kitten in the basket. What it is to have a brother who understands you. I was so absorbed I hardly heard Mack arriving home and calling me.

'She's a girl,' Piers said, equally oblivious. 'Seven weeks. The rest is up to you.'

'She's beautiful.' I lifted her out of the basket with great care and began stroking her; she started to purr immediately. I was enraptured. It was amazing to hear such a loud vibrant sound emerging from such a tiny creature.

I heard Mack saying hullo to Piers. There was an odd note in his voice – surprise, annoyance?

'Hullo, Robert, nice to see you again,' Piers said, relaxed. 'Doesn't Di look splendid? It really suits her.'

I turned to Mack with the kitten in my arms. 'Darling, look what Piers has given me. Isn't she lovely?'

'Yes.' He sounded extraordinarily unenthusiastic.

I was already considering names. 'I think I'll call her Antigone.'

'I'm not sure I like the sound of that,' Piers said. 'Didn't she bury her brother?'

'Only after he was dead.'

'Quite a long time after, if I remember rightly.'

We were enjoying ourselves, playing an old childhood game. I could see Mack looking baffled and furious, feeling out of things, but I didn't care: I was cross with him for not being impressed by Antigone.

'Come along, Antigone,' I said, 'let's see if there's some milk for you in the fridge, shall we?'

'Shall I get it for you?' Piers said, all solicitous. 'Are you sure you can manage the stairs?'

'Oh yes. I'd quite like to see the kitchen again – I haven't been down there for months.' I went slowly and carefully down the stairs and gave Antigone her milk; then I listened to the conversation in the drawing-room.

Mack was saying, 'I wish you hadn't done that.'

'What?'

'Brought that animal into the house.'

'Oh, don't you like cats?' Piers sounded so innocent I nearly laughed. 'What a frightful shame. Di's mad about them.'

'Yes, I can see that.'

'Didn't you know?'

'I know she likes them, of course, but that's not the same thing as having one.'

'Isn't it?' There was an edge to Piers' voice now which meant he was losing his temper and smiling at the same time to compensate. 'One thing generally leads to the other. I mean, presumably you like children and that's why you have them.'

There was a pause.

Mack said, 'I only meant – it would be nice to be consulted about what goes on here.'

'Oh, is that all?' Piers now sounded so excessively pleasant that I knew he must be very angry indeed. 'I didn't know I needed your permission to give my sister a present in her own house.'

The buzzer went. Mack picked up the entry phone at the same moment I did, and said furiously, 'Yes? Oh, hullo, Mrs Crawley,' deflated, just as I called up the stairs. 'It's all right, darling, it's only Mummy.' It wasn't often I was pleased to see her, but it struck me now as quite useful she had turned up in time to avert open warfare upstairs. They both disliked her and were pretty sure to suspend hostilities in the face of the common enemy. So I hoped, at any rate.

My mother saw Antigone as soon as she came in. 'Diana, what on earth is that creature doing here?'

'This is Antigone. She's a present from Piers.'

'Well, keep her well away from me.' She looked outraged. 'You know they give me asthma.'

'Mummy, that's absolute nonsense.'

She marched briskly up the stairs and I trailed behind her, clutching Antigone on top of the bulge.

'Good evening, Robert. Piers, why are you here?'

'I'm visiting Di.'

'But you're not due till tomorrow.'

'I got an earlier flight.'

They exchanged dutiful kisses on the cheek. You had to admire Mummy – when on form she never wasted time in putting people's backs up.

'You might have let me know.'

'I'm staying with friends. I won't be in your way.'

'I suppose you'll be visiting us at some point – your father would like to see you. How long are you staying?'

'Well, I'm waiting for Di to pop and then I'm off. Back to New York.'

'So you won't be here for Christmas.'

'No.'

'Coward,' I muttered.

'Well, I'm glad I've caught you all together. It saves time. Diana, you don't look well. Are you getting enough rest?'

'Yes, of course.'

'I think she looks marvellous,' Piers said loyally. 'Huge but marvellous.'

I threw a cushion at him but I was grateful.

'If that animal gets under your feet and you fall downstairs,' Mummy went on, relentless as a tank, 'you'll have only yourself and Piers to blame. Really, Piers, I thought you had more sense.'

'Yes, Mummy. Thank you, Mummy,' I said.

Suddenly Mack joined in. 'I really think your mother has a point, you know.'

She glanced at him in surprise. 'Well, at least we're agreed about something. Now, I've ordered the pram and the cot and Harrods can deliver in about –'

'We won't be needing a cot,' Mack said.

'Nonsense, of course you will.'

'I mean I'm taking care of it. I'm making my own arrangements.'

There was a pause while we all stared at him and wondered what he meant.

'I see,' Mummy said eventually, a bit tight-lipped when it was obvious he wasn't going to tell us. 'One pram, then. Is that acceptable?'

'Very kind of you,' Mack said grudgingly.

'Thank you, Mummy. Come again.' I went on stroking Antigone, who was purring herself into a stupor on my lap. Then I suddenly noticed my mother gathering herself together in that funny, self-important way she has, prior to making an announcement.

'What I really came to tell you, Diana, is that I've been to see Nanny Wilkinson. I've been down to Lyme Regis and spent all day talking to her. She wasn't sure at first, you know she's retired and her sister still depends on her, but I finally managed to persuade her to come.'

Piers and I were transfixed. It was a miracle.

'Oh, thank God,' I said. 'Mummy, you're wonderful. What a load off my mind.'

'That's pretty impressive. I didn't think you'd pull that off,' Piers said.

Mummy looked triumphant as Piers and I gazed admiringly at her. Suddenly Mack said coldly, 'What is all this?'

I'd almost forgotten he was there: I was so used to three-cornered conversations with Piers and my mother.

'Diana's old nanny – and mine, come to that – has finally agreed to look after the baby.'

Mack looked appalled. I'd never seen him so shocked. 'But Diana can do that.'

Mummy looked at him as if he were mad. Piers and I started to laugh; it seemed the safest way to react. We were also very nervous by now.

'Don't be silly, darling,' I said lightly. 'What do I know about babies? Nanny's an expert.'

All the same, after they'd left and we'd had supper and gone to bed, it was obvious I couldn't avoid the issue any more: we were going to have to discuss it. Mack was turning over restlessly and there was a sticky silence. I tried pretending to be asleep but clearly I couldn't be, with him shifting about like that. Finally he said, 'Do we really have to have this person here?'

I felt a twinge of resentment at his talking about Nanny like that instead of realizing how lucky we were, but I tried to keep calm. 'Darling, I simply can't manage without her.'

'But we'll never be alone.'

'Of course we will. We'll be alone all the time.' He was really being very obtuse. 'Nanny'll be upstairs with the baby.'

There was a pause. 'I'm sorry, lassie, I'm just not used to this kind of thing.'

'You soon will be. It's much easier, honestly. Especially when I'm working.'

'Working?' He sounded quite shocked.

'I've only got a few more years left in modelling. I mustn't waste them.'

'Diana, why didn't we talk about this?'

'What?' I didn't like his tone.

'Having a nanny – and you working.'

'What is there to talk about?'

'Whether it's a good idea. I'm not happy about it.'

The baby was kicking me and I was tired. I really didn't want Mack spoiling my joy at the prospect of Nanny making everything easy and pleasant. 'Oh, darling, you're not going to be difficult, are you?' At the same time I nudged Antigone gently with my foot and she started up.

Mack jumped as if he'd been shot. 'What's that? Something moved.'

'Only Antigone. She can't get comfortable. Come here, poppet.' I felt guilty about disturbing her and grateful she'd been so cooperative.

'I really don't like her sleeping on the bed.' Already he'd forgotten about Nanny, for the moment at least.

'She has to, while she's little. She's missing all her brothers and sisters.'

Then my father came up with the offer Mack had been waiting for, and that put everything else out of his head. It was lovely to see him so jubilant. He finished telling me all about it one evening at supper.

'So we're going to start Mackenzie Developments for the houses and Mackenzie Holdings for the parent company. The bank will have an interest in both. We've already got Mackenzie Industrial, of course.' He was afraid I might have forgotten and he was so proud of it.

'Terrific,' I said, my mouth full of omelette.

'He said in a few years' time we might be able to fund the whole operation by going public.'

'What does that mean?'

'Getting a Stock Exchange quotation.'

I liked the sound of that. 'Are we going to be rich?'

'More or less. What's that to you? You've been rich all your life.'

Even now he seemed to have no idea what being rich really meant. 'Oh, it's poor boy from the Gorbals time. Shall I get out my violin?' We both laughed, and I tried to explain. 'Actually I've never been rich. It'll be a new experience. All you poor boys made good are the same.' And when I thought about it, I'd known several. 'You think the odd title and a few acres mean wealth. You're crazy. There's never been any spare cash as long as I can remember.'

He looked amazed. 'But you never lacked for anything.'

'Neither did you. Whatever kids have, they think is normal.'

'Aye, you're right.'

I considered this sudden access of wealth. 'D'you think we could afford to buy the house next door?'

'I didn't know it was for sale.'

'It's not, but it might be. One day, I mean, not now. We

189

could make them an offer when we're rich. Only it's going to be awfully cramped here with Nanny and the baby. I mean, they'll need the whole top floor, so there goes the spare room and Piers' darkroom and everything – we can't have people to stay.'

'But we don't anyway.'

'Darling, of course we don't while I'm like this, but we will.' Was I trying to accomplish too much at once? 'And we need someone to cook. It's really much easier if they live in.'

'Can't Nanny Whatsername cook?'

He still didn't really understand. 'No, of course she can't, nannies don't. And you and I can't live on omelettes much longer.'

'We don't, we go out.'

'Well, I won't be able to go out indefinitely.' Already it was becoming an effort.

'I can always do my egg, bacon and sausage special.'

It was sweet of him to offer, but I couldn't warm to the idea. 'I'd rather you learned to cook steak and things.'

'You're bloody hard to please,' he said, but I could tell he didn't really mind, so I smiled my best sexy smile.

'Yes, but I'm rewarding.'

I went to see Mr Sinclair for a check-up. It was lovely to see him : he always made me feel secure and he'd seen me through so much already.

'Well, that's all most satisfactory,' he said after he'd examined me. 'You can get down now.'

'That's easier said than done.' I heaved myself off the couch and did up my stockings.

'Not much longer now. You've done pretty well so far.'

'Oh yes, I'm terribly fit.'

He sat down behind his desk and smiled at me. 'Amazing how nature manages these things. I'd have predicted all sorts of complications in your case and I'd have been wrong.'

I knew he was pleased to be wrong and I could feel my smug look coming on.

'All the same, I think we may have to do a Caesar.'

That was a shock. 'Oh no. I don't want a scar.'

'Big baby, narrow pelvis. Work it out for yourself.'

'I'm quite brave.'

'I'm sure you are, but it does the baby no good, if you're pushing away for hours on end, not getting anywhere. Baby gets distressed. Can't blame it really. Still, we'll see. Let you go into labour naturally and see how you get on.' He beamed at me reassuringly over his glasses. 'Don't look so worried. Scars are really quite elegant these days.'

'Still don't want one.'

'Now, Diana, if I was doing some modelling for the first time, I'd take your advice, wouldn't I?'

He could always make me laugh, too; that was another good thing about him. I suppose he was yet another father figure really.

Then we went to Glasgow for the weekend. Madness when I look back on it, but at the time it seemed positively sensible: Mack wanted to see the boys and introduce me to them and his mother before the baby arrived, and we had three or four weeks to go.

It was fun on the train. I pretended to be a strange woman picking him up.

'Are you going to Glasgow?'

'Aye, that's right.'

'Where are you staying?'

'The Central.'

'So am I. What a bit of luck. My husband doesn't arrive till tomorrow.'

You could almost see the ears of the other occupants turning pink with embarrassment at the idea of a pregnant married lady suggesting adultery with a perfect stranger. Mack and I could hardly keep our faces straight.

'Maybe we could have dinner together,' Mack said.

'Why waste time eating? I'll just give you my room number.'

I was okay till we reached the school. Then I began to lose my nerve.

'God, this takes me back.'

'Oh, yes, of course – Piers came here.'

'Every time I came to see him I thought how lucky he was to be at boarding-school so far away from Mummy.'

'Where did they send you?'

'Roedean. It was hell – she was always visiting me.' We started walking towards the front door. 'Bet you're glad I told you about this place.' It hadn't changed at all.

'Yes, I am.'

A small boy came out of the school and started walking towards us. I panicked.

'Oh God, this is it. I don't look like the wicked stepmother, do I?'

'Of course not, don't be silly.' But he looked worried all the same.

The small boy came up to us. He looked like his mother. 'Hullo, Dad.'

'Hullo, laddie. How are you?'

'I'm fine.' To my surprise he turned to me with an ingratiating smile. 'Are you Diana?'

'Yes.'

'Can I kiss you?'

'Yes, of course.' I bent down as best I could and he gave me a timid little-boy kiss on the cheek. I felt quite overcome.

'She's awfully pretty, isn't she, Dad?'

Mack said, 'Where's Jamie?'

Duncan hesitated, embarrassed. 'I don't know.'

'You must know. Where is he?'

'He's not coming.' Duncan stared at the ground.

'What?'

Duncan said, like a child repeating a lesson, 'He said to tell you he's not coming.' Then he looked up and saw the expression on Mack's face. 'Don't be cross, Dad, please. That's what he said. It's not my fault.'

'Where is he?' Mack just wouldn't let it drop.

'I don't know. Honestly. He could be anywhere.'

I watched Mack staring at the school and grounds, and I could feel his rage and frustration: somewhere Jamie was

192

hiding from him. But still, there was nothing to be done about it.

'Now look here, Duncan –'

'Leave it, Mack.' I took Duncan's hand. 'Come on Duncan, we're going out, aren't we, all three of us. We're going to have a nice drive and a lovely tea.'

I did my best. He was a nice little boy and almost frighteningly eager to please, yet not in a way that made you feel sick. It was rather pathetic really. He kept watching Mack for signs of approval and it was obvious Mack was thinking about Jamie most of the time, so I tried to fill in the gaps. I was surprised to find I could be so conscientious, but I felt sorry for the poor little thing. I thought what a difficult life he was going to have if he made a habit of trying too hard.

We had as good a time as we could in the circumstances and then took him back to school. He went off with his friends (probably to report to Jamie, I thought) and we went to see the headmaster.

Mack kept saying, 'I simply don't understand.' He was still really furious and upset. I hadn't realized before how much Jamie meant to him.

'It's quite straightforward, Mr Mackenzie. Jamie decided he didn't want to see you today.'

'I realize that, damn it, but where is he?'

Mr Hammond shrugged. 'He could be in any number of places. Woodwork, forestry, swimming, even his own dormitory.'

'Presumably someone could find him,' said Mack, glaring at him, 'given long enough.'

I said, 'Darling, let's leave it. We've had a nice day with Duncan. If Jamie wants to sulk, why not let him?'

'I'm glad you appreciate the situation, Miss Crawley.' Mr Hammond clearly approved of me, despite the bulge. 'Piers Crawley, wasn't it?'

'That's right. My brother.'

'Yes, of course. I knew I remembered the face.' Mr

Hammond gave me a lovely feeling of solidarity, a wonderful mixture of tradition and progress. Just to watch him re-filling his pipe made me think of Agincourt and the playing-fields of Eton and the Battle of Britain. Mr Hammond had Our Finest Hour stamped all through him.

Mack said, 'If you two could stop reminiscing for a minute – don't I have the right to see my own child?'

Mr Hammond looked surprised. 'Not by force, Mr Mackenzie, which is what you seem to be suggesting.'

'But I came here specially to see him.'

'I appreciate that. However, you're also paying us a considerable amount of money to teach Jamie, among other things, how to think for himself. If he's made up his mind he doesn't want to see you, that's his decision. We can't interfere.' It was almost the same speech he'd made about Piers a long time ago.

'What d'you mean, you can't?'

'All right, we won't.' The more angry Mack was, the calmer Mr Hammond became. 'If you think about it, Mr Mackenzie, you'll realize there's no point in forcing a visit. What would it achieve?'

'All I can think about is that my son is somewhere in this bloody school and you won't find him for me.'

'That's right.'

There seemed no end to it. I began to feel very tired.

'Is that all you've got to say?'

Mr Hammond gave Mack one of his sternest looks. 'No, I could say a lot more but I'm trying to restrain myself. This is a very delicate situation. I'm sure Miss Crawley knows what I mean. These two boys are having to make enormous adjustments at a very vulnerable age. They are doing it in different ways. That's all.'

We drove back to Glasgow and Mack went on about the school all the way.

'That man was bloody insulting.'

I tried to make light of it. 'Oh, he's always been like that. He just doesn't like parents very much. He once had a frightful row with Mummy when Piers was fifteen and he went vegetarian. Mummy wanted the head to make Piers eat meat and he wouldn't.'

Mack said grimly, 'I seem to have more in common with your mother than I thought.'

'Actually I think Mummy was hoping for a rebate on the fees. She thought vegetarian just had to be cheaper and the head explained it wasn't.'

'Why did she ever send him to a school like that?'

'It was Daddy's old school.' I was proud of him. 'He's very progressive in a quiet sort of way.'

'You call that progressive? I've a good mind to take them both away.'

I was horrified. 'You *can't* – they've done wonders for Duncan, you said so yourself.'

'What's the good of that if they're ruining Jamie?'

'Darling, they're not. He's upset about us and they're backing him up, that's all.' At that moment we drew up outside his mother's flat. He'd exaggerated as usual; I was quite disappointed. It wasn't the Gorbals at all, just perfectly adequate council housing for what Eliza Doolittle's father would have called the deserving poor. Ghastly, of course, but not a slum. I said, 'Oh dear, we've arrived. I'm not sure this is a good idea.'

'It's the only way. You wait here.' He got out of the car. 'I'll have a word with her first.'

I watched him go up to the front door. I felt very tired and my back ached; I wished I was at home. The whole Jamie–Duncan thing had been more than I'd expected. I wanted to meet Mack's mother, but I wished I could do it another time when I had more energy.

He rang the bell and waited. A woman finally opened the door. She looked so like him, my heart turned over. But she was only surprised to see him, not pleased : that was clear, even at long distance. They spoke, but I couldn't hear what they said. Then she slammed the door in his face. I don't think anything ever upset me more. I wanted to protect him, to comfort him : he was like my child.

He rang the doorbell again and again; he pounded on the door. Then he gave up and came back to the car disconsolate, like a puppy with its tail between its legs. I felt like crying, but I knew that wouldn't help. He looked so sad. I wanted to tell him it didn't matter, but of course it did. He got into the car and I squeezed his hand and kissed him, trying to be cheerful. An idea came to me.

'Bet you I can get in.' I saw his look of astonishment. 'Just you watch me.'

'No. I don't want her insulting you.'

It was sweet that he was so protective, but that wasn't really the point. 'How much d'you bet?' I heaved myself out of the car and I could feel his eyes boring into my back as I walked up to the front door. I didn't know what to expect and I was past caring. I wanted a resolution. I pressed the bell very lightly and she opened at once; she was so absurdly like him, I felt quite unnerved. But it was not a time for sentiment. I had not even planned what I was going to say.

She looked at first surprised and then furious, embarrassed. So was I, come to that, but for once in my life I had to forget how I felt.

'Hullo,' I said, with the first thing that came to mind. 'May I use your loo?'

She looked at me with real hatred; I'd never seen it before at such close quarters.

'You can burst,' she said, 'for all I care.'

I was used to the accent, or else I would have found it hard to interpret. 'It's your grandchild I'm carrying,' I said. At the back of my mind was the thought that if I actually fainted on her doorstep, she'd have to take me in. I was prepared to faint; in fact I felt it might very easily happen without my permission. Or I could even pretend I was in labour; then she'd have to let us both in. But while I was considering these alternatives, she opened the door wider, with great reluctance, so I went in anyway.

It was a horrid little flat, but I suppose she'd done her best with it. I caught a glimpse of poky rooms overstuffed with cheap furniture and made even more crowded by carpets and curtains whose patterns clashed. It all looked very clean, but there was a funny smell I couldn't identify – not dirt, not cooking, just something odd. I'd noticed before that other people's houses often smell odd. Sometimes you like the smell and sometimes you don't. Anyway, I went to the loo and felt instantly better, as I'd really wanted to go. Then I sat there for rather a long time thinking what to say to her when I came out. Obviously she couldn't evict me by force, but how was I going to persuade her to let Mack in? I straightened my clothes and checked my make-up while I pondered, and then as I was brushing my hair I noticed that I really felt most peculiar, as if I was about to get the curse, only I couldn't be.

I was having a pain. No, I was having a contraction. My God, I'd actually gone into labour in Mack's mother's loo and it served me right; I'd brought it on by thinking what a clever deception it would be, to get Mack into the house. As soon as I could, I came out of the loo into the hall. She was hovering.

'I'll have to ask you to go now,' she said.

'Sorry,' I said, 'I'm in labour.' I wondered if she'd believe me, but the pain must have shown on my face, for she looked searchingly at me for a moment, then helped me to the sofa in her sitting-room and gave me a cup of tea.

'I'll get Rob,' she said. 'I'll not be a minute.' And she ran out as if it was urgent.

I sat there feeling important and sipping her ghastly strong tea with milk and sugar in it, thinking she was quite sweet really, and then Mack arrived in a state. I couldn't understand why they were both so agitated. 'Isn't this exciting?' I said. I honestly thought it was.

He grabbed my hand. 'Are you all right, lassie?'

'Yes, of course, I'm fine. Bit of luck this, I'll get it over early. Are we far from the station?'

'Station?' his mother said. 'It's the nearest hospital you want.'

'But I've got to get back to London, to the clinic.' What was all this rubbish about hospitals? I couldn't go to a hospital in Glasgow of all places.

'You canna travel in that condition, lassie.' Mack was flicking through the phone book.

'Of course I can. It'll be ages yet. All night probably. I can sit on a train with a few pains, what's the difference?'

'No, you can't,' his mother said. I could see now where he got his aggression. 'It might come quicker than you think and you'll end up having it on the seat. Now you don't want that, do you?'

'I want Mr Sinclair,' I said. 'It's all arranged.' But Mack was already dialling.

By the time we got to the hospital I was having regular contractions. I was taken into a cubicle and some ghastly person prodded me, saying, 'What are the pains like?'

'What d'you think they're like? Painful.' I was too cross to be polite; I still thought Mack should have taken me to the station, and we'd argued in the car all the way to the hospital.

'How often are you having them?'

'About every twenty minutes.'

They then listened to the baby's heart with a stethoscope and came up with the brilliant deduction, 'Aye, you're in labour all right.'

'I had realized that,' I said.

'I'll just take your blood pressure.' More equipment and nonsense and fuss.

'We could have been on the train by now,' I said bitterly to Mack. He looked contrite but not very contrite, so I realized he was actually glad I was in a bloody hospital in Glasgow.

'That's fine,' the white-coated person said, unwrapping my arm.

'Of course it is. I'm perfectly all right.'

They turned to Mack. 'Would you mind waiting outside, Mr Crawley? We have to shave your wife and give her an enema now.'

'For Christ's sake, that's all I need. And I'm *Miss* Crawley. He's my lover and he's called Mackenzie.'

There was a pause while they absorbed all that and decided not to react.

'Could you wait outside, please, Mr Mackenzie?'

198

Mack looked at me pleadingly. 'I'll be right back, lassie.'

'Oh God, what's the difference? You've seen it all, haven't you?'

They fixed me up with a private room and let him stay for a while. I wanted him there, and yet I also felt the whole process was almost more of an ordeal for him than for me. It went on for hours, the contractions getting stronger and closer together. As I came out of a particularly powerful one he said anxiously, holding my hand, 'Was it bad?'

I was exhausted, but there was no point in telling him that. 'No, just the same as the others.'

He wiped my face. 'I love you so much.'

'I know, darling, I love you too.'

'It seems a long time since we began, doesn't it?'

'Centuries.'

'I hate to see you in pain.'

'All right, go away then.'

He kissed my hand. 'I didna mean that. I hate to think I'm causing you all this pain.'

'Think nothing of it – but I'm not doing it again, that's for sure.'

We laughed. Then I got another pain.

They sent him away eventually and moved me to the labour ward. I got worn out with all the pushing, and the more they encouraged me the more I snapped their heads off. I really was astonishingly bad-tempered.

'Come on now, push,' they'd say brightly, and when I got my breath back I'd snarl, 'What the bloody hell d'you think I'm doing?' They gave me stuff for the pain, but I didn't think it was much good and I said so; still, I suppose it might have been even worse without it. Who knows? The entire performance was so gruesome I wondered why I'd ever let myself in for it. By the time they wheeled me into the delivery room I was past caring if I lived or died: I just wanted the whole thing to be over, and suddenly it was.

She was born around six in the morning. She was tiny and

perfect and I couldn't believe I'd performed such a miracle.
I burst into tears.

Mack arrived mid-morning with flowers and champagne.
I was asleep, but I woke up when he kissed me and we smiled
at each other.

'Aren't I a clever girl?' I said, hugging him. 'Have you
seen her yet?'

'Not yet. I came straight to you.' There were tears in his
eyes; I was proud and grateful.

'I should think so too. Get your priorities right. I only
saw her for a minute – she's got to be in some special room
for a day or two because she was early. She's not bad-
looking though.'

'I'm sure she's beautiful.'

'Well, she's a bit wrinkled but she's not bad.' I watched
him opening the champagne, and remembered the first time
he'd done that for me. His hands were as sexy as ever,
though sex was the last thing on my mind, I was so tired and
sore. I ached as if I'd been run over. 'God, it's a weird feeling. I can't believe I've actually done it. Isn't it funny she
was so small? It was nearly all liquid or something, making
me so huge. Bit of luck, really, no Caesar, no scar. So much
for Mr Sinclair. He doesn't know everything after all.'

'Was it awful?' He looked at me tenderly and I felt quite
faint with love.

'I thought it was ghastly, but they tell me it was all perfectly normal and straightforward. God help the ones with
complications, that's all I can say.'

'You're very brave.'

Just seeing him look so proud of me made me start to forget the pain. 'Not much choice when it comes to the point,
actually. I must say I'm surprised there are so many people
in the world. I'd have thought there'd be a lot more only
children.'

We drank champagne and toasted each other and our
daughter. I was totally euphoric. He sat on the bed and held
my hand. 'I've rung your family. They're all delighted and
they're coming up tomorrow.'

'All of them?'

'Well, the big four.'

'What fun. Daddy and my father haven't met for years. Neither have Mummy and my father, come to that. I'll be able to hold court from my bed like Louis the Fourteenth.' It was rather a beguiling prospect. 'All the same, you better get me out of here as soon as you can. Breakfast was revolting, so God knows what lunch and dinner will be like.'

I can't remember when the bad feeling started. It must have been sometime that night; I suppose the euphoria wore off gradually during the day. Anyway it seemed very suddenly night and Mack had gone and I was alone. I'd had two more disgusting meals and I'd had a sleeping pill, so now I was supposed to sleep and I couldn't. I kept turning over but I just couldn't get comfortable and my stitches hurt, but worst of all I felt so terribly awake, as if there were a problem I had to work out in my head.

A nurse looked round the door. 'Not asleep yet, dear?'

'I can't sleep.'

'Did you take your pill?'

'Yes. It's not working.'

'It will soon,' she said soothingly. 'You just relax.'

'Can't you give me another one?'

'I'm sorry, dear, I canna do that.'

She went away. I was sorry; I didn't hate her like some of the others. She was nice; I'd have liked her to stay. I felt worse after she'd gone, much more alone, and I usually enjoyed being alone. I couldn't understand where all the elation had gone: I'd had the baby and she was fine and I was fine and Mack and I were both thrilled. What was wrong with me? I felt such a terrible sense of anti-climax, as if the whole thing had been for nothing, all that effort to no purpose, as if we were all going to die so I might as well not have bothered. I was so tired and I longed to sleep but I couldn't. It seemed that something dark and heavy was pressing on me and I might actually choke if I wasn't vigilant. It was such an awful, irrational feeling, I wondered if I were going mad. I put on the light and tried to read but I felt totally unreal, as if I were pretending to be someone else, so I switched it off again. Better to be in darkness and face whatever it was. Just me and it, alone.

I suppose I fell asleep eventually. I can't remember.

In the morning all the black feeling had got somehow locked in, as if someone had thrown a switch. I'd never felt so angry before. I was afraid to speak, in case I killed someone.

They complained that I hadn't eaten my breakfast, but I didn't answer and eventually they took it away. Then somebody higher up came bustling in, like a prefect.

'Now then, mother, what's all this about not eating?'

'I am not your sodding mother.'

She flinched but rallied. 'There's no call to use language like that.'

'Piss off,' I said.

She must have sent for the big guns because presently Sister came in, radiating cheerfulness.

'You can have a bath today, Miss Crawley. And then you can go and feed your baby. Now, won't that be nice?'

I shook my head. It was so black inside my head, I was surprised she didn't notice.

'Come along, dear,' she said in a bracing tone, 'you know it'll make you feel better.'

I closed my eyes and made a huge effort to speak normally. 'I'm too tired.'

'All right, then, we'll bring her in to you. She's a lovely bairn. What are you going to call her, have you decided?'

They brought the baby in. It didn't look the same. I don't mean I actually thought they'd got it mixed up (although I suddenly understood the changeling fantasy as never before), just that I felt entirely different when I looked at it. Where was the pretty child I'd been so proud of and gone through so much to produce? This was just an ordinary baby. I knew rationally it was the same one, but I didn't feel anything when I looked at it. It was terrifying to feel nothing.

Rather like falling out of love with a man. You look at the same person and they are so changed, you wonder what you ever saw in them.

The nurse said, 'Isn't she lovely?' and tried to put it in my arms. I turned violently away and began to cry.

Crying was a big mistake. Once I started, I couldn't stop. My father came in and said, 'Kisleanyom.' He hugged and kissed me. 'What is it, what's the matter?'

I just went on crying. 'Oh, Apukam, get me out of here, please.'

Piers came in. He said, 'Rabbit? What is it? You can tell me, can't you?'

But I couldn't. He held my hand. He sounded like a worried little boy again. 'Di? It's all right, really it is.'

But it wasn't.

I was still crying when Daddy and my mother came in. They stood by the bed, looking ineffectual and helpless.

'Go away, please,' I said. 'Just go away.'

'Diana, don't be silly.' As usual they fell into their parental roles, Mummy being tough and Daddy soft.

'Please, angel, we only want to help. We love you.'

I felt such anger, I wanted to injure them. 'I know, I know, for Christ's sake, just go away. I'm sorry.'

Mack came in. I saw him through a great screen of tears and rage.

'Well, she's in a frightful state,' my mother said, shrugging her shoulders. 'Maybe you can deal with her.'

Daddy said hesitantly, 'I should go easy, old chap, if I were you.'

I lost control completely and shrieked at them both. 'Oh, get out. For God's sake. All of you.'

There was a bit of shuffling and murmuring, then Mummy and Daddy left. Mack came over to me.

'What is it, lassie?'

I didn't know how to explain to him the enormity of what I was feeling. There were no words for it. And I was afraid he would think I was mad. I even wondered myself if I was mad, so why shouldn't he?

I said, 'Oh – everything they say is wrong. All of them. I can't bear it.'

He said very seriously, like a pledge, 'I love you. Whatever you want, just tell me and I'll do it.'

I said, 'Take me home.' And I pulled the covers over my head. I wanted to hide from the world.

Eventually I stopped crying. I had to: there were no tears left. I felt dehydrated, emotionally and physically. A psychiatrist came to see me. I took my head out of the bed-clothes so I could breathe, and let him do most of the talking. Apparently post-natal depression was what I had, and it was not uncommon. He seemed to find it reassuring that my ailment had a name and afflicted many people. I myself found such facts alarming, but I kept my alarm well hidden and agreed with everything he said, which pleased him. He was not a stupid man but he was clearly overworked. I would have to see my own doctor, he said, when I got back to London, and he would prescribe pills and refer me to a psychiatrist. Yes, yes, I said, anything. Eventually I would get better, he assured me. Terrific, I said. He looked a bit suspicious; he had probably never had such a docile patient. He tried to get me to talk – about depression, anger, anxiety – but I just kept saying all I wanted was to go home, which was true. I felt I possessed the legendary cunning of the insane. I knew he'd have to let me go.

As soon as the baby was fit to travel, we went home. Nanny came downstairs to meet me and we hugged each other as if it were a matter of life and death – as indeed it was. I said, 'Oh, Nanny, thank God you're here,' and I started to cry again.

'There, there, my pet, it's all right now.'

It was wonderful to see her and have her arms round me again. I could feel Mack watching us but I didn't care.

'It's all right, my love,' she said while I sobbed. 'Nanny's here.'

'I know, I know.' I managed to collect myself enough to blow my nose and wipe my eyes.

She turned to Mack. 'You give baby to me, sir,' and he handed her over reluctantly. 'Now don't you worry about a thing. What a lovely little girl.' She smiled at me in the way I remembered, infinitely reassuring. 'You just sit down, my pet, and don't you worry. Just you have a good rest.'

'Oh, Nanny, you're an angel.' I watched her go upstairs with the baby and I could feel the weight lifting from my shoulders as if by magic. I was young again and I was free: I could be myself. This terrible mistake I had made could be accommodated: Nanny would cope with it. I had not been wrong to place all my trust in her; I had not expected too much. She would never let me down and nothing I did would ever make her stop loving me.

I was so relieved, I felt almost light-hearted. I went into the drawing-room and suddenly it was wonderful to be home. Antigone came running to greet me and rub against my legs.

'Oh, Antigone. Did you miss me? Oh, baby, come here.' I picked her up; I had forgotten how lovely she was. 'Did I go away? I'm sorry. I'll never go away again, I promise.' I sat down with her on my lap and picked up a copy of *Vogue*. I felt I had been away and out of touch for centuries, not ten days. I looked up and there was Mack watching me with a strange expression on his face – amazement, concern, horror – I don't know what, but it seemed inappropriate.

I felt calm, pleasant and distant. I also wanted to lighten the atmosphere. I said, 'Get me a drink, would you, darling?'

1961

Diana

It didn't improve, but I learned to dissemble. I left Adrienne completely to Nanny, who was marvellous, of course, and I smiled a lot, and simply set about rebuilding my life. It wasn't that easy: I had to rebuild my body first. Diet and exercise and a lot of self-discipline; even so, it took me three months to get back to normal. But the satisfaction, at the end of all that effort, was tremendous. Because of course my goal was to get back to work as soon as possible and prove I was still myself. I felt as if I had been involved in a very severe accident.

Mack was no help at all. He meant to be, but he had a lot on his mind at work; at home he seemed either to be fussing over the baby or pestering me for sex. I was alarmed by the indifference I felt towards both.

Geoffrey Sinclair came to see me. He had his foot in plaster, so I had to get Nanny to bring Adrienne down. He made a great song and dance about her, as if he'd delivered her himself, as planned.

'What a lovely little girl. Aren't you the pretty one? She's a credit to you, Diana – and to you, of course, Nanny.'

Nanny looked gratified. 'Thank you, sir.'

'Sorry to bring you down all those stairs, but one flight's about my limit at the moment, I'm afraid.'

I said, 'How did you do it?' as he clearly wanted to be asked.

'Liz and I went skiing – I must be getting old. I feel a perfect fool, I can tell you, and the boys can't stop laughing.' But he looked pleased with himself, to be still so zestful, though injured.

I said, 'All right, Nanny, you can take Adrienne back to

the nursery now. Thank you so much for bringing her down.'

'It wasn't any trouble, my love. You know I've never minded stairs.'

And she disappeared with the baby. He called after her, 'You're fitter than I am, Nanny,' and we all laughed politely. 'She really is pretty,' he said to me.

'Well, I think so. And the baby's not bad either.'

He laughed. 'Nanny is a marvel – how old is she now?'

'God knows. Pushing seventy, I suppose.' I hardly liked to think about it. 'She was twenty when Granny got her for Mummy. Just as well she likes stairs, isn't it, in a place like this?' I wanted her to live for ever.

'And how are you?'

I had forgotten how abrupt he could be. 'Fine.'

'Really?'

'Don't I look it?' I hated the way doctors probed a sore place.

'You look very beautiful and very slender once again – but that's hardly the same thing, is it?'

'I thought this was a social call.'

'It is, but while I'm here –'

Suddenly all was clear. 'Mack's been on to you.'

'I'd have called anyway.'

I felt quite faint with rage. 'God, he's got a bloody nerve.'

'Would you rather he didn't care? We're both very worried about you, Diana. I asked you to come back after your post-natal and you didn't. I've had letters from the psychiatrist in Glasgow about you.' He looked hurt. 'I've begged you to talk to Gascoigne, he's a good chap; we were students together and I know you'd like him, he's very down-to-earth.'

'I don't need him,' I said. 'I told you before, it was bad enough having my body tugged apart, I'm not letting anyone loose on my head.'

He considered that for a moment. 'When I last saw you, I thought you seemed very depressed.'

'That was six weeks ago. I'm better now.'

'No, you are merely more aggressive. That's often a feature of depression.'

I shrugged. 'Can't win, can I?'

'Post-natal depression is a real illness, you know.' He leaned forward with a dreadful air of sincerity, as if addressing medical students. 'It's not imaginary, it's not a sign of weakness, and it affects quite a few women.'

'How ghastly for them.'

'Diana, you're ill and you need help. Please let me help you. Robert tells me you never go near the baby if you can avoid it, and you never talk about her. Now that can't be good for any of you, can it?'

I resented his cajoling tone. 'We have Nanny. You said yourself she's a marvel.'

'Your baby needs a mother as well as a nanny. And you need to sort out your feelings.'

I stood up. 'Geoffrey, have you ever had a one-night stand?'

'Well ... er, yes.' He looked surprised, embarrassed. 'I imagine most –'

'– most people have, yes, quite. Of course. Well, just you imagine the best one-night stand you ever had – and then in the morning you realize it was all a frightful mistake. Maybe you were drunk, or they look different in daylight, or you just want to go back to your own life. Only then someone very powerful, someone in authority, tells you that this person is going to live with you for twenty years. Wouldn't you avoid them if you possibly could? Wouldn't you get someone else to look after them?'

There was silence. To my horror I found I was close to tears.

He said, 'I've never heard it put quite like that before.'

'I feel nothing for that child. Absolutely nothing.' I started to pace about the room and ended up at the window, looking out over the garden square. 'I'm sorry, I realize I must be unnatural, but there you are, you wanted me to be honest. If I didn't have Nanny to look after it, I'd probably do it actual damage.' I tried to find a way to make him understand. 'I know Mack's hurt and upset. Well, I'm hurt and upset too. I went into the whole thing with very high hopes, you know, once I got over my nerves at the beginning. I really did. And for twenty-four hours it was fantastic. Then I suddenly realized what I'd done.' It still hurt to say it. 'It was just a monumental blunder, that's all. I should never have let Mack talk me into it. Mummy was right, damn her, and you were right, aborting me twice. Thank God you did, I think I'd kill myself if I had three of them.' The past whizzed through my head, as if I were drowning or drunk. 'I've ruined my life, Geoffrey, and nobody can help me. I've just got to salvage the bits as best I can.'

Perhaps if we'd had more time, it might all have been different. He might have said something helpful and I might have responded. But as it was, Mack chose that moment to come home. As soon as I heard the door, I said indifferently, 'Oh, good, there's Mack,' and that was the end of our conversation.

Mack came in looking worried, as he always did nowadays. It was a new look and it annoyed me dreadfully, knowing I'd caused it. I said, 'You remember Geoffrey Sinclair, don't you darling? Yes, of course you do, you keep ringing him up.'

'Good to see you,' Mack said.

'Yes,' Geoffrey said, 'I'm glad I called.'

I laughed. 'Don't believe a word. I've been giving him a hard time. Shall I get you both a drink? That *is* something I still seem to be good at.'

'I'm sorry.' Geoffrey looked doubtful. 'I'd like to stay, but Liz and I are meeting some people.'

I poured drinks for myself and Mack. 'Lucky old Liz. We never meet people at the end of the day, do we? We're always too shattered after building our empire. All we want to do is go upstairs and play with our daughter.'

Mack was disappearing downstairs. 'I'll see you out.'

'Come and see me, Diana,' Geoffrey called, departing. 'And make it soon.'

'You're a glutton for punishment, aren't you?' I said. 'Thanks, anyway.' I sat down with my drink; I was suddenly very tired and longing to be alone. I could hear the two men talking together in the hall in low, discreet voices; about me, no doubt. Antigone came in and jumped on my lap.

'Hullo, my beautiful,' I said, stroking her. 'How are you? Don't have kittens, that's my advice.'

My agent got me a job doing a series of pictures for an album sleeve. It was lovely to be working with Jake again, but the other two models, Steve and Krista, depressed me because they were so thin and young. Krista was particularly irritating, because she was stupid as well. We were supposed to be a sort of bisexual threesome, with Steve and Krista as the young couple and me as the predatory outsider, but Jake really had his work cut out getting Krista to understand the basic idea, though it could hardly have been simpler. I had to roar up on the motor bike in my leather gear while Steve and Krista were out riding. Krista was supposed to look hungrily at me while Steve looked possessively at her. We did it over and over again, but she couldn't get it right and I could see Jake beginning to lose his patience.

'Look as if you fancy her, Krista, for God's sake.'

She made a face. 'I try, but it is not normal.'

'Normal or not, ducky, it's what you get paid for. Okay, let's try it again.'

Eventually we got it more or less right. The next shot was on the tennis courts, but the scenario was much the same. Krista kept shivering and twitching and calling out, 'Jake. Can we finish soon? It is very cold, I think.'

'It's cold in your country, too, darling,' Jake said, reloading. 'It's January, that's why. Come on, give it another try. The sooner you get it right, the sooner we can all go home.'

I roared up again on the bike. I was sweating inside the leather suit, but my hands and face were frozen. This time, thank God, Krista managed a bit more animation.

'That's better,' Jake yelled. 'And about bloody time.'

Then we had to do the shots in the casino. We were all worn out with travelling and changing our clothes. By now

Steve was supposed to look interested and Krista nervous, while I was still stuck with being enigmatic. It seemed ages before Jake said, 'That's more like it,' and we could all go back to the studio for the threesome stuff. We undressed and piled into bed, Steve in the middle. I kissed him and he kissed Krista. Then absolutely nothing happened. She was supposed to kiss me but she didn't move.

'Come on, you two,' Jake said. 'Get going.'

Krista wrinkled her nose. 'I don't like to do this, Jake.'

'You're not paid to like it.' He sounded at the end of his patience, so I leaned over and kissed Krista hard on the mouth, taking her by surprise. Jake brightened up at once. 'Terrific. Right. Now do it all again. Just keep going.' Somehow I'd managed to break the tension and we all rolled about, kissing and stroking each other. There was a lot of giggling but some genuinely erotic stuff as well, which must have pleased Jake because presently he said, 'Okay, everybody, I've got what I want. You can please yourselves what you do next.'

We all laughed and I climbed out of bed at once. I was exhausted. Steve and Krista went on kissing in a desultory way. I put on a bathrobe and went across to Jake.

'She stinks of garlic,' I said in a low voice.

'Yeah, I know.'

'But she's very pretty.' That unlined childish face.

'Oh, she's that.' He grinned at me. 'And as thick as two short planks. How are things with you?'

'Oh, the same.'

Steve and Krista ran past us to get dressed in the changing-room.

Jake said, 'Can you stay for a drink?'

Progress at last. 'I'd like to, but my father's picking me up.'

'Too bad. Maybe another time.'

'I hope so.'

'Really?'

'Oh yes. Believe me.'

We stared at each other thoughtfully, remembering old times.

'Look,' Jake said, 'your father's been around. Surely he'd understand . . .'

'He's very fond of Mack.'

'Oh. Yes, of course.' There was another loaded pause. 'You're looking good, baby.'

'Thank you. So are you.'

The doorbell rang, but we didn't move. Steve reappeared, fully dressed. 'Shall I get it? I've got to dash anyway.' Off he went and let in my father on his way out. I'd never been less pleased to see him.

'Nice to see you again,' Jake said, going to meet him and closing the door after Steve.

'Jake.' My father shook him warmly by the hand. 'Has she been working hard?'

'I always do.' I gave him a quick hug. 'I'll just get dressed. Won't be long.'

In the changing-room I listened to them having drinks and talking shop, comparing photography and banking. Krista was beside me brushing her hair, then she went out to join them.

Jake said, 'Krista, may I introduce George Kovacs? George, meet Krista – all the way from Sweden – or is it Denmark? Sorry, darling, I never can remember.'

I heard the polite, moronic little voice. 'My mother is Swedish and my father is Danish, but they live in Norway.'

There was a pause. I pictured my father kissing her hand.

'I am enchanted to meet you.'

'Thank you.'

Warning bells began to ring in my head.

Jake said, 'Yeah, well . . . Krista's also worked very hard today, haven't you, doll? We're doing this album cover for Strip Cartoon, you know, the new group, and it's their first album, so naturally they want it to look like a strip cartoon, stands to reason, so – well, this is the story board, give you an idea what we're aiming at.'

'Oh no, Jake, do not show it to him.' Again the prim, hypocritical voice. 'It is not correct.'

My father said, 'Yes. I see what you mean. It looks very interesting.'

'Oh, it's interesting all right,' Jake said.

Krista sighed. 'I do not like to do such things. It is not natural.'

'But you're getting well paid, aren't you, darling?' Jake sounded impatient again. 'We tried to fit in too much today, but that's how I like to work, keeps everyone on their toes, especially me – trouble is, this time of year you don't get much daylight for the outdoor shots.'

I couldn't stand any more. I slung my coat over my jersey and jeans and went out to join them. My father and Krista were looking at each other as if they had been programmed to represent lust and avarice. I said, 'Sorry, was I ages? You've got such a fascinating book in the loo.'

'Yeah, I'm famous for my loo books.'

'Do I get a drink?'

'Sure. I thought you didn't have time.' He poured me whisky.

'You have an appointment?' Krista said carefully.

'No, not really.'

'Mr Kovacs is giving her a lift.'

'Oh, I see.'

Oh well, I thought, why not give him a treat and do myself a good turn at the same time? 'So Jake's already introduced you to my godfather.'

'Ah.' She sounded pleased. 'You did not say.'

'No,' Jake said, playing along. 'I forgot.'

'It's not important,' I said. 'Actually, I'd like to stay on and talk to Jake about tomorrow's shots – d'you mind if I don't take you up on that lift?'

'Not at all.' My father smiled at me and turned to Krista. 'Perhaps I can drive you somewhere? It would be my pleasure.'

'Krista lives in Knightsbridge,' I said helpfully.

'Then it is on my way.'

'Well, if you are sure . . .' She almost wriggled.

'Oh good,' Jake said, with relief. 'That's settled, then.'

We all kissed goodnight.

'Drive carefully, godfather,' I said.

'As always. Sleep well.'

We watched them leave together, then fell into each other's arms.

'Fantastic.' I heard myself laughing a shade hysterically. 'My God, she's just his type. I don't know why it didn't strike me before.'

Jake kissed me. 'Mm. That's better.'

'Much better.' I could feel myself slowly beginning to come alive again.

Jake poured fresh drinks. 'Isn't someone going to be awfully cross with you?'

'Oh, you mean Ruth?' I had forgotten all about her. 'If she ever finds out. Oh well, that's just the luck of the draw, isn't it? Could happen to any of us.'

I got home rather late and Mack had his brooding, sulky look. I said brightly, 'Oh, darling, haven't you had supper?'

'What supper?'

'It's all in the oven. I told you I've hired this marvellous cook.'

'Really?'

'Oh, you don't listen to a word I say. I ran into Madeleine Bradley in Fortnums the other week. I *told* you, we were at school together, only she did a Cordon Bleu thing afterwards and now she's running this agency for cooks and she's sending us one five nights a week. This is her first night. God, I hope it's not burnt.'

He looked at his watch. 'Not surprising if it is.'

'Darling, you're not sulking, are you? I know I'm late, but Jake had to retake some shots, so what could I do?'

'You could have phoned.'

'I tried to, but Jake's phone is on the blink.' I began to feel bad-tempered: all these lies were so exhausting. 'God, I'm tired. It's been a very long day. Tell you what – let's have a quick drink and unwind a bit, then all I have to do is take Virginia's stew out of the oven.'

'Is that really all you have to do?'

As he didn't move, I poured my own drink. 'Yes, I told her to make a salad and do baked potatoes.'

'Don't you have anything else to do?'

'Well, I have to boil some fish for Antigone later on.'

'And that's all?' He was positively glaring at me.

'I certainly hope so, I'm exhausted.'

'It didn't cross your mind that it might be a good idea to go up and see Adrienne.'

So that was it. 'Oh, God, you're not starting all that again, are you?'

'I think we should talk about it.'

'Whatever for? I'm doing the best I can, there's nothing to talk about. And I don't like you seeing my doctor behind my back.'

Wrong-footed, he immediately looked slightly shame-faced. 'I know, I'm sorry, but I'm so worried about you.'

'Why? I'm perfectly all right, just tired. It's not easy doing a job and running a house and keeping Nanny happy. Thank God I've got the cooking organized. I thought you'd be pleased.'

'Of course I am –'

'But what?'

'You don't have to get so tired. You don't have to do a job.'

I felt my temper straining away from my control, like a heavy dog on the end of a lead. 'I thought we'd get to that.'

'We don't need the money, lassie, and you had a rough time in Glasgow. Wouldn't you rather relax and enjoy yourself?'

'I *am* enjoying myself.' Wasn't that what he resented? 'I enjoy working. Don't you?'

'But you're not spending any time with Adrienne – you don't even say goodnight to her.'

I exploded. 'Christ, that's all you think about, that bloody child. If I went up there ten times a day, she wouldn't know who I am. She's got Nanny. She's perfectly all right. As far as I can remember, my mother didn't come near me till I was five years old.'

'Maybe that's why you hate each other.'

'We don't bloody hate each other.' I heard myself scream-ing at him but I sounded like somebody else. 'What the hell d'you know about it? Just keep my mother out of this. My mother understands me a damn sight better than you do.' It was unforgivable that he should criticize my mother: only I was allowed to do that. 'I wish to God I'd listened to her, then I'd never have had that sodding child upstairs.'

'You don't mean that.'

'Of course I do. I wish she was dead.'

Silence. We were both shocked. To my horror, quite against my will, I began to cry.

'We were all right before she was born, we were happy. Oh God, I wish I'd never had her. We could have been happy for ever. Oh God, I'm so miserable.'

I thought he'd be angry but he hugged me while I sobbed. 'I'm sorry. I'm sorry,' he said, kissing the top of my head. 'It will get better, I promise. I love you. Look – we can have a holiday. Get away – have a good rest. We both need one. The decree absolute's through – why don't we get married on your birthday and have a Caribbean honeymoon?'

I was so amazed I stopped crying out of shock; I raised my head and found him looking at me hopefully. I couldn't believe it.

'You must be mad,' I said. 'Isn't it bad enough being thirty without getting married?'

Things went steadily downhill after that. I suppose he felt rejected and I felt trapped. Anyhow, we were wary of each other. It was a bad time. My father had got off with Krista very quickly, and somehow she'd turned his head so far that he'd broken up with Ruth, so I had *her* on the phone in tears. Meanwhile, I hardly ever saw my father alone: he was either screwing Krista or talking business with Mack. I couldn't believe it was only a matter of months since everything had been all right.

One night at dinner my father tried to set Mack up to help him with his properties. He appeared to be just rambling on, but I knew what he was up to. It would even have been amusing if I hadn't felt so alienated. Mack was enthralled, however.

'Don't you find it a problem getting vacant possession?'

'Yes, of course it is a problem, but –'

'He has his methods,' I said.

'There are ways of doing it, but I have to be careful. Some landlords I know, they do it illegally, with threats, with harassment – in my position I can't afford to take such risks.'

Mack said, 'So what d'you do?'

'Well, you know, it is possible to make life difficult for a tenant without harassing them. It can happen by accident. It often does.' My father shrugged expansively. 'You do your best with the repairs, but when the builders come they make a bit of extra mess, and then they go away and they don't come back for weeks on end. It can be very annoying: they take the old bath out and they don't put the new bath in, or else there is no hot water. It happens all the time. Quite often people can be so annoyed that they leave. You would be surprised.'

Mack looked faintly shocked. I could see all that Scottish puritanism rising to the surface. 'It can't do the builder's reputation much good.'

'Don't look so worried, my friend, I am not asking you to do anything like that. Although of course it is always useful to have a new construction company to work with. I have so many little properties needing repair, it is hard to find builders to do everything and especially to do it on time. When I am so busy at the bank, I really need somebody like a deputy, a kind of first lieutenant you might say, to make sure that all my private interests run as smoothly as they can.'

I nearly laughed; my father was such a smooth operator. But I also resented being excluded from the conversation at my own dinner table.

'But why do we talk about my problems?' my father went on. 'These are trivial matters when we have so much to celebrate. Let us drink to the new companies and our future partnership.' He raised his glass and we copied him obediently. 'To Mackenzie Developments and Mackenzie Holdings. With Mackenzie Industrial already behind us, now we are like the Trinity. And yet you have still your own construction company. It's a most satisfactory arrangement.

You have come a long way in five years, my friend. We have all come a long way.'

'Too far perhaps,' I said.

Mack was looking at my father, not at me. 'I've had a wee problem with the construction company as a matter of fact. Maybe I better tell you about it.'

I let off steam to Jake the first chance I got. 'And then he simply told my father every ghastly mistake he'd ever made with this god-awful building. I didn't know where to put myself. I was so ashamed.'

'What did your father say?'

'Oh, he was very nice about it. Said it could happen to anyone and even the bank had backed a few losers, only not to do it again and not with his money. It was all a big laugh. God, I could have thrown up.' I'd known for some time that Mack was having trouble with repairs and resale on the New Cavendish Street building – it had all gone wrong while I was in hospital – but I never dreamed he'd boast about it.

'Why did he tell him?' Jake asked.

'He said he was afraid my father would find out, the property world's so small, but I think he was just showing off – look at me, see how honest I am, aren't I lovable?' All part of his campaign to take over my father. 'I don't know how he could be so bloody stupid; even I know how important it is to have a proper survey done, but no, he blamed it all on me and how worried he was about me at the time and what a lot he had on his mind, as if it was *my* fault he'd made a hash of it, and then the bloody baby cried and he wanted to go up and see it and I told him that's what I paid Nanny for – and so it went on.'

I was trembling with rage. Jake rearranged the bed-clothes. 'Not a good evening.'

'Not one of our best, no.'

'Is that why you're here?'

'What d'you mean? I thought you were pleased.' He'd certainly behaved as if he were.

'Course I am, but I still like to know where I stand. Is it

221

just a bit on the side you fancy, or have you gone off him in a big way?'

Typical of Jake to put me on the spot. 'It's different since the baby. I can't explain.'

'What are you going to do?'

'I don't know.' What indeed? 'He's so bloody cosy with my father. I don't think they even remember I introduced them. They spend all their time talking business or cooing over the baby. The other night they hardly noticed what they were eating.'

Jake nibbled my neck. 'But you don't care about food much, anyway.'

That wasn't the point. 'I went to a lot of trouble to organize Virginia. They might at least appreciate what she cooks.'

'I suppose it's fun for your old man to have another bloke to talk shop with – I mean he's always been a bit of a loner, hasn't he?'

God, the way men stuck together. Was Jake going to let me down too? 'Oh, they're like Siamese twins. They don't even see me any more – all they want is for me to go to the doctor and get cheered up.'

'Well, it might not be such a bad idea at that.'

'Oh, Jake, not you as well.'

'Why not? You haven't really been yourself since you had that kid.'

Annoyed though I was, the cliché struck home. 'That's exactly how it feels. As if bits of me are missing and other bits have got all snarled up. I'm *not* myself any more and it makes me so angry I'd like to kill someone.'

Jake said calmly, 'Who, d'you know?'

I thought about it. 'Mack, I suppose. And the baby. I don't know. Perhaps if I killed the baby I wouldn't need to kill Mack. Honestly, Jake, I feel so violent it frightens me. I have to make such an effort to control myself, I'm always exhausted. It doesn't matter how much sleep I get, I always want more.'

Silence while he cuddled me. I had forgotten how comforting Jake could be. Very warm and basic. Like Mack at the beginning. I buried my face in his chest.

222

'My sister went a bit funny after she had her youngest,' he said, 'but she's okay now. She said her doctor was really helpful.'

'I don't believe in doctors.'

'Make do with me then.'

We started to make love again.

When I got home I was late for tea with my father. Maybe I'd done it subconsciously on purpose. Anyway he was already there, in the drawing-room and playing with the baby.

'You're early,' I said accusingly. I was furious that he'd made Nanny bring her down.

'No, you are late, but it is not important.' He looked positively serene, which enraged me further.

'What's *she* doing down here?'

'I wanted to see her, and at my age three flights of stairs are too much.'

I flung down my coat and bag. 'You're fifty-five, for God's sake, that's hardly geriatric. I suppose you're saving your energies for Krista.'

'The young can be very exhausting.'

I couldn't bear his smug expression. 'Well, at least you won't be worn out by her conversation.'

'Why are you so angry? Don't you want me to be happy?'

'There are so many beautiful girls you can buy,' I said pointedly, 'd'you have to pick a moron?'

He shrugged. 'You have been talking to Ruth.'

'Only on the phone; I haven't seen her, but she sounded very upset.'

'I know, I am sorry, but there is nothing I can do.' He wouldn't look at me, but he sounded cheerful and he was still fiddling with the wretched baby.

'You're pretty callous really, aren't you?' I said.

'And you?'

'Yes, it must be hereditary. What with you and Mummy, I didn't stand a chance. Poor old Ruth, it's a case of one bad turn deserves another, I suppose. She introduced me to Mack and I introduced you to Krista.' But it wasn't Ruth I felt sorry for, it was myself.

My father got up from the floor and the baby. 'What is wrong between you and Mackenzie? I worry about you, Kisleanyom.'

'I wouldn't have thought you had time. Maybe it's Mack you're worried about. You can always find time for him.'

'What is this nonsense? You are all the world to me, you know that.' He tried to embrace me, but I moved away.

'It's time Adrienne went back to the nursery. I don't like her down here, she might mess up the carpet.'

'That is why Nanny provided a rug.'

And it was time she did more than that. 'Nanny? Nanny?'

'She has gone out.'

'What? But it's not her day off.'

'I said she could go. It was only for an hour. She wanted to do some shopping.'

Silence. I got over my astonishment, collected my temper and harnessed it. 'I'd be grateful if you don't come here and upset my domestic arrangements.'

It was clearly a challenge and he rose to it. 'Perhaps you would rather I do not come here at all.'

'Yes, that might be even better.'

We were both shocked by what we had said. The baby started to cry and he moved towards her.

'And you can start by not touching *her*.'

There was a pause. I was pleased to see he looked hurt. At the same time I wanted to cry and I wanted him to comfort me.

'Kisleanyom, you are ill,' he said finally. 'You must see a doctor.'

'I'd like you to go now.'

When he had gone I felt terribly alone. I couldn't believe what had happened: we had never quarrelled before. I stood at the window and watched him leaving; I willed him to turn round, but he didn't. Nanny came back at that moment and they stood on the pavement talking. The baby started to cry. My father got into his car and drove away, and Nanny came into the house. I went on looking out of the window.

When the crying stopped I knew Nanny must have come into the room and picked up the baby.

'Ah, Nanny, you're back,' I said, turning round. 'Another time, I really would appreciate it if you don't go out without my permission.'

She looked startled. 'I'm sorry. I thought if Mr Kovacs –'

'And I'd also be grateful if you don't bring Adrienne down to the drawing-room. Not for Mr Kovacs, nor for Mr Sinclair. Not even for Mr Mackenzie. Adrienne belongs in the nursery. That's why we have a nursery.'

'Very well.'

'And that's where she ought to be now.'

Her face closed in somehow: hurt, self-protective, blank. 'Whatever you say.' She started up the stairs with the baby. Suddenly I couldn't bear it any more: I had taken advantage of my position and I had wounded the one person in the world I could rely on. I flopped in a chair and burst into tears.

Nanny came back at once. She dumped Adrienne on the sofa and put her arms round me. I sobbed, 'Oh Nanny, I'm sorry, I'm so miserable.'

'There, there, my love. It's all right.' She stroked my hair and rocked me like a baby. 'It's all right. Don't you worry about a thing. Nanny's here.'

Things drifted on. Sex with Jake cheered me up quite a lot, but didn't make me any keener for sex with Mack. He gave up trying at night and started trying in the morning, but it wasn't any better. On what turned out to be the fatal day I got so desperate to be let off that I said, 'This is ridiculous. I think we better stop.'

We stopped.

'Well, you're not helping much,' he said accusingly.

'Neither are you. Oh, never mind, we're both in the wrong mood, that's all.' I wanted to make light of it.

'You're always too tired at night and now you're too tired in the morning as well.'

'I didn't say I was too tired, I said I was in the wrong mood.'

'You're always in the wrong mood these days.'

Why couldn't he leave well alone? 'I don't know why you bothered to try. You didn't really want to, you were just trying to prove something.'

'I love you, but –'

'That's not my idea of love.'

'– but you've got to have something done.'

The whole thing was escalating as usual. 'Why? Is it getting uncomfortable for you?'

'For your own sake, I meant. You're not happy and you're not well, and it's not going to cure itself.'

The phone rang. Not knowing the horrors ahead of us, I was actually pleased and relieved. I thought it would provide a diversion. Then I saw the look on his face as he listened, and I was frightened.

'Darling, what's happened?' I felt a rush of love for him, almost like the old days.

He told me Duncan had had a climbing accident. I didn't know it then, but that was the beginning of the end for us.

Jean

Christmas and Hogmanay were difficult for Jean, as Robbie moved between his two families. She felt he was bribing the boys with presents, which Duncan didn't need and Jamie despised. She thought continually of the new child and envied the mother, although Robbie said she had been very ill after the birth. Such an event must surely set a seal on the relationship. Her own feeling of defeat made her realize that she must have been secretly hoping for something to go wrong, and she was ashamed of her lack of charity.

One afternoon in January Robbie arrived at the back door earlier than expected. He had taken to knocking and letting himself in before she could answer. She wasn't sure if that pleased or annoyed her. Now she felt flustered because she was still making the cake she had planned to offer him.

'D'you know where Jamie is?' he said, without any greeting.

'Aren't they both in the garden? They were just now.'

'Only Duncan.'

'Well, I didn't tell them you were coming.' That was a new policy, agreed between them, designed to prevent Jamie going out to avoid his father.

'He must really hate me.' He sat down heavily on a kitchen chair and she poured whisky for him automatically. 'I wish I'd never given him the bloody bike. Now he can get away from me even faster.'

'It's just a phase,' she said, unconvinced.

'Aye, well, it's been going on a long time.' He looked at her with a touch of embarrassment and he knew he was going to ask her a favour. 'Could you talk to him for me? Make him see sense?'

'I've already tried.'

He looked surprised. 'What did you say?'

'Oh – that you're still his father and you still love him and you want to see us all, the three of us, not just me and Duncan. And if he's angry with you, that's all right, he should see you and tell you, and not keep running away.' She sighed. 'I really did try, Robbie.'

'Aye, it can't have been easy. That's more than I deserve.'

She longed to put her arms round him. 'I'm sorry it didn't work.'

'He's very stubborn.'

'Aye, he takes after his father.'

Robbie smiled faintly. 'I don't know which is worse – him avoiding me like this or all that phony politeness over Christmas – yes, sir, no, sir, thank you, sir – as if I was a perfect stranger.'

She wanted to remind him of the other child in the garden, needing him so much, but she knew it was not the moment. Instead she poured more whisky. 'Have you had a bad day?'

'Why?'

'You sound tired.'

'I've had a bloody awful day, if you really want to know. A deal's just fallen through and the bank are screaming for eighty thousand pounds. I've got repair work costing twenty thousand pounds and I'm being sued for damages.'

She was horrified; she could hardly have been more surprised when he suddenly burst out laughing.

'What's funny?'

'Oh – you have to laugh. I sounded so damn sorry for myself.'

'I'm sure it'll all work out,' she said inadequately.

'Course it will. And everything else is going fine. I shouldna complain.'

Was it her eager, hopeful imagination or did he sound a shade too emphatic? 'How's the bairn?'

'She's a wee beauty.'

'Have you fixed the wedding date yet?'

'No. No, we haven't. Not yet. We've been so busy.'

She still thought that was strange. 'When you do, don't tell me, will you? Not till afterwards. I mean, I do want to know, of course, but not till it's over.' In some ways it would almost be a relief, like an execution.

At that moment, mercifully, Duncan ran in. 'Dad, I got down the tree all by myself. I shouted, but you didn't hear, so I just climbed very slowly the way Jamie told me and it was all right.' Jamie had been teaching him all through the holidays.

'What's the matter with your knee?' Jean said suspiciously.

'Oh, I grazed it a bit, but it doesn't hurt.' He was glowing with pride in his achievement, gazing anxiously, adoringly, at Robbie and longing for praise. She prayed Robbie would respond.

'You did fine, laddie.' Robbie ruffled Duncan's hair.

It was enough. Later she was to look back on the moment, clear and permanent as a photograph, with a mixture of gratitude and horror. At the time she only thought how happy Duncan looked and she was content.

It seemed no one could be happy for long. Ruth phoned, inviting her to lunch on Saturday but sounding very strange, and when Jean arrived the door was opened by Lisa, who took her coat and led her into the sitting-room in a very grown-up way, announcing, 'Mummy's still doing her face. She didn't sleep very well so she stayed in bed this morning.' She poured whisky and water for Jean, and orange juice for herself. 'Daddy won't be back till one o'clock. He has to work on Saturday mornings. Isn't that rotten?'

'It does seem a bit hard.' Looking at Lisa, nearly twelve and already so self-possessed, Jean thought yet again of the daughter she had never had. And now she never would.

'It's because they're short-staffed at the moment – oh, good, here's Mummy.'

Ruth came in, beautifully dressed as ever, but Jean was shocked to see dark shadows under the careful make-up, and eyelids swollen as if from crying.

'Hullo, Jean, sorry I wasn't ready.'

They kissed on the cheek.

'That's all right, Lisa's looked after me beautifully.'

'Oh, good. Thank you, sweetheart.'

'Can I go now, Mummy? I don't want to be late for ballet.'

Left alone with Ruth, Jean didn't know quite what to say. She complimented Ruth on Lisa, quite sincerely, and then felt obliged to ask, 'Ruth, are you all right? Lisa said you didn't sleep well.'

Ruth seemed relieved to be asked and not in the least embarrassed. 'No, I didn't. I'm not sleeping at all well these days. The doctor's given me some pills but they don't work properly, not even when I take two. They knock me out all right, but I wake up later.'

'What are they?' Jean didn't like Ruth's careless tone.

'I've no idea.'

'I only meant – are you sure it's safe to take two of them?'

'Oh, God, what does it matter? He's left me.'

Jean was amazed and horrified. 'David?' She couldn't believe it.

'No.' Ruth almost laughed. 'Of course not.' She poured herself a drink. 'The man I told you about.'

'I'm sorry.'

'Are you? You could say it serves me right.'

'No, of course I'm sorry.' She had never seen Ruth look so ill. 'Why didn't you ring up and put me off?'

'I wanted to see you.' Ruth started pacing about the room. 'No, that's not strictly true, I don't want to see anyone at the moment, not even Lisa, but if I have to see someone I'd rather it was you. I mean you're bound to understand.' She took a big gulp of her drink. 'Just forget about David for a minute. I'm feeling the way you felt when Robert left you. I'm sorry I never sympathized enough – I simply didn't realize anything could hurt as much as this.'

Jean didn't want to be reminded; at the same time she couldn't help but sympathize. 'D'you want to tell me about it?'

'He's gone off me, that's all. Just like that. After ten years. He's fallen in love with a girl of sixteen.' Ruth seemed quite wild with grief. 'Oh, I knew he had them now and then, but I tried to pretend it wasn't important; if he could put up with me being married to David, I could put up with him having the occasional fling. It wasn't ideal but it was bearable. It didn't affect us. I never dreamed this could happen.'

Jean found herself using the same empty words others had used to comfort her. 'Maybe it won't last.'

'That's what he said, but I don't believe him.'

'Why not? It's a very big age gap.'

'He's besotted with her.'

'Well, she might get tired of him.'

'How could she?'

'Maybe she doesn't see him the way you do.'

Nothing she said got through and it was awful to be reminded how little anyone could help you.

'I don't know what to do,' Ruth said. 'I can't eat, I can't sleep. I hurt all over – it's like flu – everything aches. I don't know where to put myself to stop the pain. No, it's not like flu, it's more as if all my skin has been stripped off. I feel quite frantic. I just want to run around screaming. Sometimes I wonder if I'm going mad.'

Jean shivered at the description. She would have preferred not to be reminded. 'Ruth, I really am sorry and I know how you feel. I felt just the same –'

'And even if I do get a few hours' sleep with those wretched pills,' Ruth went on as if she had not heard, 'then I have to wake up and remember what's happened. I wish I didn't have to wake up.'

She sounded as if she meant it: Jean was alarmed. 'You mustn't say that. You've got David and Lisa to think of.'

Ruth smiled bitterly. 'Are you going to tell me I'm lucky?'

'Well, I think you'd feel worse if you were alone.' Jean hated to hear herself sounding severe, but she did think Ruth still had a lot to be grateful for. 'Whatever does David think is going on when he sees you in this state? What on earth do you say to him?' It seemed to her quite bizarre enough to have a ten-year affair, but to flaunt your grief when it broke up was even worse.

Ruth shrugged. 'I've got insomnia. He won't ask questions, he's too afraid of the answers.'

'You're very sure of him.'

'Now you're angry with me.'

'No, just envious. I was sure of Robbie once.'

Ruth poured another drink. 'Oh, look, I don't suppose I'll kill myself, I haven't the guts, and if I don't, then one day I'm bound to feel better. I can't spend the rest of my life like this, that's obvious, nobody could. Perhaps we'll even make it up. But it won't be the same. I'll be waiting for this to happen again. Or perhaps I'll learn to live without him.' She looked at Jean bleakly. 'But I can't see how.'

'Couldn't you learn to be happy with David?'

'I am – I never said I wasn't. Oh, I'm sorry, you don't understand, do you?'

'I *am* trying to.' Jean wondered if she sounded cross.

'Don't bother, it's not worth it. One day I'll feel better, presumably. Only what do I do in the meantime? How do I get through the bit between now and then? It's unbearable.'

Well, she could only be truthful, whether it went down well or not. 'Can you pray? It helped me. Not a lot, to be honest, but just enough to stop me going over the edge, I think.'

Ruth looked astonished, as if she had suggested something weird. 'No. I haven't prayed for years.' The front door opened and closed at that moment and she seemed relieved. 'Oh, there's David.'

'Look, I don't have to stay to lunch.' Jean felt uncomfortable.

'Nonsense, we want you to.' Ruth put on a hostess smile as David came in; they kissed on the cheek.

'Hullo, Jean, nice to see you.'

'Hullo, David.'

'How was your morning?' Ruth asked brightly.

'Oh, pretty hectic as a matter of fact.'

'I'll get you a drink.'

'No, you stay there, I'll get it. D'you want another one?'

'No, thanks. I've got to see to lunch.'

'I can do that.'

Jean was amazed how ready he was to wait on Ruth even now.

'Don't be silly, darling, why should you? I've done nothing all morning.'

'Did you get any more sleep?'

'Yes, I'm fine.'

She went out of the room and into the kitchen.

David said, 'She always makes light of everything.'

'Yes.' Jean was uncertain how to react.

He sat down opposite her and said earnestly, 'Jean, d'you think you could possibly keep an eye on Ruth for me? She's a bit low, she's not sleeping well. I thought it might be an early menopause, but she says it isn't.' He smiled apologetically. 'I don't know, I'm not very good on these things, but she isn't herself. I just think ... maybe friends are more use than I am right now. Especially old friends.'

Jean, feeling no use at all, said, 'Yes, of course. I'll do anything I can.' She wasn't sure whether to admire or despise him, but she envied Ruth.

'Thank you. I'd be so grateful.'

Ruth came back. 'Well, we can eat.'

'Good.' David smiled at Jean. 'I'm starving. Aren't you?'

There was nothing, in the weeks that followed, to prepare her for what happened. The boys were back at school and writing cheerful letters; she was telephoning Ruth regularly, though not to much avail; Robbie was visiting her once a week as usual, and she was enjoying her work at the hospital. Everything was as nearly normal as it could be.

She had seen him only the day before, so she was astonished when he came into the ward where she was on duty. He looked so grave that she knew at once it must be bad news. He told her very gently what had happened, but it was so terrible that she could not take it in.

'I can't tell you how sorry I am,' the headmaster said. 'We all are. Nothing like this has ever happened here before.'

'There must have been something you could have done,' Robbie said. 'There must have been.'

'Believe me, we did everything we could.' Mr Hammond was obviously distressed but trying to keep calm. 'It's an easy climb in normal conditions, but the weather changed, so the master in charge naturally told the boys to turn back. They were all roped together, of course. Then it began to get dark and the mist closed in. There was no way Mr Rees could count heads – besides, he had no reason to suppose there was anyone missing. It was only when he got back to base that he found your son had cut the rope and gone on to the summit alone.'

Jean was numb with shock. She stared at the headmaster and rocked silently to and fro.

Robbie said, 'But the other boys must have known – some of them anyway. D'you mean they said nothing?'

'The party was very near the summit when they had to turn back. Mr Rees was quite right, of course, but several of the boys wanted to go on. They probably felt that Duncan was only doing what they would have liked to do. They certainly wouldn't report him.'

'God Almighty,' Robbie said, closing his eyes. 'God Almighty.'

'I'm so very sorry,' Mr Hammond repeated. 'There was nothing we could do overnight, but we thought he had a good chance. They've all been well trained for survival in the open. We sent up a search party at first light, of course, but it was too late – he'd fallen.'

Jean heard herself wailing, 'No ... no ... no ... no.' Robbie put his arms round her.

They stood beside the bed in the sanatorium and looked at the pale, unmarked face: Robbie stroked Duncan's hair.

Jean said, 'I can't believe it,' and bent to kiss him, but she broke down and clutched the body to her, weeping and rocking it as if to sleep. Robbie watched her with tears in his eyes.

'Come on, hen,' he said, tenderly after a moment. 'Leave him be. Let the laddie have his rest.'

Very slowly Jean let go of Duncan. Robbie settled him back in bed and tucked him in as he had so often done before. The door opened and Jamie came in.

'Mam.'

'Oh, Jamie.'

He came to her and she hugged him tight.

'It didn't hurt him, Mam. I'm sure it didn't. You can see how peaceful he looks. He wasn't scared at all.'

Jean nodded and groped for a handkerchief. Jamie went over to the bed where Robbie was still arranging the bed-clothes and ruffling Duncan's hair. 'Don't touch him any more.'

Robbie looked up, startled.

'It's all your fault,' Jamie went on. 'You killed him.'

Jean said, horrified, 'Jamie . . .' but he went on as if he had not heard her.

'He only did it to impress you. He'd have done anything to make you notice him. You're a rotten murderer. First you go away and leave us all, and then you make him kill him-self. I hate you.'

He ran out of the room. Jean and Robbie stared at each other in shocked silence.

Mr Hammond lent them two guest-rooms in the school. They were both exhausted but felt as if they would never sleep again. Jean unpacked the few things she had brought while Robbie watched her.

'I don't know,' he said wretchedly. 'Maybe he was right. Maybe it was all true.'

Jean felt calmer now, and drained. 'You must stop tormenting yourself. There's nothing you can do now. He's gone. Jamie's grieving so much he doesn't know what he's saying.'

'I feel so guilty I believe him.' He buried his face in his hands.

'No, you mustn't. He has to lash out at someone. He knows you loved them both really.'

'Oh, God, I can't bear it.'

Jean went to sit beside him and they put their arms round each other. 'I know. I know.'

There was a long silence. Finally he roused himself. 'Well,

I must let you get to bed.' He got up and moved a few steps to the door, then stood there irresolutely, turning back to look at her. 'Will you sleep? You must try.'

It was all totally unreal.

'Robbie – I don't want to be alone tonight.'

There was a pause.

'Neither do I.'

He came back to her and they embraced.

1963

Diana

I suppose Mack never really recovered from Duncan's death. I didn't know how to comfort him: I certainly couldn't say I knew how he felt. It was probably worse than if it had been his beloved Jamie: there was a lot of guilt connected with Duncan. I got an awful feeling I was supposed to make up for what had happened, so we had sex a lot, though I knew that wasn't enough to take his mind off it all. Still, it was all I could do. I've never been very good at responsibility.

Really it was a dreadful time for us. I still couldn't feel anything for the child and Mack blamed me for that, and fretted, while I thanked God for Nanny every day of my life. Mack's companies were thriving; he was expanding financially all the time. But I didn't listen when he talked to me about work: I was bored with that by now, and I resented the way he questioned me about what I did when he wasn't there. I realized I was in a trap, but I couldn't see how to escape, and besides I still loved him, in a way.

So we did what lots of couples in our position do, I suppose: we bought another house. In our case it was the house next door, which I had long coveted, only by the time we got it, the moment had passed and it was already too late. But he didn't know that and I wouldn't admit it, so we soldiered merrily on, exclaiming with delight. It was such a good way of affirming we were going to stay together, without actually saying so, which would have suggested there was the possibility of doing otherwise.

Once we were inside the house, genuine excitement took over. 'At last,' I said. 'I thought they'd never go.'

He looked at me indulgently, as if I were a child. 'They moved quite fast really.'

'Not fast enough for me. Oh, it's all going to be wonderful.'

'You really like it?'

I brushed past him, running in and out of rooms, poking about. 'There's a lot to be done. Come on.'

He followed me up the ordinary staircase into the rather dingy drawing-room. I knew we were both remembering the time we had stood in my empty drawing-room next door, before it all began. Centuries ago.

'Well,' I said lightly. 'Here we are again.'

He kissed me. I hugged him back, but he felt so desperate that I couldn't sustain it and detached myself in a hurry. 'Now – there are two ways to do this – the hard way and the easy way.'

He said, 'Tell me the easy way.'

'You amaze me – where's your pioneering spirit? Well, it's very simple. We install Nanny and Adrienne at the top, a housekeeper on the floor below, let them all bounce around down here, and we have our house to ourselves again. We can always put mirror down the party wall to make it look bigger. Then our house would be just for us and this would be very elaborate servants' quarters. Much cheaper like that.' I saw his disapproving face. 'Joke, darling. Just a joke. We do it the hard way. Rip out the staircases and put in spirals, and knock down the party wall. Make everything double and matching. Like *Alice Through the Looking Glass*. After all it *is* a bit of a fairy tale.'

He said after a moment's silence, 'We'll need an architect for all that.'

'Yes,' I said, very casually. 'I thought we might use Peter Langton.'

Peter was thrilled. He walked around measuring things, while I purred to myself at the success of my plan. I didn't feel strong enough yet for anyone new. Old friends and lovers like Jake and Peter were best, till I regained my self-confidence. Besides, they reminded me of the good old days, when I had been free.

I said, 'Well, what d'you think?' But I knew it was a good building, so I watched his face with confidence.

'I can do it,' he said, 'but it's a big job, and it's going to cost you a packet.'

I smiled. 'Not me, Mack.'

'Peace-offering?'

'Sleeping tablet.'

Somehow we were in each other's arms. Peter had never been special to me, but he was young and beautiful; besides, the sense of freedom I got from being unfaithful to Mack mattered more than anything.

Peter said, 'Oh, I have missed you.'

My father was still obsessed with Krista. He had set her up in a flat and he visited her all the time. It really made me sick: he deserved better. He used to come round and see us and then telephone her. She hardly ever answered. I just wanted him to give her up; I wanted it so much I got a pain in my stomach.

'Not in?' I said, one evening after his latest attempt.

'No reply. It's not quite the same thing.'

'I don't know why you bother with her, I really don't. Oh, of course she's young and beautiful, but dear God, is that enough?'

He said humbly, proudly, 'It seems to be.'

I was so angry. 'I know it's the space between her legs you're interested in, but don't you ever think about the space between her ears? It's like the Grand Canyon.'

Mack handed us drinks. I had almost forgotten he was there.

My father said, 'They say there is no fool like an old one.'

I said furiously, 'You needn't sound so smug about it.'

He looked quite unperturbed. 'Haven't you ever cared enough to make a fool of yourself?'

'Too often,' I said. 'That's why I'm anxious not to do it again.' Mercifully Nanny arrived with Adrienne at that moment and diverted us from further wrangling. 'Heavens, is that the time? Bedtime already. Goodnight, darling.'

Nanny brought the child over to me and I offered my cheek. I could feel Mack watching me and I hated being obliged to display affection I did not feel. As I had feared, Adrienne clutched me passionately around the head and kissed me several times: she had turned into a very demonstrative child. I disentangled myself with some difficulty, saying, 'Goodness, mind my hair, angel.'

Nanny moved round to Mack, who kissed Adrienne several times. He was really sloppy about her. She hugged him back, but nothing like as violently as she'd hugged me, and she only gave my father a token hug, while he of course made a great fuss of her. It was ironic, really, the way she distributed her affections: ironic and most unfortunate.

My father said, 'Goodnight, my love,' and Nanny, thank God, took Adrienne back to the nursery. My father sighed. 'She is so delicious I could eat her.'

I was annoyed and vaguely jealous: after all, he'd told me once that he used to feel like that about me when I was little. 'Now, there's an idea,' I said lightly, but Mack looked daggers at me. 'Joke, darling. Only a joke.' I got up. 'Well, time I was off.'

My father said, 'Where are you going?'

'Paris.'

'Very nice.'

'Only for two days and I'll be working flat out.'

Mack said, 'I thought you were leaving tomorrow.'

'No, darling, we're *starting* tomorrow, early, so we have to be there tonight. Get our beauty sleep and all that.' I picked up my suitcase, which I'd packed earlier and hidden behind a chair. 'Bye, darling. Be good.' I kissed Mack on the cheek and my father on the top of his head. 'That goes for you too.'

Mack got up. 'I'll give you a lift to the airport.'

I hadn't expected that and it threw me a bit. I said the first thing that came into my head. 'And leave my father by himself?'

'Oh, I'm not staying to dinner,' my father said.

'Well, actually,' I said, improvising wildly, 'I'm going to the airport with Robin and Jenny.'

242

Mack looked blank. 'Who are they?'

'The people I'm working with. Darling, I told you.'

'I don't think you did.'

'Well, anyway, all I have to do is get a taxi to Chiswick, so I don't need a lift.'

'Why Chiswick?'

'Because that's where they live.' I was beginning to feel exhausted. 'Heavens, what a lot of questions.' I picked up my model bag; I thought I looked very convincing.

'Leave me a phone number so I can get in touch with you,' Mack said.

Alarm. 'Why should you want to?'

'Just in case.'

'In case of what?' It was all I could do not to lose my temper. 'Anyway, I can't, I don't know which hotel we're in yet. I'll ring you when I get there, darling, okay? Now don't work too hard.'

Outside on the pavement I seethed with rage, then made a conscious effort to control myself. I had not been prepared for an interrogation, but I had come through it and I mustn't let it spoil my treat. A parked car flashed its lights at me; I went over to it and got in.

Peter hugged me and we had a long kiss. Then he drove off. We were both too excited to say much at first; then I asked him, 'Where does Anne think you are?'

'In Bath.'

'Why?'

'Well, I go there a lot on business. And that's where the chap whose flat we're borrowing lives. So he'll cover for us if she rings. Why did you say Paris?'

'It's so corny and obvious. Oh, isn't this fun? Like playing truant from school.' I actually giggled; I could hear myself becoming hysterical with relief that all had gone according to plan. 'I said I was going to be working flat out.'

'We'll have to make that come true.'

Silence, then, and more sober thoughts.

'Why did you marry her?' I asked him suddenly.

'Because I couldn't have you.'

I was delighted. 'What super lies you tell.'

We had terrific fun. We made love and slept and made love again, and all the time there was this wonderful sense of irresponsibility. When we finally surfaced, I knew it must be mid-morning, but my watch had stopped. It seemed like an omen. I wished I could have made time stand still with Mack, back at the beginning.

'What's the time?' I asked Peter.

'Half past eleven.'

'Champagne time.'

'Isn't any time?'

'That's what I mean.'

He got up and went to fetch it. I lay there thinking how nice and cheerful he was, and eager to please. Mack had been awfully dour lately. I couldn't stand depressed people near me; it was bad enough having to cope with my own depression. That was why I hardly saw Ruth any more. 'Wonderful,' I said as Peter returned with the bottle and glasses.

'Here's to us.' He got back into bed. 'And here's to the next time.'

He was probably only being polite, but even that much anticipation made me nervous these days. How was I to know what I'd want in future? It would be ghastly if the whole thing became routine – just what I was trying to escape. 'Oh, let's not make plans. That always spoils everything.' I sipped the delicious champagne; it always cheered me up. 'Do you and Anne ever stay in bed and drink champagne?'

He laughed. 'With two kids and an au pair? You must be joking.'

'Mack and I used to, but not any more. God, bloody kids. They ruin everything, don't they?'

'Yes, in a way. But they're worth it.'

'Are they?'

'Well, I wouldn't be without them.' He said it so easily and naturally.

'Wouldn't you?' It seemed everybody loved their kids except me: I felt like an outcast. 'I would.'

But the mood passed and we had two good days. When I got home I felt really tremendous: rested and satisfied and refreshed. I found I was actually humming to myself as I put my clothes away. When Mack arrived I called to him down the stairs, 'Hullo, darling, I'm back,' and when he came into the room I gave him a big hug and kiss. I was in such a good mood. But he didn't react.

'Missed you,' I said. 'It's nice to be home.'

'Is it?' He was stony-faced.

'I think I'd forgotten how hard you have to work in Paris. It's really like nowhere else – except New York maybe. The pressure, I mean, not the atmosphere.' Was I overdoing it?

'Maybe next time you'll go to New York.'

'Doubt it, darling. I think they want younger people, more's the pity.'

He looked at me strangely. I can't describe the look, but it made me feel uneasy. 'Oh well, when you're too old for modelling, you can always earn your living as an actress.'

'D'you really think so?'

'Well, you're doing pretty well at the moment. Or maybe you could be a courier. It's pretty clever, being able to travel without one of these.' And suddenly he took my passport from his pocket and threw it on the bed.

Silence.

'Oh dear,' I said, shrugging. 'Well, if you will go poking about . . .' I was so outraged that I felt quite calm.

'Where were you?'

'Away. I need some time to myself now and then.'

His jaw set stubbornly. 'I want to know.'

'I don't think you do. Not really.'

'Who is he?'

'Darling, this is a silly conversation. It's not going to get us anywhere. I've been away and I'm back. Let's leave it at that, shall we?'

Suddenly, to my amazement, he rushed round the bed, seized me by the shoulders and shook me violently.

'Oh, terrific,' I said. 'Nothing like a bit of brute force when you can't get your own way. Is that how you treated your wife? Well, I'm not your wife, just remember that, and this is my house you're living in.'

He said quite savagely and as if he meant it, 'I'd like to kill you.'

'Then you better hurry up, because any more of this and I'm going to take out an injunction to stop you molesting me.'

We stared at each other. He was breathing hard and I was reminded of a bull in a field, thwarted when you climb over the fence in time. Then it was finished, all at once: he hugged me tight and I stroked his hair. I felt very tired.

'I love you, I love you,' he said, his voice muffled in my neck.

'I love you too, darling, most of the time, but you don't make it easy. Now come on, let me finish unpacking.'

He let me go reluctantly and I got on with sorting my clothes and hanging them. They were pretty creased as of course they'd been in the case for two days.

'What are we going to do?' he asked in a heavy voice, as if we were in the midst of some tragedy. I'd been hoping he would change the subject.

'How do you mean?'

'I can't stand the thought of you with other men.'

He really did look wretchedly unhappy, but I could hardly sympathize when he was torturing himself. 'What other men?'

'Oh, why won't you tell me the truth?'

My brain was racing. All he really wanted was reassurance and I mustn't confuse that with making concessions. 'D'you want to go to bed? We can make love right now if you like.' But he hesitated, then shook his head. Maybe he thought I was too polluted just then. 'All right, as you please. I'm available when you want me. But I'm not going to have you behaving like a policeman. This is my home. I'm a free agent and so are you.'

'I don't want to be a free agent.' He seemed to be wallowing in self-pity and I've never cared for that.

'That's your problem, not mine.'

We avoided each other as best we could for a few days, then we had an uneasy truce. The atmosphere was strained and I kept thinking what a dismal way we were living, but I couldn't see what to do about it.

One evening my father came to dinner and we all pretended to be bright but ended up being merely polite. He praised Virginia's cooking like a guest and I smirked like a hostess. It was awful. Mack said it seemed a long time since his last visit

'It *is* a long time,' I said resentfully. 'You've been such a hermit lately.'

'Oh, I have had many things to do. And you, aren't you busy with the house next door?'

'Aye, we had a friend of Diana's draw up the plans. It's coming along fine.'

'It's going to be beautiful,' I said proudly, thinking of Peter's skill and my good taste.

'Are you going to do the work yourself?'

'Aye – maybe in the new year. I should be able to get a few of my men in there and make a start anyway.'

My father sighed. 'Another new year – they come round so quickly. Do you have any plans for Christmas?'

Mack said, 'No, not really?'

Well, it was as good a chance as any. 'Yes, I thought I might go to New York and stay with Piers.'

Mack looked surprised, but I avoided his eyes. My father said 'Why don't you both go? Then you could take a Caribbean holiday afterwards. It would do you good.'

'Do we need doing good to?' I asked pointedly.

He smiled. 'Everyone needs a Caribbean holiday.'

'I don't think I'm invited,' Mack said.

'Well, you're not very fond of Piers, are you? And you hate New York. Besides, don't you have to visit Jean and Jamie?'

Silence. We all studied our plates. There was no warning.

'My children, I have been thinking,' my father said. 'With all this travelling you do, perhaps I should change my will.'

The word fell between us. We both looked up at him.

'The little one upstairs needs two parents, of course,' he went on smoothly, 'but if something should happen, God forbid, that she has only one, perhaps her grandfather's money might be some comfort.'

I said, 'What d'you mean?'

'At the moment, Kisleanyom, as you know, everything I have goes to you. But it is a lot. More than you need. I could of course make a separate bequest to the little one. But she is so young. There would have to be trustees, administration. I think it is simpler that I leave half to each of you. Then whatever happens in the future, you are both provided for and the little one as well.'

My heart was beating very fast. 'This is all rather sudden, isn't it?'

'No. I have been thinking about it for some time. Life is so unpredictable.'

I swallowed. My throat was dry and I drank some wine. Mack said, almost stammering with embarrassment, 'It's very generous of you – more than I can say – but I honestly don't think I'm entitled to anything. I mean that.'

'It's my wish to do it this way,' my father said. 'You are my son now.'

My head swam. For a moment, briefly closing my eyes, I thought I was going to be sick. Then I got up. 'Excuse me.'

I left the table and went upstairs.

I lay on my bed and lost track of time. I had astonishingly physical symptoms: I felt hot and cold alternately and presently I developed a blinding headache and had to take aspirin, which I hate. Antigone came and lay on top of me. I stroked her a lot; there was something faintly consoling about all that warm fur. I played the scene over and over again in my mind, as if I could change it, but it always came out the same, like the re-run of an old film.

It was unbelievable.

Eventually Mack came up the stairs and into the room. I said, 'Has he gone?'

'Yes. He wanted to say goodnight, but you didn't come

248

down and the stairs are too much for him.' He sat on the bed, looking awkward and shamefaced. 'I'm sorry. He meant well, but he was clumsy.'

'Sorry? Don't be such a hypocrite, you're delighted.'

'I'm trying to talk him out of it.'

'Don't bother, it's his money, let him do what he likes with it. I don't care about that. But he's on your side.'

'No –'

'He is. He knows we're fighting and he wants you to win.' The full horror of it swept over me: no wonder I felt ill. 'You've stolen my father.'

I met a rich American in the Ritz bar. He was a friend of Piers, and Piers had told him to look me up. He wasn't anything special, but he was pleasant and at least he helped to take my mind off what had happened. We drank and chatted and flirted. Finally I said, 'When are you going back to New York?' I was still trying to make up my mind what to do.

'At the end of the week.'

'Give Piers my love.'

'I sure will. It's been really great meeting you. He's talked about you a lot.'

I forced myself to smile and be charming. 'Not too much, I hope.'

'Not nearly enough. I hope we meet again, Diana.'

I hate the way Americans use your name to give spurious intimacy to a conversation. 'I might be in New York for Christmas.'

'No kidding. We must get together.'

'Don't you have a wife?'

'Not any more. Just a load of alimony to remind me of my mistakes. All three of them.'

'Oh dear. That sounds expensive.'

'Yeah, but as long as the oil keeps flowing I can keep pace with it. And there's always a sporting chance one of them may remarry.' He paused, trying to tread delicately. 'Piers tells me you're not married but you have a little girl.'

It seemed a curiously brief summary of my state. 'That's right.'

'Pretty courageous of you.'

'No, bloody stupid.' Then I laughed because he looked so surprised. 'Sorry, have I shocked you?'

'Not at all. It's just not often you meet a woman who's prepared to be really honest about her life.'

Oh dear. How I wished Americans wouldn't overstate everything. It was such a tedious habit. 'Are you serious about investing in this model agency?' Piers was hoping to start up in business and it looked like a life-saver for me.

'I think it's a great idea. I want to diversify in any case, and Piers has the know-how, I have the cash.'

'Sounds perfect,' I said. 'Could you use an ex-model?'

Nanny and Adrienne had more luggage than I would have believed possible. By the time I had finished piling it into their taxi I was quite exhausted.

'Happy Christmas, Nanny.' We embraced. 'Give my love to Mummy and Daddy.'

'I will. Happy Christmas, my pet. D'you know when you'll be back?'

All these people trying to pin me down. 'Not yet, Nanny, but I'll send you a telegram.'

'Give Master Piers my love, now don't forget, will you?' She turned to Adrienne. 'Say goodbye to Mummy now, lovey.'

Adrienne grabbed me round the knees and I kissed the top of her head. It wasn't my fault I couldn't feel what I was supposed to feel. It was nobody's fault. But it was very inconvenient for everyone.

'She's very attached to you, my love,' Nanny said eventually, detaching her. 'You do know that, don't you?'

It was the nearest she had ever got to pointing out my duty, and was not to be encouraged. 'Take care of her for me, Nanny.' I handed over the cat basket containing Antigone. 'Now remember, as soon as you arrive, let Antigone out.'

'Shouldn't I butter her paws and keep her in for a while?'

'No, that's all rubbish. Let her go and chase rabbits and have a good time. She'll come back – if she wants to.' It cheered me to think of Antigone enjoying the country, but the parting was still painful. All that black and orange fur to stroke, and those slanting eyes watching me. I kissed the wicker basket. 'Have fun, precious.'

From the taxi Adrienne wailed, 'Mummy, Mummy.'

'Thanks for everything, Nanny.' For a moment I wanted to cry: she had done so much for me and I had known her all my life. But the moment passed. The taxi drove off, with both of them waving, and I went back briskly into the house.

Mack came home while I was packing. He had on his shut-down face.

'Do you really have to go tomorrow?'

''Fraid so.'

'Can't you get a later flight? Then at least we could spend Christmas Eve together.'

What was the point of sentimentality at this late stage? But men always behave like that. 'It's all arranged.'

'The house seems very empty without Nanny and Adrienne.'

'They'll have a good time in the country. Mummy and Daddy haven't seen them for ages. And you can go down there whenever you like.'

He said bitterly, 'Oh aye, that'll be great.'

'Anyway, you've got Jean and Jamie to visit, and my father, and David and Ruth. Jews are very comforting at Christmas, I always think. That should take up three days. Then you'll be back at work.'

'And when will you be back?'

God, it was never-ending. 'I'm not sure, darling, in a couple of weeks, I expect.' Now for it. 'But when I do get back, I think we should separate.'

He looked absolutely aghast, as if I had hit him on the head. 'What?'

'Sorry, was that a shock? It wasn't meant to be. I just think we should live apart and meet now and then for sex and conversation and dinner, the way we used to. It'd be much more fun like that.'

He actually sat down on the edge of the bed, very suddenly, as if his legs had given way. 'My God, what a Christmas present.'

'I wanted to give you time to think it over while I'm away. I could even live next door, if we don't go ahead with the conversion.' I had thought it all out very carefully and it seemed like our last chance. 'We could meet all the time. But I must be entirely separate. Living like this is killing me.'

He looked quite bemused. 'What d'you mean, killing you?'

'I just can't do it any more, the wife and mother bit. You've had seven years of my life, that's enough for anyone.' Oh, why couldn't he understand? 'You're forever breathing down my neck if I meet another man, you whine about me not loving the baby, you go through my things when I'm out to check up on me ...'

'Only once –'

'Once was enough. And now you're my father's heir.'

'Ah, now we're getting to it.' There was a touch of malicious satisfaction in his voice. 'This is all about money, isn't it?'

Typical of him to think that. 'No, it's about jealousy. Yours and mine. It's poisoning everything. Don't you see, it's bound to be easier if we're not living together? It doesn't work this way. I've had to give up too much.'

'And what about me? I've given up my wife and two boys for you.'

'I didn't ask you to do that.' God, I had even tried to prevent it.

'And I've lost Duncan. It was your idea to send him to that toffee-nosed school. He might be alive if he hadn't gone there.'

'The way you were treating him, he's better off dead.' But I was so shocked by the look on his face that I stopped. 'Sorry. I didn't mean that. Oh, look, you can see it's no good if we start saying things like that to each other.'

He said very soberly and humbly, 'I can't do without you, lassie.'

'You won't have to. I'll be around. Only not like this. It's so ... domestic.'

'But I need to be with you.'

Then he went out to see Jean to discuss the arrangements for Christmas, but I could feel that when he came back he'd be all set to argue until I gave in. It amazed and depressed me that he understood me so little after all this time: I felt I had no choice about what to do next. I wrote him a note on a Christmas card, saying, 'Sorry, Mack, you didn't buy my idea, so I'm not coming back.' Then I finished packing in a great rush and took a taxi to the airport. If I couldn't change my flight, then I could sleep in an airport hotel and leave tomorrow as planned. I cried all the way and had to put on dark glasses because my eyelids were so swollen. But I was running away to preserve myself, before he swallowed me alive. No matter how painful the escape, it was worth it. I felt like an animal in a trap, willing to bite off one of my own limbs to release the rest of my body.

Jean

Ruth was helping her to pack. Or rather, Ruth was watching her pack and admiring everything she put in her suitcase. Ruth was being determinedly cheerful and unselfishly pleased on Jean's behalf.

'Are you driving?'

'No, it's too exhausting. I thought I'd take the sleeper and maybe hire a car when I got there.'

'Yes, you want to arrive nice and fresh.'

'Don't be silly.'

Ruth smiled. 'Well, you look smashing, anyway.'

'Do I really?' Jean surveyed herself critically in the mirror. 'I'm not sure about this dress. I like the colour but it does crease.'

'He won't notice. He'll be so pleased to see you.'

'Ruth, you really mustn't imagine things. I'm only going to see Jamie.'

'Rubbish – it's been going on for two years now.'

'Nothing's going on.'

'Then why are you blushing?'

It was true: Jean could feel her face getting hot. She snapped the suitcase shut and took another look at her dress.

'It's no good; I'll have to change.'

'You *are* going to a lot of trouble – for Jamie.'

'Shut up.' But she was glad to be teased, glad there was someone to be teased about. After so long in the desert, it was wonderful to feel like a woman again. She did not want to spoil it by thinking too far ahead.

'It's just nice to see you looking happy again,' Ruth said. 'It's been a while.'

'Yes, I know.' She was filled with concern for Ruth and amazed at her generosity of spirit. 'I wish you were happier.'

'Oh.' Ruth shrugged. 'Don't worry about me. I'm a lost cause.'

Once safely on the train she relaxed and some of her initial excitement began to drain away. She half admitted to herself how much she would prefer to be on her way to meet Robbie. But the night together after Duncan's death had not led to any sort of reconciliation, as she had afterwards hoped; it had turned out to be merely what it seemed at the time, an attempt to blot out the unbearable with animal warmth and comfort.

She told herself sternly that she was lucky to have Francis Hammond in her life. He was a good man, and kind; he occasionally made her laugh and he took a great interest in Jamie. To ask for more was greedy – or at least unrealistic.

When she arrived at the school, he and Jamie were playing squash. She stood and watched till they had finished, admiring their skill. She felt better about Francis Hammond now that she actually saw him. It was only when she compared him to Robbie in her head that it all went wrong. They came across to greet her, when the game was over, and she knew from the look on Francis Hammond's face how pleased he was to see her; and from the look on Jamie's face how pleased he was about her and Francis Hammond.

It was nice to be taken out to dinner, she had to admit that. Nice to be dressed up in a candle-lit restaurant with an attentive man she could control. Nice to start with fresh salmon mayonnaise and move on to rare steak. Each time they met, she feared the conversation might become too intimate, and each time she was wrong. They talked about Jamie, as if there was a rule that they should, or as if someone might be listening who would disapprove if they didn't.

'He really is adamant he doesn't want to go to university,' Jean said.

'Oh, we'll talk him round eventually.' Francis seemed easy and relaxed about it.

'I hope so. It would be such a waste.' And his father would be so disappointed, she kept thinking.

'Yes, he's a bright boy.'

'He keeps on about wanting to leave and earn money, but that's absurd, my husband's very generous.'

Francis frowned slightly, looked blank. 'Your ex-husband.'

'Yes.' It was still hard to accept that word.

'Forgive me. For a moment – well, I only thought you might have remarried without mentioning it.'

'No. You know I'm a Catholic and we . . .'

'Yes, of course.' He looked thoughtful. 'Not that Jamie . . .'

'No, he doesn't go to Mass very often, I'm afraid. It worries me a lot, but I've tried talking to him and it just doesn't work. His father's Protestant, of course.' Too late she thought that sounded like a condemnation.

'Oh, I shouldn't worry if I were you. It's probably just a fit of adolescent rebellion.'

'Really?'

'Happens all the time. Leave him be and he'll go back to his religion later on, when he needs it.'

'I do hope so.'

'Well, you've done all you can – given him a good grounding. The rest is up to him.'

'I suppose so.'

He looked at her compassionately. 'Your faith means a great deal to you.'

'Yes.'

'You're lucky. My wife and I weren't religious at all and when she died – well, I felt I had nothing left.'

'That must have been terrible. I mean it's bad enough even if –' But she had to stop.

'Yes.' He stared at his plate, then looked up and smiled at her. 'How's your steak?'

'Fine. It's really good.'

'That's a relief. It's such a responsibility – like the weather. Don't worry about Jamie. He's a credit to you. Let's wait and see how he does in his "O" levels.'

What a nice man you are, she kept thinking. So why don't I love you?

Next day Jamie took her to see the canoe he had made. She could tell how proud he was of it from the way he was pretending to be casual.

'Did you really make that yourself?' she said, impressed. It looked so professional.

'Yes. It wasn't very difficult. Old Marilyn's pretty good.'

'Old Marilyn?'

'Mr Monroe, the woodwork master.'

She laughed. 'Did he help you?'

'He told me what to do, but I did it all myself. D'you want to try it?'

'Now?' she said nervously.

'Mm.'

'But I'm not dressed for it...' She was wearing a dress and coat, with sensible shoes, but surely she should be in trousers for canoeing. Even oilskins, she thought.

'You never are,' he said.

'All right.' It was clearly a challenge. Suddenly she noticed that the stream seemed to be flowing awfully fast.

'We won't go very far,' he said, following her glance. 'Just down to there. It's easy to stop there.'

'I hope so.' She couldn't see why, and besides, it seemed a long way off.

Jamie helped her in; she wobbled and squealed with fright. But he hung on to her and settled her down; then he got in behind her and paddled off. She was surprised how quickly fright turned to enjoyment. She was even sorry when they stopped. He was right: it was easy.

'Oh – I was just getting to like it.'

'You'll only get cold,' he said protectively, honour satisfied. 'Come back tomorrow properly dressed and I'll take you all the way down.'

'All right.'

He helped her out and they started walking back to the school.

'Your father'd be really impressed with that,' she said.

'I didn't make it to impress him.'

'I know, but he'd be very proud of you all the same.'

He said savagely, 'Then I might as well smash it up.'

'Jamie –'

'It's a pity he wasn't more proud of Duncan.'

'He was – in his own way – only –'

'Only I was always his favourite, yes, I know, don't remind me. How d'you think I feel, knowing Duncan might be alive if I hadn't been Dad's favourite?'

Grief made her angry. 'That's not true – and even if it was – I'd rather you didn't say it. You've got to stop hating your father, Jamie.'

'Why?' There was a sneering tone in his voice. 'Because he doesn't like it?'

'Because it's bad for you.'

'You still hate that woman, don't you?'

How tough and direct he was. 'Yes, God forgive me, and it's very bad for me too.'

'It's all Dad's fault. If he hadn't gone off with her, none of this would have happened.'

She said sharply. 'Nothing is ever all one person's fault, Jamie. Just you remember that.'

'I don't believe you.' But he softened his tone to pacify her. 'The Organ was ever so pleased to see you yesterday, wasn't he?'

'I wish you wouldn't call him that.'

'Why? You usually laugh.'

'Well, I shouldn't – and I'm not laughing now.'

'Oh, all right, Mr Hammond then. He's not bad, for a teacher. I mean he really listens, even if he doesn't agree with you. And he's still pretty fit, for his age.' He looked at Jean hopefully, but she stared straight ahead, pretending not to have taken the hint.

When the visit was over, Francis carried her suitcase to the car. Now that she was leaving they both felt a little awkward, not knowing quite what to say.

'I don't suppose you'll be up here again before Christmas.'

'No, probably not.'

He hesitated. 'D'you have any special plans for the holiday?'

'No. I usually stay at home. Jamie's father visits, of course.'

'All the time?'

'No, just now and then. He's mostly with his –' How to put it? 'His other family.'

'I'm sorry, perhaps I shouldn't have asked, but I do so enjoy seeing you, and since I've been on my own, I normally spend Christmas with my sister in Epsom.' He gazed at her hopefully. 'I was wondering – if you're free any time over the holiday, whether we could meet. Maybe have a meal together?'

Jean felt a thrill of alarm mixed with pleasure. 'That would be very nice.' They had never met on her territory. It seemed an amazing step forward, an extraordinarily intimate suggestion.

'Good,' he said briskly. 'That's settled then.' He stowed her suitcase in the boot. 'Is Jamie coming to see you off? He's got a free afternoon, if I remember rightly.'

'No, we said goodbye after lunch.' An uneasy goodbye, full of affection and hostility. Jamie needed a father.

'Let's hope he's studying, then.'

'Yes.'

They both laughed at this implausible idea.

'Not very likely. He's probably knocking hell out of someone on the squash court.'

Suddenly she wanted to say, 'Help me with Jamie. Tell me what to do.' Instead she shook hands with Francis Hammond, got into the car and drove away.

On her way back to Glasgow she made her usual detour to the cemetery and changed the flowers on Duncan's grave. She still found it hard to speak about him and easier to do things for him; she wished now that he had been buried in London, but at the time a train journey with the body had seemed unthinkable. Besides, he had loved the countryside up here.

Some people might think the inscription inappropriate

because it was taken from Christ's words to the Good Thief, but she still found it deeply moving. It was exactly what she had wanted to say. Surely there could be no Purgatory for Duncan: what did he know of sin at ten years old?

'This day thou shalt be with me in Paradise.' It could not be otherwise.

While she was praying at the graveside, she had the oddest feeling that someone was watching her. But when she opened her eyes there was no one there.

When she got home she phoned Ruth, wanting to discuss the weekend and her own ambivalent feelings. But first she had to listen to Ruth, who was nearly hysterical with joy. Her lover had broken with his young mistress, following a heart attack, and he and Ruth were reconciled. Jean had never imagined herself so eager to encourage adultery. She had feared for the sanity of Ruth without him. Her own news seemed tame by comparison.

When Francis Hammond came down for the Christmas holidays, Ruth invited him and Jean to dinner. Lisa and Jamie were going to a party that night, so it was a convenient arrangement, but Jean also felt that Ruth was trying to recognize her and Francis as a couple. She was pleased and disturbed by the gesture.

David opened the door to them and they went in; Jean did the introductions. Then Ruth said, 'I'm afraid I've got a very shy young lady hiding behind me. Come on out, darling, and say hullo.'

Slowly Lisa emerged from the dining-room. 'Hullo.'

They all stared, transfixed by her beauty, silent, awed.

'Don't you look lovely,' Jean said weakly. She hardly dared glance at Jamie. His childhood playmate had grown up.

They had a good evening with David and Ruth. There was nothing special about it, but everyone felt comfortable, ate and drank a lot, made jokes. She was pleasantly surprised how well Francis fitted in, as if he had already met them; she had never seen him in a social situation before. She could tell that David and Ruth liked him, and she was pleased and proud, yet at the same time she felt disloyal to Robbie. It was all very confusing.

Lisa and Jamie came back at eleven as promised, full of chatter about the party. Gazing at Lisa's effortless fourteen-year-old beauty, Jean wondered briefly what it must be like for Ruth to have such a daughter: was she jealous or proud or both? Then she found herself curious about Robbie's daughter by that woman: what was she like? But she stamped quickly on that thought. Absurd to be jealous of a three-year-old. Then something in Jamie's face caught her attention and she got the oddest premonition: that although he was only sixteen, the die was already cast, and Lisa would always be important to him, though she might not bring him happiness. She shivered in the warm room. They made their farewells and left soon after.

Francis drove and Jean sat beside him, with Jamie in the back. The silence was easy, as if they were a family.

'So you had a good time,' Francis said eventually, sounding pleased for Jamie.

'Yes, it was terrific. She's a jolly good dancer.'

'And she's bonny as well,' Jean said, unable to resist teasing him.

Jamie didn't answer. Jean and Francis smiled at each other.

When they got home Jamie went straight to bed, and for the first time that evening Jean felt awkward with Francis. He looked so at home in the big armchair. What was she doing? Why was he here?

'That was a really enjoyable evening,' he said, stretching. 'I liked your friends.'

'Yes, they're nice. They've been very kind to me.'

'They seemed so happily married. That's always a refreshing change these days.'

261

Not a subject she wished to explore. 'Would you like a nightcap?' She wasn't sure if she wanted him to go or stay.

'Thank you. I must say, this is the best Christmas holiday I've had for a long time.'

She was flattered. 'It's only just started.' She handed him his glass and picked up her own. 'Cheers.'

'Cheers.'

They both took a sip. There was no warning. He said abruptly, taking her entirely by surprise, 'I suppose you wouldn't consider marrying me?'

She was dumb with shock.

'Oh, I'm sorry,' he said quickly, 'I didn't mean to spring it on you like that, I've spent weeks planning how to lead up to it gradually, but when I'm actually with you...'

'Francis, I –'

'Look, don't say anything now, you're bound to refuse if you answer in a hurry, and I couldn't bear that. Take your time and think it over and give me your decision at the end of the holiday.'

She felt quite dazed and yet at the same time stupid not to have seen this coming.

'Look,' he said again, 'I know I'm a fair bit older than you and I'm not as ... dynamic as your ex-husband' (did he hate Robbie? she wondered), 'but I do have a good salary and an adequate pension to look forward to, I could make you very comfortable and ... you're very dear to me.'

That made her want to cry.

'These last two or three years,' he went on, 'well, I've just lived for your visits. And I haven't forgotten you're a Catholic, but there must be a way round that. I – I suppose I must have been afraid I wouldn't ask you at all, if I put it off.' He paused and looked at her very directly. 'Look, I can't speak for you, but I don't like living alone.'

She thought about it. She thought about nothing else. She was still thinking about it when Robbie came, two days before Christmas, to discuss the holiday arrangements.

'I don't know what to say about Christmas,' he said distractedly. 'She's supposed to be going to New York tomorrow, but now she's got this crazy idea about us separating when she comes back and I need time to talk her out of it.'

Why now? Jean thought. All these years she'd waited and hoped in vain to hear that word *separating*. Why now, when she'd almost given up, when she had a chance of something else?

'If I can persuade her not to go away for Christmas,' he went on, 'then I'll be pretty tied up; but if she goes I could come and see you any time till she gets back. Any time that suits you, I mean, of course.'

Jamie came in at that moment. 'Don't do us any favours.'

'I didn't know you'd taken to listening at keyholes,' Jean snapped at him, her nerves raw.

'We've got Mr Hammond visiting us for Christmas,' he told Robbie proudly, 'so we don't have a lot of time for you.'

'Jamie.' It was more than she could take. 'If you can't be civil to your father, you can go out.'

He went. Silence. She was trembling.

'Mr Hammond?' Robbie said.

'He's staying with his sister in Surrey. It seemed only polite to ask him to a meal. Don't take any notice of Jamie.'

They tried to talk of other things but they were both too tense, absorbing each other's news. He looked terrible, she thought, exhausted. Was that woman really going to leave him after all these years? And what about the child? Jean's mind raced ahead.

At the door, as he was leaving, he suddenly said, 'Is Hammond serious about you?' as if he had the right to know.

'He's asked me to marry him.' Strange how the truth could sound like a lie wantonly invented, a piece of coquetry.

'What did you say?'

Oh God, was he actually jealous? 'Nothing. I had to have time to think.'

'You deserve to be happy,' he said after a long pause. 'He's a good man.'

'Do you really think you're going to separate?' That seemed to be suddenly all that mattered.

'Oh no, not like that, just live apart, maybe next door. I don't know.' He looked oddly as if he were back on a building site, bracing himself to lift a heavy weight. 'She's a great one for her freedom. But I'll talk her round.'

1966

Diana

Deciding to go back wasn't easy, but I had pressing reasons for it. In the end it seemed simpler and more fun just to turn up: I did not want to be warned I was unwelcome, nor did I want a special display put on for me. I don't know what I expected as I rang the bell: Mack or another woman or Nanny. I waited, but no one came, so I rang again. Still no one came. It was late evening and it hadn't occurred to me the house might be empty. I got out the keys I hadn't used for two and a half years.

Once inside the house I had a frightful shock. All the furniture was covered in dust sheets. I went from room to room, unable to believe what I saw, and everything reinforced the impression of disuse. Why was nobody living here? Why hadn't someone warned me what a state my lovely house was in? It was dreadful, like coming home to find a relative you loved and believed to be healthy was in fact suffering from a terminal illness.

I'd got as far as the drawing-room and was beginning to feel anger as well as distress when I heard a car draw up outside. I glanced through the window and saw Mack: my heart lurched a bit and I dodged back quickly before he saw me. He came into the house at once: I heard the door slam and the familiar voice calling, 'Who's there?' in a threatening tone that I knew well. I felt myself beginning to smile as I imagined him getting ready to knock hell out of an intruder. 'Surprise,' I said, just before he reached the top of the spiral staircase.

His face was wonderful to see: utter amazement that turned quickly into joy. I tried not to notice how shaken I felt: it was like meeting him all over again for the first time, my brown gorilla at Ruth's party ten years ago.

'It's like a morgue in here,' I said lightly. 'What *have* you been doing?'

I saw his face begin to shut down, assume the old look of mistrust. 'Living next door.'

'Why?'

'It seemed easier.'

Suddenly all I could think of was the waste. 'But you could have let it. I thought you were still here, otherwise *I'd* have let it.'

'Why didn't you tell me you were coming?'

'You might have told me not to.' But it sounded inadequate; I wanted to change the subject. 'How is everyone?'

He looked sober and burdened now, as if I had asked the wrong question. 'Nanny's gone. Her sister had a stroke. Adrienne's staying with the Isaacs.'

'So we're all alone.' I wanted to cheer him up. 'A plague on both your houses.' But it came out sounding merely nervous. 'Sorry, that was a bad joke.'

Silence, while he stared at me. I had never felt myself so minutely examined before. 'You look wonderful.'

'Just older.'

'No, more ... established somehow.' He hesitated. 'I can't explain.'

'It's my new high gloss finish, to go with New York. My business woman image.'

'How's it going?'

'Very well, at last. It was tough starting. I've been working my tail off, as they so quaintly put it.' I wanted to make it sound amusing for him. 'I must say, I look at my agent with new respect these days. I'd no idea it was such hard work.'

More silence. We were both very tense.

'I've missed you,' he said.

'I've missed you too, darling. You look a bit haggard, actually – been living it up?' He looked more than haggard; he looked ill. But attractively ill. I was amazed how attractive he looked.

'Not exactly.'

'Neither have I, there hasn't been time.' That wasn't strictly true, but never mind. 'Well. We must stop meeting like this.'

He said as if it had only just entered his mind, 'Would you like to come next door for a drink?'

'Yes, I would, it's terribly gloomy in here.' And I thought you'd never ask, I nearly added, picking up my bag and going downstairs before he could change his mind. He was slow to turn out the lights and follow me, so I had another look at the kitchen and dining-room. They felt so desolate, it was really depressing. When he joined me in the hall I said, 'Poor old house. What a shame. It looks so unloved.'

He put out the hall light and we gazed at each other in the gloom, then suddenly embraced. After that it was easy.

We had a wonderful night. We didn't talk very much, just made love and slept and made love again. It was like old times, back at the beginning, before we had any problems. I felt such goodwill and freedom.

In the morning I said, 'Now that's what I call a warm welcome,' and we laughed and hugged each other closer. 'You *are* lovely. I'd forgotten how lovely you are.'

'I hadn't forgotten anything about you,' he said, studying me. 'How you look, how you feel, how you taste, how you come ...'

'Don't get me excited again. I simply haven't the energy.'

'Are you sure?'

I smiled. 'God, I'm worn out. What with the flight and visiting Mummy and now all this ...'

'Was it worth it?' He was teasing me, sure of his ground.

'Oh yes. You could say that. Don't you think so?'

'I'd call it good value myself.' He kissed me and we giggled like children. 'I'll make some coffee.'

'Oh, that would be nice. It might just pull me together.' I watched him climb out of bed and put on a dressing-gown, one of several, while I lay there, yawning, and looking round the room. 'You haven't done much to the house.'

'It's only been somewhere to eat and sleep.'

Now, was that the first note of reproach? Before I could investigate, we heard the front door open and close two floors below.

'Visitors,' I said, intrigued.

'It must be Lisa bringing Adrienne back. I'll go down. Prepare the ground.'

He went, looking positively eager. I stayed in bed, listening to the childish footsteps running up the stairs from hall to drawing-room, and began to wonder what I had got myself into.

I listened to the voices below for a while. Then I got up and put on a dressing-gown and some scent and brushed my hair, but not too much, noticing I looked rather attractively dishevelled. Then I went downstairs.

The child noticed me first. She was sitting on Mack's knee and she stared at me with fascination till I felt almost embarrassed. Lisa was watching me closely too, and I could feel her hostility right across the room.

Adrienne said to Mack, after a long stare, 'Is she my Mummy?'

'That's right.' He was delighted.

'What a good memory she has,' Lisa said. 'For her age, I mean.'

I smiled at her. 'You've grown up quite a lot, haven't you, Lisa? I believe you've been helping out. That was very kind of you – we do appreciate it.'

'It was a pleasure.'

'I expect it was.'

'Mummy,' said Adrienne in wonderment, still staring at me. She had improved a lot: I was quite impressed.

'My goodness, you're a big girl now, aren't you?' I said, going over to her. 'And very pretty.' As I leaned towards her, my hair fell forward and she slowly reached out and touched it.

'Well, I'll be off now,' Lisa said sharply. 'I'll pick her up Monday morning early – that is, if you still want me to.'

Mack looked bemused. 'What? Oh yes, thank you, Lisa – that is, I'll ring if there's a change of plan.'

'Right.' She hesitated. 'Bye.'

'Goodbye, Lisa,' I said firmly. 'Have fun.'

She ignored me. 'Bye, Adrienne.'

But Adrienne was busy stroking me and didn't answer.

When Lisa had gone, Mack amused Adrienne while I got dressed and did my face. Then he went to make coffee and I tried to read the paper while she climbed on my lap. I felt utter confusion at seeing her: the mixture of Mack and me in her face was simply too much. It was amazing to think we were responsible for her existence. When he came back with a tray of coffee for us and milk for her, I said almost in a panic, 'That looks wonderful. Could you take her, darling? She's awfully heavy.'

He lifted her off my lap. She went reluctantly. 'Come on, now, let Mummy have her coffee in peace. There'll be plenty of time for a cuddle later on.'

'Oh, don't tell her that, darling. I've got to go in a minute.'

'Go?' He was holding Adrienne on his knee while she drank her milk, and he looked at me as if astonished.

'I've got business meetings all day,' I said. 'Look, we really must talk about the house.'

'Yes, you're right. I've been thinking about that. Let's try it your way this time. I was maybe too stubborn before. Let's have half each and visit the way you wanted.' He looked at me hopefully.

'Are we at cross-purposes? I want to sell my half. I was going to ask if you minded.'

'No, of course I don't mind, it's yours to do what you like with, but it won't leave us very much space.'

I wasn't sure what he meant. 'But you haven't been using my half all this time and I really need the money so I can buy a place in New York.'

Silence. He looked really shocked. 'You're not staying.'

'No, of course I'm not. What on earth made you think I was?'

'Maybe last night had something to do with it.'

'Oh, darling. That was for auld lang syne.' I simply refused to let him make me feel guilty. There was no time for all

271

that. 'Look, I must go, I'm going to be late and you know how I hate that. I'll ring you about the house, okay? When you've had time to think.'

I got up, but he put Adrienne down and followed me. 'You're not going anywhere.'

I began to feel crowded. 'I'm leaving, Mack. Now get out of my way.'

'Bitch.' He grabbed me round the throat with both hands as I tried to pass him on the stairs. I'd forgotten how strong he was. The hands I used to love for being so sexy and well used seemed now to be squeezing the life out of me. I was frightened. I punched and kicked as hard as I could, but I could feel myself passing out, see everything going red and black before my eyes. Then suddenly the child was between us, yelling, 'Mummy, Mummy.'

My father was wonderful as ever. I curled up on the sofa beside him and we held hands while I told him all about it.

'It was awful. I thought he was going to strangle me. But the child made so much noise he suddenly let go. I've got ridiculous marks on my neck, like something in a movie.' I was rather proud of them, though not at all proud of my moment of terror and my undignified exit.

'Why didn't you tell him at once you were not going to stay?'

'It honestly never occurred to me he'd think I was.'

My father smiled. 'When people say "honestly" with such conviction, I generally find they are lying.' But he sounded tolerant.

'Well ... I did mean to tell him straight away, but we got talking and he looked so attractive ... I just wanted to make love again.' Surely he would understand that. 'And I thought it might put him off if I said, "Look, I'm only back for a week and I want to sell the house," just like that.'

My father said indulgently, 'You're impossible.'

'I must take after you. You're not angry with me?'

'I could never be angry with you, Kisleanyom. But you stayed away too long.'

I tried to be honest. 'Well, there was all that business about your will. I was terribly angry about that.'

'D'you want me to change it?'

'No, it doesn't matter any more. And after that I was so busy working, I wanted to prove I could do it. If I'd seen you, well, you'd only have offered me money and I might have taken it. You know how weak I am.'

He laughed and kissed my hand. 'Well, you must come back more often now you are rich and successful. I'm just an old man and I'm tired of flying the Atlantic.'

'You do go on about being old.' It worried me a bit, when I paused to think about it. 'You're not ill, are you?'

'Of course I'm not ill. The doctors say I will make medical history by being the oldest hypochondriac in the country.'

'It's not enough to be Hungarian. You must also live for ever.' I leaned my head on his shoulder. 'Please live for ever, Apukam.'

And then it was time to go back to New York.

Jean

Over the years, as Robbie's visits became less frequent, she grew to depend on Francis Hammond. She even promised to marry him if and when she could get an annulment, though even using the word made her feel fraudulent. Meanwhile they devised a vaguely sexual relationship which left them both unfulfilled but made Jean feel guilty enough to go to Confession from time to time. Like most compromises, it satisfied neither of them, but it still seemed the least and the most she could do in the circumstances. Most of the time, however, they were more comfortable together sharing meals and watching television like an old married couple.

'Well, time I was off, I suppose,' he said one evening, as he always did, tightening his arm round her while he attempted to peer at his watch.

'Already?' She liked the undemanding arm round her shoulders, the undemanding television programme, the feeling of being with someone, a couple again, normal. 'Oh, stay till Jamie gets back. He'd like to see you.'

'Bit late, isn't he?'

'Well, he's got to take Lisa home.'

Jamie and Lisa had been visiting Cambridge for the day so that Lisa could see Jamie's college.

'Is it serious, d'you think?'

'Heavens, no, they're much too young.'

'You were only twenty when you got married.'

She wondered why he should want to remind her of that.

'And we still haven't fixed a date,' he said later, pouring himself a final drink and giving her one.

'No.'

'We really can't leave it much longer. Look, lovey, if the annulment doesn't come through soon, we'll just have to go ahead without it. I mean, we can't wait indefinitely.'

'I know.' If she didn't marry him soon, one of these days he would go away and there would be no arm around her, no one to call her lovey. 'You've been very patient.'

'Don't look so worried.' He smiled at her encouragingly. 'If we have a civil wedding now, we can always have a Catholic one later on, just as soon as you get your bit of paper.'

Mercifully, at that moment, she heard the front door. 'Oh, there's Jamie now,' she said with relief.

Francis put down his drink and turned off the television as Jamie came in. They greeted each other warmly, casually, like the old friends they almost were by now. For a moment she felt excluded.

'Did you have a nice time?' she asked Jamie.

'It was all right.'

'Was Lisa impressed?'

'Oh aye, she thought it was all fantastic.'

He sounded so bitter that they both looked at him curiously, with concern.

Francis said, 'Is there anything wrong?'

'No.' Jamie had on Robbie's brooding look. 'But you may as well know right away – I've decided not to go there.'

They were shocked and amazed, not sure they had heard correctly. Then they both spoke at once.

'What?'

'Now look here –'

'It's all right,' Jamie said, 'really it is. I've just changed my mind, that's all.'

'About *Cambridge*?' Jean felt as if he had suddenly gone mad.

'Yes.'

'But you were always so set on it . . .'

'No, *you* were. You and Dad. And you, sir,' he added, turning to Francis. 'So I thought I was too. I didn't really have a choice. Anyway, it was a challenge, seeing if I could get in.'

Francis began to sound like a headmaster again. 'Jamie, this isn't the kind of opportunity you turn down lightly, you know.'

'No, I realize that. I've been thinking about it for months. Ever since my interview really. Today was just the last straw.'

'Whatever happened?' Jean asked.

'Nothing. Absolutely nothing. I just decided it's not the place for me. I don't feel at home there.' He looked almost pleased with himself at this discovery.

'I don't think that's quite the point,' Francis said. 'You've got your whole future to think of –'

'That's exactly what I *am* thinking of, sir.'

'But, Jamie, how can you throw away a chance like this?' Jean couldn't bear it. 'You worked so hard for it. You were so pleased when you got in . . .'

'Look, Mam, I don't want to spend three years messing about, that's all. I want to start working and earning money right away, not being dependent on Dad and mixing with a lot of stuffed shirts. I can get all the qualifications I need at night school and be learning a trade during the day.'

Francis said, 'Your father's not going to like this.'

Jean had never seen Robbie so angry. The kitchen seemed too small to contain his rage. She wanted to hide in a corner while he shouted at Jamie.

'You must be out of your bloody mind.'

'Then it's just as well I'm not going. They probably wouldn't take me anyway.'

Robbie banged his fist on the table. 'Don't you get clever with me. I've spent a lot of money on your education and I'm not having it all thrown away just when it's starting to pay off.'

'Who needs it? You didn't go to Cambridge, did you, or bloody public school? You started work at fourteen and you seem to have done all right.'

'Aye, and I've worked hard for it. All the more reason for you to do better with all the advantages I've given you.'

'What advantages? Going to a posh school? You had

your reasons for sending me there, and Duncan too, or have you forgotten about him? You were glad to see the back of us for reasons of your own and they didn't have much to do with education.'

'That's enough,' Robbie said. 'Now look here, laddie. You've got a place at Cambridge, you're bloody lucky to have it, and you're going to take it up. Now that's all I've got to say on the matter.'

'I'm sorry, Dad. I'm not going.'

'Jamie, please. Your father's right.'

Jamie looked at her pityingly. 'You always stick up for him. I wonder you aren't sick of it by now.'

Robbie rose to the bait. 'By God, I've been too soft with you. It's a pity I didna take my belt to you when you were a lad.'

'Yes, you'd have enjoyed that, wouldn't you? Well, it's too late now. You lay a hand on me and I'll take you apart.'

'Oh aye, you and who else?'

They were so absurdly alike as they squared up to each other that in another mood she might have laughed, but she was too tense to be amused. 'For God's sake, you two, I'm ashamed of you. Have you both gone raving mad?'

Silence. They looked embarrassed.

'I'll make a cup of tea.' She put the kettle on while they fidgeted and shuffled their feet and avoided looking at each other.

'So, you're not going to Cambridge,' Robbie said at last in the grim, contemptuous tone that signalled defeat. 'You're going to throw away the chance of a lifetime and I canna stop you. Well, don't you imagine I'm going to keep you in idleness while you strum that guitar of yours or any nonsense like that.'

Jamie said coolly, 'I rather thought you might give me a job.'

'What?'

'Why not? Sons often go into the family business, don't they? I could be very useful to you.'

'Oh really? Doing what?'

Jamie ignored the sneer. 'Something in your finance department, I think. You've got a lot of fuddy-duddies in there, I noticed the last time I was in the office. And that old guy in charge of it all, what's his name –'

'Are you talking about my chief accountant?'

'That's right. Mr Hunt, is it? Well, he's okay and all that, I'm sure he was all right in his day, but I bet you I could show him how to cut a few corners. Just put me in there to learn the ropes and have a good look round, and in three months I'll have a plan to ginger the whole place up and save you a packet.'

There was an ominous pause before Robbie said, 'You've got no qualifications.'

'Oh, come on, Dad. If I was good enough to read Maths at Cambridge, I'm good enough to work in your finance department. They didn't all go to university, those guys. I was chatting them up the last time I was in and they told me. You can do all that at evening classes. What really counts is practical experience.'

The kettle screamed. Jean made the tea.

'I'll tell you what I'll do,' Robbie said, and she knew from his voice there was no hope of peace. 'Since you're so keen on practical experience, I'll give you a job on one of my building sites. You can be a tea-boy. You can learn how to hump bricks and mix cement and put window frames together. You can start at the bottom and work your way up, *if* you're good enough. That's what people with no qualifications have to do.'

Silence. She could tell from the stiff way Jamie answered exactly how hurt he was. 'I think I'm worth a bit more than that.'

'Not to me, you're not. You're still wet behind the ears. You've never done a day's work in your life. That's not your fault, but it's a fact. Now, turning down Cambridge is another matter. That *is* your fault. And if you do that, you're worth no more to me than any other lad off the street.'

They were both so stubborn, Jean hardly knew if she wanted to hug them or bang their heads together.

'Right,' Jamie said. 'Then at least I know where I stand.

You can stuff your job.' He slammed out of the house and roared off in his car.

Robbie stayed to supper, but they were both miserable and hardly able to eat. He picked at his food and finally pushed it away. 'I'm sorry, hen. I've lost my appetite. That business with Jamie – well, it just makes me sick to my stomach.'

'I'll try and talk him round. Make him see sense.'

He looked relieved. 'You do agree with me?'

'Yes, of course. It's a wonderful opportunity. We can't let him throw it away.'

'I'd have given my eye-teeth for a chance like that when I was his age. And he just doesn't care. I suppose it's my fault. He's had everything too easy.'

'He'll maybe come round,' she said soothingly, not believing it. 'If we play our cards right.'

'Aye. I should never have lost my temper.'

'Well, he was very provoking.' She struggled to finish her steak.

'Have you fixed the wedding date yet?'

Now, why should he suddenly want to know that? 'No, but nearly.'

'You know I wish you well, don't you? Both of you.'

'Yes.' She hesitated. There was something faintly obscene about the conversation, she felt. 'Thank you.'

'You've had a rough time. I don't know how you've stuck it all these years. He's a good man, you should be very happy.'

She didn't know how to answer that. 'I think so.'

After supper he drank too much whisky while she sat and watched him. The evening seemed to grow sadder and sadder. There was so much of the past in the room with them.

'Where are you going to live?'

'Well – at the school during term-time, of course. Now that Jamie's left, it won't be so embarrassing; that's one of the reasons we waited. And we thought we'd buy a small place on the south coast for the holidays. We'd both like to be near the sea.'

'It sounds ideal.' He was still being polite; then he suddenly stunned her with a question. 'Have you got the annulment?'

'No, not yet.'

'I never thought I'd see you going against your Church.'

She felt he was attacking her; she felt guilty, indignant and shamed all at once. How dare he judge her? But how dare she pretend their marriage had never existed?

'No – well – it's not an easy decision. But we *have* waited a long time – and it's something we can always put right later.'

'Oh, I'm not blaming you. I think you're absolutely right.' Silence.

'I'm only sorry it's happening just now,' she said, 'when *she's* not with you.' Was this a safe topic? 'D'you ever hear from her?'

'No.' He poured more whisky. 'Oh, I know she's in New York, and she's running a model agency. But she hasn't been in touch, she takes no interest in the child – well, she never did.' He emptied the glass in one movement. 'It's over. It's been over for years, but I wouldn't admit it.'

How long was it that she had longed and prayed to hear that? Yet now she could feel no satisfaction, only sympathy for his pain. 'I'm sorry. You loved her very much.'

'Och, it serves me right.'

He drank more and more, and began to drowse. She watched him anxiously.

'Robbie. Are you all right?'

'Aye. Just tired.'

'How about some coffee?'

'I'm not drunk, if that's what you're thinking.' But he was, and they both knew it. 'It's just that I don't want to go home. It's not a home any more, now she's not there. It's just a house with me and the child and the nanny in it. But I'm all alone there, Jeannie.'

And no more is this a home without you, she wanted to say but couldn't.

'It's like a judgement on me,' he went on presently. 'I should never have left you and that's all there is to it.'

She watched him fall asleep in the chair. His words went round and round in her head, making Francis recede like a figure in a distantly remembered film. She tried to hang on to her common sense, but hope was stronger.

By morning she had convinced herself there was a real chance of a reunion with Robbie. It seemed like fate. That must be why she had postponed her wedding so long. Robbie had been too drunk and exhausted when he left for her to ask him outright, but she would, as soon as possible, or more likely he would contact her. After all, he must know how she felt. Her feelings had never really changed.

She slept badly but woke up very cheerful. When breakfast was ready she shouted upstairs to Jamie, through a blast of flamenco, that his food was on the table and went back into the kitchen to finish her coffee. He clattered downstairs, still wearing his dressing-gown, and looked appreciatively at the plate of bacon, eggs, sausage and tomato.

'That looks great.'

'I hope it's not cold.'

He watched her adjusting her nurse's uniform and said with his mouth full, 'Mam, have you thought about bridesmaids at all?'

She was startled. 'What?'

'Only I was thinking – you like Lisa, don't you – and I know she's going to be upset about me not going to Cambridge, she'd set her heart on the May Ball and all that rubbish. So I thought it might cheer her up if you asked her to be a bridesmaid at your wedding.'

Jean turned round from the mirror, shocked, but he didn't see; he was too busy eating.

'Well, all this Jewish–Catholic nonsense won't matter in a registry office, will it? And Lisa loves dressing up. I know it's silly but I think she'd like it, that's all. You wouldn't mind, would you?' He looked up confidently.

'Jamie, I can't talk about this now, I'll be late for work.'

'What's the matter?'

'I don't have time to go into it all just now.'

'What's there to go into?' He began to be angry, like his father, at not getting his own way at once. 'You either want Lisa for a bridesmaid or you don't. You can't be narrow-minded like her mother, you just can't. I know you're not.'

She said reluctantly, 'Jamie, I'm sorry, but I can't have Lisa as a bridesmaid.'

'Why not? What's wrong with her?'

'Nothing, nothing.'

'You like her, I know you do.'

'Yes, I like her.' She took a deep breath. 'Only I'm not getting married.'

'What?' He looked as shocked as she must have done when he announced he was not going to Cambridge.

'I'm sorry.' It was not how she had planned to tell him, but he had left her no choice.

'But the Organ,' he burst out, so that she didn't know whether to laugh or cry. 'He loves you. He's been waiting and hoping all this time. You promised. Mam, you gave him your word.'

'I'm sorry, Jamie. I've changed my mind, that's all.'

'But you can't. It's too late for that.'

'No.' She thanked God that it wasn't.

He said savagely, with such hatred that she was frightened, 'It's Dad, isn't it? Christ, I could kill him. What's he been saying to you?'

Telling Francis was more difficult because it was not forced upon her: she had to create the opportunity. She decided to do it on their next evening out rather than at home, so that she could walk away if need be, rather than wait for him to leave. She also thought he would be less likely to make a scene in public. Not that she was expecting a scene, but it did no harm to narrow the odds still further. This amount of calculation, however, was so foreign to her nature that by the time they reached their usual restaurant her throat was so constricted with terror that she could hardly swallow.

Francis ate heartily and talked a lot. She could scarcely

take in what he was saying, she was so busy planning her own speech.

'Suppose we make it the third week in August,' he went on. 'Then we'll still have plenty of time for a proper honeymoon before term begins. Will that give you long enough for shopping?'

A moment's hesitation, but her nerve failed her. 'I don't know.' The indecision made her heart race painfully.

'All right, then, the last week in August and that's my final offer.' He peered through the candlelight at her stricken face. 'Come on, cheer up, it's a wedding, not a funeral.'

'I'm sorry.'

'My sister wants to give a party for us, did I tell you?' Suddenly he noticed her plate. 'Hey, you're not eating. You hardly touched your prawn cocktail and now you're letting your chicken get cold. There's nothing wrong with it, is there? This place is usually so reliable.'

It was like him, she thought, to describe a romantic, candle-lit Italian restaurant as reliable. She needed a flash of irritation, however tiny, to spur her on. He had always behaved so correctly.

'I can't go through with it,' she said rapidly before she lost her nerve again. 'I'm sorry, Francis, I can't marry you. I've been trying to tell you all evening but I couldn't get up my courage.'

There was a ghastly silence. She stared at her plate, unable to face him.

'This isn't a joke?' he said at last. 'No, I can see it's not. Well. I don't know what to say.'

'I can't tell you how sorry I am.'

They had both put their knives and forks down by now. A zealous Italian waiter dashed up to their table.

'Is everything all right, sir?'

'Yes,' Francis said, 'everything's perfect, thank you.'

'Thank you, sir.' The waiter bounced away. They were alone again in their suffocating silence.

'Is it the annulment?' Francis asked gently. 'Because I don't mind waiting a bit longer if it really bothers you.'

'No, I – I've written to say I don't want to go on trying for that.'

'Why?'

She tried to be honest. 'I think – even if I got it, I wouldn't believe it. I don't really want a decision, I'd rather leave it as it is. I think I knew all the time I was trying to cheat.'

Suddenly, as if enraged by her last word, or perhaps because he had had time to absorb the hurt and disappointment, he became angry. She had never seen him angry before. Theirs had been a very peaceful relationship.

'You're still hung up on him, aren't you?' he said loudly. 'That bloody ex-husband of yours. Christ, you've made a fine fool of me, stringing me along for three years, making me behave like a schoolboy.'

She admired his anger and thought it justified, but it scared her all the same. Even so, she wished he had shown it before: she might have seen him differently.

'Please don't shout, please,' she said.

'Shout? I'll raise the roof if I like. My God, you've taken me for a ride. And all the time you were stuck on your ex-husband. Maybe if I'd treated you as badly as he did, you'd have been stuck on me.'

Other diners were looking at them by now. 'I hope we can still be friends,' she said inadequately, suddenly afraid Robbie didn't want her back after all and the sacrifice was for nothing, or rather only to please God, who was even more remote than Robbie.

'Friends? What else have we ever been? Is that supposed to be some sort of long service medal you give men who are stupid enough to think you mean what you say?'

Jean got up and struggled into her coat. The whole restaurant was watching, fascinated. Francis flung a handful of fivers on the table and rushed after her as she ran out through a group of excited waiters.

In the street she found she was crying. She hadn't realized she'd be so upset. She was looking round blindly for a taxi when Francis caught up with her.

'You don't get away from me as easily as that.'

'Don't go on, please.' She was now hideously embarrassed by the entire scene.

'I'm sorry. I didn't mean what I said.' He was breathing hard, trying to calm himself. 'It was such a shock. Please. We've got to talk about it calmly –' And he took her by the arm.

At the same moment Jean saw a cruising taxi and hailed it. Francis shook her. The taxi stopped alongside them.

'Please help me,' Jean said.

'You having trouble, love?'

Francis let go of her arm.

'No,' she said, weeping. 'We're saying goodbye.'

'Jean, please –' Francis said. But she got into the taxi and it drove off, leaving him looking so lost and miserable on the pavement that when she looked out of the back window and saw him, she cried all the more with guilt and remorse, as if she had truly loved him. But she was also crying with relief.

'Some people don't know when to leave off, do they?' the cabbie said, after a decent interval. 'Now, where we going?'

In the days and weeks that followed she realized that Robbie was not going to seek a reconciliation, and it became increasingly impossible for her to approach him on the subject. She had, after all, made her sacrifice for God alone; or in earthly terms, merely exchanged imperfect reality for a mirage of love.

Lisa

July

At last! Jamie took me to Cambridge for the day. It was even better than I'd imagined. He's so lucky to be going there. It's full of lovely buildings and it's very peaceful and sort of unreal. We wandered about holding hands and looking at everything, and I tried to pretend I was going there too. I went on about how beautiful it was till Jamie got fed up with me. That's my trouble. I always overdo everything.

He said, 'What, the dreaming spires and all that rubbish?' in a funny sneering voice.

I said, 'Idiot. That's Oxford.'

He said it was all the same to him, but I don't believe him. He must be thrilled about it. He couldn't not be. Only he likes to make out he's too grown-up to get excited. He kept teasing me as if I was a little girl because I want to go to the May Ball, so I told him about Judy and her boyfriend at Peterhouse, and how they used to spend weekends sporting the oak till her parents found out and made her give him up because he's not Jewish. I was just showing off but I wished I hadn't, because he said immediately, 'D'you think your parents will make you stop seeing me?' He's really worried about that. So I explained how Mummy's a bit old-fashioned but I can always get round Daddy, and anyway he's on our side.

Then we went to look at the college Jamie is actually going to be at. It was so lovely, I said, 'Jamie, you *are* lucky, I wish I could be here,' and he laughed and said I'd be a sensation. I wanted us to go in but he wouldn't. He said a funny thing: 'We're bound to run into some old retainer babbling on about his young gentlemen.' I couldn't see what was wrong with that, but he said he'd had enough of it at his interview. 'They're so bloody obsequious,' he said. 'As if you were better than they are, only they don't mind because it's an act of God.' Then somebody on a bicycle nearly ran into us. He looked so funny with his gown flying behind him, I laughed, but Jamie was furious. He shouted at him, 'Hey, why don't you look where you're going?' and the man said sorry and pedalled off. Jamie said, 'Bloody fool. What's he doing here anyway? I thought they'd all gone down for their long vac by now.' He sounded full of scorn. I said I thought the man was probably a postgraduate and Jamie said, 'Bloody chinless wonder. Fancy staying on here when he could get a job. You'd think three years would be enough for anyone.'

I was upset because he was spoiling our day and I'd looked forward to it, so I said, 'What's the matter with you? You're in a rotten mood,' but he didn't answer properly. He wanted to go home early, but I persuaded him to take me in a punt and after that it was better. I think he's upset about his mother going to marry his ex-headmaster, but when I ask him about it he just says how pleased he is and how he wishes she'd done it before.

It's not easy being in love. On the way home we parked the car and we were kissing and everything and then Jamie tried to go too far. After he'd promised he wouldn't. It's difficult enough wanting to, anyway; sometimes I get such an ache, I don't need him trying to persuade me as well, when he knows we can't, not yet. It just makes it worse. I tried to explain and I said I was sorry, but he was furious and drove off terribly fast. So it was a funny sort of day really. Lovely to see Cambridge, but sad we weren't getting on better.

I can't believe it. Jamie's decided not to go to Cambridge! He really means it. He's had a terrible row with his parents and persuaded Daddy to give him a job. Mummy's very cross because she thinks it will make bad feeling between our two families. I do wish he'd talked to me first. I'm sure he's doing the wrong thing. How can *anyone* want to give up Cambridge? I'm not surprised his parents are furious with him. He could always have gone to work for Daddy after Cambridge, if he still wanted to.

He didn't say a word to me about it, didn't even ring up, just told his parents and came round and saw Daddy while I was out at Youth Club. The first I knew of it was when I got home and my parents told me. I felt so silly not knowing, when we're meant to be going steady, that I pretended he'd told me he was having doubts, but I don't think Mummy believed me.

It's been a dreadful week, full of shocks. Jamie's mother isn't getting married after all. Jamie was so upset when I saw him, I simply couldn't be cross with him about Cambridge although I'd meant to be. I was quite wrong to think he didn't want her to get married again – I suppose I was thinking of my parents and how I'd feel if they did something like that, only of course they wouldn't – he really was pleased about her and Mr Hammond and now it's all off. I remember they came to dinner with my parents two years ago when Jamie and I first went out together, although it was only to that party down the road and not like being alone. But still, that shows it's been going on a long time.

Jamie says his mother is still hoping his father might come back to her. I didn't know what to say. After all, it's six years since he left. That's an awfully long time. Why should she think he might come back? And if she did, how could she get engaged to someone else? But I have to be careful what I say about Jamie's mother, he's so fond of her. She's all right, I quite like her – I don't see her very often really – but he goes on about her as if she's perfect and his father is just awful. It can't be as simple as that. And what about Diana? Suppose she comes back from New York? *Then* what would happen? But no one ever talks about Diana so I can't find out.

August

We'd been playing tennis and when Jamie brought me home he asked me to go dancing tomorrow. I said I wasn't sure if we were going to the cottage for the weekend and I'd ring him, or he could come in and ask Mummy now, but he suddenly noticed his father's car parked outside our house, so he wouldn't come in because his father would only want to know how the job was going. I said '*I'd* quite like to know how it's going,' and he went into a great list in a sing-song voice: 'I know how to work the copying machine. I know how to work the duplicating machine. I make the best cup of tea in the place. I'm even very good at holding the end of a tape for measurements.'

I said, 'I suppose it's bound to be like that at the beginning.' I meant to be soothing.

He said, 'I never get to do any negotiating because none of the clients know my name. And they never will until I do some negotiating. It's a bloody vicious circle.' He sounded quite savage. 'Sometimes I get the feeling I'll have to wait for someone to die before I can even answer the telephone. The switchboard put all the calls through to the old people. There's got to be a way round that.'

He drove off and I went in, shouting to Mummy about the cottage. Then I noticed she wasn't alone. She had Jamie's father with her. I'd forgotten about his car outside because of talking to Jamie about the job, so I got quite a shock. I hadn't seen him for ages and I hadn't remembered him properly. He looked younger than I remembered, well, not *young*, of course, but not like somebody's father either, and certainly not like Jamie's father. Jamie was always describing him as such a monster. But he looked nice and kind and terribly sad, as if something dreadful had happened to him and he was waiting for someone to put it right.

Mummy said, 'You remember Jamie's father, don't you, darling?'

I said, 'Yes, of course. You used to come and see us a lot and then you stopped.' I was trying to remember how long ago it was. Certainly several years. Maybe five or six. I must have been quite little.

He said, 'Hullo, Lisa,' as if I was important. 'You're quite grown-up now.' He has the most lovely Scottish accent that makes you feel warm. I don't know why Jamie wanted to get rid of an accent like that, but he has.

I said, 'Yes, I'm leaving school next year,' and Mummy said, 'Only if you pass your exams,' so I made a face at her, and then I could have kicked myself for being so childish.

He said, 'I'm sorry you couldn't persuade Jamie to go to Cambridge.'

'I did try, but he wouldn't listen. Isn't he silly?' Then I felt terribly disloyal to Jamie. I did think he was silly not to go to Cambridge, but I shouldn't have said so. It was like ganging up with his father against him. Then I noticed a child of about six in our garden. She wasn't playing with the puppy as you would expect. She was pulling the heads off Mummy's precious flowers and stamping on them. I went out to see if I could distract her attention.

It's all settled. I'm going to look after his daughter till the end of the holidays. Her nanny's retired and she's missing her, so he doesn't want to get a new one straight away. She's going to stay with us Mondays to Fridays and I'm going to take her back to him for weekends. I've even got a key to the house, so we can go and fetch things if we need to during the week when he's at the office. She's a strange child. Very solemn. I suppose having your mother leave you when you were a baby would make you solemn. I've never really thought about it before. I'd like to make her laugh and play games like other children.

She came in my room this morning. I was ever so surprised. She must have been watching me asleep because when I opened my eyes, there she was. She said, 'When's

Nanny coming back?' and she sounded so sad. Maybe losing Nanny is as bad as losing her mother, in a way. Anyway, it's more recent and it probably feels like the last straw.

I said very gently, 'I don't know, darling. She's got to look after her sister. Her sister's not very well. D'you want a cuddle?' She nodded. 'Come on then, get in my bed.' She got in and I held her tight and rocked her. She felt very, very tense. She didn't relax at all. It must be awful to have people keep leaving you. I can't imagine Mummy going away ever, especially not when I was little.

I took her to the park and tried to make sure she had a good time, but I'm afraid I enjoyed it more than she did. Sometimes I think I'm not very grown-up. We went on swings and slides and roundabouts. She did everything I suggested, but she didn't smile once.

On a wet day I got her to do some drawing because I remembered how much I used to enjoy that when I couldn't go out. She got in a corner with her paper and kept her hand round it. Eventually I said, 'What are you drawing?'

'Mummy.'

I thought that might give me a clue how she was feeling. 'Can I see?'

'No.' She screwed up the paper and put it in her pocket.

I tried to talk to my mother about her. I asked if Diana was ever coming back.

'I shouldn't think so,' Mummy said.

'Will they get divorced?'

Mummy looked embarrassed. 'Well, they weren't actually married.'

I was amazed. Now why had no one ever told me that? Not even Jamie. I'd just assumed they were. People get divorced and they marry other people, especially if they have children. Was that why Jamie's mother had been hoping his father would come back to her, because he hadn't married Diana after all?

*

An awful weekend. So much has happened, I don't know where to start.

I took Adrienne back to her father early on Saturday because Jamie and I were going out for the day. As soon as she saw her father she lit up and told him what a lovely time she'd been having. I was amazed. He scooped her up and gave her a big hug. It was so nice to see them together. You can tell they're really fond of each other. And I was so pleased she'd enjoyed herself with me after all, even though she hadn't seemed to.

Then to my absolute horror he sat down with her on his knee and said, 'I've got a surprise for you. Somebody's come back. She's upstairs. Can you guess who it is?'

Adrienne got a funny look on her face, sort of hopeful but scared. She said, 'Nanny?'

He said, 'No, it's not Nanny,' and he looked very happy. 'Better than that. Who d'you most want to see? If you had a wish and you could magic that person here right now, who'd it be?'

I got the most dreadful, cold, sick, lurching feeling in my stomach. Then there was a movement on the staircase and of course it was Diana. I saw her just a second before Adrienne did. She was wearing a man's dressing-gown and no make-up and her hair was all over the place, but she still looked wonderful. I couldn't believe it. It was like a bad dream, as if I had conjured her up by talking to Mummy about her.

She said to Adrienne, 'Hullo, darling, d'you remember me?' and Adrienne asked her father, 'Is she my mummy?'

He was delighted with her. 'That's right.'

I said, 'What a good memory she has.' Then I thought I'd been really rude so I added, 'For her age, I mean,' to soften it a bit.

Diana said, 'You've grown up quite a lot, haven't you, Lisa,' and she looked at me appraisingly. Then she said they were both grateful to me for helping out. I said it was a pleasure and she said no doubt it was, with a nasty smile on her face. Adrienne kept staring at her and saying, 'Mummy,' as if she was magic. It really upset me.

Diana said, 'My goodness, you're a big girl now, aren't you? And very pretty.' You could tell she hadn't a clue how to talk to a child. But she went over to Adrienne, who was still sitting on her father's knee, and sort of bent over her.

Adrienne put out a hand and touched Diana's hair.

I said, 'Well, I'll be off now. I'll pick her up Monday morning early – that is, if you still want me to.'

He was looking sort of bemused. He said thank you and he'd let me know if there was a change of plan. I said goodbye but he didn't answer.

Diana said, 'Bye, Lisa. Have fun.'

I said goodbye to Adrienne but she didn't answer. She was actually stroking Diana now. I left them all looking like a happy family. Nobody noticed me go.

Of course I was in a foul mood after that and took it out on poor Jamie. But he didn't help much. I told him what had happened and he said thank God for that, I wouldn't have to look after that bloody child any more and now his mother might marry Mr Hammond after all. I was so furious I said, 'Can't you stop thinking about yourself for one minute? She went off and left that child. Just walked out. She's a rotten mother. Why should she expect to come back and pick up where she left off?' Of course after that we had a rotten weekend. Jamie was sulking and I couldn't stop thinking about Adrienne and Diana and Robert all together. It would have been better not to go out, but I didn't want my parents to know we'd had a row.

On Sunday evening I said I had to be back home for supper, so Jamie dropped me at the gate. My mother was cooking. She was surprised to see me home so soon when I'd been out late at the dance the night before. I usually stay out with Jamie as late as I'm allowed to. I said I wanted an early night because I had to fetch Adrienne first thing in the morning.

Mummy said, 'She's here. Robert brought her over. Apparently Diana's been and gone again. Adrienne was in a frightful state and he didn't know what to do with her.'

I don't know how I kept calm. There was so much to take in all at once.

I said, 'Poor little thing. Shall I go up and see her?'

Mummy said, 'Not now, darling. I've only just got her off to sleep. She cried so much, she's exhausted.'

I said how awful and was Robert very upset. Mummy said he was quite calm when he brought Adrienne over, but he'd rung up since and he sounded as if he was drinking heavily. She told me to go and talk to my father, he'd hardly seen me all weekend. I made up my mind very quickly and I said after supper I might go and see Judy, now I didn't need an early night.

It was about nine when I got to Robert's house. I'd had to ring Judy from a call-box and ask her to cover for me, just in case. Of course she was very excited, she loves secrets, and I had to promise to tell her all about it later.

There was a light on in the first-floor drawing-room. I rang the bell but nobody answered, so I took a deep breath and let myself in with the key he'd given me. I knew I was taking a chance and he might be furious – or out – but I had to risk it. I could hear the television was on and I called up the stairs, 'Robert, are you all right?'

He didn't answer. When I got into the room I saw why. He was lying in front of the television with his eyes shut. I said, 'Are you asleep?' and then I saw the whisky bottle, nearly empty, on the coffee table. I put the top back on it and turned off the TV. I thought the sudden silence might wake him, the way it wakes Daddy when he goes to sleep in the evenings, but he didn't stir. He looked so tired and lonely and sad. I went upstairs and got a quilt and covered him up. Summer evenings get quite chilly. Then I sat on a stool and watched him for a long time. I kept hoping he'd wake up so we could have a talk about Adrienne and what to do and how much Diana had upset her, but he didn't. Maybe it was just as well. He might have been cross I'd let myself in and seen him asleep, though of course he'll know in the morning because of the quilt.

He looked so unprotected lying there asleep. Watching him made me feel very old. It was about half past ten when I crept out.

I've got to find a way to help him.

1969

Lisa

April

Robert is going to go public! It means being quoted on the Stock Exchange so people can buy shares in the company. It's a wonderful achievement. I tried to explain to Adrienne about it so she could be proud of him too, but of course she didn't really understand.

It's quite hard getting round there to see her as often as I'd like these days. I thought it would be easier once I'd left school, but Mummy and Daddy keep on about how lucky I am to have got into art school, as if I didn't deserve it, and how I must work hard. But they want me to do all the social things as well. I think they're hoping I'll meet a Nice Jewish Boy and forget all about Jamie.

I got round there today about five and got my usual frosty welcome from Mrs Deacon. She's so tight-lipped she hardly opens her mouth and she doesn't say hullo or anything normal, just 'Miss Isaacs' in that terribly disapproving tone of voice as if I was a slug or something she'd found in the lettuce, or she had a piece of lemon in her mouth, or both. I'm very polite to her, but cool. 'Hullo, Mrs Deacon,' I say, and I smile, but she knows I don't mean it. Maybe I'm worse than she is. At least she's honest and shows how much she dislikes me.

'Mr Mackenzie isn't home, yet,' she said pointedly.

'It was Adrienne I came to see.' But she still didn't move and I actually had to say, 'May I come in?' before she opened the door wider than a crack. She's unbelievable. Of course I pretended not to notice.

I went straight into the kitchen and Adrienne came running to meet me. 'Lisa, Lisa, I knew it was you, I'm so glad you've come,' and I swung her off the ground and gave

299

her a big hug. Mrs D. looked sourer than ever and said, 'I didn't say you could get down, did I?'

I said, 'Well, she's down now.' I couldn't resist it.

'She hasn't finished her tea.'

'Maybe she's not hungry.'

Adrienne said, 'No, I'm not.'

'There you are,' I said.

'It's a waste of good food,' Mrs D. said, as if she were paying for it. I thought of Robert going public and I said, just to annoy her, 'Never mind, it won't break the bank.'

She made her mouth look even narrower and she said, 'It's very bad for her to get her own way all the time.' I thought, What rubbish, and I nearly laughed in her face. 'Oh, Mrs Deacon,' I said, 'it's lovely to get your own way, we all like it. I'm sure you'd like to clear up now, so you won't want us under your feet. We'll go in the garden, shall we, sweetheart? I'll give you an aeroplane.' Adrienne was very excited. She said, 'Ooh, yes please.' She likes them as much as I did when I was her age.

When we were safely in the hall she put her tongue out in Mrs D's direction and started to giggle. I said, 'Ssh, she'll hear you,' but I was giggling myself. Then she talked me into doing the grenade joke yet again. I mimed pulling the pin out with my teeth and chucking the grenade into the kitchen, and we both crouched in a corner, with our fingers in our ears, so we wouldn't hear the blast. We were laughing so much, but silently, we were nearly hysterical. Then I opened my eyes and there was Mrs D., just standing in the hall, looking at us. I nearly choked.

'We were just playing a game,' I said innocently.

'So I see.' She stalked into the dining-room and started laying the table. We followed her through – we were still squeaking a bit – and went into the garden.

Adrienne's getting quite heavy, so the hard bit is lifting her as a dead weight. Mummy's always saying I'll do my back in, but I don't believe her. Anyway, it's worth it, and once I've got her swinging round and round by one arm and one leg, it's easy and I could go on all day. Afterwards she told me Mrs D. had been making her eat a runny egg when I arrived.

Honestly, that woman. She knows Adrienne only likes hard-boiled eggs. I think she only does it to have a battle. I don't know why Robert hired her, I really don't. You only have to look at her to know she doesn't like children. He says she was the best of a bad bunch, but I think he was probably too busy to look properly.

Mrs D. had her revenge though. The phone rang about quarter past six and she called me in. It was Robert. She watched me all the time I was talking to him. He said he was very sorry but his meeting wasn't over and he'd be late for supper. I was so disappointed I could hardly speak. Then he said, 'I'm sorry I won't see you,' and he sounded all warm and like himself. 'How's Adrienne?'

'She's fine.'

'I hope she's behaving herself.'

'Yes, we've been having fun.'

'I'm glad. Wish I could say the same. Well, I better go. Bye for now, lassie.'

'Good luck with your meeting.'

I hate phones. You can never say what you want to. I told Mrs Deacon he'd be late and she said that was nothing new. Then I said I'd have to go soon and she said, 'Yes, I expect you will,' very meaningfully, as if she knows more about me than I do.

I was so miserable, when I got to bed I just cried and cried. I thought I was being quiet, but suddenly Mummy came into the room. She said, 'Sweetheart, what is it?'

I said, 'Nothing.' I'd got my face buried in the pillow so it came out muffled.

She said, 'You cry like this for nothing?'

'I didn't mean you to hear. Truly I didn't.'

She gave me a handkerchief out of her dressing-gown pocket and I blew my nose.

I said stupidly, 'I don't know what to do,' and she got all alarmed and said, 'Is there something you want to tell me?'

'No.'

'Are you sure?'

I said, 'I'm not pregnant, if that's what you mean.' It

was awful; one minute she was all nice and sympathetic and the next minute she was like a policeman.

'Thank God,' she said, as if it would have been really terrible.

I said, 'Oh, Mummy, you're so old-fashioned. I wouldn't be such an idiot – and anyway, Jamie's not like that.'

Then I started to cry again and she gave me a lecture, like a sort of prepared speech.

'They're all like that. But deep down, they all prefer girls who say no, they all want to marry virgins. It's stupid, it's unreasonable, but that's how they are, and we have to put up with it. No matter what the papers say, it's all nonsense, the permissive society and all that. It just doesn't work. Believe me.'

I just cried more and more, I couldn't stop, and she gave me a big hug. I said, 'Oh, Mummy, I'm so miserable.' I was thinking of Robert, but of course she thought I was crying about Jamie.

'D'you really love him that much?'

'Yes.' I was still sobbing. 'But it's hopeless. It's impossible.'

She rocked me like a baby. She's really much better at cuddles than chats. 'Don't be silly, darling. Of course it isn't. I'm sorry. I just didn't realize.'

Now I don't know what to do. Mummy and Daddy are being so sweet. Of course I love Jamie; we always said we'd get married one day, and this other feeling is just silly, like a crush at school, it's not real, it's not grown-up. I wish so much I could talk to Mummy about it, but I daren't. I can't talk to anyone. That makes it worse, as if I've imagined the whole thing. Maybe I have. I just don't know how to compare feelings. I don't know how I ought to feel. And then *ought* seems wrong. Why isn't it all easy and natural the way you read about?

I *ought* to be able to sort this out by myself but I can't. I know Jamie so well, we've loved each other such a long time, it's as if we were married already, even though we haven't gone all the way yet. I know when he's happy or sad without looking at him, just by the way he moves, or the way he says hullo on the phone. I know how to cheer him up. I know how to upset him, too, but I try not to. He's so vulnerable underneath that big tough front. I can hurt him so easily and I don't want to. I know he loves me and that's very important. I love him too. But do I love him *enough*? The French say there's always one who kisses and one who turns the cheek. I never used to believe that. But now I think it's true. I think Daddy loves Mummy more than she loves him. And I think Jamie loves me more than I love him. But it doesn't always have to be that way round. Héloïse loved Abelard more than he loved her. You can tell because after they castrated him he made her go in a convent and she went because she loved him. But if he'd really *really* loved her, he'd have wanted her to be happy with somebody else.

Would I want Robert to be happy with Diana again?

The thing is, I know if Jamie and I get married we'll be happy because we suit each other. Is that enough? Should there be an extra magic something or is that just silly and childish? I wish I knew.

Adrienne and I were doing finger-painting on the drawing-room floor and having a lovely time when Mrs D. burst in squeaking, 'Oh, Miss Isaacs, and you promised me you wouldn't make a mess.'

I said, 'It's all right, Mrs Deacon, we've spread plenty of newspaper.'

She went on and on. 'You know I don't like painting in the drawing-room. All that water. It's not the place for it.'

'I'll clean everything up, Mrs Deacon. Don't worry.'

'She's got a perfectly good play-room upstairs for messy games like that.'

I couldn't resist it. 'Oh, but it's much nicer down here, Mrs Deacon, don't you think?'

Adrienne grinned and I tried to look innocent. Mrs D. glowered at us both.

'Five more minutes and then it's bedtime.'

'Not till Daddy gets home,' Adrienne said.

'Five minutes.' She stalked out and Adrienne did that thing of putting her thumbs in her ears and wiggling her fingers while crossing her eyes and putting out her tongue. I laughed. She does it very well. She said, 'Mrs Dragon caught me doing that one day. She said I'd stick like that, and I said don't care and she said don't care was made to care, don't care was hanged. What did she mean?'

'She was just cross.'

'She's always cross. I hate her. I wish she'd go away. I wish she'd die.'

I felt obliged to draw the line somewhere. 'You mustn't say that.'

'Why not?'

'It's just too bad a thing to say about anyone.' I couldn't really explain.

'Even Mrs Dragon?'

''Fraid so. Even her.'

'She wouldn't really hang me if I don't care, would she?'

'No, of course not.'

She said with satisfaction, 'Daddy wouldn't let her, anyway.' Then we heard the front door, and Robert and Mrs D. saying good evening to each other. Adrienne jumped up shouting, 'It's Daddy,' and of course she knocked the painting water over. I kind of saw it happening in slow motion, that funny way you do without being able to stop it. I mopped up as best I could while she went flying to the door just as Robert came in. He gathered her up in his arms, saying, 'How's my wee lassie, then? How's my best girl?' but he looked at me over the top of her head while he was saying it, and gave me the most lovely smile. My heart lurched. He sat down with Adrienne on his knee and said, 'Oh, sometimes I wonder if it's worth it, this whole business of going public – it's all bloody meetings.' He looked so tired. 'D'you know, there are times I wish I was back on a building site – anywhere – anything to get away from great heaps of paper and people yattering on at me.'

I said, 'It sounds awful, but you know it's worth it. It must be.'

Adrienne tugged at his arm. 'We've been painting.'

'So I see.'

'Mrs Dragon didn't want us to, not down here, but we did anyway.'

He laughed. 'You better be careful. You'll call her that to her face one of these days, and then where will we be?'

'She might leave,' Adrienne said hopefully.

'I don't think so, but she might be very upset. You don't want to upset her, do you?'

'Yes.' Gleeful tone of voice.

Mrs D. came in. 'Bath time and bedtime, young lady.' I don't know why she doesn't join the army and have done with it.

'Oh, Daddy, must I?'

'I'll come up and tuck you in presently.'

'Will you come too, Lisa?'

'Of course I will.'

Mrs D. said, 'I see you had an accident with the painting water, Miss Isaacs. Just as I knew you would.'

I gave her a beaming smile. 'It must be wonderful to be always right, Mrs Deacon.'

When we were alone he poured drinks for us and said, 'Don't you get enough painting at art school?'

'No, I don't. Besides, it's much more fun here.' I wanted to have a really good talk with him and I thought this might be the moment. 'Robert, I know it's none of my business, but would it really matter if Mrs Deacon left?'

'Of course it would. She's a very good cook.'

'I'm serious.'

He sighed heavily. 'Oh, Lisa, I know she's not perfect, far from it, but she's the best of a bad bunch as far as I'm concerned.'

'Adrienne doesn't like her.' I thought that was the only thing that really mattered.

'Adrienne doesn't like anyone except you. And I can't employ you twenty-four hours a day, more's the pity.'

I felt encouraged. 'She nags Adrienne all the time. I don't think she's got any idea about children.'

'Probably not, but she's a widow, she has to earn a living,

she tries her best. It can't be much fun having to cook endless meals and look after someone else's child.'

He's too kind-hearted, that's his trouble. 'D'you really think she tries her best?'

'Oh, I don't know, I'm hardly ever here, am I? Obviously she's always on her best behaviour with me. But think of all the others we've had in the last two or three years. Adrienne played them all up in different ways and they left. If Mrs Deacon has the guts to stay, how can I sack her? What good would it do? It would only mean yet another change and that's the last thing Adrienne needs.'

'Yes, I know.' He was right about that.

'She *is* a very difficult child.'

'I don't see her like that.' I wondered if he meant it. Surely it would be fairer to say she's had a very difficult life so far.

'Well, of course, she isn't like that with you. But ever since Nanny left, she's been so unsettled she's taken it out on every new person I've hired.'

I decided to take a risk and I said, 'I think it made it worse for her – Diana coming back for a day – just after Nanny left.'

'Aye.'

I could tell I shouldn't have said it. He didn't want to be reminded and his face sort of closed up. I thought, well, it's got to be said, in for a penny and all that, and anything would be better than the awkward silence.

'My parents have agreed to Jamie and me getting engaged on my birthday.'

He said, 'Congratulations,' with no expression at all. Absolutely neutral.

'You don't approve, do you?'

'It's nothing to do with me. Jamie's nearly of age.'

'But you think I'm too young.'

'That's not for me to say. If your parents agree, that's fine.' Then there was a long pause and we just stared at each other. My heart was thumping like mad.

He said, 'I think Jamie's very lucky.'

*

When I got home Jamie was already there having drinks with my parents. I could see at once that I was in for trouble. Mummy was in one of her moods and Daddy was trying to keep the peace. Jamie was furious and pretending not to be. Only the dog was pleased to see me.

I said, 'Hullo, sorry I'm late.'

Mummy said, 'Why bother to be here on time? It's only your engagement we're celebrating.'

Daddy said, 'Now let's not spoil the day,' and poured me some champagne.

'What happened to you?' Jamie was doing his best to sound casual.

'Nothing. I went to see Adrienne.'

'Till this hour?'

'I had to read her a bedtime story.'

Daddy said gently, 'Another time, darling, you could phone us, you know. It's not very polite to keep Jamie waiting.'

'I'm sorry, I didn't think –' Daddy can always make me feel guilty just by being so gentle. I drank some champagne, trying to make amends. 'This is lovely, Daddy. Thank you.'

'Jamie brought it.'

'Oh.' I felt them all watching me, making it worse, as if they were saying 'so get out of that if you can.' I said brightly, 'Well, I'll just run upstairs and have a quick shower and change and then I'll be ready.'

'I don't think we have time,' Jamie said. 'I've got tickets for that play you wanted to see – if we don't leave now, we'll be late.'

'I'll be ever so quick. I can't go like this, I feel so scruffy.'

'You look perfectly fine to me.' He was all charm. Very phony. 'You always do.'

'Well,' I said, 'it looks as if we're leaving right away.'

He drove fast as usual and sulked. I watched him for a bit, then I said, 'Are we really going to the theatre, or did you just say that to get me out in a hurry?'

He didn't answer. I put my hand on his thigh.

'Not while I'm driving.'

'You spoke.' But I wasn't out of the wood yet. I put on a funny accent. 'Ah, you are so handsome when you are angry.'

He started to laugh. I could always make him laugh. I leaned against him, resting my head on his shoulder, and I laughed too, out of sheer relief.

He took me to see the new flat and it's really nice. Two large rooms painted white, and very little furniture. A small kitchen and bathroom. Very simple. I like it a lot.

I said, 'Oh Jamie, it's wonderful.'

'Hardly.' He was pleased. 'But it'll do for a start. I thought if I got somewhere decent to live, your parents might let us get married sooner.'

'When are you moving in?'

'At the weekend.'

'I wish I was moving in with you.' I felt a sudden wave of panic and I kissed him hard. 'Oh, Jamie, I do love you.'

'Do you? Sometimes I'm not sure.'

'When?'

'When you're late.'

I thought, Oh God, I've hurt him, and it hurt me too. 'I've said I'm sorry.'

He gave me a hug. 'D'you have to see that child so often?'

'She's your sister. And I'm nearly family.'

'She's nothing to do with me. She's the reason my parents got divorced.'

'Oh, Jamie, that's so long ago. And it wasn't her fault.'

'I don't want you seeing her after we're married.'

I thought about it. I was going to have to choose; he was right in a way, it would be too painful to go on seeing Adrienne with Robert there. I had to sort out the whole thing now. It wasn't a choice between two sorts of love, the sane and the mad, it was a choice between reality and fantasy. When I'm with Jamie I know I love him and we belong together. It's only when I'm with Robert or alone in my room late at night writing my journal and playing music that I get confused. I couldn't bear anyone else to have Jamie: that proves I love him, doesn't it?

I said, 'Let's get married now.'

'What?'

'All right, tomorrow. Next week. Let's run away. We could go to Gretna or somewhere like that.' I really meant it.

He was so relieved. I could see him relaxing. 'You're crazy. That's hardly the way to make your parents learn to love me.'

'I don't care about them. Oh Jamie, I'm so scared that if we don't get married soon we never will.' But once we were married I'd be safe for ever and I'd forget all my silly ideas once and for all.

He looked amazed and said, 'What are you talking about? We've just got engaged and you'll soon have a ring to prove it.'

I started kissing him and stroking him, undoing a few buttons. He was responsive at first, then he suddenly pushed me away. 'You're not playing fair.'

'Jamie, please. I'm not teasing. Make love to me.'

After a long silence he said, 'You always said you wanted to wait.'

'I was wrong. I've changed my mind.' I was quite convinced now that if only we did make love everything would be all right, it would make a bond for ever and I'd never feel confused again. It would cast a spell. It would make us magic as well as suitable.

He said, 'No, I think you were right,' and started buttoning himself up. 'Your parents trust me now, they might let us get married in just a few months. Let's not spoil anything.'

'How could we?' I was furious and so disappointed, I was nearly in tears.

'I don't know. I just feel – oh, we've waited this long, we can wait a bit longer. Do the whole thing properly.'

'Oh, you don't understand.' I turned my back on him.

'Yes, I do. And I feel the same as you.' He put his arms round me from behind. 'But I want everything to be perfect. Not furtive, not secretive. I want your parents to feel they were right to trust me. It's not for long.'

He kissed the top of my head. He couldn't see how miserable I was. Why does he have to go on about my parents? What about *me*?

'I'll make it up to you, I promise,' he said. But I don't see how he can. I'm really frightened now it's all going to go wrong. We've missed the moment.

I told Jamie I had to spend the weekend at the cottage with my parents, so I couldn't help him with the move. Then I went out with Robert and Adrienne on Saturday for a long walk in the park. We took the dog. She quite likes the dog now. There was a time she used to throw stones at dogs. That's how miserable she used to be.

Robert told me how he'd had to scramble all over a building site posing for photographers. I said I'd get all the papers and he said they'd give me a good laugh. Adrienne ran ahead with the dog. Anyone watching us would have thought we were a real family. I asked him when the great day is and he said next Friday. My birthday. I was horrified.

'Does that mean you can't come to my party?'

'No, of course I'll be there.'

I didn't want to think about the party so I said, 'It sounds awfully grand – going public.' But he only said he'll be glad when it's all over.

I said could I ask him something and he said yes of course. I was very nervous.

'D'you ever tell lies?'

'Not often. You need a good memory to be a liar and I've got enough on my mind already.'

'I told Jamie a lie about this weekend. I said I had to go to the cottage with my parents.' It was a stupid lie, too. He can so easily check up. Do I want to be found out?

'Why did you do that?'

'Because I should have been helping him move into the new flat. Only I wanted to be here with you and Adrienne.' And because he wouldn't make love to me.

He said, 'I'm very glad you are.'

'Are you?'

'Aye. It's no fun without you.'

But I never know if he's just being polite or if he really means it.

I said, 'Promise you won't lie to me,' and he said all right. I thought, I've got to know, I've only got till Friday and I can't let Jamie down for nothing. I don't want to lose him if I'm just imagining things, I must know where I stand, so I said, 'Robert, d'you want me to marry Jamie?'

There was a long pause and my heart was beating so fast I felt really peculiar.

Eventually he said, 'No,' very reluctantly.

'Why not?'

'I can't answer that.'

'Because we're too young?'

'Something like that.'

I said, 'I worry about it too. Not being too young, just – not having the right feelings. I do love him, but ... I've known him all my life, I feel safe with him. It's not dangerous, it's not romantic. Just ... terribly comfortable and reassuring. D'you know what I mean?'

'Aye. Very well.'

'It scares me because I'm not sure that's how I ought to feel about someone I'm going to marry. Or maybe it is, and the other feeling's wrong. I just don't know. When you've never been in love before, it's awfully hard to tell.' It was such a relief to say all this to him after bottling it up for so long, I felt immensely lighter, as if I were going to float.

He said presently, as if he'd thought hard about it, 'If it's any help, the way you feel for Jamie is the way I used to feel for his mother.'

'And is the other feeling ... the way you feel about Diana?'

'Aye.'

'D'you think you'll ever feel like that about anyone again?'

Silence. If he said no, then that was it. I'd get engaged and married and live happily ever after. But if he said yes, then I'd pluck up my courage and ask if that person could be me. I felt he was just on the verge of answering and I held my breath. Then Adrienne came running towards us, shouting for us to look at something she'd found, and the moment was gone. Maybe he was relieved, I don't know. But after that we talked of other things. I felt very, very tired and I went home early.

May

I don't know how to write about my birthday. So much has happened and I've thought about it for such a long time. I feel incredibly elated and terribly sad all at once.

On the actual day the party went very well, but it was a bit overwhelming. Too many people, and I knew they were wishing Jamie was Jewish and every time they examined my diamond they were sure to be working out what it had cost. But everyone was very nice to us.

I went up to my room just for a break, to have a rest from them all. I sat in front of my dressing-table and brushed my hair and admired my engagement ring. It was only a small stone, of course, but in a very pretty setting, very delicate, and it shot wonderful colours in all directions when I moved it. I knew Jamie must have been really extravagant, even though he'd gone to Daddy's friend Danny Rosen, where he'd be sure to get a good price. Daddy'd made certain of that.

The only thing was, why hadn't Robert arrived yet?

I heard footsteps on the landing and Jamie's voice. 'Lisa?'

'I'm in here.'

He came in. 'What are you doing?'

'Nothing. I just felt like a break.'

'*You* did. How about me? At least you know everyone.'

'I don't. Most of them are my parents' friends. And there are lots of old relations I haven't seen for years.'

'I get the feeling some of them would like to circumcise me on the spot.'

I laughed. 'Are you hating it all?'

'No – but it's better when you're there.' He kissed my hair.

'I'll be down in a minute.'

'They're all asking for you.'

'I won't be long.'

'Okay.'

When he'd gone I waited a moment, then I carefully

opened my secret drawer, the one Mummy can't unlock, and I took out a photograph of Robert. I had saved it from one of the newspapers. It wasn't very good but it was better than nothing. I stared at it for a long time. Why aren't you here? I thought. Why aren't you here?

When everybody had gone, Mummy and Jamie's mother sat around saying how tired they were and Daddy poured drinks. Then they all started discussing why Robert hadn't come and Jamie said he was glad. That started a row between him and his mother and she apologized for him to all of us. I was very embarrassed, so I just kept on looking out of the window. I had the oddest feeling something was wrong. It wasn't that he'd been too busy with the going-public celebrations, and he couldn't have forgotten. Something must have happened, and it must be something important or serious enough to stop him telephoning.

Eventually Jamie's mother rang Robert and got Mrs Deacon. She said Mrs Deacon sounded very odd, as if she'd been crying. We all waited. Then Robert came on the line. Jamie's mother asked him why he hadn't come to the party. There was a long pause and she looked very shaken and said things like, 'Oh my God', and 'Is she all right?' and 'What a relief'. We all watched her, even Jamie. I was trembling. Then she said a lot of soothing things and hung up. She told us Adrienne had been knocked down by a car but she wasn't hurt. The others said how concerned they were, but they didn't sound as if they really cared. I said I must go to her and they all argued that I shouldn't, she had her father, she didn't need me, she'd be asleep, as if I was a stranger to her or as if she wasn't important. I said I was going anyway and Jamie said he'd come with me, which was sweet of him, so we just rushed out, ignoring all the disapproving looks, and jumped in the car. It's the first time I've been glad Jamie drives fast.

When we got to the house he said, 'I'll wait outside. I don't want to see him. You won't stay long, will you?'

I dashed up the steps, but as I got to the front door it opened and Mrs D. came out carrying a large suitcase. She was crying. I'd never imagined Mrs D. could cry. I asked her where she was going and she said, 'You can see the rest of my things are sent on, now you're here. I'm not staying another minute where I'm not wanted. It wasn't my fault what happened, but I get the blame. You're making a rod for your own back with that child, you mark my words.' And she stomped down the steps and started looking for a taxi. I actually felt sorry for her. I'd never imagined I could, but she looked suddenly old and crumpled and vulnerable. I'd have liked to help her but there wasn't time. I ran upstairs calling to Robert, and there he was in the drawing-room with Adrienne on the sofa wrapped in blankets. She was so pleased to see me, she kept saying 'Lisa, Lisa,' over and over again. I gave her a big hug and she hung on so tightly I could hardly breathe. She said, 'I knew you'd come if I wished hard enough. Will you stay till I go to sleep?'

I don't know how long it was but eventually her hand let go of mine and Robert poured us a brandy each. He told me all about what had happened and how he'd given Mrs Deacon the sack. The doctor had been and said Adrienne had been very lucky and only had bruises and shock, but they were going to have x-rays just to be sure. She'd run out in front of a car while Mrs D. was supposed to be looking after her. We both kept pausing while we talked and I knew we were both thinking the same thing: how easily she might have been killed, or injured for life. I kept shivering and Robert poured two more brandies. Then I suddenly realized what the time was.

I said, 'I ought to go. Jamie's waiting.' I had forgotten all about him.

Robert said, 'Oh yes, of course. Jamie. It was good of you to come round.'

'How could I stay away?'

We just stood there looking at each other. There was terrific tension between us, but I didn't know if it was just because of Adrienne.

Robert said, 'Well, you've worked magic as usual. I don't know how we're going to manage without you.'

'Why should you have to?'

'Jamie won't let you come here once you're married. We both know that, don't we?'

'That's a long way off.'

Then I knew from the way he was looking at me that it wasn't just Adrienne and it hadn't been my imagination all this time.

He said, 'I'm glad I missed your party. I'm so jealous, I might have made a scene.'

It was such a relief to hear him say that, and yet it seemed only right and appropriate, as if everything was falling into place, and yet I was amazed – oh, I felt so many different things at once and the brandy had gone to my head because I'd had champagne at the party and I hadn't eaten very much. I just said, 'Oh, Robert,' and he put his arms round me and we kissed.

It was just as wonderful as I'd imagined it would be, if I'd dared to imagine it at all. Then we just stood there holding each other and both talking at once about how long we'd been in love, only we'd thought it was hopeless. We were so happy. It was like being drunk with happiness.

Then the doorbell started ringing and there was pounding on the door. I dashed to answer it. I wanted to open it before Robert could.

I said, 'What's the matter with you? There's a sick child in here – we've only just got her to sleep.'

Jamie was very pale, very dignified. He was so angry I was afraid of him. He said, 'It's time to go home, Lisa.'

I said, 'I'm sorry, I can't. I'm needed here.'

'Oh really? Who by?'

I could hear Robert coming downstairs, so I said, 'You'd better come in.'

In the hall Jamie said, 'Well? Is the brat going to die?' as if he really hoped she would.

'No, thank God.'

'No, that would be too much to hope for.'

'Jamie – I didn't mean to hurt you but I have.' I took off my engagement ring. 'Please forgive me. I've been very confused.' I held out the ring but he wouldn't take it, so I put it on the hall table. All the excitement and happiness with Robert had gone. I felt miserable and guilty. Jamie looked so upset and it was all my fault.

Robert came up to us. 'If you want to blame someone, Jamie, blame me.'

'Don't worry, I will.' He looked at Robert with real hatred.

Robert said, 'I'm truly sorry. We're both as surprised as you are.' He put his arm round me to stop me trembling.

Jamie said, 'Surprised? I'm not surprised. I could see it coming. Only I hoped I was wrong. God, you're disgusting. You make me sick. Both of you.' And he gave us a dreadful look as if we were something slimy.

Robert said very quietly, 'I think you better leave.'

'It'll be a pleasure.' Jamie was shouting by now. 'But this isn't the end of it, you know. Don't imagine you're going to get away with it. By Christ, I'll get even with you for this, if it takes me a lifetime.' Then he went out and slammed the door so hard the whole house shook. I burst into tears and Robert hugged me. He kept saying 'It's all right, lassie, it's all right.' But I cried for a long time.

I don't know what's going to happen now. I wrote Jamie a long letter trying to explain and apologize, but he sent it back unopened. My parents are furious. Anyone would think they'd been longing for me to marry Jamie. I've tried ringing him up but he won't speak to me, and his mother sounds as if she thinks I'm the lowest of the low. I've managed to upset everyone just like that, without meaning to, and all because I didn't know my own mind. But I do now. Robert and I haven't had time to make any plans yet, but we're in love with each other, and that's all that matters.

Jean

It was hard not to grow bitter as the years passed. Her life was empty, though on the surface it went on much the same and others might have envied her. She had a satisfying job, good friends, a loving son and enough money. She was grateful for all those things. She could have been alone, poor and ill. But the knowledge that Robbie would never come back made her realize how much she had been hoping he would. She tormented herself by wondering if he might have drifted back more easily had she never actually divorced him. It was ironic to have made such a sacrifice, only to see Diana leave him. But if he had come back, could she have truly forgiven him? Could she have accepted Diana's child?

At other times she wondered about Francis Hammond and whether she should have sent him away or not. Perhaps they could have been happy together after all; she might have surprised herself by forgetting about Robbie and the Church. But if she had let him go because it was the right thing to do, then why had she not been rewarded with peace of mind?

Some nights she cried herself to sleep like a child, wanting to scream that it wasn't fair. Her religion was a comfort to her, but not enough. She was so lonely that it seemed at times as if her bones ached with it. To accept that there could never be anyone new she could love without guilt was such a heavy punishment she did not know how to bear it. What had she done to deserve that? Had she been careless or complacent in the marriage? Had she in some way been partly responsible for the misery she now had to endure? Was there something she could have done at the time, if she had been clever enough, to change the whole course of events?

It made matters worse that no one she knew could really understand her predicament if they did not share her beliefs. To anyone who believed in divorce, nine years was a ridiculously long time to spend yearning for an ex-husband. She was not even sure in her own mind any more whether it was Robbie himself she still wanted or merely someone, and he was the only person she was allowed to want. To stop wanting him, to learn to want no one at all, would be peaceful, certainly, but it would also be a kind of death.

She watched Jamie's growing love for Lisa with envy and approval. All she wanted was for him to be happy. She didn't see him as too young: at his age she had been married. She liked Lisa and they had known each other all their lives. What could be more natural?

'I gather you're all for it,' Ruth said to her one day, sounding hostile.

'Not exactly.' She felt accused of renegade behaviour, of letting down the parental side.

'That's what David seems to think. Jean doesn't mind, he keeps saying, so why should you? I must say, I do hate being the odd one out, the rotten spoil-sport, when I'm only trying to be sensible.'

'All I said was, as Jamie'll be twenty-one in a few months there's not much point in my objecting.' It seemed tactless to add that she wouldn't anyway. 'You can make Lisa wait more than two years. That's a very different matter.'

'I wonder.' Ruth sounded grim.

'Oh, surely. A lot can happen in two years. She might change her mind.'

'I meant, can we really make her wait? Oh, legally we can, of course, but what good is that? She'll make life unbearable. She might even elope. Everyone thinks she's so sweet and amenable, but underneath she's so pig-headed you wouldn't believe...'

'I'm sorry.' She didn't know what to say for the best. 'You're really worried, aren't you?'

'It's not that I don't like Jamie, you know that. But they *are* too young, they've hardly been out with anyone else, and these religious differences *do* make problems, I don't

318

care what anyone says. Well, you found that out with Robert.'

'Yes.' She wished Ruth wouldn't go on about it.

'Oh, it's all ridiculous. It's *your* wedding we should be talking about.'

'It's much too late for that.'

'D'you ever hear from him?'

'Not any more.' If only she would drop the subject. 'We wrote for a while, but it was so pointless it got a bit embarrassing, so we stopped.' And yet she had kept his letters. Sometimes, to her shame, she even re-read them. Living on crumbs ...

'I wish you'd married him,' Ruth said. 'He was such a nice man.'

'Yes, he was, but it wouldn't have worked.'

'Because of Robert or the Church?'

'Both, I suppose,' Jean said evasively.

Ruth got up and began wandering about the room, fiddling with various objects, looking out of the window at the spring sunshine as if she disapproved of it. 'Oh, I don't know, maybe it's just a case of sour grapes.'

'What?'

'About Lisa, I mean. Maybe I'm jealous because she's young and pretty and thin – and look at me –'

'You look fine.' In fact Ruth had put on weight just as Jean had lost it, but neither of them was looking her best, Jean thought. It occurred to her that Ruth had not meant to be tactless but had asked probing questions from a sense of duty, because she really wanted to talk about herself.

'Thanks. You're a true friend. Anyway, it's all ahead for her, isn't it, whichever way you slice it, and downhill for me.'

Jean said, 'Has something happened?' She sounded so agitated, quite unlike herself.

'Oh – the man I told you about, I still see him but it's not the same, not since he had his heart attack and that teenage girl left him.'

'I'm sorry.' She felt inadequate.

'Well, it serves me right, doesn't it? It's a judgement on me, don't you think?'

'No. I never said that.'

'Sorry, I'm being unfair.'

Jean couldn't stop herself from saying, 'You've still got David.'

'Yes.' Ruth did not sound consoled at all.

'There was a time when I thought Robbie and I might get back together ... but it didn't work out.' She hadn't meant to say that but she felt better afterwards, as if she and Ruth were on more equal terms and the friendship repaired.

'Oh Jean, I'm sorry. I didn't realize.'

'No, well, it was silly of me.'

Silence, while they looked at each other sympathetically. Ruth sighed. 'Oh God, what a long time ago it seems we were all in Scotland together.'

'Fourteen years.'

'We were all so carefree then.'

'Were we?'

'That's the way I remember it. Don't you?'

That night as she lay in bed reading to stop herself thinking, she heard Jamie come in.

'Is that you, Jamie?'

'No, it's a burglar.'

She smiled: it was an old family joke, a well-loved ritual. She and Robbie – no, close the door on that quickly.

Jamie came in and she put down her book. He said, 'You always say that.'

'So do you. How was night school?'

'Okay. I'm glad you're still awake. Can I talk to you?'

'Is it about Lisa?'

'Not exactly. Mam, I've found a flat.'

'Ah.' She had seen it coming, they had even discussed it, but she had still thought maybe not yet, maybe not so soon.

'It's only two rooms, k. and b., but it's nicely furnished and it's only ten minutes from here, so I'll be able to pop in and see you every day.'

She said indulgently, wanting to set him free even if it hurt, 'Once a week will do fine.'

'You don't mind?'

'No, of course I don't mind. You were bound to leave home one day.' But she had thought not till the engagement at least, maybe even the wedding. 'Can you afford it, that's all?'

'Just about.' He looked pleased with himself. 'It's a third of my salary – well, a bit more actually. But I'll be getting a rise soon. Mr Isaacs is very pleased with me.'

'I'm sure he is.'

'You won't be lonely?'

'That's my problem, Jamie. Nothing to do with you.'

'Maybe you could share with someone from the hospital.'

She smiled at his concern for her – and his relief that she would let him go so easily. 'Don't you worry about me, I'll be fine.'

'Well, I'll say goodnight then.' He kissed her. 'Thanks, Mam.'

'What for?'

'You know.' He went out.

She put down her book and set the alarm clock for the morning. Then she turned out the light and lay down. Well. It was all going to be very different. She would be alone in the house. Now she would really have to come to terms with herself.

Ruth and David surprised her by suddenly agreeing to let Lisa and Jamie get engaged on Lisa's nineteenth birthday. It chanced to be the same day that Robbie was to go public. Jean felt confused. Too much was happening in her life all at once, after years of nothing, but none of it was happening to her.

Robbie came to see her – one of his rare visits. She had been reading about him in the newspapers: 'Canny Scot floats his empire', and similar nonsense, complete with pictures of Robbie grinning and waving a trowel or climbing on half-built walls. It was like a fantasy. They were trying to turn him into a film star. When he actually arrived at her door in a second-hand Rolls, the illusion was complete.

'Very nice too,' she said sourly.

'Can I take you for a ride?'

'No, I don't think so, thanks all the same. Not again.' But the bitterness was lost on him. He was like a child with a new toy. 'I suppose it ought to be champagne these days,' she added.

'I still prefer whisky.'

'Just as well, that's all I've got.'

While she poured the drinks he took an envelope from his pocket and put it down on the table.

'I've brought you some shares.'

'Thanks.'

'And I wondered if you'd like to come to the lunch on Friday.'

'Sorry, I'm on nights.' She heard herself sounding sharp. 'And I'll have to catch some sleep before Lisa's party.'

'Oh. Yes, of course.' He looked crestfallen.

'Well, here's to your flotation or whatever it's called.' They drank. 'Anyway, I'll see you at the party, won't I?'

'Aye.'

'She's a lovely girl. They ought to be very happy.' It was odd: she didn't even know how he felt about it. They had never discussed the matter, as if that part of Jamie's life had become nothing to do with his father. 'Do sit down, Robbie, you look so uncomfortable standing there. I've been wondering what to do about the house. Now that Jamie's moved out, it's much too big for me.'

He sat, awkwardly. 'Would you like me to buy you somewhere smaller?'

'Good heavens, I can sell this place myself and buy another, I'm not helpless.' The sudden burst of anger nearly choked her; she had to take a deep breath to calm herself. 'I've been thinking of moving back to Scotland, as a matter of fact. I'd be nearer your mother and all my old friends. And Duncan's grave, of course. I mean, there's nothing to keep me here, is there?' But he didn't answer. 'Well, is there, Robbie? I would like to be sure.'

'No.'

'That's what I thought.'

'I'm sorry, have I said the wrong thing?'

'Not at all. I like to know where I stand.' A sudden awful

suspicion occurred to her. 'I'm surprised you invited me to the lunch, actually.'

'Why?'

'I thought you'd have some glamorous new person lined up for that.'

'Well, I obviously haven't.' He sounded cross.

'You surprise me. There must be someone in your life.'

'Not really.'

'What does that mean?'

'I don't know, Jean. I'm very confused.'

So she was right. Oh God, it was dreadful. The more she attacked him, the more she hurt herself. But she couldn't stop.

'I can see that. Who is she?'

'Why are you so sure there is someone?'

'Oh, come on, Robbie, I've known you a long time. And you've got the same shifty look you had before you went off with Diana.' It was the first time she had used the name to him and they were both startled. 'Don't tell me she's coming back?' To share in the glories of the flotation, perhaps. That would be the final irony.

'No.'

'Then it must be someone new.'

Silence. He looked relieved as if she had guessed wrongly, yet also curiously embarrassed.

'Not really. I've known her a long time. But she's unobtainable.'

She felt sick. It was horrible to have proof that she was not immune to jealousy after nine years apart.

'Oh, I wouldn't have thought anyone was unobtainable now that you're so rich and famous.'

The engagement party was a great success, considering that Ruth still did not approve and Robbie did not turn up. Jean thought that Jamie seemed nervous and Lisa preoccupied in a dreamy way, but she put that down to young love and worries about the religious problem, although all the Isaacs' friends and relations were tactful about that. When everyone had finally gone and Ruth had recovered from fussing with the caterers, they all flopped into chairs and David offered brandy.

'Oh, yes please.' Ruth was pulling off her shoes. They had such ridiculously high heels that Jean wondered how she managed to walk in them, but they did make her legs look marvellous.

'Jean?'

'No, thanks.'

'Whisky, then?'

'No, really. Nothing.' Now that it was all over she felt very flat and obscurely worried. 'Well, Robbie missed a good party.'

'Was it really all right?' Ruth sounded so eager for reassurance, anyone might have thought she had never given a party before.

'Of course,' David said. 'You worry too much.' He poured her a very large brandy and looked at her fondly. The unfairness of life impressed itself on Jean once again.

'I can't think what happened to Robbie though,' she said, unable to leave the subject alone. 'He promised faithfully he'd be here.'

Ruth put her feet up. 'Oh, I suppose his lunch must have dragged on.'

'Aye, but he could have phoned.'

Lisa was fiddling with her tiny diamond and staring out of the window. Jamie said abruptly, 'I think he did us all a favour. I didn't want him here, anyway.'

'Jamie, you know I don't like you to speak of your father like that.'

'He gave up being my father nine years ago.'

'For heaven's sake. Do we have to have all that nonsense again?' She turned to Ruth and David. 'I'm sorry. I apologize for my son.'

They tried to talk of other things, but Jean could not get Robbie off her mind. It was so unlike him not to arrive and not to phone. Eventually she couldn't stand it any longer and rang him. Mrs Deacon, his housekeeper, answered in a strange, snuffling voice, almost inaudible, as if she were crying. Jean was alarmed. Then Robbie came on the line.

'Robbie, what on earth's going on? We've been expecting you.'

'Adrienne's had an accident,' he said, sounding very far away, very closed-up inside himself.

'Oh, my God. Is she all right?'

'I think so. The doctor's been and he's coming back tomorrow.'

'But what happened?'

'She was knocked down by a car. He says it's just bruises and shock but she could have been killed.' His voice shook.

'Is there anything I can do?' She wanted so much to comfort him, but it was no longer her place.

'No, I ... thanks all the same. Look, I'd better go. Will you tell David and Ruth I'm sorry ...'

'Yes, of course. You get on back to her.' She put down the phone. Terrible memories of Duncan's death flooded back to her. Diana's child would be luckier, of course. 'Well,' she said to the row of anxious faces. 'No wonder he never turned up. His daughter's had an accident. Apparently she was knocked down by a car but she's okay. Very shaken, of course.'

'What a frightful thing to happen,' Ruth said. 'Poor Robert.'

David said, 'How awful.'

Jean felt the silence from Jamie, so strong that he almost seemed pleased. But she noticed Lisa was trembling.

'I must go to her,' Lisa said.

Ruth said, 'Darling, I don't think that's necessary. She's got her father with her and she'll only want to sleep.'

'But she needs me.'

David said, 'Lisa, just for once, can't you take your mother's advice?'

'I'm sorry. I have to go.' Lisa was twisting her engagement ring round and round.

Jamie said, 'I'll come with you.'

'Oh, Jamie, thank you. Then you *do* understand.'

'No, but I'll come with you anyway.' He turned to the others with a curious air of authority. 'Don't worry, we won't be long.'

They went out in a hurry, Lisa actually running ahead.

'Well,' Ruth said, 'it's nice to have so much influence over your only child.'

'She's very soft-hearted.' David sounded almost approving.

'Pig-headed, you mean.' She turned to Jean. 'Didn't I tell you she's pig-headed?'

Jean said faintly, 'Yes.'

She went home early, unable to shake off a feeling of impending calamity and unwilling to share it with David and Ruth. She had known, of course, that Lisa took a maternal interest in Adrienne and that Ruth and Jamie disapproved. But she had never before imagined... Well, of course, it was ridiculous. Lisa was young and tender-hearted; she had grown up in a close, warm family and felt sorry for a motherless child. It was only natural.

Yes. Hang on to that.

But the look on Lisa's face when she heard the news, the degree of concern, of involvement, of responsibility... It was as if Lisa were rushing to help her own child.

Jean was terrified. She couldn't be right. She was imagining absurd things. Lisa and Jamie were in love, they had just got engaged. What was she thinking of?

It was evening when Jamie came home. He went straight upstairs to the bathroom and she heard him being sick. Then he came down to tell her the engagement was broken. His father and Lisa were in love. He looked so white and so hurt she wanted to hug him like a baby, but he stood stiffly apart from her, somehow diminished, as if his whole frame had shrunk inside his skin. She began to tell him that she knew how he felt, that it was almost as great a grief to her, that she understood, but he said abruptly that he never wanted to speak of it again and went out of the room.

1973

Diana

This time I meant to stay, I really did. Selling the London house was intended to make me feel I had burned my boats. I found myself a nice apartment and I furnished it; I even bought a car. I stopped behaving like a tourist and referring to London as home.

It simply didn't occur to me that Piers might feel threatened by all this, that for him I was forever cast in the role of visitor. I assumed he'd be pleased to see me putting down new roots. He had never cared much for Mack, so he must be glad that the break was final. Who could be closer than we were, brother and sister, business partners? I took it for granted that nothing could ever come between us.

In many ways, New York suited me well. I liked its frenetic energy: I had never been afraid of hard work and New York respected that. I liked its honest acknowledgement of the fact that money was important, instead of pretending it didn't matter while insisting you had plenty of it, as in dear old hypocritical London. I even liked the violent, aggressive rudeness that coexisted with the cosy, ethnic jokes.

But of course New York was not America, as Americans never tired of telling me. So I took fly-drive vacations in an attempt to get to know this big country of theirs that they boasted about so much. It was certainly very beautiful; I had to grant them that. There was every kind of scenery you could wish for, and the cities were crammed with museums and art galleries, as if they had just discovered culture and valued it all the more for having so little of it. But you couldn't blame them for being a young nation; only time would cure that. And meanwhile, the much-vaunted efficiency of their telephones and their plumbing made up for a lot.

It wasn't that I was homesick exactly; after all, I could visit London whenever I wished, though in practice I seldom did. It was just that in America I felt European, while in England I merely felt English. And being reconciled with my father meant I was kept up to date with news of Mack and Adrienne. My mother had pursued a policy of never mentioning either unless I specifically asked. I knew that in fact she saw Adrienne regularly and avoided Mack, but from her letters you would never have guessed they existed.

So there I was, a permanent expatriate, getting regular bulletins on the progress of my daughter and my ex-lover three thousand miles away. I could have asked my father to stop the bulletins, I suppose, but that might have indicated distress and, besides, I was curious. Sometimes I wondered what my father was trying to achieve and whether he thought that even now there was a chance that I might go back, especially after Mack went public.

I wasn't really surprised when Mack and Lisa started living together. I realized with hindsight it had been on the cards when I last saw them: the way Lisa looked at him, the way she reacted to me, the way she tried to take over Adrienne. If that was what she wanted, she deserved to get it. She had been very diligent and would probably make them both very happy. Mack needed to live with someone, and Adrienne needed a mother. So why not Lisa? A bit of a joke for Ruth, though, in the circumstances, and a bit odd for me, when Lisa had been a mere child of six at the time our affair began. Like a true outsider, she had come up on the rails and overtaken the leaders. I had no cause for complaint: I had chosen to live alone and have a succession of lovers because true love and living together were too much for me. The fact that I actually missed the experience of being loved, much to my surprise, was neither here nor there. I would still have found it overwhelming.

When everything went finally wrong, it was very sudden.

Lisa and Mack got married, Piers started living with Leroy and I noticed a lump in my breast. Any one or even two of these events I could have handled, but not all three at once. They fed off each other and became disproportionately disturbing. Mack's wedding came as a shock because after five years together I'd assumed they simply wouldn't bother, and I liked to think that was in some way due to me: I had managed to turn Mack off marriage for life. So I was irrationally put out to hear that he'd finally taken the plunge. But I wouldn't have minded so much if Piers hadn't suddenly become a couple. I'd taken it for granted that Piers, who had never lived with anyone for more than a week, never would, and now here was Leroy moving in.

It would have to be Leroy, of course. Piers had got through well over a thousand partners, man and boy, in the last ten years, to my certain knowledge, and some of them had been charming, though of course there had never been time for me to meet them all. But of the ones I disliked, Leroy was the one I disliked most. He was absolutely the worst product of the civil rights and gay liberation movements. Very young and very pretty, in tight trousers and open shirts, with masses of gold chains round his neck and a provocative manner that positively screamed, 'Go on, insult me, and then I can prove you're anti-gay and anti-black.' There was no winning with Leroy. If you were pleasant to him, you were being patronizing; if you were unpleasant, you were being prejudiced. Impossible to be normal with him because he simply wasn't normal, in the human sense, I mean. He was a monster: lazy, selfish, greedy and dishonest, and he brought out the worst in me on purpose.

Leroy was from the deep South and had one of those maddening accents that I'm sure he exaggerated because he thought it sounded cute – one of his favourite words. One of his grandfathers or great-grandfathers – some ancestor anyway – had been a slave, so he claimed, and that was apparently enough to justify Leroy in making sure that everyone else was a slave to him. I realize of course that being black and gay in America was still no joke – well, it wasn't in England either – but it made me sick to watch Piers fetch and carry for him, leaping up to light his cigarette or refill his glass.

Officially Leroy was a model and actor, but forever out of work because he was no good, though of course he pretended that was all due to prejudice too. It turned out he wanted a share of the business that Piers and I had built up so slowly and painstakingly: he had always fancied himself as an agent, giving or withholding the jobs he had failed to get for himself. At first I couldn't believe it: it seemed like a bad joke. But Leroy was serious (he had no sense of humour) and Piers was in love with him. Whatever Leroy wanted, Leroy must have. Leroy was here to stay, ordering silk shirts by the gross and hiring decorators to transform the apartment. I can only assume that Leroy was very good in bed, although I truly believe he was much too idle to exert himself even there.

Nothing on earth would have persuaded me to give up my share of the business to Leroy – nothing, that is, except Mack's wedding and the lump in my breast, plus the fact that Piers sulked continuously until I agreed. Leroy of course had no money of his own, so Piers had to buy me out at a bargain price, to prove I wasn't prejudiced, and because he couldn't afford to pay me more. I might have held out, I suppose, if I'd been feeling fit and cheerful, but it did occur to me that my working days might be numbered and I certainly don't want to spend them with Piers in a sulk, or Piers and Leroy gloating. I could have waited for the Leroy phase to pass, only I didn't believe it would: Leroy looked to me like a permanent fixture, a true parasite who had found an ideal host. Besides, suddenly I didn't have much spare time.

So I saw a doctor and a specialist, and I sold out my share of the agency to Piers and Leroy, and I boarded a plane for London, leaving one of my ex-lovers, who was in real estate, to find a buyer for my apartment. Watching the Manhattan skyline disappear, I found it hard to believe I had spent ten years of my life in New York.

*

Arriving in London I felt very odd, neither visitor nor resident. All the élan of the Sixties had vanished, and there was a new atmosphere of anxiety and austerity which I felt very strongly but could not pin down. Perhaps I was imagining it because I had heard so much about it from my father.

As usual I had told no one I was coming home in case I changed my mind at the last moment. I knew I wouldn't, but I liked to feel I could. I checked into my usual room at Claridge's but it felt like an anachronism, although it was lovely as ever. I had never been much troubled by jet lag before but this time I was, and although I meant to stay up and adjust to English time, I found to my surprise that I was suddenly waking up on the bed, in my clothes, and it was evening.

I felt instantly alert but very disconnected, rather like a ghost with a high I.Q. I unpacked, thinking of all the clothes I had left behind in New York and the nuisance it would be to collect them or have them sent. Better to forget about them, perhaps. I had brought all my favourite things, and possessions had never mattered to me that much.

I rang for room service and ordered some champagne; then I rang my father. He wasn't at home, so I rang the club and after a moment or two he came on the line. I said hullo and found myself quite overwhelmed by the sound of his voice, his surprise and his joy: I had tears in my eyes.

'Where are you?' he said, as if it was a matter of urgency.

'At Claridge's.'

'When did you arrive?'

'This morning. But I've been sleeping.'

'But why didn't you let me know?'

I smiled. 'I wanted to surprise you.'

'Well, you have succeeded. And how long are you staying this time?'

The sixty-four thousand dollar question. 'Who knows? Perhaps for ever. I've sold my share of the agency and I'm looking for somewhere to live.' A gross over-simplification, but it would serve.

'Really? That's good news. You mean it? Well, when do we meet?'

'Tomorrow for lunch? If you're not too busy.'

'Yes, I am busy, of course, but for you it can all be arranged.' I could hear the pleasure in his voice and I wanted to hug him. 'Till tomorrow. Goodnight, my love.'

I hung up. Suddenly it occurred to me that Mack might be with him, sitting beside him and listening to every word. I could have gone round and surprised them that very minute: the club was not far away.

But of course I didn't. Instead I rang Mummy and had to endure an inquisition about Piers' behaviour which Mummy described as very silly, her most damning adjective. Mind you, she also thought I was rather silly to let him get away with it. She said she was disappointed in both her children, but that was nothing new. Daddy was at the House, so I couldn't speak to him, but I promised to visit them soon, maybe next weekend. Finally I managed to get Adrienne's number out of her, the purpose of the call.

She had been five or six when I last saw her, on that ill-fated visit, and now she was nearly thirteen, a much more interesting age and well worth a visit, especially if I didn't have all the time in the world left to play with. I prevaricated, pacing the room and looking out of the window, rearranging things on the dressing-table and brushing my hair. I stared at my reflection. It was hard to believe I was forty-two. I didn't feel old at all, just tired. Very tired. But luckily I did not look it. My mother's metabolism had preserved my body, her bones had upheld my face.

Finally I sat down on the edge of the bed and dialled the number. They were living in the depths of the country, for some extraordinary reason, so it took a while. I kept wondering if my instinct was right and Mack was at the club with my father. If so, Lisa would answer, little Lisa, grown-up Lisa, the official wife at last. Unless my daughter answered.

A sleepy voice said, 'Hullo?'

I said, 'Surprise. This is Diana.'

After a short pause the voice, now totally awake, said,

'Yes, it is a surprise.' It was cold, polite and wary. It was Lisa all right. No doubt about that.

'Can I speak to Adrienne?'

'No, I'm afraid you can't, she's asleep.'

I glanced at my watch. 'Already?'

'Yes, we're very old-fashioned, we believe in early nights.'

How she must have relished that 'we'. 'Well, I'd like to talk to her.'

'But you've never shown any interest in her before, quite the reverse.'

'Well, I'm showing it now.'

Silence. I sipped my champagne. At least that hadn't changed. I could almost hear Lisa thinking.

'I'm sorry,' she said finally, not sounding sorry at all, 'but I can't give you an answer now. I'll have to ask her first and talk to her father. Can I ring you back in a few days?'

'Why not tomorrow?'

'No, I can't do it sooner.' It was amazing how authoritative she sounded. The wedding ring must have turned her head. 'It's taken you so many years to ask, I don't think a few more days will matter, do you? Would you like to give me your number?'

I gave it to her and hung up before she could say goodbye, or worse still, hang up on me. I found I was shaking with rage and yet I also felt a certain amount of grudging respect, even amusement. It was odd how things turned out.

Well, if Lisa thought she could stop me seeing my daughter, she was wrong. What had started as a mere whim, a piece of idle curiosity, assumed a fixed purpose. I drank more champagne and lay on the bed, thinking. I needed a plan.

I told my father all about it over lunch. 'Yes, they refused all right. You bet they did. Lisa rang back this morning, pretending to be sorry, but you could tell she was delighted.' Still, it had been a minor triumph to get a decision so soon. I was quite surprised, after her playing for time. 'I admire Lisa – she's got spirit. There was a nice touch of malice in her voice. I wonder if she's as sexy as her mother.'

'Unfortunately, I have never had a chance to find out.'

I laughed. Above all, I wanted to be cheerful for my father. He mustn't be worried about me. 'What a shame. Never mind, the fantasy's probably better.'

'In this case I think the reality is perhaps quite good also.'

'Mm.' I could do without hearing Lisa's praises sung: the only way, given my father's affection for Mack, was to sing them myself. 'It must be great for Mack – the Jewish mother and the child-bride all in one package. Cooking and sex.' It was certainly ironic. 'My God, he's fallen on his feet this time.'

My father stared at his plate. We'd been having such a lovely jokey lunch and I was looking my best especially for him, but suddenly I knew he was about to tell me bad news.

He looked up at me. It was a heavy, anxious look. He was older than I remembered. He didn't want to hurt me and he was afraid he would.

'Did you know she's pregnant?'

Well, there was no better person to tell me. I kept my face blank, grateful for all my training. 'No. How very interesting. You'd think he'd had enough of that.' The obvious reason for the wedding, and I had not allowed myself to think of it. Pathetic.

I drove down the same afternoon. No time like the present, as Nanny had always said when she wanted me to do something now that I'd rather postpone. It was a fine November afternoon but I couldn't appreciate the scenery much; I was too busy thinking of the meeting ahead of me. How bizarre that Ruth's daughter should now be stepmother to my daughter and actually presuming to stand between us. It wasn't as if I wanted to take the wretched child away, after all; only to see her. Or was it Mack who was putting his heavy foot down, making sure I wouldn't contaminate his brave new world?

I was impressed when I saw the house, large and rambling, built of warm old mellowed stone and set in lovely grounds. I parked near the gate and walked up the drive: any element of surprise I could get would be useful, I thought. With any luck Adrienne should be due home from school soon after my arrival. I rang the bell and waited, but no one came so I rang again. What an anti-climax it would be if there was nobody in: the one thing I hadn't anticipated.

Lisa opened the door. She was wearing a long dress and no shoes and she looked flushed and vague, as if she had just woken up.

I said, 'Hullo, Lisa, I've come to see my daughter.'

Clearly I had given her a shock but she pulled herself together quickly. 'She's out.'

'When will she be back?'

'She's staying with friends. She won't be home tonight.'

Transparent as glass, our little Lisa. Always was. 'You're not a very good liar, are you? I suppose you don't get enough practice.'

'Look, I explained to you on the phone. She doesn't want to see you. And she's not here.'

'Then I'll come in and wait for her.' But Lisa didn't move and I was suddenly reminded most uncomfortably of Jean on my doorstep thirteen years ago. I should never have let her in, and if Lisa had any sense she wouldn't let me in. It was a time for swift action. 'I hope we're not going to have an undignified tussle in the doorway, with you in your delicate condition.' And I marched in as if there were no question about it. She didn't try to stop me: as usual, good manners prevailed, out of habit, as they had with me and Jean.

'Oh, this is very nice,' I said, looking round. 'I really like this house. I bet you chose it and everything in it. Mack never could see houses as homes, only as properties. I suppose it's an occupational hazard – like shoe salesmen having scruffy shoes and psychiatrists being neurotic.'

She followed me into the drawing-room, letting me ramble on, as if struck dumb by shock. 'Cat got your tongue?' Nanny would have said.

'Lovely. You've got much better taste than your mother.

Still, I suppose that wouldn't be difficult. What time will Adrienne be back?'

That got her going again, 'I've told you – she won't.'

I sat down and removed my gloves. 'You know, I really wish we hadn't called her Adrienne.'

'I think it's a pretty name.'

'Yes, but it's so . . . oh well, her father chose it, of course.'

She bridled slightly. (Was I beginning to get through to her?) 'I don't suppose you cared much at the time.'

'I had post-natal depression, I didn't care much about anything at the time.' How pretty she looked, and how absurdly young. 'I hope *you* don't get post-natal depression, it's extremely unpleasant.'

'I don't think I will.'

'No one ever does think they will. When's it due – in the spring, I suppose?'

'April.' She was still standing, eyeing me warily. It was annoying: it meant I had to look up at her. But I had to prove I was staying for a while.

'Clever you – at least you avoid carrying all that ghastly weight through the summer.' I could see her making up her mind she'd have to be rude to get rid of me.

'I'd like you to go now.'

'Go? I've got no intention of going.' I lay back in my chair to look more relaxed. 'Lisa, why all the hostility? We're not enemies, we're not even rivals. I've never done you any harm. In fact I've done you a favour – if I hadn't gone away you wouldn't be married to Mack, and I assume you're glad about that. I don't want him back, so you needn't be afraid. I just want to see my own daughter. Is that so very unreasonable?'

Her expression hardened and she suddenly reminded me of Ruth in one of her stubborn moods. 'You don't even remember her birthday.'

'Yes, I do, she's just had one, she's thirteen.'

'You've never sent her a present – you've never been in touch.'

'And don't you prefer it that way?'

Obviously she did, but she wouldn't lie, so she changed

the subject instead. 'Never mind what I prefer, how d'you think *she* feels? No wonder she hates you.'

'Don't be silly, of course she doesn't hate me.' I'd never heard anything so ridiculous.

'Well, she doesn't want to see you. We asked her and that's what she said. D'you know, she actually pretends you're dead.'

She looked shocked. I smiled. 'Now's the time to show her I'm not. I shouldn't get so excited if I were you, it's very bad for you. Sends up your blood pressure or something.'

'Look, you've never been a mother to that child, you ran away and left her to nannies and housekeepers and then I took over. We're a happy family and you're not welcome here.'

She was beginning to get on my nerves. 'Yes, you've made that perfectly clear, now do calm down. I'll go just as soon as I've seen her.' It was delicious to know that she couldn't get rid of me, short of physical ejection, and she obviously wasn't up to that. 'Thirteen is a very interesting age, you can't blame me for being curious. Has she got the curse yet? I do hope she has.'

An amazingly resentful look, as if I had no right to ask such intimate details. 'Yes.'

'Oh, good. I bet she started early, just like me. What have you told her about sex – take the pill or cross her legs? Funny to think if they'd only invented the pill a bit sooner she'd never have been born.' No doubt my mother could have said the same about me.

Lisa didn't answer. She looked very tense and I was irritated, after all the years I'd known her, that she wouldn't relax and have a normal conversation. It wasn't as if I was a stranger or an enemy. She'd taken my child and my lover and she couldn't even be civil to me. I looked idly round the room and noticed a photograph on a nearby table.

'Oh – is this the wedding? My God, she's pretty, my daughter.'

'Yes.'

'At least I've done one thing well.' I studied the photo-

graph more closely: there seemed to be someone missing.
'Where's Ruth?'

'She didn't come.'

Still the stony, po-faced stare. Oh, let her have it, silly
little cow. She probably knew already and if she didn't, she
should. 'Why not – because she's my father's mistress or
because she had a quickie with Mack? I thought she'd have
risen above all that for her only daughter's wedding.'

Well, there was no doubt about it, the whole thing came
as a complete surprise.

'Are you all right? You've gone awfully pale.'

She didn't answer, just suddenly sat down. She looked
white, shocked and bruised, as if someone had punched her
in the face. It was such an extreme reaction I could hardly
believe it, except that I knew she was no actress.

'For God's sake, don't tell me you didn't know. We all
move in such small circles – can I put it like that? – I naturally assumed ...' For one ghastly moment I thought she
might be going to be sick. 'Look, it was ages ago, you were
a tiny child, it was even before I met him; in fact Ruth
passed him on to me, I bet she's kicking herself now. Still,
she's always loved my father best – apart from your father,
I mean.' I wasn't even sure now if I was trying to make
matters better or worse, but her look was beginning to irri-
tate me. She was over-reacting. 'Oh, come on, don't look like
a stricken deer. I know you're young, but people have to do
something to prove they're alive. Look, it's all water under
the bridge. What does it matter now?' At least she didn't
have a lump in her breast.

Silence. I didn't know what to say next. She was still
looking as if I'd stuck a knife in her when we heard the front
door open and slam.

'Lisa?' It must be my daughter. 'I'm back. Did you watch
it?'

Footsteps. Adrienne came in. She was even prettier than
her photograph, but she stopped dead in the doorway when
she saw me.

'Hullo,' I said, 'I'm back too. D'you remember me?'

She stared at me for a moment. I thought she might hug

me or, equally, tell me I was meant to be dead, but instead she turned suddenly on Lisa and shrieked, 'I told you. I *told* you. How *could* you?' Then she burst into tears, rushed out of the room and slammed the front door behind her.

'Oh dear,' I said mildly. 'She's rather hysterical. Is she always like that?'

With a sudden burst of energy Lisa got up and yelled, 'Damn you. Are you satisfied now? Have you done enough damage?' She looked at me with absolute hatred, and then she ran after my daughter.

I waited for a while, but they didn't come back, so in the end I got bored and went home. The whole expedition had fallen rather flat. I sat on my hotel bed and considered what to do next. It was too late to ring my doctor and make an appointment, which was what I should have done already, if only to see whether he agreed with the doctors in New York. Well, I could do that tomorrow. Or next week. Why rush to hear bad news? Sufficient that I had to spend the weekend with my mother.

I slept late, surprised how tired I felt these last few months. I certainly wasn't bouncing back the way I used to in the good old days.

To cheer myself up I rang a few estate agents and asked them to send me lists of flats and houses; I would need somewhere to live pretty soon. I certainly couldn't stay at Claridge's indefinitely.

Around lunch-time I was still in my bathrobe and had just finished washing my hair when the telephone rang. They told me it was Mack and I said he could come up. So my visit had borne fruit after all. I was a bit agitated and over-excited at the thought of seeing him again and I wished he'd given me more notice. There was no time to do my face, but perhaps I looked younger without make-up, or so I told myself. My skin was still good. So I merely sprayed on a little scent.

There was a huge sudden bang on the door, as if someone had fallen against it. I opened it and Mack burst in, knocking me across the room. I was so surprised I hardly felt any pain, just total shock and breathlessness. Then I heard him slam the door and come towards me.

'My God, I ought to kill you for this,' he said, sounding as if he meant it. 'D'you realize what you've done?'

My turban had come off and my wet hair was dripping down my neck. I picked myself up and threw an ashtray at him, but he ducked. I tried to grab the phone, but he got to it first, with such a murderous look on his face that I dodged behind a chair. He pursued me. It was ludicrous and terrifying all at once, the worst fight we'd ever had. We were both smashing everything we could lay our hands on, and part of my mind was still detached enough to feel sorry for Claridge's, though no doubt they'd get their revenge.

It was probably only a few moments before he had me cornered, with his hands round my throat and this time no child to save me. I thought I was going to faint, and it occurred to me that it might be no bad thing, taking the long view, if he did in fact murder me after all, when abruptly his expression changed, my bathrobe fell open, he stopped trying to choke me, and suddenly we were making love.

It had been so long since we were together that the first time was very quick, but the excitement was tremendous. Afterwards we lay still and contemplated the wreckage of the room.

He said very softly, 'I think I really hate you,' but it sounded like love to me. When we started again it was slow and deliberate. When he went down on me, I remembered how much I had missed him; when he entered me, I felt I had come home.

Lisa

September

I re-read my old journals the other day and I was appalled
how self-centred I was. Poor Jamie. How badly I treated
him. Even at nineteen I should have known better than to
get engaged when my feelings were in such a muddle. I
can't understand why I was in such a hurry, why it had to be
Robert or Jamie, there and then, in a sort of panic, as if it
were wartime and I might never meet anyone else, ever. Was
I so anxious to leave home? I always thought I was happy
there.

Reading what I wrote four years ago is really shaming. I
can't avoid the impression that I was simply using Jamie and
the engagement to get what the Victorians would have called
a declaration out of Robert. It's such unpleasant scheming
behaviour and yet I don't remember myself being that kind
of person. It's obvious to me now that Jamie and I must
have been like brother and sister all along and when I
thought I wanted us to make love it was just a generalized
teenage sex urge, quite normal but not at all personal. I had
to make it respectable by calling it love.

The irony is that I've done the right thing, though inad-
vertently and clumsily. Robert and I *are* happy. But we've
paid a heavy price. Jamie is completely alienated from us
both, which makes me very sad. I miss him as a friend and
I know it's a terrible thing to have come between father and
son. There's nothing I can do about it. I just have to wait
and hope that one day it will all come right. And my parents
only tolerate our situation.

There hasn't been much time for keeping a journal over
the past four years. That shows how happy we've been. Also
that I hadn't the remotest idea how much time it takes to

343

run a home properly, even with plenty of money and help, and even though I'd watched my mother doing it all my life. I think I moved in with Robert too quickly because life at home became unbearable very soon after the big row, but he was right to make me complete my course at art school. It did mean I got very tired, though, because I wouldn't have a housekeeper; I wanted to look after Adrienne myself and do all the cooking, so we just had someone to clean, and of course there was all my college work as well *and* we were making love all the time, so I never got enough sleep but it was wonderful. We don't make love so often now, I suppose the novelty has worn off a bit and I know things are going badly in the property world, but it's still wonderful when we do. Moving to the country was a stroke of genius, as soon as I finished art school, and I really adore this house, although it's much too big for us.

It amazed me to think how little I knew about Robert when I moved in with him. It was like going to live with a stranger, though of course I didn't think that at the time. He's very affectionate but very moody. Sometimes he just shuts himself off from me and I can't reach him. I used to think it was all my fault, something I've done, but I've learnt that it usually means he's worried about work and it's better to leave him alone till he comes out of it. That's quite hard to do, but I try.

He talked to me a lot at first, about his childhood in Glasgow and how he always vowed to be rich because he saw what being poor did to his mother. It was the constant anxiety, he said, about making ends meet, rather than actually going without anything basic. The other awful thing was losing his father in the war and trying to be the man (aged twelve) of the house for his mother and three sisters. When his mother remarried he felt as if all his efforts just hadn't been good enough, so in a way he lost father and mother. I think it's made him very insecure, which he tries to cover up with a big tough front (like Jamie). He also feels inferior about not having had a proper education. He's spent all his time working and making money, so he doesn't know about books and music and art and history. Diana used to tease him about that, he said. He envies me my education, which is ridiculous because I'm really very ignorant, there are great gaps all over the place, but he won't believe me when I say that.

He hasn't talked much about Diana. He told me all about Jean and how happy they were at first and how guilty he felt about leaving her and the boys. He went on at great length about the horror of Duncan's death and how it seemed like a judgement. (He's a great believer in crime and punishment, almost old-fashioned.) But he hardly ever mentioned Diana. In a way I was relieved because I knew it would be painful. At the same time I longed desperately to know. I think I hoped that telling me about her would exorcise her. But obviously it's too deep and private.

Well, nothing can ever be perfect. I've learnt that much. Maybe I'm beginning to grow up at last. When we were first together I wondered if we made love so often because he was trying to forget about Diana. It was as if he were trying to bury himself in me.

One of the great joys has been watching Adrienne blossom. She's so self-confident now. I think I've really made up to her for being deserted, as far as you ever can. I love the feeling that I've been able to heal them both, Adrienne and Robert, after they'd both been badly damaged.

That's why I feel so nervous now. I was sure already: seeing the doctor was just a formality. I've got to tell Robert and Adrienne the news pretty soon and I really don't know how they're going to react. I'm thrilled, of course, but I've taken a big risk.

I made a specially nice stew and I was just putting it in the oven when Adrienne came in. I asked her about school.

'Oh, you know what it's like first day back,' she said. 'Pretty useless really. Nobody can find anything, and the teachers don't want to be there any more than we do.'

She sat down at the big oak table and I poured tea for us both. 'Bread and butter?'

She looked tempted but shook her head. 'No, I'm on a diet.'

I remember how my mother had dealt with me when I tried all that. 'Honey's good for diets. I'll cut the bread very thin.'

Adrienne said, 'I used to think teachers liked teaching, but they don't, they hate it.'

'Some of them, maybe.'

'Why do they do it then?'

'Well, they have to work at something – to earn a living. Lots of people hate their jobs.'

'Daddy doesn't.' She sounded approving. 'He loves his job.'

I put two slices of bread and honey in front of her. 'It's a bit different for him. He's working for himself.'

'How soon can I leave school?' She was eating ravenously.

'Not until you're sixteen at the earliest.'

She made a face.

'I thought you liked this school.'

'It's better than the last one.' She shrugged as if she were a veteran of a dozen schools.

'Well, then. Give it a chance. Was everyone there today?'

'Mm, but there wasn't enough time to talk. Karen was ever so miserable. Her mother's got a job. Poor old Karen.'

'Why?'

'Because her mother won't be there when she gets home from school, of course. It's rotten for her. They don't need the money, either – her father's rich.'

'Maybe her mother got bored. Some people do work for fun, you know.'

'It's still rotten for Karen.' She looked at me anxiously. 'You're not bored, are you?'

'No, not a bit.'

'Oh, good. I'd hate it if you weren't here when I got home. You won't get a job, will you?'

I smiled. 'No. I'm much too lazy.'

'That's all right then.' She finished her tea and the bread and honey and got up. 'Is it okay if I go round to Lucy's?'

346

'What, now?'

'Yes, she needs cheering up. Her mother's going to have another baby.'

Well, thank you, God, that's all I need right now. 'Isn't Lucy pleased?'

'No, of course she isn't.' She sounded as if I were an idiot. 'It's going to be awful.'

'Don't be late for supper,' I said faintly. 'We're having something special.'

Supper was a huge success. We all stuffed ourselves rotten and had seconds. Adrienne even helped me clear away.

'It was smashing. Maybe I could finish it up tomorrow.'

'Too late. I'm going to have it for lunch.'

'Couldn't I come home to lunch?'

'No, you could not.'

We were all laughing. I put the dishes through the hatch and brought in the next course.

'Gosh.' Adrienne was impressed. 'You've done a special pudding as well. What are we celebrating?'

'Nothing. I just felt like it.'

Robert said, 'Thank God for that. I thought maybe I'd forgotten our anniversary.'

I served the pudding; Robert poured more wine. Adrienne said, 'How can you have an anniversary if you're not married?'

'Oh, you'd be surprised,' Robert said.

'Is it a secret?'

'Sort of.'

We smiled fondly at each other. So far so good . . .

'How was Kovacs?' I asked.

'Fine. We had a good meeting.'

'Is he coming for the weekend?'

'Damn, I forgot to ask him.'

'Oh, Robert, it's his birthday, he might be lonely.'

'I'll ring him later.'

Adrienne swallowed the last of her pudding. 'Well, I better go and finish my homework.'

I was surprised. 'On your first day back, they gave you homework?'

'Well . . . not exactly.'

'You either have homework or you don't, that's how I remember it.'

She looked shifty. 'Mm, well, it's my holiday essay. I haven't quite finished it.'

'Oh, darling, you told me you had.'

'Well, I have *nearly*.'

'I'd never have let you go off to Lucy's if I'd known that.'

'Yes, I know.'

'And it's lights out at nine-thirty in term-time.'

'Ten,' she said, wheedling.

'No.'

'Oh, go on, please. Just this once. I can get it done by then and I've got to give it in tomorrow.'

Robert said nothing. He never interferes. I said, 'Quarter to ten and that's my final offer.'

'Oh, thank you.' She hugged me. It's such a tight hug. I don't think she's quite forgotten the desperation of those early days, even now. 'Night.'

'Night, darling.'

She hugged Robert. 'Night, Daddy.'

'Goodnight, lassie. Sleep tight.'

When she had gone I said, 'I'm too soft with her.' But I was still smiling.

'Rubbish. You're perfect with her and she adores you. Almost as much as I do.' He kissed me. 'And that was a wonderful meal.'

I said, 'Has it put you in a good mood?'

'Why?'

'Oh – I find I'm pretty conventional when it comes to the crunch, so I thought I'd give you a nice dinner first.'

He looked baffled. 'What are you talking about?'

'Adrienne was right really. We *are* celebrating something. At least, I am. I'm not sure about you, hence the meal. You may blow your top.'

'I will if you go on like this.'

'I meant to wait till we got to bed but I'm too nervous.' I

had a whole tribe of butterflies in my stomach. 'Oh well, here goes. I'm pregnant.' I watched his face. All I saw was shock. Not delight, but not horror either. Just shock. 'Yes, I was afraid you'd take it like that.'

He said, 'But you can't be pregnant, you're on the pill.'

'Not any more.'

'Since when?'

'Three months ago.'

He began to sound angry. 'You might have told me.'

'Yes, I might.' I had prepared for this moment for a long time. 'But every time we talked about it, you said maybe next year. I thought you meant sometime, never. I got tired of waiting. I know. It was wrong of me. I took a calculated risk.'

He said, 'I didn't realize you wanted a child that much.'

'Yes, you did.' It was our first real confrontation. For four years we'd been blissful and I'd made all the concessions.

'I'm sorry. Have I been very selfish?'

He's always fair. It's one of the things I love about him. 'Not really. I see your point. You've got two already, why have three? But I haven't had any. And you love Adrienne and Jamie so much, I thought you'd probably love another one, once it's real.'

'Maybe I will. Only I wanted to go on being alone with you.'

'But we aren't alone now. Not really.'

'You know what I mean. It's all so perfect – I don't want to change anything.'

'It can still be perfect. Just a bit different, that's all.'

'And I would have liked a say in the matter.'

When it comes to the point, regardless of age, he and Adrienne are both deprived children, really. I've got to make them believe there'll still be enough love to go round.

We had a strange, reserved evening and we didn't really make it up till we were in bed. I snuggled up to him in our big four-poster. 'Robert? Are you still cross?'

'I'm just getting used to the idea. It's very exciting.'

I was so happy I couldn't believe it. But he *is* surprising – that's another thing I love about him. 'Really?'

'Of course. The minute you told me, even though I was furious, I was still excited. And very proud.'

I said, 'Oh, darling, thank you. I'll make it ever so easy for you. You'll hardly know it's there.'

'In my experience that's not possible, but you're welcome to try.'

We both laughed and we had a good cuddle. Then he said, 'D'you want to get married?'

'Wow. You're actually prepared to make an honest woman of me.'

'Why not?'

I felt dishonest, trying to be fair when I only wanted to be self-indulgent. 'We always said that wasn't important.'

'Well, maybe we were wrong.'

'That wasn't why I got pregnant, honestly.' But I wondered, and I crossed my fingers as I spoke.

'Are you spurning my offer, woman? I know my track record's not so hot, but all the same . . .'

'Oh, we'll soon change all that.' I found I was almost in tears. 'Yes, I would like to be married, thank you.'

'You're very formal all of a sudden.'

'Well, it's a solemn moment.' Was it so important to me to be his wife because Diana hadn't been? 'Adrienne's going to be furious, I'm afraid.'

'Rubbish. She'll love being a bridesmaid.'

'No, I meant furious about the baby.'

'What makes you think that?'

'Oh – just something she said. I've been stupid. Just because I hated being an only child, I shouldn't have assumed she does. In fact she probably loves it. She certainly wants all my attention.'

'Don't worry about her, she'll be fine. Your parents are going to be the problem.'

I wondered why he thought that. I was so sure a baby was all we needed to bring my parents round. I was sick of their frosty tolerance. I wanted them all warm and relaxed, the way I remembered. They'd never be able to resist a grand-child. I went to sleep smiling.

Robert was right. My parents hit the roof. Or rather my mother did. It was unbelievable. Worse than when we told them we were going to live together.

Mummy said, 'Well, what d'you want us to do – congratu-late you?'

Daddy tried to calm her down but it didn't work. I said, 'I was hoping you might be happy for me. Because I'm so happy. We both are.'

She turned away from me.

Daddy said, 'Of course we're happy for you. It's wonder-ful news. We need time to adjust, that's all.' But he didn't sound as if he meant it. He was just being soothing and polite.

Mummy said, 'Don't be such a hypocrite. It's a dis-aster.'

I felt as though she was actually hitting me, which she never has. Robert could see me shrinking into a corner. He said, 'We didn't come here to have an argument. We wanted your blessing ... and we'd like you to come to the wedding; that's about it.'

Mummy said, 'I'd rather go to your funeral.'

'That's nonsense.' Daddy put his arm round her. 'Now stop it.'

I couldn't take any more. I started crying and I ran into the garden. The dog made a big fuss of me. Dogs always know when you're upset. Then Daddy came out and hugged me and talked about how Mummy'd come round if we only gave her time. I tried to find out why she was so angry and he said because Robert wasn't Jewish, of course, and he was so much older than me. But Jamie wasn't Jewish either and they let me get engaged to him, God forgive me. So it can only be the age gap. I can't understand it. It just doesn't seem a big enough reason for all this fuss. Daddy said he'd talk her round and he'd come to the wedding even if she didn't. It was awful – him even suggesting she might not come. After I've been happy with Robert all this time. She must know it's going to last.

Then Daddy said, 'Have you told Jamie yet?'

'No, I don't know how to. I was hoping you could do it for me.' It seemed a good moment to ask him, while he was trying to cheer me up. 'Sort of casually, at the office. *You* know.'

He said, 'Oh, Lisa. You don't ask much, do you?' And he sounded burdened.

I said, 'But we're hardly on speaking terms and he never sees Robert. It's all so awful and I'd like to make it right, I really would.'

'Perhaps there are things even you can't make right.'

'But I've got to try. Jamie can't go on avoiding us indefinitely.'

'Maybe he finds it too painful to see you.'

'Oh, Daddy, surely not. Not after all this time.'

It's odd the way Daddy seems to understand Jamie better than I do.

But he must have talked to him all the same because today when I was in the garden Jamie zoomed up in his sports car. He honked the horn and I looked over the wall and there he was. I was *so* happy to see him.

'Hey, you,' he shouted, smiling and waving. 'Little mother. Little Mother of all the Russias. Mazeltov.'

I laughed and nearly cried. I ran out to the car, calling, 'Jamie. Oh Jamie ...'

'Well,' he said, looking me over. 'You don't look so bad. Not about to burst, anyway.'

'No, of course not, it's ages yet. Don't be silly.'

He looked older, and even better-looking. More grown-up. A bit sad. I don't know. Maybe I imagined it. He was staring at me, too. Evaluating my face. It had been such a long time since we had seen each other.

He said, 'Well. You're a crazy lady.'

'Oh Jamie. D'you forgive me?'

'No.'

'Oh, please.'

We hadn't hugged or even touched. Now he got back into the car. 'Come for a drive.'

'I'd love to but I can't.'

'Why not?'

'I've got to be here when Adrienne gets in from school.'

'Ah yes. God forbid the brat should have to spend even ten minutes alone. Have you thought how much time I've spent alone in the last four years?'

'Not much, I bet.'

'Shows how little you know.' He revved the engine.

I was surprised by how moved I was to see him. 'Jamie, stay to supper. Your father'd love to see you.'

He actually laughed. 'Now that *is* an exaggeration. Not to say an untruth.'

'Please.'

'I only came to see if you were all right. And you are. Obviously.'

'Will you come to our wedding?'

'No. I'll be in Scotland.'

'But you don't know when it is yet.'

'That's when I'll be in Scotland.'

'Oh, Jamie.'

Suddenly he said, very briskly, as though he were in the office, 'You know, this baby and the wedding and all that. It doesn't make any difference. You're just wasting time. We're meant for each other. Don't you realize that?'

It was such a shock. We hadn't seen each other for four years and he comes out with all that. I said, 'No,' but I was fascinated by the unlikeliness of it all.

'Oh, yes,' he said, totally confident. 'It's only a matter of time. I'll be back to claim you, like a demon God.' He laughed, but I could see he was serious.

'Don't be silly,' I said, ashamed of myself for being flattered, however remotely. It's not every day someone talks about undying love. I didn't feel disloyal at that moment. It was all too sudden and a bit unreal. Like running into someone you knew at school who has turned into a film star.

'When you least expect it,' Jamie said. 'You wait and see. Marriage, babies, what the hell. You belong to me.' And he roared off up the road. After he'd gone, I could hardly believe I'd seen him and he'd said all those things. It had all been so quick and bizarre. Like a genie from a bottle in a pantomime.

Adrienne came home shortly afterwards looking miserable, refused tea in the garden and went straight indoors, saying she had a lot of homework to do. I got the impression she was angry with me. She hardly spoke at all at supper, ate very little and went to bed early. All most uncharacteristic. I tried to talk to Robert when we were in bed, but he'd had a hard day and he was half asleep. Then I thought I heard muffled sobs from her room, just for a moment.

'There's something wrong, I'm sure of it. She was so quiet at supper and she hardly ate a thing.'

'It's a teenage mood. Or that silly dieting they all go in for.'

'No, it was more than that.' The sound started again. 'Oh, Robert, do listen.'

But he didn't answer. Apart from his being very tired, I get the impression he doesn't take as much interest in Adrienne as he did when she was little. Either he finds her too difficult now she's nearly a teenager, or he simply handed her over to me when I moved in. I feel more and more that she's my responsibility, not his. Yet he used to be such a devoted father. I hope he's going to take a proper interest in our baby.

In the end I got up and went into Adrienne's room. The crying stopped before I opened the door.

I said, 'Darling, are you all right?' but she didn't answer. 'Please don't pretend you're asleep, I could hear you crying.' I sat on the bed beside her in the darkness, but she turned violently away from me. 'What is it? Please tell me. I love you very much and I can't bear you to be unhappy.'

'You don't love me.' Her face was buried in the pillow.

'Yes, I do. You know I do.'

'No, you don't.'

We went on like that for a bit, then there was a long silence. Finally she said accusingly, 'You're going to have a baby, aren't you?'

354

'Who told you that?'

'Jamie did.'

'I see.' He must have passed her on the way home from school. He certainly hadn't wasted any time. What a spiteful thing to do.

'It's true, isn't it?'

'Yes.'

She burst out, 'Why didn't you *tell* me?'

'I meant to, darling, but I was waiting for the right moment.'

'I don't want you to have a baby. I hate babies.'

'Why?'

'They make everything different.'

'Yes, they do, but that doesn't mean it won't be nice.'

'Yes, it does. It'll be horrible.'

I stroked her hair. 'Are you afraid I'll love the baby more than you? That won't happen, darling. I can promise you that. I won't love it more than Daddy, either, just differently. Don't you see? You'll always be special because you were first. And because you're you.'

She sniffed disbelievingly. Of course it was all just theory to her. I cast around for a way of proving it.

'Look. Daddy loves both of us, doesn't he? That doesn't make us jealous of each other, does it?' Thank God, that seemed to get through to her. She accepted my handkerchief and blew her nose.

'That's better. Now listen. We're going to get married next month and we'd like you to be our bridesmaid. Will you do that for us? In a lovely new dress. We'll be awfully sad if you don't.'

She didn't answer but she gave me a hug and I sat with her till she fell asleep. I was reminded of myself and my mother, only the roles were reversed. Then I went downstairs and rang up Jamie and told him what I thought of him. He pretended he'd assumed I'd told Adrienne already, made out he was quite innocent, didn't do it on purpose at all, and implied I was making a fuss about nothing and he didn't much care for being rung up at midnight. I was so angry I put the phone down on him.

Now I've upset three people: my mother, Adrienne and Jamie. I suppose he just might have been telling the truth and I shouldn't have lost my temper; I'm going to have to be extra loving and tactful with Adrienne; I'm worrying already in case my mother doesn't come to the wedding. Oh dear. This poor baby. What a lot of trouble it's causing. Was I very selfish to start it?

October

Well, we're married. Mummy didn't come to the wedding and Adrienne sulked all through it. Daddy and Kovacs were there, plus a few friends, but it was very quiet, which was what we wanted. Jamie was in Scotland with his mother, of course. As weddings go I can't pretend it was a huge success. It's lovely to know we've done it and it's official, and I've got a beautiful ring, but it was hard to rejoice properly with those three special people absent or furious or both. I feel as if they all tried to ruin my big day. I'm quite angry with them all, as a matter of fact. In the middle of the ceremony at the registry office I suddenly felt as if I'd lost patience; I was worn out with trying to see other people's points of view instead of my own.

November

I'm surprised how tired I am. I've already been so strong and healthy and I'm the ideal age to be pregnant, I never imagined I'd find it so exhausting. I don't seem to have any energy. I fall asleep at odd times of the day and it takes a real effort just to get through my normal routine. And the middle three months are supposed to be the best, everyone says, when you should feel really well. Maybe I'm feeling tired because I wasn't sick at all. Maybe it's justice. They have to even up the score somehow.

A dreadful thing happened last night. Diana rang up. Robert was out seeing Kovacs and I was having my usual sleep in front of the television when the phone woke me. I got such a shock. I didn't even know she was back in London. We had a very chilly conversation. She wants to see Adrienne – after all this time. I told her I'd have to talk to Robert and I'd ring her back.

Adrienne came in to say goodnight shortly after that. The noise of pop music from her bedroom was deafening when she left the door open, but she said she'd finished her homework.

I said, 'I don't know how you can work through all that noise.'

'Didn't you when you were young?'

'Yes.' I didn't know whether I was amused or hurt. It seems I've turned into the wicked pregnant stepmother, so I'm suddenly old as well.

She said, 'I looked in earlier but you were asleep.'

'I'm sorry. It's just that the baby makes me awfully tired at the moment.'

'I told you it would make a difference.' She sounded coldly smug, like an expert who had been proved right. I was the bungling amateur who'd stupidly imagined everything could go smoothly. 'Who was that on the phone? Daddy?'

I should have said yes. Instead I said, 'No. A wrong number.' Such a stupid lie, and lies don't come easily to me. I was amazed how quickly I lied, but why didn't I accept the lie she offered me?

She said, 'You were talking for ages.'

'They were very argumentative.'

'You should have hung up on them. I always do.' As if her life was plagued by wrong numbers.

Robert came in soon after she'd gone to bed. He was very depressed because Kovacs had been full of gloom about the economy. I broke the news to him about Diana, but he already knew she was back because she'd rung Kovacs at the Club. We talked about her wanting to see Adrienne. He was dead against it, purely on the grounds of her being a rotten mother. In my heart, of course, I agreed with him, but I felt obliged to be fair and put the other point of view.

'I'm only a stepmother, and pregnant, and Adrienne hates me being pregnant. Who am I to stop her seeing her real mother, just because I'm jealous?'

He sat beside me and held my hand. It was very comforting.

'I don't want them to meet.'

'Darling, are you afraid of Diana?'

'No, of course not. But she's bad for Adrienne. She's an intrusion.'

'I'm afraid of her. That's why I was so nasty on the phone. But she has a perfect right to see her own child.'

He said very deliberately, 'I love you.'

'Yes, I know. But she was always the special one.'

'She was a disaster.'

We were both silent. That was the most we'd ever said about Diana.

I said eventually, 'I think we should ask Adrienne what she wants to do. She might like to see her mother.'

'Rubbish.'

'Then she can say no.'

'Oh – let's leave it a bit.'

'We can't, darling. Diana might always ring back. And Adrienne might answer the phone.'

'She'll be at school.'

'Not tomorrow. They've got the day off for Princess Anne's wedding.'

He got up and poured himself a drink, then paced about with it. He hadn't done that for a while. It's always a bad sign.

'Christ, I wish Diana'd leave us alone.'

'Maybe it's you she wants to see.' The thought had occurred to me before, but I'd pushed it away.

'Then she could come to my office and I'd soon tell her where to get off.'

I hope he means that. He sounded almost too emphatic.

We told Adrienne about Diana over breakfast. She said she'd known I was lying about the phone call. She also said she hadn't got a mother.

I said, 'Darling, you know you have, only she's been away in America, and now she's back.'

She said, 'I always tell people she's dead. It makes them feel ever so sorry for me.'

Robert looked at her in astonishment, 'Why on earth should you want people to feel sorry for you?'

'It's fun. Anyway, she might as well be dead.'

I said, 'Don't you remember her at all?'

'No. Why should I?'

'Well, you were five – nearly six – when you saw her last. I thought you might remember.' And I'm sure she does. Only it's too painful, so she's buried it. 'Anyway, she wants to see you.'

'Too bad.'

'I promised to ring her back.'

'Well, you can tell her to piss off then.'

Robert left for work, saying he approved her sentiments but not her language. I should feel triumphant but I don't. Adrienne may be rejecting Diana but she's rejecting me as well. She's gone to spend the day with a friend. It's more fun, she says, to watch the wedding on television there than here. She's probably right. Now all I have to do is ring Diana and say no. I think I'll go back to bed after that.

December

I've been too depressed to write anything since I got out of hospital. I've lost the baby. Diana came to see me and told me my mother is Kovacs' mistress and has also had an affair with Robert. I didn't believe it at first. Then Adrienne arrived home, took one look at Diana and seemed to think I'd invited her round. She rushed screaming out of the house and I rushed after her, leaving Diana sitting there. I was so afraid Adrienne would have an accident, the state she was in. She dashed across the road without even glancing at the traffic. I didn't have shoes on, so I got in the car and drove after her, but that only made her start running across the fields so I parked and chased her. It was stupid of me but I didn't think. It seemed so important to catch her and calm her down and explain I hadn't asked Diana to see her against her wishes. But I couldn't run very well in the field, it was uphill and I twisted my ankle and fell very heavily and then I got a terrible pain.

They were very nice to me in hospital but they couldn't save the baby. I was very unlucky. I can't be as strong as I thought. Losing the baby was dreadful. On top of all the pain I kept thinking it was all for nothing. Then I thought about my mother and what Diana had said. I tried to believe she was lying. She had to be.

Robert and Adrienne came to see me and brought flowers. Adrienne said, 'I'm sorry about the baby,' as if she meant it. She said it was all her fault and could I have another one. I said I didn't know. 'You've still got me,' she said.

When she'd gone back to school Robert went on about how he'd like to kill Diana for calling on me, but of course he didn't know what she'd said. He told me my parents sent their love and would be visiting me, so I asked him not to let my mother come.

'Why not? I thought you were so keen to make it up with her – and now she really wants to – it's the one good thing –'

I said, 'D'you remember you once promised never to lie to me?' and he said yes. 'Is my mother Kovacs' mistress?'

He looked genuinely surprised. 'I've no idea – what makes you say that?'

'Diana told me. She seemed to think I knew. She seemed to think everyone knew.'

'Well, I certainly didn't. Look, don't get upset, it may not be true ... and even if it is, you mustn't let it affect the way you feel about your mother.'

'That wasn't all Diana told me.' I was reliving the scene. I thought I had probably been running away from Diana as much as after Adrienne. My heart felt tight in my chest and I couldn't breathe properly. 'She said you were my mother's lover long ago. Is that true?'

He was silent but it was enough, the look of anguish and guilt, the obvious uncertainty whether or not to lie.

'I see.'

He said, 'You must let me explain.'
'Please go away.'

I dreaded coming out of hospital: at least I could be alone there. I've moved into the spare room to give myself time to think. I can't bear to be anywhere near Robert. I feel sick at the thought of him touching me.

At first he was very hang-dog and shamefaced, creeping round the house and waiting on me. Then he started insisting we talk about it.

'There's nothing to talk about. You had an affair with my mother. That says it all.'

'No, it does *not* say it all. It lasted about three weeks, I was flattered, she was bored, and it meant nothing to either of us.'

'Is that supposed to make me feel better?'

'I don't know, but it's the truth. Are you going to punish me and your mother for the rest of our lives for something we did when you were five years old?'

Put like that, yes, it sounded unfair and unreasonable. I tried to explain. 'I can't help it. I can't sleep with you at the moment, not because I don't love you but because ... she knows about you in the same way I do.' It was unbearable to think about it even for a moment. 'I don't mind about the others because I'm not close to them, but she's my mother. It's as if you and I aren't private any more, we aren't alone in bed, she's there with us.' And it made me feel sick.

'What can I do?' He looked stricken, but at least he seemed to understand.

'I don't know.'

And I really don't. I didn't say that just to punish him. When I don't feel sick I feel numb. I'm so tired it's all I can do to be up and dressed by eleven and by about half past two I want to go to bed again. It's even an effort to drag myself up again by five. My doctor says exhaustion is a symptom of depression and she can give me some pills to help, but I said no. I don't want to be doped, I want to

361

know how I really feel. She thinks it's all to do with losing the baby, of course; she goes on about how easy it will be to start another one as soon as my system gets back to normal. She doesn't know about the other thing. I couldn't tell her about that.

Every morning when I wake up I have to remember about my mother and Robert. There's always a split second when I've forgotten and I feel almost all right. I don't know what to do. I can't imagine life ever being normal again, but we obviously can't go on avoiding each other indefinitely. He's very quiet now, just waiting for me to 'come round' or 'forgive and forget' or whatever he calls it in his head. Adrienne's got bored with being guilty and sympathetic and she's started slamming doors and playing loud music again. I don't really blame her. I'm not exactly ill and I must be pretty boring to live with from her point of view.

The worst irony of all is I need my mother more than anyone else at this time and she's the one person I can't even speak to. At first I cried and cried, but now I just sleep.

Well, something had to be decided. We couldn't all go on staring at each other. I'm going to Geneva on the seventeenth to stay with Judy and her husband for three or four weeks. Robert isn't coming with me. It wouldn't work. In any case, things are going very badly at the office, so he couldn't get away even if he wanted to. It seems Kovacs was right to be pessimistic. My father is very depressed too. Property values are really tumbling and we could all be in serious trouble quite soon. It's all I need really and yet in a sense it's irrelevant. Things are so black they can't get blacker. We may as well have all the disasters at once.

Jamie sent me a huge bunch of flowers, which was nice of him, and I'm going to have lunch with him on my way to the airport.

Jean

When Lisa went to live with Robbie, Jean sold the house in London and moved back to Scotland. She was disgusted with herself for not doing so before. It was humiliating to wait until such an event forced her to act. She should have moved long ago, on her own initiative.

All the same, her feelings were very mixed. She could not be jealous of Lisa, she found, as she had been of Diana. She was surprised but not wounded. And she did not think it would last. Maybe that was the greatest source of comfort. She saw it as infatuation on both sides: Robbie trying to recapture his lost youth, Lisa romantically bemused by the older man. It was a cliché, so it had to be temporary. But the effect on Jamie wrung her heart. When he came to see her, she hardly recognized him. The loving, warm-hearted young man she had been so proud of had gone, to be replaced by a self-contained, embittered adult.

She was glad to be in Scotland again. When she was alone, she could almost pretend that none of it had really happened. She saw London now as a terrible maelstrom of emotions: she was lucky to have escaped. David and Ruth had reacted almost as strongly as Jamie. Ruth, in particular, was distraught. Jean thought it ironic that she had objected to Jamie as a son-in-law, but now would be positively grateful to have him. She was implacably opposed to Robbie – on the grounds of age, Jean supposed. She could find no other reason, from Ruth's point of view. The religious problem was surely much the same. In fact, it should be easier for Ruth, since there was, presumably, no question of marriage.

Back in Scotland, very slowly, she learned resignation. It was painful but necessary. To find peace she had to face the fact that her emotional life was dead. She had put off the moment as long as she could, but it was finally here. She had to stop wanting Robbie and she had to leave the space unfilled. It was like cutting a piece out of her heart.

Unwelcome information filtered through to her. Robbie and Lisa had moved to a house in the country. They were reputed to be idyllically happy. Years passed. For them, there would be anniversaries. Already it was lasting longer than she had thought it could. They began to seem glamorous and unreal to her, like people she had read about, with photographs, in the gossip columns.

Then, after they had been together four years, she heard that Lisa was pregnant and they were getting married. Jamie came to stay with her for a few days. While the wedding was taking place she was carefully weeding Duncan's grave and arranging new flowers. Jamie didn't help, merely stood and watched her. The pain in his face helped her to forget about any pain of her own.

'D'you spend a lot of time here?' he asked her.

'I like to come up once a week, make sure it all looks nice.' She had bought her cottage because it was near the place where Duncan was buried. Sometimes she came here every day, but she would not tell Jamie that.

'Poor little sod. Lot of good that'll do him.'

'It helps *me*,' she said, chilled by his tone.

'I'm sorry, Mam. Of course it does. I didn't mean it like that.'

He was restless: he kicked at the turf and stared into the distance, then back at the grave. She got the feeling he was tormenting himself by picturing the wedding. She found that her grief for his loss, and his jealousy, was greater than any she had felt for herself. She really would have suffered anything to spare him this.

He said, 'Is that why you moved up here – to be near him? Or to get away from Dad?'

She thought about it. 'Both. Oh – there were lots of reasons. I'd had enough of London, that whole . . . part of my life was over. I wanted to come home and be peaceful.'

'Don't you get lonely?'

'Not a bit.' She tried to sound cheerful. 'I see a lot of your grandmother and all my old friends. I've got a nice job at the hospital. Even my parents aren't so bad now I only have to pop in for ten minutes.'

'You've given up,' he said severely.

'I have *not*. What d'you mean by that?'

He didn't answer. He had his father's brooding look. She was shocked that at his age he had not recovered from the loss of Lisa yet, after four years. Then she thought of Robbie and Diana. He might be marrying Lisa because she was pregnant, but it was probable he still loved Diana. Or was it too much to bear, that she had actually divorced him for someone he had now forgotten? No, it wasn't possible. And what about her own behaviour over the past thirteen years? Jamie gets it from both of us, she thought, this fatal tenacity. It's like a curse and he's got a double ration of it.

They walked back from the cemetery to the cottage in the autumn sunshine. He said, 'D'you want Dad back? I bet you could get him if I took Lisa away.'

'You do talk nonsense sometimes.'

'Oh, I'm going to have her eventually and then he'll be all alone.' He sounded absolutely matter-of-fact, not dramatic at all. Like someone who had worked out how long it would take him to save up for his dream car.

'Believe it or not, Jamie,' she said, praying it was true and crossing her fingers, 'I've stopped thinking about your father, and I only wish I'd done it sooner. If you take my advice, you'll put Lisa out of your head.'

'How d'you manage for sex?'

'That's none of your business.'

Over supper she tried to divert his attention to more cheerful topics.

'How's that nice girl-friend of yours?'

'Cathy? She's okay.'

'Why don't you marry her?'

'Why should I?'

'You've been together quite a while now.' There had been a lot of girls in Jamie's life since Lisa, but Cathy had lasted the longest and she had met her once and liked her.

'I don't love her.'

'Then why live with her?'

He shrugged. 'It suits me – for the moment.'

'That's not very fair on her, is it?' She didn't like to think she had produced such a hard-hearted son.

'It's a free country. She can always walk out if she's not satisfied.'

When he left, she watched until his car was out of sight. She was very worried about him: he seemed all set to ruin his life in exactly the same way that she had ruined hers, and she was powerless to prevent it. Why couldn't he see from her example how futile it was to go on pursuing someone, whether husband or sweetheart, who had rejected you? It could never be the same again. All that wasted time and effort and feeling – and all for what?

In November she heard that Diana had returned and Lisa had miscarried. It was as if all her worst fears had been realized. Diana had told Lisa about Ruth's lover and Lisa was so shocked that she and Ruth were not even speaking, now, at a time like this, when she surely needed her mother most. But Jamie was jubilant. He would be spending Christmas and Hogmanay in Scotland with Jean. She couldn't understand it. He had given up Cathy; Lisa was going to Geneva to recuperate; the property business was in the doldrums – and yet Jamie was jubilant.

Jean was puzzled, but she couldn't concentrate on Jamie for once; instead she kept thinking about Diana. Back to square one. Diana in London. Diana visiting Lisa. Diana with Robbie perhaps? She felt a melancholy satisfaction at being right. She had always believed Diana would come back.

1974

Diana

It turned out Lisa had a miscarriage after chasing my daughter across a field or something equally stupid and unnecessary. Mack was very upset and I pretended to be sorry, but privately I thought it served her right. In any case she was young enough to have a dozen children if she wanted them, so I couldn't see what the fuss was about. It looked to me as if the main object of the exercise had been to get safely married at long last, and she had accomplished that.

However, it seemed she was brooding about what I'd told her about Mack and Ruth, wouldn't sleep with him, and even took herself off to Geneva for a Christmas holiday with one of her cousins. All of which suited me perfectly: she could hardly have done me a bigger favour if she'd tried. From November to January Mack and I had a wonderful fling, meeting three or four times a week. It was just like the old days. I didn't ask to see Adrienne again: I couldn't insist and I wasn't going to beg. Besides, I thought if I left well alone and she was anything like me, one day she'd suddenly change her mind.

It was so lovely being Mack's mistress again, and back in London and free, that I tried to forget about the lump in my breast. I thought it was growing, but it wasn't obvious yet and Mack didn't notice it. I wanted to tell him about it, but I also didn't want to spoil the Indian summer we were having: we were surely entitled to that. Besides, there were enough other clouds on the horizon. The bank was getting heavy with him and he was having big financial problems. My father was also deep in gloom about the state of the economy, and worried about Ruth because Lisa wasn't speaking to her. But at least he was happy about Mack and me.

Well, the state of the property market had to benefit someone. I got my money out of New York and bought a small mews house in Kensington. It was reassuring to have a home of my own again, though I didn't have much left to spend on it.

Then in January Lisa came back from Geneva and she and Mack had a reconciliation. That meant he had to be more careful and spend more time at home, so we could only meet twice a week, but that still suited me fine, and my father was very cheered. He thought it was perfect for Mack to have Lisa as a wife and me as a mistress. So did I, really; I only wished we hadn't wasted so much time achieving a perfect balance, when I had said long ago that this was how it should be. We were getting on better than ever, now that it was nearly too late.

All the same, there was something about Lisa's return that made me face facts, so in February, round about my birthday, I saw my doctor. He was very cross with me about the delay and sent me to the inevitable specialist, who was even crosser. They both echoed what the American experts had said, only rather more vehemently because of the time lapse. I must go in at once for a biopsy. It might be benign or malignant. If it was malignant I might lose the breast or merely part of it: I must give them permission to do as they thought best according to what they found. I said I needed time to think about it. They said I had wasted too much time already, but if I hurried now and did what they said, all might yet be well. They tried to be very cheerful and encouraging, which didn't quite go with the urgency.

I went home and wondered why I had waited so long. Was I simply a coward or did I have a death wish? Everyone I had spoken to seemed to assume that life was worthwhile at any price; I was not so sure. Would Mack still love me with a mutilated breast? Would I still love myself? What was there really for someone like me to look forward to, my career over, getting older and older, eventually losing my looks? No one but my father had ever loved me for my character. It was only logical to assume that the best part of my life was already behind me.

Still, I might have faced up to it, I suppose, if Mack had been more supportive. I had taken a short holiday in March because the weather was so foul and I needed some sun: looking brown always made me feel better. I came back almost resolved to tell him, if only I could get over the idea that he might feel sorry for me: I couldn't have borne that. Whatever else, I had always been strong in his eyes. He had never seen me as pathetic.

But when I came back, he was changed. Oh, he was still sexy and attractive, but there was a subtle difference, as if his mind were far away. It was odd, because lately we'd been having some good conversations. It disturbed me, so I didn't tell him anything. I waited, suspiciously, like an animal trying to sniff out what a new scent might mean.

Early in April he told me. He arrived one day with flowers, which was totally out of character. They were red roses, really good ones, three dozen of them, as if he were copying someone he'd seen in a film. When I kissed him he was tense and unresponsive, and I knew the writing was on the wall. I almost laughed. What a sublime sense of timing we both had.

'I must talk to you,' he said.

'Yes, you do have that faintly ominous look – I remember it of old. D'you want a drink? Would it oil the wheels?'

'Thank you.'

I put the flowers down and poured whisky while he paced about my drawing-room.

'Do sit down, Mack, you make me nervous when you walk up and down like that. I get the feeling you're about to condemn my brickwork.'

'Sorry.' He sat on the edge of a chair, looking uncomfortable. I handed him his drink and he thanked me in a funny, embarrassed way.

'Darling, you do look gloomy.' He was still my brown gorilla, I thought as I studied him, but going grey now, and looking as if he had the weight of the world on his furry shoulders. I sat opposite him in the big armchair, sipping my drink and suddenly wondering if all this gloom could possibly be related to things I had seen in the press, and therefore in a sense not bad news at all. At least, nothing to do with me, nothing personal.

'Are you really bust?' I said. 'I saw the papers but I couldn't believe it.'

'Oh, it's true enough. If anything, they underplayed it.'

'God, how awful. I *am* sorry. It seems incredible.' But newspapers always exaggerated everything, and most people I knew who were said to have gone bust seemed to go on living in much the same way. It couldn't actually mean he had no money left.

'Aye, it seems that way to me too.' He drained his glass: he was drinking faster than I had ever seen him drink before.

'Why don't we just go to bed and take our minds off it?' I suggested. 'Bound to cheer you up, it always does.'

'No, I ...' He lapsed into nervous, anxious silence.

'You're not in the mood. Okay.' I got up. 'I'll just get some water for the flowers. Help yourself to another drink if you like.'

When I returned with the two vases filled with water he was leaning forward, his face buried in his hands as if he wanted to hide from the world. I felt really sorry for him.

'Isn't there something you can do?' I started arranging the roses. 'I'm sure my father'd lend you money. I could even let you have a little – not that I've much left after buying this place, but you're welcome to it. What does it cost to start again – in a small way, I mean? We could call it Phoenix Erections or something like that.'

'No. Thanks all the same.' His voice was muffled.

'Surely you *want* to rise from the ashes.'

He took his hands away from his face. He looked terrible.

'Diana, I'm trying to say goodbye. Only I don't know how to.'

I was shocked. It was all the worse because I'd suspected something like this when he walked in and then I'd persuaded myself it was only money worries. Besides, I'd never really believed that this could happen.

'So you decided to "say it with flowers". Good for you. I should have guessed.' And I almost had.

'It's not easy.' He sounded almost as if he felt I should comfort him.

'Oh, you seem to be managing. May I know why?'

'You'll only laugh.'

'Let's hope so.'

'I feel guilty.' He looked at me wretchedly. 'The thing is ... Lisa's going to have another baby and –'

'Oh, she's always doing that, isn't she?' Sneaky little cow. 'Starting them, I mean. D'you think she'll finish this one?'

'I hope so.'

'Well, well. The demon father strikes again.' I went on arranging flowers as if my life depended on it. 'Forgive me for being dense, but just exactly what does Lisa's pregnancy have to do with you and me together?'

'To put it very crudely ... I'm afraid she might find out, and after what happened last time, that could be the end. I'm not prepared to risk it.'

I was impressed by his practicality and his devotion. 'You really love her.' I'd never considered that seriously before; I'd always assumed sex and cooking and a mother for Adrienne were all he wanted.

'Yes,' he said, shamefaced, as if caught out in some misdemeanour. 'But I love you too.'

'So much you're going to give me up. I see.'

'I can't cope any more, lassie. You enjoy this kind of double life but I don't. It doesn't suit me – it never did. Don't you remember? And the way things are now – it's all too much. I've lost the company; if I lose my wife and child as well – I don't think I could take that.'

'She *is* important ...' I still didn't seem to grasp this amazing fact.

'She doesn't replace you but ... she's never let me down, she's always been there when I needed her, she made me feel life was worth living again after I lost you. I feel she's my last chance. If I mess it up, that's the end of me.'

I could have done without the litany. 'Tremendous.'

'I'm sorry.'

'So am I. I enjoyed being your mistress again. Twice

weekly visits are just about my limit. Oh well, can't win 'em all. Funny really. There was something I wanted to tell you too.'

'Tell me now.'

That would be a real joke. 'No, it's irrelevant now.'

He got up and came towards me. 'I hope you know just how much you mean to me.'

'Oh, for God's sake, you don't have to make a speech.' I wondered if he could see how much he'd hurt me. 'Full marks, anyway,' I said brightly. 'You've finally managed to surprise me.'

'I best be on my way.' But he didn't move. We just stood there looking at each other.

'It's the end of an era, Mack,' I said. 'What do we do – shake hands?'

So we went to bed for the last time. It wasn't one of our best sessions, but we couldn't have said goodbye any other way. When it was over we were both crying and he held me in his arms and kissed me as if he could never let me go. Then he got up and got dressed and went home.

After that, there didn't seem much point in opting for surgery. I might have been able to face it with Mack holding my hand, assuring me it wouldn't make any difference to us; it was a different matter facing it alone. So much of my life had depended for satisfaction upon work and lovers. Well, my modelling career had been over long ago and Leroy had put an end to my share of the agency. I'd never imagined Mack could reject me, no matter how often I rejected him; it had seemed like the law of gravity. I couldn't imagine embarking on new love affairs with such a blow to my self-esteem as well as the problem with my breast.

I didn't go out much for a while and I didn't ring anyone. I felt safer at home, not talking, not having to react, while I thought about what to do next. It was wonderfully peaceful, but of course it couldn't last. One evening when I was curled up on the sofa, wallowing in champagne and Sinatra, my father arrived on my doorstep. He looked anxious, so I tried to give him a big welcoming smile.

'May I come in?'

'Of course.'

'You're not entertaining?'

'Not very, no.' But it wasn't his sort of joke. We hugged and kissed on both cheeks and I closed the door behind him. 'Why didn't you ring?'

'Because you don't answer the phone any more.'

'Oh, that.' So it had been my father, not Mack. 'Sorry. I've been very busy.'

'Doing what?'

'Thinking.' I turned off Sinatra who was nearing the end of 'Here's that Rainy Day', almost too much of a good thing, even in my present mood, 'Have you had supper?'

'Yes, I dined at my club.'

'Ah, you don't trust my omelettes. A glass of champagne then?'

'Thank you. So – what have you been thinking about?'

'Oh, this and that.'

He raised his glass. 'Your health.'

I couldn't help laughing; I hoped I didn't sound hysterical. 'To life. God, who invented these toasts? What a macabre sense of humour they must have had.'

He looked very serious. 'Tell me what's wrong, Kisleanyom.'

'Yes, I suppose I'll have to.' It felt very odd, now that the moment had actually come. I'd been alone with the problem for so long. 'Well, I've been trying to decide what to do. You see – I've got a lump in my breast.' I was watching him closely: for a moment there was a flicker of intense alarm, but he concealed it so quickly I almost felt I had imagined it. But then, he was a poker player, of course. 'The left breast, to be precise. It's not very big but it's growing and they want me to have it removed.'

A moment's silence. 'Then you must, of course.' He sounded completely matter of fact.

'Mm. I'm not so sure.'

'But you can't neglect these things. You catch it early and it's a simple matter. It happened to Ruth years ago. There was nothing to it.'

I poured more champagne. 'Come on, you're just saying that to cheer me up.'

'You can ask her yourself.'

'I don't think I will.' Ruth had made it clear that she blamed me for the rift with Lisa. 'Somehow I get the feeling I'm not Ruth's favourite person right now.'

He looked at me imploringly. Suddenly I thought that the worst part of the whole business was going to be upsetting him, of all people. No one else had loved me truly all my life.

'Kisleanyom, it's a simple operation, believe me, but you must have it done quickly.'

'Yes, that's what the specialist said. He was madly cheerful, of course, the way they always are, but he did manage to convey a feeling of urgency.' And an air of disapproval, rather like a headmaster, I thought.

'You must go in immediately. I'll pay for everything of course. You'll have the best.'

'That's sweet of you, but I think I'd rather not.'

'What?' He looked horrified.

'I'm fond of my breasts. I know they're not very big, but they *are* pretty. I'd rather keep them that way.'

'In a few years, you will hardly notice the scar.'

'Especially if I don't have the operation.' I was hoping we could leave it at that, but he stared at me in such alarm that I had to go on. 'Look – say I let them cut it out and it's harmless. I'm disfigured and all for nothing. They could have left well alone. On the other hand, suppose it's ... not harmless. I could end up losing the whole breast.'

'That's most unlikely.'

'But it's possible. I couldn't live like that. I'd feel ... mutilated.' I tried to smile. 'I wasn't cut out to be an Amazon.'

My father put his arm round me. 'My love, if you are so determined to look on the black side of things, you have to admit it's better to lose a breast than lose your life.'

Odd how everyone but me seemed to believe that. Did no one else consider the quality of life, merely the length? 'Ah.

Now I'm not sure about that. I've been giving that a lot of thought.'

His expression became severe and he let go of me. 'You mustn't frighten me like this, it's bad for my heart.'

'What do you mean?'

'I had a big heart attack a few years ago and they told me to be careful.'

I was so shocked I could hardly breathe for a moment, let alone speak. I just stared at him. 'Why didn't you *tell* me?'

'Oh – there was nothing you could do and you had your own problems.' He shrugged. 'I didn't want to worry you. But now it's a different matter.'

Words started tumbling out of me. 'Did Mack know you were ill?'

'Yes.'

'And Ruth?'

'Of course.'

'And they didn't tell me.' I was filled with rage; I felt sick. 'I asked them not to.'

'It's unforgivable. I had a right to know. I'm not a child.'

'If you can speak so carelessly of your own life, then you *are* a child. A spoilt and foolish child.' He sounded angry and loving. 'What does Mackenzie say about this nonsense? I'm sure he agrees with me.'

I turned away. 'He doesn't know – and you're not to tell him. That's only fair. He kept your secret. You've got to keep mine. I couldn't bear it if he pitied me.'

'But he will have to know – he will notice –'

'He won't be around. It's over.'

'Oh, you've said that so often, but you always go back.' He didn't sound at all perturbed about that.

'This time it's final.'

'Did you send him away because of this?'

'No, he left me. He's scared his little pregnant creature might find out and drop her foal.' For a dreadful moment I thought I was going to cry, but I hung onto my anger and the moment passed.

'Ah, now I understand.' My father's voice was full of tenderness. 'Listen, my love –'

I said rapidly, 'Please don't imagine I'm heart-broken. It's just ... inconvenient. I was rather hoping he might be a tower of strength.'

It was certainly my year for surprises. A few weeks later my daughter appeared on my doorstep. I had just finished drying my hair when the bell rang and there she was. I was so astounded I couldn't speak at first.

'Hello,' she said. 'You don't mind me just turning up, do you? I wanted to surprise you.'

It was so much my own sort of behaviour. 'Well, you've certainly done that.'

'Can I come in?'

'Yes, of course.' She was even prettier than her photograph, and thinner: all traces of puppy fat had gone. I was proud of her. It was a strange feeling.

'I was just drying my hair,' I said, as I shut the front door behind her.

'It's lovely. I'm trying to grow mine, but it takes ages.'

'Yes, it does.' We stood there appraising each other. 'How did you get my address?'

'Grandfather gave it to me. I asked Granny and Grandpa first, but they said they didn't know. Granny said you'd moved so often, she'd lost track of you. You were very elusive, she said.'

I caught the whiff of a plot, though the child obviously didn't. 'I probably am, where she's concerned.'

'Don't you like her?'

'Only now and then.'

She looked relieved. 'I know what you mean. She's all right but she's a bit prickly, isn't she?'

'That's a very good description.'

Then it seemed we had run out of conversation. There was a terrific atmosphere of goodwill but an awkward silence. It was weird to look at her and remember this was the foetus I'd nearly aborted, the baby I'd given birth to with such pain, the child who'd caused what almost amounted to a nervous breakdown and whom I'd finally deserted. There she was, a thin, pretty teenager in my drawing-room, pretending not to be nervous.

'Well,' I said, 'would you like a drink – orange juice or something?' I had no idea what children of her age drank these days.

She said indignantly. 'I'm not a child. Can I have a glass of wine?'

'Why not?' I was amused. 'Red or white?'

'White, I think.'

I went into the kitchen to get the bottle and glasses. I felt very smug to be proved right: she had come to me of her own accord. Then I suddenly wondered if someone (my father) had given her a nudge.

I returned with the wine and she tasted it carefully as if copying some expert she had seen. 'It's very nice.'

'Good. Why don't you sit down?'

We both sat, facing each other, meaning well, but uneasy all the same, as we could expect to feel after so many years apart.

'I like your house,' she said, looking round. She was obviously determined to be complimentary, which I found rather charming.

'Yes, I'm pleased with it. It's small but it's all right.'

I had obviously struck a chord. She said eagerly, 'Ours is too big, that's why we can't stay there. Daddy's gone broke. Did you know?'

'Yes.'

'It's rotten luck, isn't it? We can't do anything any more – not even have a holiday – and Lisa keeps drooping about 'cos she's having a baby again.'

'Yes, I can imagine.' I felt myself warming to her indignation. 'Not much fun for you.'

'No. I don't like babies.'

'Neither do I.'

She hesitated. 'Is that why you went away when I was little?'

I liked her directness and I wasn't going to lie to her. 'Yes, partly. And partly because your father and I didn't get on.'

379

'I always wondered.' She looked relieved. 'I thought maybe I did something awful or you didn't like me.'

In spite of myself, I was moved. 'No, darling, it wasn't that. I was a bit strange in those days. I wasn't very well. It all got a bit much for me.' How about that for the understatement of all time? 'I'm sorry if you minded.' It was all I could offer her, but quite a lot, for me. I wasn't much given to apologies.

She said bravely, 'Oh, I didn't really mind, I just wondered why, that's all, I mean later. I do wish people would tell you things properly, not just keep pretending it's all right or it's something else.'

I knew just what she meant. 'Yes,' I said, 'I wish that too.'

After that, I couldn't really think what to do with her. We could hardly sit there drinking wine all afternoon. There was, of course, a lot we could have talked about, but it seemed too soon and too dangerous, as if we had already said enough for one day. It was, after all, our first conversation. So we played cards, and I studied her face. The mixture of Mack and me was potent and confusing. We won three games each, which was just as well: we were rotten losers, having an identical urge to win. But playing cards gave us a breathing-space, a chance to be together without having to talk.

When she was leaving, she suddenly turned to me on the doorstep. 'I'm sorry I ran away when you came to see me last year.'

'It doesn't matter.' But it was strange to think of the chain of events she had precipitated.

'I was younger then. I was a bit silly. Can I visit you again?'

'Yes, but ring up first.' Just what I used to tell Mack. 'I might be out.'

'All right.' She hesitated, unsure, I suppose, whether she should kiss me. 'Well, goodbye then. I've had a lovely time.'

'Goodbye.' I couldn't quite bring myself to hug her: it

seemed too soon, artificial. But watching her walk away, I felt her courage and her vulnerability and I wanted to give her a present. 'Oh, by the way,' I called after her, 'you're awfully pretty.'

She turned round; she was so pleased; she radiated joy. 'I take after you.'

I watched her out of sight, thinking that might well be true, and not just in looks. Then I went back inside, shut the door, and had a good cry. Why should this all happen now? It was much too late.

All the same, I made a point of taking my father to task about it the next time we had lunch together.

'Don't you think you're exceeding your grandfatherly duties?'

'How do you mean?'

'Putting my daughter on to me.'

He shrugged. 'She has a right to see you.'

'And I have a right to be warned she's on her way.'

'Weren't you pleased to see her?'

'Yes, I was, quite.'

'She's beautiful, isn't she?' He was watching me closely.

'Yes. I didn't know whether to be envious or gratified. It's a bit of a shock, seeing oneself when young. She's also very well-mannered. I suppose I have Lisa to thank for that.' I had to be fair. 'Can't imagine Mack exerting himself to instil any social graces.'

'She used to be very close to Lisa,' my father said thoughtfully. 'After you left, Lisa was wonderful with her – I think she really loves the child. But now with the baby coming, Adrienne is so jealous, it is all spoilt.'

'Yes, I gathered that.' It was the first time he had mentioned the new baby to me.

'That's why she needs you now.'

'Maybe she does, but do you really think it's fair to encourage her?'

'Why not? It won't take up much of your time and it could make all the difference to her.'

Well, it had to be said. 'But I may not be around very long. I'm not having that operation, I've definitely decided. I'll just go on as I am till it all gets too much and then pop a few pills. I've had a good run for my money – why be greedy? I never fancied being middle-aged anyway.'

Oh God, the look on his face. 'I can't believe you mean this.'

'Oh, it wouldn't be everyone's choice, I grant you. Most people go for "where there's life there's hope" and all that, but I've got a definite feeling the best is over for me.' If only I could make him see it was a perfectly valid point of view. 'And I've always thought you should know when to leave a party. Much better too soon than too late.'

'I can't bear to listen to you.' He looked so stricken I felt terribly guilty, but I still wanted him to understand how I felt.

'Did you send that child round to give me a sense of purpose? You did, didn't you?' Then I saw he was crying. 'Oh, that's not fair, that's blackmail.'

He said slowly, 'The whole point of having a child is for them to outlive you.'

I wanted desperately to cheer him up. 'Come off it, you didn't think of that when you were sliding into Mummy's knickers.'

'Does she know about this?'

'No.' I considered the fewer people who knew, the better; I couldn't stand any more arguments. 'But it wouldn't surprise her. She's always thought I'm deeply neurotic.'

'Kisleanyom, listen to me. My heart is not good, it can only be a few years. I beg you to wait. If you do this terrible thing, you will kill me.'

'I was hoping you might hold my hand when I do it, and tell me Hungarian fairy tales, the way you did when I was little. I had it all planned. Champagne, and everything blurred at the edges.' It seemed to me a very good way to go. The Romans ... the Japanese ... they had had the right idea. 'Wonderful.' I didn't want to live in pain or disfigured, bored and lonely; I wanted to go in style at a time of my own choosing.

He said, 'Stop it. You make me angry.'

'That's better.' I held his hand and kissed it. 'It's all right, it's not imminent. But you're tough as old boots, you might live to be ninety. You can't expect me to hang on till then.'

A few weeks later he was dead.

Losing my father made everything else that had happened to me quite unimportant. The pain was intolerable, as if I had never felt pain before. It changed my entire perspective on the world. The agency crisis, the loss of Mack, the lump in my breast – all were suddenly trivial. I could not remember why I had found such things distressing. None of them mattered at all in comparison to this. I had lost the only enduring mutual love I had ever known.

Worst of all was the feeling that I had actually caused his death by my selfish honesty. He must have worried his way into the grave because of me and my decision. It was as if I had literally broken his heart. Now that I knew what it was like to live without him, I was appalled that I had expected him to live without me.

After the funeral there was still the business of the will to be got through. I sat in the lawyer's office wearing dark glasses, because I had cried so much that my eyes had swollen till I looked like a boxer.

'Lionel, can we get this over quickly? I'd like to get home.'

'Yes, of course – as soon as Mr Mackenzie gets here. I don't know what's keeping him.' He looked at me sympathetically. 'We could have done it by post, you know.'

'It's better this way. I'd rather see you.' I found I was obsessed with formalities – something to hang on to, I suppose.

Lionel's secretary buzzed him to say that Mack had arrived and in a moment she was showing him into the room. I felt nothing. We were all non-existent people.

Lionel shook hands with him. 'Mr Mackenzie, we meet under unhappy circumstances, I'm afraid.'

'Aye.' Mackenzie turned to me. 'Diana – I'm so sorry.'

I didn't answer.

'Well, do sit down,' Lionel said. 'We can get this over in a few moments, if you're agreeable.'

'Aye. Sorry I was late, but my wife went into labour prematurely and I had to drive her to hospital.'

No wonder he looked preoccupied. I still felt nothing, but Lionel, who must have known something of our history from my father, was clearly embarrassed.

'Ah. In the midst of death we are in life, as you might say ...'

Neither of us answered.

'Well, I take it you don't want me to read the will to you. It's here if you want to refer to it. If I skip the legal formalities and give you the gist of it, will that suffice?'

I nodded. I had never liked Lionel, but my father trusted him.

'Well, to put the matter in a nutshell – it's very simple – Mr Kovacs left you, Mr Mackenzie, the sum of ten thousand pounds in recognition of your long friendship.' He looked at Mack as if he should be pleased. 'And the rest, after the various expenses and death duties have been paid, of course, to Miss Crawley.' He smiled; he obviously thought justice had been done.

If I had not reached the stage where pain turns to numbness, I might have laughed. Mack was so shocked. He was the original banana-skin casualty, or a child who sees its birthday treat whipped away from under its nose. Amazement and horror were written all over his face.

'But,' he said, 'but ... he promised ...' as if it were an unfair world and there should be some redress.

I said, 'He changed his mind.'

Afterwards I walked in the park, where my father and I had walked so often, and cried until I was exhausted. Then I went home.

In September, after Lisa's baby was born, my daughter came to see me quite often. In a way I had been expecting her, but it was as if she had been waiting for the way to be clear. We had a carefully casual relationship, very offhand yet intimate. She particularly liked watching me do my nails.

'Why can't I get mine to look like that?'

'It's only practice.'

'But you're so quick.'

I felt she deserved some instruction. 'If you do it slowly, you get brush marks. Three strokes per nail and make sure you don't touch the cuticle.'

'Why?'

'Because if it's stuck down it's going to tear as the nail grows out.'

She looked at me enviously. 'My nails never grow as long as yours, they just break.'

'They'll be better when you leave school and stop playing all those silly games. Either that or you're filing the sides too much.'

'I wish I could leave school now.' She sighed, looking at me for approval. 'It's so boring.'

'I know. I hated it too. Being herded together with a lot of other women and crammed full of useless facts is a real turnoff. The only consolation is you're getting the worst bit of your life over right at the start.'

She said eagerly, 'Really?'

'Oh yes.' Provided your father didn't die. 'Nothing is ever so bad again, once you can make your own decisions.' I poured two more glasses of wine.

'Can I stay to supper?'

'Isn't Lisa expecting you?'

'Oh, she's so busy with the baby, she doesn't notice if I'm there or not. It's funny ... she never stops moaning how much she has to do, but she won't let me help.'

'Do you really want to?'

There was a pause and she looked guilty. 'No.' Then we both laughed. 'But it's sort of insulting – as if she doesn't really trust me.'

'I don't suppose she does – but isn't that better than being slave labour?' Maybe I could get this across to her. 'Babies are jolly hard work. It's her baby – why not let her get on with it?'

'Can I stay then?'

Oh God, it had come out wrong. 'Sorry, darling. I've got someone coming.'

'A boy-friend?'

'No.'

'I've got a boy-friend.' She sounded as if she hoped I had too. 'Well, sort of.'

'Terrific.' I was really pleased she had started so soon. 'Is he nice?'

'He's all right. He's only one of the boys from the farm but he's quite good-looking.'

I saw my duty looming. 'Don't get pregnant, will you?'

'Of course not.'

'I mean enjoy yourself, but stick to what we used to call heavy petting.' How long ago it seemed. My God, another world, another life. What did it all matter now? 'D'you know what I'm talking about?'

'Mm.' She wouldn't look at me.

'If you want to go further than that – I mean if *you* want to, not merely if *he* wants to – just ring me up and I'll take you to my doctor, make sure you're safe.' There was at least *that* I could do for her. 'Have I embarrassed you?'

'No.'

I knew she was lying. 'Well, someone had to say it, and your father and Lisa won't. They'll bang on about being under age and waiting for true love. All very fine, but a lot of accidents happen that way.'

There was a long silence. Then she said, 'I wish I lived with you.'

I felt pain; I felt guilt. But there was so little time left. No more choice. No point in her getting attached to me now, even if it was mutual. 'Oh, darling, it's much more fun just to visit, don't you think? More special.'

She said as if she were much older, 'Don't you ever get lonely?'

'Yes, of course.' I had to be truthful. She deserved that. 'But living with someone doesn't cure that.'

Time was passing, though, and I had plans to make. Ruth and I had been reconciled at my father's funeral (I was impressed by the sight of David holding her while she sobbed) so I asked her round to choose souvenirs from his things. There was an awful lot to sort out, much more than I had bargained for. We stood together gazing at the suitcases on the floor full of papers, jewellery, oddments.

'Well, those are all your letters,' I said. 'In those two cases.'

'I'd no idea he'd kept them.' She sank to her knees. 'My God, they're even numbered.'

I'd been impressed by that too. 'He was always methodical.'

'But I told him to burn them. He said he had.'

'Never trust a Hungarian.' I handed her a drink, just as she started to cry. 'Oh don't, for God's sake, you'll set me off.'

She was turning the letters over as if bemused by them. 'I didn't know I'd written so many.'

'Well, it was twenty years, wasn't it?'

'Twenty-one.'

She blew her nose and I poured myself a drink. 'There's all his jewellery. Rings, watches, cuff-links. Help yourself.'

'But what about you?'

'When someone leaves you everything, you're a bit spoilt for choice.' I watched her handling his things. She touched them with such tenderness. I was glad he'd had someone like Ruth to appreciate him. 'I know he'd want you to have whatever you like. I'm sure he'd have left you something in his will if he hadn't been trying so hard to be discreet.'

She said hesitantly, 'If I could have his signet ring and the watch he wore most often ... and perhaps his favourite cuff-links. Would that be all right?'

'Have the lot if you like. Now – about his flat.'

'God, you're so brisk.'

'It's the only way I can do it. Would you like to have the flat? I can't live there, so I've either got to let it or sell it.'

'Oh no –' Poor thing, she looked years older since the funeral. But then, no doubt I did too. Not that it mattered.

'Then you'll have it?'

'I don't know.'

'I wish you would. I'd rather not go there again.' But she still looked doubtful, so I added to persuade her, 'I haven't changed anything. It's still full of his clothes, books, records. It's as if he might walk in any minute.'

'I'll have it,' she said instantly. 'Thank you. You're very generous.'

'I feel as if I killed him.' I hadn't meant to say it but it was a great relief when I did. She didn't ask what I meant, just looked as if she understood, making me wonder what my father might have said to her. Of course, in a sense she was my stepmother, though I had never thought of her like that.

It was a strange evening. We drank a lot and cried a little and talked about old times. It was comforting to be with someone who'd loved my father as much as I did. There was still the problem of what to do with her letters. She said I should burn them; she couldn't bear to read them again.

'All right. It's not long to Guy Fawkes. I'll have an erotic bonfire.'

After a long pause she said, 'It's funny . . . I never thought we'd be friends again after what you did to Lisa.'

'I didn't do anything to Lisa.'

'Come off it, you know it was your fault she had that miscarriage, after what you told her.'

'Rubbish. There was no need for her to go racing after my daughter like that – she'd have come back much sooner if nobody chased her. Lisa should just have put her feet up and told me to piss off.'

'God, you're a hard bitch.' But she didn't sound resentful any more.

'I'm honest, that's all. People can't get used to it. Anyway, Lisa's a lot tougher than you think. She can take care of herself.' I truly believed that. 'Under all that meringue there's a heart of steel. That's the secret of her success. With me it's the other way round and that's why I flopped on Broadway.'

'What *did* happen?' She sounded really curious. 'I've always wondered.'

'In New York? Oh, a few hundred men and a few thousand dollars.'

'Did Piers let you down?'

I was impressed. 'That was clever of you. Yes, he did, as a matter of fact. I thought we were partners and I worked my guts out. But I also leaned on him too much, probably. Cried on his shoulder too often.' I was trying to be fair, now that none of it mattered any more. 'Suddenly all he wanted was for me to sell out to his boy-friend at a bargain price. I thought I'd come home to lick my wounds – or get someone else to do it – and then, among other things, I found Mack didn't love me any more. Funny thing about love.' I poured more wine for us both. 'When you've got it, you suffocate, but when it's gone, you really miss it. At least, I do. This is my big year all right. This one's a winner.'

She said abruptly, 'Diana, you must have that operation. Your father told me.'

'He had no right to.'

'He was frantic, he had to talk to someone. Please. Have it done for his sake.'

'That's not fair.' Besides, what was the point? It wouldn't bring him back. But mercifully, being drunk took the edge off the whole conversation.

'God, you're so like him,' she said, staring at me. 'I keep seeing him in your face.'

She started to cry and I held her hand. I'd never imagined we could be so close again.

'You know,' she said. 'I used to envy you because he loved you best.'

'You can't compare a mistress and a daughter. He needed us both.'

'Yes, but if we'd been drowning, he'd have saved you.'

'Lucky we could both swim.'

She managed to laugh at that and got out her handkerchief. I opened another bottle, wondering why I didn't get drunk more often. It blurred the pain wonderfully.

In the morning I remembered exactly why. I felt terrible. I didn't even remember the end of the evening, what time

Ruth had gone home or how I had got to bed. I was surprised and pleased, though, to find that the habits of a lifetime had prevailed and although I had fallen asleep in my clothes, at least I had removed my make-up first. Then I remembered that of course it hardly mattered any more. Whatever state my skin might be in, I wasn't going to need it much longer.

Well, a hangover might be just the excuse I needed to make plans. People with hangovers often wished they were dead and they always resolved to have no more hangovers. I would achieve both desirable objectives. The only problem now was to choose an arbitrary date and stick to it. Not today – I felt too ill. That was a joke. But I also naturally wanted to look my best.

I got out of bed, took various hangover cures, undressed and crawled back into bed, trying to avoid touching my left breast. Working backwards, I certainly didn't want to be around on my next birthday: I was quite old enough already. It would also be best to avoid another Christmas and New Year's Eve, both gruesome festivals at best. But I wanted to go on some occasion, not any old day. Well, that didn't leave me much choice. It would have to be Bonfire Night, unless I opted for Halloween, and I didn't fancy the connotations of that. Better to go with a bang. I smiled to myself. It was only a feeble joke, but in the circumstances any joke was better than none.

I had enough pills saved up for the occasion. When the time came I would burn Ruth's letters, do my hair and face very beautifully, put on my best Janet Reger, take all the pills and drink some champagne, but not enough to make me sick. I would listen to Sinatra by candlelight and hope I was unconscious before the tape ran out. It would be an anticlimax to be left there in one's final moments in total silence. I would take the phone off the hook as well. Dreadful to be plagued by a last minute call and die wondering who on earth it might be.

But first I would make a will, leaving everything to Adrienne. She deserved it, my father would have wished it, and it would set the cat among the pigeons nicely with Mack and Lisa. Had I overlooked anything? No, I didn't think so. Better not to leave a note; it would be tedious to write and there was always the chance that everyone (except Ruth) might think it was an accident. Much nicer for them all.

I felt myself getting drowsy again. If I could sleep now, when I woke the hangover would have gone. I hoped it would be like that when the time came. I hoped I would have the courage to do as I had planned. Most of all I hoped there might be some afterlife in which I could be with my father again.

Lisa

She gave up keeping a journal that year. The thoughts that revolved in her head were too terrifying to be recorded. Judy teased her and asked if it was a New Year resolution. Lisa said she had decided that she was too old to keep a journal any more, it was an adolescent thing to do, and Judy, who still kept one, pretended to be offended. It was the first time in Lisa's life that she couldn't be entirely frank with Judy. To explain the rift with Robert would be to implicate her mother. Judy would promise secrecy till death, but sooner or later she would tell someone on the phone in greatest confidence and the news would be all round the family in no time at all. However, no one questioned her depression: losing the baby was sufficient explanation.

Judy and Rolf were newly married. Seeing their happiness made Lisa feel very old. Was it really only a few months ago that she and Robert had been as happy as that?

She worried about her father. Did he know about her mother's behaviour or not? Was he hurt or uncaring or ignorant? Did he too perhaps have a secret life? She felt as if she no longer knew her parents. So many things fell into place now: in particular her mother's hostility, out of all proportion to the age gap, and her refusal to attend the wedding. It must have seemed disgusting, even incestuous, to her. But how did her father interpret Lisa's refusal to be reconciled with her mother now?

Thinking about her parents at least stopped her thinking about Jamie. But eventually she had to think about Jamie. She had really done this terrible thing. That was why she no longer dared to keep a journal. She was as bad as her mother and Robert now. Worse. Was that why she had done it? Had she been incapable of forgiving until she needed forgiveness herself? She didn't want to believe that. If it was true, then it had been unconscious, but that didn't seem to make it any better.

Looking back, however unwillingly, she couldn't imagine what else she had expected from Jamie, and yet at the time she had convinced herself it was an innocent expedition. She arrived just as he was opening the champagne.

'Perfect timing,' he said, letting her in, bottle in hand.

She wanted to be amusing for him, not the misery she had become at home. 'I heard a bang and I thought, surely he hasn't shot himself just because I'm ten minutes late.'

He laughed, taking her parcels from her and closing the door. 'What have you brought?'

'Just a few things for the holiday.'

'What made you pick Geneva?'

'My cousin Judy lives there now – she married a Swiss banker.'

'Very nice, too – he and Dad should have plenty to talk about.'

'Oh, Robert's not coming.' There, she had said it. Was that what he wanted to know? 'But I've got to meet him later – he's driving me to the airport.'

Jamie poured champagne. 'How long will you be away?'

'I'm not sure. Three or four weeks.'

'Well, I'm glad you weren't afraid to beard the bachelor in his den.'

'Why should I be?'

'You know I'm planning to seduce you, of course.'

'Don't be silly.' And she had actually laughed, as if he didn't mean it. 'Are we eating here?' As if it wasn't obvious. The whole table was loaded with expensive cold food, carefully arranged.

'That's up to you. If you want to go out, there's a rather swish place round the corner and I can devour all this stuff for my solitary supper. I just thought you might like to put your feet up after all that shopping.'

'Yes,' she said, like an accomplice, 'I am a bit tired. I haven't done much for the last month and I didn't realize quite how I'd feel.' It was true, and yet ... there was no need to say it, to give in so easily.

He said smoothly, 'Also, you never know who you're going to run into in a restaurant. I saw Dad and Diana the other day.'

Now, was that true?

'Oh, they didn't see me,' he went on. 'They were tucked away in a corner, deep in conversation. About the brat, I suppose. Didn't Dad tell you he'd had lunch with Diana?'

'No.'

'D'you think I'm lying?'

'I'm not sure.' It was such an obvious threat that she had already imagined it.

'Well, it would be one way of trying to get you into bed.'

'Don't tease me, Jamie. I'm very low at the moment.'

'I'd never tease you, you're the love of my life. Don't you know that by now?' The matter-of-fact tone made it all the more convincing. 'Have some more champagne anyway.'

'Thank you.' She watched him refilling their glasses. She noticed he gave her rather more than himself. I shall get drunk, she thought. I've got such a weak head for drink and I didn't have any breakfast. Was that the moment when she abandoned responsibility?

'Will you tell Dad you had lunch with me?'

She hesitated. 'Yes, of course.'

'Did you tell him we'd arranged it?'

'No.'

'I wonder why not.' He moved closer.

'I don't know.'

'I think you do.'

She said faintly, 'I forgot.'

They kissed and four years were instantly wiped out.

'Oh, Lisa, I want you so much.'

'Jamie – please – I can't. It's too soon.'

'You've got to be joking. I've waited years for you.'

'No, I mean...' But he kept on kissing her and it was hard to think. 'I haven't felt like it since I lost the baby. And anyway, the doctor said I should wait at least –'

But he didn't pay any attention. And she wanted him so

much, more than she had ever wanted him before. So why did she see Robert's face when she closed her eyes? Revenge? The thought disgusted her, but it also seemed to make her more excited. She wanted Jamie. She wanted to make love. She wanted to do it all with Jamie at last and forget everything else. She wanted to be a helpless victim and have Jamie do it and do it and do it to her till she was exhausted. Jamie obliged. She found him more exciting than Robert. She felt dirty and ashamed. She wanted to feel dirty and ashamed. Just before he came she had a moment of panic, but then it was too late and he was making her come again too. He seemed to know just what she liked. She felt used and abused and it was wonderful.

She might just have persuaded herself that the first time was a kind of violation, but the second time was at her instigation, so there could be no excuse for that. She thought while he was sucking her, My God, I'm using him again, I've always used him, one way or another. And she thought, I must have gone mad, this is very dangerous.

When they were quiet, he stroked her hair and kissed her. She had only to look at him to see that he really loved her.

He said, 'Stay with me.'

She was tempted. But of course she couldn't stay with him; it was crazy. She left in a panic, damp and exhausted, late for Robert, pretending her shopping had delayed her. They had to drive fast and nearly missed the plane. Once she was safely past the barrier she had time to think. What have I done? I must be out of my mind.

And so it still seemed. An afternoon of insanity. A couple of hours of total madness. She had never felt like that before or since.

Three weeks passed. She breathed clean Swiss air, admired the scenery, talked guardedly to Judy and Rolf and tried to relax. Robert wrote and phoned. Jamie didn't: he had his pride. Besides, she had not given him her address.

Three weeks passed and she did not bleed. But of course that was only to be expected: her system had not yet returned to normal. There could be no other explanation. She began to sleep badly and sometimes she woke in the night, sweating, after terrifying dreams that she could not remember.

Robert met her at the airport. It was clearly the end of everything or else a new beginning. Adrienne was staying with Caroline, so they had the house to themselves. They went home and went straight to bed. Lisa wasn't entirely sure of her motives. Afterwards he cried and asked her to forgive him and she said they could make a fresh start.

In March the doctor confirmed her pregnancy and the bank called in Robert's loans. He was obliged to suspend dealings in his shares on the Stock Exchange. Bankruptcy seemed imminent and receivers would have to be appointed. The bank would pay him a pittance to wind up the company. Only the house was safe, because it was in Lisa's name.

Early in April she went to see her mother. Ruth opened the door while Lisa was still walking up the path. She looked radiant and tearful.

'Darling.'

'Hullo, Mummy.' She gave her flowers.

'Oh, it's so lovely to see you. I couldn't believe it when you rang up. I was beginning to think I'd never see you again.'

Inside the house they stood and looked at each other for a moment before they hugged.

'You look well,' Ruth said. 'You look wonderful.'

'I couldn't stay away any more. I've been longing to talk to you.'

'Oh, sweetheart, I've missed you so badly.'

'I've missed you too. I'm sorry. I've been horrible.'

'No, no, it was all my fault.'

They were both in tears now.

'Let's pretend it never happened,' Lisa said.

They tried to talk about the property crash, but it was too depressing and conversation kept returning to the baby.

'Of course it might be September,' Lisa said suddenly. There was no one else she could talk to. Her own crime had cancelled out Ruth's: she found she could look at her mother without remembering what Diana had said, if she tried hard.

'Darling, are you sure?'

'Well, I got in a bit of a muddle after ... the miscarriage. My doctor said I should wait at least till I get the curse so we'd all know where we were, but –'

'– but you didn't,' Ruth said cheerfully. 'Good for you. I never did either. It's so depressing, losing a baby; the only cure is to bash straight on with the next one, that's what I think.'

Lisa was startled. 'Did you lose one as well?'

'I lost two before you. You were third time lucky.'

They hugged each other again. 'We do have a lot in common,' Lisa said.

'Anyway, what does it matter, September, October? Who's counting? Robert must be so pleased.'

'Yes, he is.' Lisa thought about it for a moment. 'It's ironic, he didn't really want the last one, but this time he's over the moon.'

Ruth poured tea. 'Well, I expect he's had time to get used to the idea. Men are funny creatures. They can be a bit jealous at first. Beats me how anyone can be jealous of their own child, but they are.'

'I think he sees it as a fresh start ... after all the trouble we had.'

'Well, that's lovely, darling, just as it should be.' Outside the door the whining dog reached a peak of frustration. 'I'll have to let that animal in, do you mind? He knows you're here and he's so excited he's going to blow a fuse.'

'I'd like to see him again.'

Ruth opened the door and the dog burst in, giving Lisa an ecstatic welcome, licking all exposed areas of skin within his reach and whimpering with pleasure. It was almost too much of a good thing.

'Wow,' she said, 'hullo, there's a good boy,' as he nearly laid her flat on the sofa, 'you remember me then – all right –

calm down.' Ruth was smiling. 'Does he still get on your nerves? Because I could always take him home with me – he could be a country dog. He might like that.'

Ruth looked at him thoughtfully. 'I'm sure he would but – you know? I've got rather fond of him at long last.' She cut large slices of cake despite Lisa's protests about putting on weight.

'It's a crazy time to be having a baby, really,' Lisa said. 'I mean financially.'

'Nonsense, it'll cheer you both up.' She made it sound like going to the pictures. Lisa had to smile.

'Yes, but things are going to be awfully tight. I never realized it could get as bad as this – you always think it can't happen to you. I've told Robert we ought to sell the house but he won't hear of it. He says everything's going to be all right and I'm not to worry.' They were both busy pretending things were not as serious as each knew them to be.

'I should take his advice if I were you.' Ruth was enviably calm: after so many years in the property business, Lisa supposed, she was used to ups and downs. But bankruptcy ... receivers ... those were terrifying words. Could they really take away all Robert had worked for, or did it sound worse than it was? He put on a brave face and so did she. How could she tell if he had told her the whole truth? How could she know how worried she ought to be?

'But I want to do something to help,' she said. 'There are lots of things I could do – like teaching art ... or ... running a nursery school. And we could grow all our own fruit and veg., if we really tried, and keep chickens and...' She stopped, thinking how feeble it sounded.

Ruth said gently, 'Darling, see how you feel when you've had the baby. You must take it easy till then, don't you think? Just to be on the safe side.'

'I suppose so.' She paused, gathering her courage. 'Mummy ... you don't happen to know if Diana's still around, do you?'

'I've no idea, I'm not in touch with her.' Ruth looked

startled, then embarrassed. 'I wouldn't trust myself, after the way she behaved.'

They avoided each other's eyes. A dangerous subject, best avoided, best forgotten.

'Only I wondered,' Lisa said. 'Everything's gone so quiet. We haven't heard from her since November and she hasn't tried to contact Adrienne again.'

'That doesn't surprise me. Must have been one of her passing fancies.'

'I wondered if Robert might be seeing her.' There, she had said it. As if fears about the baby and fears about bankruptcy were not sufficient.

'Surely not.' Ruth looked shocked.

'Well, she's his great love.'

'Not any more.'

'Oh, I think she always will be, till the day she dies. I'm only second best. I accepted that when I married him. He only wanted me because he couldn't get her back.' She wondered if she was saying all this now to justify her own behaviour.

'Did he say so?'

'No, of course not, but I could feel it. I think he saw me as a kind of romantic cure. Don't look so worried. It's all right. I can live with it.'

'I don't know,' Ruth said, 'how I managed to produce a child with such a low opinion of herself.'

'It's not that at all, I'm just being realistic.'

'Are you? Then look at the facts. Robert didn't leave Jean for Diana till Diana was pregnant, right? And he didn't marry you till you were pregnant. Doesn't that prove the woman who's having his child will always be first in his life?'

Ruth's words haunted her all the way home. As she entered the house the phone was ringing.

Jamie said, 'Why didn't you tell me?'

'What?'

'Oh, come on. Don't play coy with me. It's mine, isn't it?

Is that why you wouldn't see me again, so you could pin it on the old man? Bit sneaky, don't you think?'

'You're crazy. I shall have to hang up if you go on like this.'

He actually laughed. 'Oh, Lisa, you are sweet. You sound so indignant. But all I have to do is wait. If your baby arrives in September by any chance, then your baby is my baby, isn't it?'

She began to tremble. 'Don't be so silly. Babies are early or late all the time. Everyone knows that.'

'And this one's going to be early, isn't it? Say – three weeks early?'

'Jamie, I really am going to hang up on you.' She'd known he would hear about the baby from her father but she hadn't been prepared for this conversation.

'There's no way this baby can be late, is there? We both know that. Did you tell my father about us?'

'No, of course not.' She was terrified.

'Be an awful shame if someone else did. I imagine he'd be quite upset. Still, nobody'd do a thing like that, would they? Kick a man when he's down? That's a terribly unsporting thing to do.'

'Jamie, please...' Was she really reduced to pleading with him?

'When are you going to come back to me, Lisa? You know we belong together.'

'If you felt anything for me at all, you wouldn't frighten me like this.'

'I don't like being rejected. Now that's not unreasonable, is it?'

'Look, I made a mistake and I'm sorry. That's all I can say. Please leave me alone.'

'Tell you what,' he said, brisk and cheerful as if he were doing a deal in the office. 'I'll make a bargain with you. If it's October, I leave you alone. If it's September, I come and collect you. Now I can't say fairer than that.'

She put down the phone. The nightmare had begun.

*

Adrienne was reacting to the new pregnancy with rudeness and detachment, making sharp-edged jokes and spending most of her time with her friends. Often she was hardly in the house five minutes before she went out again.

'I'm going round to Lucy's, okay?'

'What about your homework?'

'We haven't got any today.'

'Are you sure?'

Adrienne did an exaggerated Jewish shrug, which Lisa felt was more of a jibe than a joke. 'Would I tell you a lie?'

'Don't be late for supper.'

'Oh, I'm having supper there.'

'Look,' Lisa said, feeling it was time she made a stand, 'you've been out every night this week.'

'So what?' Adrienne marched briskly through the gate.

'Doesn't it occur to you your father might like to see you now and then?'

'Wouldn't you rather have him all to yourself?'

She gave up. When Adrienne had gone, she went to look at the cottage, struck by a sudden idea. At least she had more energy with this pregnancy. She examined all the rooms. It was so obvious. Why had she not thought of it before?

When Robert arrived home she waved to him from the cottage, noting how tired and anxious he looked before he saw her and brightened.

'What are you doing in here?'

'Inspecting our new house. Honestly, darling, it's the only way. What's the point of a staff cottage? We can't afford any staff. Anyway, I'd rather do everything myself, you know I would.'

He took a cursory look round but she could see his heart wasn't in it. 'Just give me time. We'll get out of this mess somehow, I promise you.'

'I know we will. And we'll start by selling the house.'

'But you love the house.'

'Of course I do, but it *is* only a house. It's madness to keep it on when we can't afford it.' She was talking as much to convince herself as him. It would be extremely painful to let go of the house. 'Must be worth a fortune by now.'

'And who's got a fortune to buy it?'

'Oh, some oil-rich Arab, I expect.'

'God, you'd love that.'

'Oh well, needs must.' She could see she was convincing him: he began to look tempted.

'But could you really stand to live here and see someone else in our house?'

They stood together at the cottage window and looked out at the house in all its rambling, expensive, wasteful splendour. Tears came to her eyes. Yet if she offered up the house, perhaps she would be spared, perhaps the baby would arrive in October and they wouldn't be destitute.

'I think so.' She made herself sound cheerful. 'At least that way I'd feel we hadn't lost it completely.'

'You're amazing.' He hugged her tight. It was rewarding to feel she had eased even a little of the burden for him.

'It's about time I did my bit for the war effort,' she said. 'I've had it easy all my life, remember?' Sometimes she felt guilty about that, too.

'We won't decide anything in a hurry.'

'It's decided already. Come and have a drink. You look awfully tired.'

'It's not easy – winding things up.'

They walked up the drive with their arms round each other. It was the nearest she had felt to peace since she returned from Geneva.

He said, 'Adrienne will hate it if we move.'

'She's so busy hating my being pregnant, moving house will be a mere detail.'

'I think we should take a firmer line with her.'

She shook her head. 'No, we've got to be gentle. Jealousy hurts a lot.' For whatever reason, she couldn't get Diana out of her mind.

By June it was impossible to keep the grim realities of life from Adrienne any longer. Lisa braced herself for a scene. Their mornings already followed an unwelcome pattern.

Adrienne came down later and later, preferring to stay in her room and play pop music very loud while Lisa cooked her breakfast.

'It's on the table,' Lisa yelled at the last possible moment. 'You're going to be late. And deaf.'

There was no reply. She sat down with her second cup of coffee and the paper. She knew she should leave Adrienne's breakfast to get cold but she couldn't bear the sight of it congealing on the plate, so she always ended up putting it in the oven on a low heat. Invariably, the moment she had done that, Adrienne would come downstairs. For such a slim, delicately built teenager she was remarkably heavy on her feet.

'You said it was on the table,' she exclaimed indignantly, staring at the empty space.

'It would have frozen over by now. I put in in the oven.'

'Thanks.' She went to fetch it. 'Ooh – the plate's hot.'

'Use a cloth.'

Then Adrienne sat and picked at her food while Lisa poured her coffee and juice.

'Aren't you having any?'

'I had breakfast with your father.'

'Why does he go to work so early if he's bankrupt? I'd have thought he could stay at home.'

Lisa hoped the coldness of Adrienne's tone indicated anxiety rather than indifference. 'He's winding up the company. There's a lot to be done.'

'I don't understand. You said we were broke.'

'Yes, we are.'

'What are we going to live on then?'

Now for it. 'We're going to sell this house and live in the cottage.'

'Oh no.' Adrienne put down her knife and fork. 'You're joking.'

'It'll be nice, you'll see.'

She pushed her plate away. 'Oh, God. I can't eat any more of this, it tastes funny.'

'There's nothing the matter with it.' Dear God, and she had always despised Mrs Deacon for having battles about food.

'You eat it then, you're eating for two, aren't you?'

'I've told you before, that's all nonsense.'

'Well, I feel sick.'

Silence. Lisa made a big effort and said gently, 'Darling, how long are you going to keep this up?'

'What?'

'Being rude and angry and hurt.'

'I'm not.' She stared at her plate.

'Look, I know you don't like me being pregnant, but Daddy and I love you just as much as ever, you're not going to lose out.'

'Can we have a summer holiday?'

'Darling, we can't afford one. And I don't want to travel like this, just in case.'

'There you are, you see.' Adrienne sounded triumphant. 'You just said I wouldn't lose out, but I *am* losing out, all the time.'

'Not on affection. That's what I meant.'

There was such a long pause that she began to hope she had won. Then it came. Spoken as a challenge.

'I'd like to see my mother again.'

In July Robert tried to borrow money from Kovacs in a last desperate attempt to save the house or buy back one of the companies. Kovacs refused. Lisa tried to be cheering, but it was uphill work.

'It's nice to have you home early.'

'Even with bad news?'

'It doesn't matter. We'll think of something else.' It nagged at her that they had not seen Kovacs since April. Had they offended him in some way? If so, what an unlucky moment. At first, she had been embarrassed with him, after she knew about her mother, but she was so used to him as Adrienne's grandfather that she had almost managed to forget his other role. 'Did he say why he couldn't help?'

Robert shook his head and leaned back in his chair, closing his eyes. He looked drained.

'I'm sorry,' Lisa said. 'You're tired. I shouldn't be asking you questions.'

'It's so humiliating.' He beat on the arm of the chair with his fist. 'I bloody crawled to him.'

'Don't think about it any more. Let me ask my father instead.'

'No, I don't want you to do that. If he sells this house for us, he'll have done more than enough.'

'But I'm sure he could lend us something.'

'Lassie, he's in enough trouble already – they're laying off people right and left. Even Jamie.'

'What? Daddy'd never sack *him*.'

'He can't afford to keep him on. There's not enough work to go round.'

So that was why she had heard no more. Jamie had problems of his own. 'Did Jamie tell you that?'

'No, I haven't seen him. Your father mentioned it the other day. But we really should ask Jamie round, you know. It's ridiculous having a feud when we're all in the same boat – and it's bloody sinking.'

'Yes, I know.' The moment was bound to come, but oh, please God, not yet. 'Only – can we leave it for a while? I don't feel up to entertaining just yet.'

Adrienne was late home. Lisa rang Karen's mother and Lucy's mother. No Adrienne. It got later and later.

Robert was pacing. 'I'm going to ring the police.'

'No – give her a bit longer.'

'But anything may have happened.'

It was only a hunch but it felt like a certainty. 'I think she's gone to see Diana. She told me she wanted to and I didn't react very well. After ... what happened last time I felt, well, it seemed an unlucky thing to do. But I was just being selfish.'

'Bloody sensible if you ask me. Anyway, she's got no right to go if you told her not to.'

She was surprised how angry he was. She tried to be fair.

'I didn't exactly tell her not to. I just said I'd rather she didn't – at least till after I've had the baby.' A pointless superstition, really, but that was how she felt.

'Same thing.'

She thought suddenly how his world had dwindled. He had lost his parents, Jean, Duncan, Diana, Kovacs, Jamie. Now she seemed all set to alienate him from Adrienne and he was still loyal. The responsibility was too much. Soon she would be all he had left. The business was going. The house would have to go. There would only be herself and the baby.

'But don't you see,' she said desperately, 'by saying that, I made it impossible for her to tell me the truth.' At that moment she heard Adrienne coming in. (Not dead in a ditch, then. Relief flooded over her.) 'Oh, thank God, there she is. Don't say anything, please.'

Adrienne strolled in, too nonchalant to be innocent. 'Hullo.'

'Bit late, aren't you?' Robert said, deceptively calm.

'We had supper late.' She took an apple from the fruit bowl and started eating it.

'Then why are you still hungry?'

'I didn't eat much. Karen's mother doesn't cook very well.'

Robert suddenly smashed his fist on the table. They both jumped. 'You're a bloody liar.'

'Have you tried her cooking?'

'Don't you get clever with me.' He was squaring up to Adrienne: he suddenly reminded Lisa of a boxer. 'You weren't at Karen's tonight and you weren't at Lucy's either. They haven't seen you since four o'clock. Now where the hell have you been? We've been worried sick.'

Lisa said, 'It's all right, darling, we won't be cross. Just tell us the truth.'

'I went to see my mother.' Adrienne sounded defiant and pleased with herself.

'After Lisa told you not to.'

Lisa tried to intervene. 'I didn't exactly –'

'Leave this to me. You knew Lisa didn't want you to go and you went.'

406

Adrienne wasn't in the least intimidated. She had, Lisa thought, inherited both her parents' temper. 'Why shouldn't I see my mother? Just because you don't like her any more, she's still my mother, isn't she? Last year Lisa said I ought to see her and I didn't want to then. Whatever I do is wrong. It's not fair. My mother's lovely. You can't stop me seeing her. I'll see her whenever I like. She said I could go any time, so there.' She burst into tears and rushed upstairs to her room.

Ruth had been away at the cottage. When she came to see Lisa in August, she took one look at her and said, 'My goodness, are you sure it's not twins?'

'Quite sure.'

'Well, you've certainly put on a lot of weight since I saw you last.'

'Yes, I know.' That was all she needed to hear after seeing her doctor yesterday.

Ruth looked at her anxiously. 'Are you all right, darling? You look a bit down.'

'I'm worried about the house. We haven't had any offers yet and loads of people have seen it.'

'August's always a bad time for property, even when the market's normal. What does Daddy say about it?'

'Not to panic and not to drop the price just yet.'

'Well, he knows what he's talking about.'

'Mm.' It was too dreadful to contemplate, having made the sacrifice of putting the house up for sale, that no one might want to buy it or they might have to let it go for less than its value. And whatever they got for it, it was worth more to her. 'Shall I get you a drink?'

'You stay where you are. I'll get us both one. What would you like?'

'Just lemonade. There's a big jug in the fridge.'

'How lovely,' Ruth said cheerfully. 'I think I'll put some gin in mine.' She went indoors. Lisa lay back in her deck-chair and tried to relax. Ruth returned presently with two tall glasses clinking with ice. 'Where's that horrible child?'

'Oh, Mummy, don't.'

'Sorry. I only meant – are we going to have the garden to ourselves for a change, or will she suddenly leap out of the bushes?'

'She's down in Sussex with Caroline.'

'How sensible of you to pack her off.'

'We didn't – she asked to go. She's very fed up with us at the moment.' It was sad to admit defeat after being close to Adrienne for so many years. Could she ever repair the damage?

'You've spoilt her, you know,' Ruth said. 'That's the trouble.'

'She was perfectly all right before I was pregnant.'

'Well, you're not going to be pregnant much longer, so I'd better get on with this.' Ruth took her knitting out of her handbag.

'Don't be silly, you've got plenty of time.'

'About three weeks, from the look of you, and I knit very slowly.'

'Oh, don't say that, please.'

'Darling, I'm sorry, I'll try to speed up.'

'No, about three weeks. It can't be as soon as that.' If her mother agreed with the doctor, there was no hope at all.

'Believe me. So it's Virgo instead of Libra. Never mind.'

Sheer terror made Lisa make a sudden decision. 'Mummy, you've got to promise me something. If – if the baby comes in September you must tell everyone it's early.'

'Why? You've been married a year now, anyway, nearly – besides, people knew about the miscarriage.'

'Please, Mummy. Promise me. You must tell ... Robert it's early. My doctor will. She gave me her word.' And what an embarrassing interview that had been.

'Lisa, what *is* this? You said from the beginning it might be September.'

'Not to Robert. Only to you.' She felt trapped, everything closing in. 'Oh, Mummy, I'm so frightened. I wasn't going to tell you, but I feel as if I'm going mad. Last December – I went to bed with Jamie. It was only once but I was still upset about losing the baby and – what Diana said. Then I went on holiday. Robert and I didn't make love after the miscarriage till I got home in January. I didn't get the curse at all. I don't know when I got pregnant but I've been praying ...' She started to cry. Ruth got up and hugged her. 'I can't believe I can be so unlucky.' That, even more than guilt, was her strongest emotion. The unfairness of it all. She sobbed in Ruth's arms.

'Hush, it's all right, darling, you mustn't upset yourself. Look, I'm not an expert. Maybe it *will* be October.'

'No, you're right. I know you are. It's going to be September. I can feel it.'

'So it's early.'

'Oh, thank you.' She stopped crying, out of sheer relief.

'I mean it. Genuinely early. It's much more likely to be Robert's than Jamie's, isn't it? I mean if you think about it logically. Statistics are on your side.'

But Lisa was beyond logic and statistics. 'I just have this terrible feeling.'

'Darling, listen. Which one d'you love?'

'Robert.'

'Then it's Robert's. Just keep telling yourself that. In the end you'll believe it.'

'Even if it's not true?'

'It will be true.' She gripped Lisa's hands tightly. 'We've all made mistakes, God knows. I'm not going to let you punish yourself for this one.'

She was so calm that Lisa began to see a glimmer of hope. She put some more objections quickly, to test the glimmer. 'But I'm so bad at lying.'

'You won't have to. I'll do it for you.'

'But if it's normal weight ...'

'You were nine pounds. If you'd been early, you'd still have been normal weight.'

There was still the ultimate threat to be considered. 'Jamie said – if it was September, he'd come and take me away.'

'Oh, now that's ridiculous. You wouldn't go, would you?'

'No, of course I wouldn't go. But he might tell Robert. He really hates him, you know. He's never forgiven him for leaving Jean, and he blames him for Duncan's death, and for not giving him a job when he wanted one – and most of all for marrying me. He's got a lot of grudges and I've given him the perfect way to get his revenge. God, how could I have been so stupid?'

'He doesn't mean it. He just enjoys tormenting you. I've always thought he was a nasty piece of work.'

'I think he does mean it.' But even as she spoke, Jamie began to shrink and recede. It was amazing how Ruth managed to defuse him. He ceased to be demonic and became merely tiresome.

'He can't prove it,' Ruth said. 'That's all that matters. If the worst comes to the worst, and I'm sure it won't, you'll just have to lie. It's easy. He'll be telling Robert a spiteful piece of wishful thinking, that's all.'

Lisa allowed herself to be comforted. She wanted so much to believe Ruth was right. And it was such a relief to have shared her secret.

The rest of August passed peacefully enough. Perhaps her hormones were taking over. Perhaps it was the absence of Adrienne, reducing stress. Perhaps their financial worries really were drawing her and Robert closer together. She felt like a large, contented vegetable. She was sure Robert had no suspicions. They discussed October and argued about names.

In September Adrienne returned for the new term, but she was very subdued. Lisa suspected that a month with Caroline had worn her out and she was glad to be home, though she wouldn't admit it. Lisa wondered how much she had seen of Diana. It was sad to find that Adrienne's mere presence made her uneasy. She didn't know how to cure that. It was difficult, too, to go on talking about next month when she felt she might go into labour in a matter of days.

One night when they were about to go to bed, the phone rang. It was too late to be good news: Lisa had a sudden premonition. Robert listened intently and looked shocked, made a few exclamations of regret and hung up. 'It's Kovacs. He's dead. Apparently they just found him sitting in an armchair at his club. It must have been another heart attack.'

'My poor mother.' What a heavy blow after all these

years. Would she break down? Would David comfort or reject her? Lisa didn't know what to think. She pitied them both.

'Aye, it's a terrible shock.'

'Oh, darling, I'm so sorry. We'll really miss him, all of us.' She was surprised how sad she felt on her own account. And it was yet another piece of bad news to be broken to Adrienne.

'But don't you see,' Robert said, 'with a bit of luck, this might save our skins.'

She was shocked. 'Oh, how can you say that?'

'I'm sorry, lassie, I'm desperate.'

She was too pregnant to attend the funeral, which was a relief. She hated funerals, and besides, Diana would be there. She couldn't have faced Diana. To compensate for her lucky escape she spent a lot of time on the phone trying to console her mother. But Ruth wept constantly and didn't seem to hear what she said. Lisa thought, Well, if my father didn't know before, he certainly knows now. But he sounded calm when she spoke to him. She began to think it must be a good omen. If her parents' marriage could survive all that, then she and Robert would be all right too. Jamie couldn't harm them.

She went into labour on the day that Robert had to see Kovacs' lawyer about the will. Diana would be there too, but she chose not to think about that. She had enough to do, concentrating on her breathing and making sure Robert didn't panic. He drove her to the hospital and wanted to stay with her, but she made him keep the appointment with the lawyer, saying she would be ages yet and it was better for him to have something to do. Then she surprised herself and everyone else by having a very short labour. It was extremely painful but over so quickly that she felt she could hardly complain. They put the blood-stained child on her belly. A girl. With all the right fingers and toes. Susan then, not Samuel. She felt a mixture of exhaustion and triumph. She didn't, at that moment, think of Robert or Jamie;

merely, my daughter. Mine. Now I have a child of my own. When Robert came to see her and the child, she said, 'Everything's going to be all right, isn't it?' Even hearing that Kovacs had left almost everything to Diana did not disturb her.

Her stay in hospital was idyllic and she wished it could have lasted longer. She thought she must be the most appreciative patient they had ever had. She felt safe, warm and protected, the recipient of flowers, fruit and congratulations from visitors who were obliged to be nice to her and to go away before she was tired. She was living in a controlled environment and it was wonderful. She was probably the only new mother not longing to go home. Anything could happen there: it was a dangerous place.

And she was right to be apprehensive. As soon as she went home all her old worries crowded in. She lived in terror of a phone call from Jamie. She tried to convince herself that living a lie with Robert and the baby was morally justifiable, or at least that the alternative was worse. She attempted to cope with Adrienne, who was jealous of the baby, grieving for Kovacs and truanting from school to visit Diana. Such anxieties did not make for peaceful breast-feeding and within a few weeks she was exhausted. Then they got an offer for the house, but a low one, and it was up to her to decide.

'You're late,' she snapped at Adrienne when she strolled in that evening about seven.

'That's right. And you've taken to drink.' She eyed Lisa's glass of wine with disapproval. 'Won't it curdle the milk?'

'I don't know why you bother putting on that uniform when you hardly ever turn up at school.' She heard herself nagging, knew it was wrong, but couldn't stop.

'Oh, they rang you again, did they?'

'I was worried. Where've you been all day?'

'With Mummy, of course.'

'But you can see her at weekends.' Useless, of course: weekends were permitted and therefore no fun.

'I just felt like it. Fridays are a waste of time at school, anyway.' Adrienne thumped her way upstairs. In a moment her latest record was blasting down the stairs. Lisa got up and went to the door.

'Adrienne, please turn that down – you'll wake Susie.' She had only just got the baby to bed.

The noise stopped abruptly. Adrienne yelled back with what sounded like real hatred. 'Oh, you mean my music wakes her, but your shouting doesn't.'

Lisa didn't answer. She thought, I deserved that, I am handling the whole thing badly. But she had run out of energy. She poured herself another glass of wine. Presently Adrienne came pounding back down the stairs. She had changed into a dress. She poked her head round the door and gave Lisa a cheery wave.

'I won't be late back.'

'Where are you going?'

'There's a village hop. It might be better than nothing. I told you but you never listen.'

That was a lie. Or could it possibly be true? Oh, God. 'Adrienne, we've got to have a talk.'

'Oh, by the way. Mummy asked me if I'd like to live with her.' She stared at Lisa with malicious satisfaction. 'I said I'd think it over, but it's probably more fun to visit.' And off she went, slamming the front door.

Lisa lay back on the sofa and closed her eyes. She thought it most unlikely that Diana could want a noisy, truculent fourteen-year-old to live with her, and yet, maybe she did. You never could tell with Diana. She might have suggested it just to be provocative. Was it perhaps even a pity Adrienne had decided not to go? Life would certainly be more restful without her. A disloyal thought: she pushed it away. In any case, Robert would presumably refuse to let her go. Poor Robert. He was late again; she was always sad when he missed the baby's bedtime. How hot it was now. She had put too many logs on the fire. In a few moments she was asleep. When she woke it was to the sound of a car drawing up outside. She went to the window and saw Robert walking up the path with Jamie.

*

Supper-time. They had managed to get through the pre-dinner drinks, the polite inquiries, the anecdotes about Jamie's new job as a used car salesman, and now they were eating Lisa's stew and drinking Jamie's champagne. Or rather the two men were eating and drinking. Lisa could hardly swallow. She was remembering the last time she had shared champagne with Jamie. And Robert was so pathetically grateful to see him again, gazing at his son with pride and affection as if they had never quarrelled, hanging on his every word.

'So you might be back in business soon,' Jamie was saying. 'That's great news.'

'Aye, if I can get the bank to agree a reasonable price for the construction company.'

'I knew they wouldn't keep you down for long.' He sounded exactly like the devoted son. Lisa was terrified. She felt she was sitting next to a time bomb.

'Of course it's all up to Lisa, really, it's her money,' Robert said cheerfully, referring to the house sale.

'What fun. How does it feel to hold the purse strings, Lisa?'

She wouldn't look at him. 'I don't think of it like that. When you're married, you share everything.'

'Well, we've certainly got a lot to celebrate.' Jamie was radiating goodwill in the most alarming way. He refilled their glasses like a host – or a member of the family. 'A new house, a new business, a new baby. Can I propose a toast?'

Lisa said, 'We've only just had the offer. There's nothing definite yet.'

'The baby's definite enough.' Jamie raised his glass. 'To Susie.'

They were both watching her. Lisa raised her glass reluctantly.

'Susie.' Robert looked so happy.

'Don't I get to see her?' Jamie asked.

Lisa said, 'She's asleep.' But, as if on cue, sounds of crying began upstairs.

'Not any more.' Robert got up. 'I'll fetch her down, shall I? She'll be wanting her next feed.'

'I can hardly do that down here,' Lisa said sharply.

Jamie smiled. 'I'll make myself scarce.'

'No, I meant you can just have a quick look at her.' Robert went out, eager to show the baby off. Lisa wanted to scream: Don't bring her near Jamie. Don't leave me alone with him.

The silence between her and Jamie seemed endless. Finally she said, 'I'd like you to go as soon as possible.'

'I can't do that. My father might be hurt. We don't want that, do we? Not now – when he's so pleased to have me back in the fold.'

She looked him straight in the eyes for the first time that evening. She saw no sign of mercy. She thought: If I had a weapon I really might injure him. I understand now how people get themselves killed. Murderers aren't full of hate. It's terror.

Robert returned with the child in his arms, wrapped in a shawl. He was so delighted with her. 'Here we are. Isn't she bonny?'

'She certainly is.' Jamie looked at Susie with alarming interest. 'I don't usually reckon babies much, but this one's special. She's really got the family face, hasn't she?'

Robert looked gratified. 'David and Ruth think she looks like Lisa.'

'Oh no,' Jamie said. 'She's a Mackenzie all right.'

The phone rang in the other room. Robert gave the baby to Lisa and went to answer it.

Jamie said, 'She's mine, isn't she?'

'No.'

'You're a rotten liar. And I can do my sums, even if the old man can't.'

Robert came back. 'It's your father, lassie. He was wondering what you thought of the offer.'

'Tell him I'll probably accept it but I'll ring him tomorrow.' It was twelve thousand pounds below the asking price but the only offer they had had.

'D'you not want a word with him?'

'No, not now. Give him my love.'

'All right. I'll tell him you've got your hands full.' He smiled at them both, kissed Susie and went out.

Jamie said, 'I promised I'd come back for you.'

When he had gone Robert said, 'You didn't mind me bringing him home, did you?'

'No, of course not.'

'Only – he obviously wanted to patch things up at long last. It's the least I could do, to meet him half-way. He's had a raw deal.'

She wanted to fight Jamie but she couldn't, so she fought Robert instead. 'Perhaps. But you shouldn't let him make you feel guilty. Adrienne's had a raw deal too, but you don't feel guilty about her.'

'I've always done my best for her. But I let Jamie down very badly.'

The front door crashed. Adrienne strolled in, looking dishevelled and pleased with herself.

'Hullo,' Robert said. 'I was just coming to fetch you.'

'Well, I've saved you the trouble.'

'You didn't walk home alone, did you?'

'No. Alan brought me.'

Lisa said, 'Oh good. He's a nice boy.' She wanted to offer Adrienne approval of some sort to make up for their earlier conversation.

Adrienne shrugged. 'He's all right. Night.' And she went up to bed.

Robert looked dubious. 'Are we giving her enough supervision?'

'Short of locking her up.'

'What's the matter?'

'Nothing.'

'You sound so angry.'

'I'm just tired. Coping with Susie and coping with Adrienne just about wears me out.'

He came and sat beside her. 'I'm sorry. You really didn't

want Jamie here, did you? D'you think he's still in love with you? Is that it?'

He was so direct. It frightened her. She made an effort to keep her voice steady. 'No, of course not. I don't think he ever was – not really. Not the way we are.'

'Then why can't you make him welcome? It means such a lot to me.'

'Yes, I know.' Trapped and doubly trapped.

'Please don't spoil it. I felt really great tonight. It all seemed to be going right for a change. Getting an offer on the house and making things up with Jamie all in one day – that must be a good omen.' He held her hand. 'It's an awful thing to have a feud with your own son, especially when you know it's your fault. It's like a judgement on you. But tonight I felt we'd really turned the corner. Only none of it means anything if you're not happy.'

She put her arms round him and he hugged her. She hung on very tight. Keep calm and lie. Her mother would lie. The doctor would lie. Keep calm. Jamie's just playing cat and mouse. It may never come to the crunch. But if it does . . .

'Of course I'm happy,' she said.

They decided to accept the offer for the house, after trying and failing to bargain. It went against the grain, but they had very little choice. It was a cash sale, to Americans, who wanted completion by Christmas. Lisa argued that it was worth losing the twelve thousand pounds to have peace of mind, and the ten thousand pounds from Kovacs' will would almost make up the difference. To her it seemed a generous bequest, but to Robert, who had once stood to share Kovacs' fortune equally with Diana, it was derisory, almost an insult.

As the winding-up process went on, the bank began to relent. They agreed to get an independent estimate for the construction company and offer Robert first refusal. If he could buy that back, he would be able to start again in a small way. David advised them to transfer the mortgage from the house to the cottage, so that Lisa's profits from the sale would be free to invest in the new business. Lisa wondered how much to hold back to pay the mortgage and survive. Robert was full of optimism again, now that there were practical possibilities in view, but they had no way of knowing how long it would be before they had an actual income again. The idea of living on capital terrified her. One day it would run out and then what?

She might have been more worried about money had she not been so worried about Jamie. After his visit she expected repercussions almost hourly: she trembled and rehearsed her lies like an actress with stage fright. She consulted Ruth, who declared herself convinced that Jamie was merely bluffing. It was an obscene game he was playing, to frighten Lisa. He did not seriously intend to tell his father anything. Lisa wondered how Ruth could be so sure. Ruth merely argued that no one, even Jamie, could actually take such a revenge on his own father, no matter how much he hated him. Lisa wished there were some more positive factor to inhibit Jamie, such as sudden death.

But days passed and weeks passed and it began to look as if Ruth was right. There was total silence from Jamie. Lisa started to relax. For the past month she had been so tense that she felt as if she had forgotten to breathe properly. She tried to detach her mind from Jamie, lest even thinking about him might impel him to act; she concentrated instead upon Adrienne, who seemed to be running wild. Lisa remembered her own meek, chaperoned self at fourteen and wondered what Adrienne might be doing with Alan, or any of the other village boys for that matter. Rows with Robert seemed to make no impression. She simply went on coming home late and saying, more often than not, that she had been with Diana, which might well be a lie, since she knew both Robert and Lisa would hesitate to check up. Lisa dreaded to think how Robert would react if Adrienne (God forbid) were to get pregnant. She tried to talk to Adrienne about virginity and heard herself sounding like Ruth, so she switched to the fact that Adrienne was under age. Adrienne merely laughed. It's only bravado, Lisa told herself, they don't really *do* anything much at fourteen, but she wasn't sure any more. The ten years that separated her from Adrienne already seemed like a generation gap.

On Bonfire Night Adrienne went to a fireworks party in the village, which sounded innocent enough. Lisa was alone in the house with Susie, because Robert was dining with David and Ruth. It was tacitly agreed between them that she still preferred not to see him and Ruth together; besides, he had a lot of business to discuss with David. Lisa thanked God every day of her life that whatever her father might know about Kovacs, he knew nothing of her mother and Robert. At least she presumed so: it was impossible to imagine he could have behaved so naturally with Robert all these years if it were otherwise. She hoped the day would come when she could forget it had ever happened, and then she reminded herself that she had no cause for complaint: her own secret was worse.

When Susie was asleep, Lisa had supper on a tray in front of the fire. She wondered guiltily if she and Robert were somehow silently urging Adrienne to go out because the house was so much more peaceful without her. The house. She would have to settle her mind to losing it. They had exchanged contracts already and would be in the cottage by Christmas. She looked round the room she had furnished with so much love and attention: only a few more weeks to enjoy it. Outside, fireworks exploded spasmodically and there was the glow of a bonfire across the fields.

Suddenly the doorbell rang. She went to answer it, expecting to see one of Adrienne's friends.

It was Jamie. He must have parked in the road and walked up the drive to surprise her.

'Your father's not in,' she said, stupid with shock, the first thing that entered her head.

'What a bit of luck.'

'And I've nothing to say to you.'

'Don't worry, I'll do all the talking.' He pushed past her into the house, reminding her oddly, just for a moment, of Diana. She followed him into the drawing-room. 'When are you expecting him?'

'In about half an hour.'

'Perfect. That gives you time to pack. I've come to fetch you and Susie. I said I would.'

To her surprise she was calmer than she had been when she played the scene in her head. She felt as if her brain were packed with ice. 'You're mad.'

'Where's the brat?'

'At a bonfire party.'

'Great. So we're alone – apart from our daughter asleep upstairs.'

The thing was, she must not panic. If she could get through this and win, she'd be safe for ever. 'I've told you before – she's not yours.'

'The dates fit.'

'She was early.'

'Four weeks early? An amazing coincidence.' He gave her a positively indulgent smile. 'D'you know what gives you away? Apart from looking guilty, I mean. You're too positive. If you were being honest, you'd have to admit you aren't sure whose she is, but the odds are she's mine. However, you're so certain she's my father's child ... you just have to be lying.'

His confidence unnerved her. He was proceeding so smoothly, pre-programmed, like a robot.

'Please go away. Please leave me alone.'

'I don't think it's fair to my father, you know. You really shouldn't go on deceiving him like this.'

'I made one mistake and I've suffered for it every day.' Surely the truth could move him.

'Rather a large mistake. With far-reaching consequences.'

'I love your father very much.'

He poured himself a drink; he seemed very relaxed. 'I wonder if he'd believe that, if he knew about us. I've been very patient, Lisa. But it's time you made a decision. Come away with me now and we won't mention last December, we won't *confuse* him about the baby. We'll just pretend it all started here and now, all nice and clean.'

She had accused him of being mad; now she wondered if he really might be. 'Come away with you? I don't even *like* you any more, the way you're behaving.'

'Never mind, a little hostility can be quite exciting. And I like you enough for both of us.'

'That's rubbish. If you did, you couldn't possibly treat me like this.'

'My father stole you from me. Now I'm claiming you back. That's all there is to it.'

His arrogance made her angry. 'I'm not a parcel, Jamie. I do have a choice.'

'I doubt if you'll have much choice after I tell my father the truth. I don't think he'll want you any more. Or *my* daughter.'

'I don't believe you'll tell him.'

'You just watch me.' He sat on the sofa, crossed his legs and leaned back, drink in hand. He regarded her almost benevolently. 'You're wasting time. You could have been packed and away by now, left him a note. It's much kinder that way. You can always send for the rest of your stuff later on.'

'You can't mean all this.' She was pacing up and down like Robert. 'It's like a dreadful joke.'

'Come on, you know me better than that.'

'What would you have done if he'd been here when you arrived?'

'Told him the truth.'

Suddenly she believed him. He couldn't have known whether Robert was in or out. Mad or sane, he really meant to do this terrible thing and she had only about twenty minutes to talk him out of it.

'I warned you I'm tired of waiting,' he said. 'And I've given you long enough to think it over. It's action time.' He grinned. 'That's why I picked tonight. Thought I'd let off a few fireworks of my own.'

Would it help to reason with him? 'Jamie, look. This feud with your father, it's nothing to do with me really. It all goes back to your mother and Diana and poor little Duncan. I know your father behaved badly, but it's so long ago. If your mother could forgive him, why can't you?'

He sipped his drink. 'You're still wasting time.'

'But this can't possibly work. You won't tell him anything

421

when it comes to the point.' If only she were convinced of that. 'And if you do, I'll deny it. He's bound to believe me, not you.' She was saying the lines Ruth had prepared for her, but they did not sound right.

'I wouldn't be too sure about that. I'm a much better liar than you – and besides, I've got a huge advantage this time – I'll be telling the truth.'

'I really think you're mad.' She glanced at her watch. 'Suppose he does throw me out – please God he won't – how can we ever live together? I'm going to hate you for what you've done. Can't you see that?'

He put down his empty glass. Suddenly he looked human, real, suffering. 'I used to love my father, I really did. He was like a hero to me. Then he walked out. He'd found a woman he liked better than my mother. The hell with my brother and me. The new woman's brat was all that mattered. But of course he couldn't be blamed. He was in love. He couldn't help himself.'

Lisa said faintly, 'I don't think anyone said that.' He had never talked so much about his feelings before, even when they were teenagers together and supposed to be in love. She felt his pain; she was alarmed by her own flood of compassion.

'How would you know? You were ten years old at the time, tucked up at home with two cosy parents. You didn't have to listen to your mother crying herself to sleep every night. No one ever walked out on you.'

The depth of his bitterness shocked her. 'You sound as if you hate me.'

'And you didn't have a brother who killed himself either, did you? And you didn't have a father who wouldn't give you a job because he reckoned you weren't good enough. All my life I've had to watch my father doing exactly as he pleased and getting away with it. And I might have gone on watching and doing nothing if he hadn't picked on you.' He paused, staring at her. He went on more gently, 'I've never loved anyone but you, Lisa,' and she knew it was true. 'It's not easy for me to love people, but I love you very much.

And the day my father took you away from me, I promised him I'd get even. Don't you remember?'

She wanted to deal with his feelings, poor hurt Jamie, she wanted to comfort him, to beg his forgiveness for the way she had used him, but the threats were more immediate. She had to deal with the threats. There was no time for the feelings.

'Jamie, please. That's not love.' She heard a car draw up outside. 'You don't love me at all, you just want to hurt him. Please don't.' Now she heard the front door open and close. 'I'm begging you. You'll hurt yourself as well.'

Robert came in, full of goodwill, delighted by the surprise visit. He poured himself a drink and offered Jamie one.

'No, thanks, I must be on my way. I only called in because I was in the neighbourhood.'

Was it possible he was going to let her off and simply go? Of course, now it came to the point, he couldn't do it, or he had never meant to. She had been a fool to take him seriously.

'It's good to see you,' Robert said.

'I'm welcome then, am I? You don't mind me being alone with Lisa?'

'Should I?'

No, he was not going to let her off.

'You must know I'm still in love with her.'

Robert said calmly, 'I thought you might be.'

'But you trust me, do you?'

'I trust Lisa.'

Lisa said, 'Jamie, for God's sake –'

Jamie paused like an actor, making sure he had the audience's attention. 'Then why don't you ask her what happened last December. The seventeenth, to be exact. The day she went away on holiday. The day she came to my flat.'

'Lisa?' Robert looked rather more puzzled than suspicious even now. 'Did you go to his flat?'

'We had lunch.' Her mouth was dry with fear; she could hardly speak.

'And then we went to bed.'

She said, 'No –'

'I wasn't going to tell you,' Jamie went on. 'But I don't think it's fair to let you bring up my child as your own.'

Robert was staring at her. She couldn't meet his eyes. She said, 'He's lying,' as she had promised herself she would, but it didn't sound convincing. What use were words, in any case, when she could feel guilt and misery all over her face for Robert to see?

'She got out of my bed,' Jamie went on as if he had rehearsed it, 'and let you drive her to the airport. She was carrying my child on that holiday, and when she came back she got together with you pretty fast and pretended it was yours. That's why it was early. Didn't you ever wonder?'

With no warning at all, with amazing force and agility, Robert sprang at him. They grappled together and a terrible fight began. Lisa screamed. They were fighting as if they meant to kill each other. They stumbled against furniture, smashing lamps and glasses, breathing heavily, grunting with effort. Jamie's nose was bleeding. There was a cut above Robert's left eye and the eye seemed to be swelling and closing as blood dripped into it. She didn't know how to stop them; she backed away as they lurched round the room, attacking each other with almost professional savagery. She was horrified, and yet with part of her mind she noticed that they looked comic and grotesque as well as terrifying.

Suddenly the baby started to cry and the telephone rang. The two men went on fighting, crashing into the coffee-table. Lisa didn't know what to do first. She picked up the phone out of habit. It was Adrienne: sobbing, hysterical, incoherent.

'Darling, what is it? Calm down, I can hardly hear you – look – hang on – just a minute.' She was suddenly very angry. She had lived in terror for months and now the worst had happened. She didn't have to dread it any more. Instead she had another crisis on her hands. It was almost a relief. She covered the mouthpiece and shouted at Jamie and Robert, 'For God's sake, stop it. What the hell d'you think it proves? I've got Adrienne on the phone. She's in London. Something's happened to Diana.'

They stopped, panting, and the room was abruptly quiet. She listened to Adrienne repeating, 'It's Mummy. She's taken some pills and I can't wake her up.'

'Darling, don't panic. When you put the phone down, ring 999 and ask for an ambulance, okay? Tell me where you are.'

Adrienne said, 'I'm so frightened.'

'I know, darling, but you mustn't panic. I'll ring them as well, all right? Adrienne, are you there?' She heard a faint sob. 'Okay, now listen.' Both men were watching her, not moving. 'Daddy'll be there as soon as he can. Ring me back when you've rung the ambulance and we'll talk. Don't move her. Just put a blanket over her.'

Adrienne said again, 'She won't wake up.'

'Try to keep calm, darling, please. I'm sure she'll be okay. All right, sweetheart? Ring the ambulance now.' She put down the phone. 'Diana's taken an overdose.'

Robert said, 'Oh, Christ.' He grabbed his car keys and ran from the house, blood still dripping down his face. Jamie took out a handkerchief and began to attend to his injuries while she rang for an ambulance.

He said, 'Lisa? I'm sorry.'

'My baby's crying.' And she went upstairs to Susie.

She expected him to go but when she came back with the screaming baby he was still there. He had finished mopping up and was pouring drinks for them both.

She said, 'God, you look a mess.' She felt tough and angry and exhausted.

He said with oddly social interest in his voice, 'Is Diana going to die?'

'How should I know?' She watched him swallowing the whisky and pouring more. Everything about him enraged her. 'Well, are you satisfied? Have you done enough damage for one evening?'

'I'm sorry. I really am.'

What could he possibly mean by that? He had done what

he set out to do. It had all been entirely predictable, apart from Diana. So how could he now regret it? She looked down at the crying child. 'She's hungry. I'll have to feed her.' Still he didn't move. 'Well? What are you waiting for?' Then, as he went on standing there, looking at her, she suddenly shrieked at him, 'Get out of my house. I hate you. Get out. Get out.'

But he wouldn't go. He said she might need him and she shouldn't be alone because she was in a state of shock. She wondered if he had some mad idea that she might yet go away with him. She went back upstairs, fed Susie and changed her and persuaded her back to sleep. The events of the evening revolved in her head. When she returned to the drawing-room, Jamie was still there. She ignored him and drank brandy because she needed it; she was too tired to be angry any more. Then the phone rang again. She thought it must be Adrienne or Robert, with news of Diana. But it was a strange voice, asking for Mrs Mackenzie, telling her there was bad news. She listened and suddenly she was grateful that Jamie was with her.

She said, 'You can drive me to the hospital. Your father's had an accident.'

It was the worst night of her life. The thought tormented her: if Robert died, she would never know if he forgave her, if he forgave Jamie. They would have to live with that for the rest of their lives. And Adrienne would never see her father again, because she was at another hospital, waiting for news of Diana, and they could not trace her in time.

She rang her parents and they came to share the vigil with her. Ruth took one look at Jamie and knew what had happened. Only Susie, warm and replete, slept through the whole ordeal until Ruth took her home.

By the time Robert was out of danger, Diana was dead. Jamie went home to sleep: he looked pale and stricken, as if he had got more, much more, than he bargained for. Lisa was left to cope with Adrienne, who was distraught. It was difficult to piece the story together; Adrienne wept for hours at a time, till she was exhausted, then she slept. When she woke, the whole cycle of weeping began again.

Lisa found out she had gone to London after the bonfire party on the back of some boy's motorbike. She had never met him before; he was part of a gang who had gate-crashed the party and started a fight. Every detail that Lisa elicited brought on a fresh burst of tears as she relived the evening. They had run out of petrol and money, so phoned Diana, hoping to borrow from her or stay at her house. The phone was engaged, so Adrienne assumed her mother was in. They went round to the house and found it in darkness: the boy picked the lock. When they saw Diana was unconscious, the boy ran away.

Lisa thought as she listened, what an alarming story it was, how in other times she would have reacted violently to it, how easily Adrienne could have been raped or murdered or involved in an accident or an arrest. Yet as things stood, she could not even be angry with Adrienne for putting herself in such danger. Diana's death and Robert's injuries made everything else seem trivial.

She spent most of each day with Robert. Adrienne came only once: it upset her too much and the doctor recommended rest and sedation. Lisa was relieved; she preferred to be alone. Sitting beside his bed she thanked God he was still alive and she found it soothing to reflect what a long road they had travelled. Perhaps there was still hope. He could not have been spared in order to reject her. Or was that to be her ultimate punishment?

Jamie had visited his father while he was in a coma, but once he was conscious, Robert refused to see him. Lisa wondered if he remembered anything. They had already had a few sketchy conversations, but Robert slept so much, she had the impression that even his waking moments were dream-like and easily erased.

One day, however, she found him much improved and very inquisitive, as if he had arrived back from a long journey and was anxious for news of home. Her relief was mixed with apprehension.

He asked first about Diana.

'I'm sorry. She died in hospital. They did everything they could.' So she had been right to think he did not remember. Or had he blocked it out because it was too painful? 'I tried to tell you before, but I don't think you took it in.'

'How long have I been here?'

'Nearly a week.'

Silence. She looked at the familiar landscape of bandages, the bed-clothes over their wire cage.

He said, 'God, why did she do it?'

She was shocked to find she could still be jealous: she was actually glad Diana was dead. But she tried to be calm and explain what had happened.

'Mummy says she was ill. She had a tumour and she couldn't face the operation. Then after her father died she got very depressed.'

'I can't believe I'll never see her again.' He wept.

It was hard to be patient, to be fair, but she managed it. She let him cry for a while, then she held his hand. Even his hand was cut and bruised from the accident. 'I know. She didn't leave a note, so we're not sure … They recorded an open verdict at the inquest. It may have been a mistake.'

'Diana didn't make mistakes.'

Except for you, she thought. You and Adrienne were the big mistakes of her life. She waited for him to ask her about the funeral, but he didn't. His eyes closed again and she began to tiptoe away.

'Lisa …'

'Yes, darling?'

'Don't go. I like to know you're there, even if I'm too tired to look at you. I canna seem to keep my eyes open. What did I do? I must have been driving like a maniac.'

She sat down again beside him. 'You had a very bad accident but you're going to be all right. You'll just have to take it easy for the next few months.'

'God … I canna remember anything after I got in the car. I canna feel my legs.' Sudden panic. 'I'm not paralysed, am I? You must tell me.'

'No, of course not. It's just going to take a while. You'll have to be patient.'

Silence. She suddenly knew this was it.

'Lisa ... about what Jamie said. I do remember that.'

Now for it. 'Can you forgive me?'

'Then it's true.'

'I wish to God it wasn't.' It had been too much to hope for, that he might have forgotten the whole thing. 'I'd do anything to change it.'

'I was so proud of Susie,' he said, as if she had died.

'I don't know how to explain. I think I went a little mad after losing the baby. I kept thinking about what Diana had said. I kept seeing you and Mummy together in my head. It was awful. I don't know why I went to Jamie, only I was angry with you and I wanted someone to comfort me. It was such terribly bad luck getting pregnant. I wouldn't have hurt you like that for the world. I should have had an abortion, I suppose, but I just couldn't, so I kept telling myself it might be yours after all. I was so frightened. I wanted it to be yours so much.'

He said like a child asking for a bedtime story, 'I wish we could pretend.'

'Can't we? I know I've let you down terribly but I don't love Jamie, I don't even like him.'

'But she's his. How can we live with that?'

Silence. She waited for his verdict.

'I canna blame you,' he said eventually. 'After you lost the baby, I went back to Diana. In spite of everything she'd done.'

So that haunted feeling she'd tried to quell at the time had been justified. But he did not sound repentant at all, merely stating a fact.

'How long did it last?'

'A few months. I left her when I knew you were pregnant again.'

'I wasn't sure but I thought you might be with her.'

'We've both got a lot to forgive, haven't we?'

Silence. She tried to believe that the scales were balanced

equally but she couldn't. When they spoke, they both spoke at once.

'Please don't leave me.'

'D'you want me to stay?'

When she got home in Ruth's car, Jamie was waiting outside the gate.

'How is he?'

'What are you doing here?'

'Your mother wouldn't let me in.'

'I asked her not to.' She made to open the gate but he stood in front of it.

'How's Dad? I've got a right to know.'

'He's got multiple fractures of the pelvis and both legs. I told you that. The hospital told you.'

'But how *is* he?'

'Improving.'

'Can I see him?'

'No. He doesn't want to see you.'

He began to seem quite frantic. 'But I want to tell him how sorry I am. I mean it.'

'I'll give him a message.'

'Will he ever walk again?'

'Yes, of course.'

'Are you sure?'

'It's just going to take time, that's all.'

He gave her an odd look, almost as if he knew about her new jealousy of Diana. 'My mother wants to come and see him. She's very upset.'

'Not yet, Jamie. I'm tired. Wait till he's home and we'll talk about it.'

'I still love you, Lisa. I always will.'

'Please get out of my way.'

'Are you going to be able to stand living with a cripple?'

The word shocked her. 'He won't be a cripple.' Were the hospital telling her the truth?

'I'm going to wait for you, Lisa.'

'Then you'll have a long wait.' She pushed past him and he let her go: evidently he had made his point.

'I don't think so,' he said, very positive. 'We belong together. And my mother belongs with my father. It's very simple.'

She walked up the drive and felt him watching her. Inside, all was peace and sanity. A different world. Why did Jamie disturb her so much? There was nothing more he could do to her.

Ruth was sitting with the baby. She looked up as Lisa came in. 'Sweetheart – you look exhausted.'

'Yes, I am.' Lisa sat down and fussed over Susie. It was reassuring to see her again, as if she had been in danger. 'Was she good?'

'Fine. No trouble at all.'

'And Adrienne?'

'Still in her bedroom. I've never heard anyone cry so much. She wouldn't let me in.'

'She's going to make herself ill.' And she probably wasn't taking the pills her doctor had prescribed. 'I'll go up presently.'

'Have a drink first.'

'No, I don't want one. I wish I could sleep for a week, that's all.' She closed her eyes.

'How was Robert today?'

'Better, I think. We had a talk. At long last.'

Ruth said eagerly, 'Is it going to be all right?'

'As far as I can tell. We're going to try. We both want it to work. Oh, Mummy. I just don't know any more.'

She started to cry. Ruth hugged her. 'You're just tired, sweetheart.' She stroked Lisa's hair. 'I heard from the lawyer. Diana left everything to Adrienne, in trust till she's eighteen. Everything Diana's father left her. That means a very great deal.'

'My God.' Lisa was shocked. 'But she's only a child.'

'Yes. It's going to make problems, I'm afraid. Diana appointed me to be executor, would you believe?'

Suddenly it was all too much. 'I can't take any more right now, I really can't. There seems no end to Diana. I'm sorry, Mummy, you've been wonderful.'

Ruth got up. 'I'll be off now, darling. Ring me.'

'I don't want to drive you away, truly.'

'No, I've got things to do. When do they think Robert can come home?'

'In five or six weeks, all being well.'

'In time for the move, then.'

'Just about.'

Ruth kissed her. 'Don't worry, sweetheart. Try taking a day at a time.'

'Yes, I've been doing that.' She hesitated. 'If Jamie's still there, could you get rid of him please?'

Ruth brightened. 'Leave it to me. It'll be a pleasure.'

Lisa watched from the window. Ruth and Jamie had a few moments conversation and then he drove off. Lisa felt relief, yet an odd pang of loss. Ruth waved triumphantly and got into her car; Susie woke up and started to cry. Lisa picked her up. The small warm body was comforting.

'Oh, Susie.' Suddenly everything was perilous and uncertain and the two of them were adrift together. 'What are we going to do then, hm?'

It looked as if they would have a white Christmas. The countryside was thick and pretty with snow, like an advertisement.

Packing up had almost defeated Lisa. There was so much rubbish. In the end she made a bonfire in the garden and heaped as much as possible on to it. After a moment's doubt, she even included her old diaries. What was she keeping them for, when everything was geared to a fresh start? She kept looking at the cottage and wondering, trying to see them all there, all four of them, living happily ever after. But the smoke from the bonfire obscured her vision. And she was so cold, even in her sheepskin jacket, that she had to keep going inside to thaw out.

Robert sat in his wheelchair by the fire. He looked gloomy. The baby was beside him, asleep in the carry-cot. Lisa came in from the garden and the bonfire, determinedly cheerful.

'It's freezing out there, but it's so pretty I don't mind. Hope the snow lasts for Christmas.'

He didn't answer. Since he came home he had been very difficult, moody and withdrawn. She tried to make allowances – he was exhausted, depressed, worried – it was a big upheaval for him. But she felt like that, too, and she would have liked a little more support.

She climbed the step-ladder and began taking down the curtains. They were moving the very next day and there was still a lot to be done and no one to help her: Ruth was nursing David through a bad bout of flu.

Robert said suddenly, 'I hate leaving this house. We were happy here.'

'We'll be happy in the cottage, too. It's a new start.'

Susie started to cry. Lisa, poised at the top of the step-ladder, waited for Robert to do something. He was so near, he had only to reach out a hand.

He didn't move. He went on staring into the fire. Lisa came down the ladder, picked up the baby and soothed her. But she was resentful.

'How long are you going to ignore her?'

'You can't expect miracles.'

'But it's not her fault –'

The phone rang.

'If that's Jamie,' Robert said, 'I don't want to speak to him.'

'Neither do I.' Jamie had rung every day since the accident. She wasn't sure what he hoped to achieve.

But it wasn't Jamie this time; it was Jean.

'For you,' Lisa said. 'It's Jean.'

Robert wheeled himself briskly across the room to take the call. Lisa went to stand by the window. She heard him being very bright. He was never so cheerful to her. 'Hello, Jean, how are you? Aye, it's great to be home ... Och, the worst is over now, I'll be up and about in no time at all ... Did you tell your mother I'd had an accident? That should give her a good laugh ... Aye, there's nothing to worry about, I'm as right as rain ... the same to you. Take care of yourself, hen.'

He hung up. Lisa was still staring at the red heart of the bonfire, the dwindling smoke, the small snowy shape of the

433

cottage in the distance. She had the sensation of being be-
sieged.

Robert wheeled himself over to her. She thought: if you
can't accept my child, this isn't going to work. Then she
pushed the thought away. It was too soon, much too soon, to
make judgments like that.

He said, 'I'm sorry, Lisa. It's going to take time, that's
all.'

She held out her hand. After a moment, he took it.

Jean

With prayer and practice, the equanimity she had forced upon herself became a reality. Her father died and she solved the problem of her mother by becoming matron of an old people's home in which her mother could live as happily as her nature permitted. It was near enough to the cottage for Jean to commute, so that she could spend her off-duty time alone. Even after searching her conscience, she could not believe that God expected her to give up her own home, or live with her mother.

She wasn't surprised that her father had died first. Worn out by a lifetime of service, she thought. She was surprised how much she missed him, though. As soon as he was dead, her mother stopped complaining about him, and conversation focused upon how different and wonderful life would be if only he were alive.

She ceased to speculate about Diana. There were no rumours to feed her imagination: Ruth was no longer in touch with Diana, as she still blamed her for Lisa's miscarriage, although Lisa was expecting another baby in the autumn and she and her mother were on good terms again. Besides, it seemed self-indulgent to dwell on the subject when there were more practical problems. Jamie had lost his job, a casualty of the property recession, and Robbie's business empire had crashed. Although she read the papers and tried to understand what was going on, Jean was astonished that such huge disasters could occur so suddenly, as it seemed to her. It was only a few years since Robbie had gone public amid such rejoicing and ballyhoo; since Jamie had rented an expensive flat in confident expectation of his rosy future as an estate agent. To think of them both in financial distress was amazing to her.

She tried to salvage something from the wreck by attempting to persuade Jamie to get a job in Scotland. She was convinced it would be good for him to be far away from Lisa. But within a few weeks of being declared redundant at Isaacs, he told her he had become a second-hand car salesman in London and was full of stories about huge profits and the gullibility of the general public. She wasn't sure she approved of this new career. But perhaps she didn't know enough about it and it really wasn't much different from the property business. At least Jamie was cheerful again. He seldom mentioned Lisa but seemed undisturbed by her pregnancy. Jean hoped he had a new girl-friend. She even hoped he might get married.

Lisa's baby was born in September. It was a girl. Jean caught herself thinking, at least no one else gave him sons. Then she quashed the thought. It was unworthy. And she should not be thinking of him at all. She tried instead to concentrate on Ruth, whose lover had died. Ruth seemed inconsolable, sobbing down the phone, and writing long letters about how he had said he regretted not asking her to live with him. Jean didn't know what to say. Apparently David was being wonderful, attending the funeral, holding Ruth's hand while she cried, sitting up with her night after night. Jean didn't understand either of them, but she thought they were very lucky to be still together.

Then it seemed as if at least one of her prayers had been answered. Jamie and his father were reconciled. The rift had hurt her very much; she thought financial problems almost unimportant compared to a family feud. She felt cheerful and light-hearted when Jamie arrived for his regular autumn visit. On average he got up to see her about once in three months, which seemed reasonable. She had an open invitation to visit him in London but seldom took him up on it. A hostile environment. She was better off staying in her own safe space.

'You're looking well, Jamie,' she said when he picked her up from the nursing home. She was carrying flowers and they were driving first to Duncan's grave.

'That's more than I can say for you.'

'Thanks a lot.'

'What are they doing to you in that place?'

'I'm working hard – that's all.'

'I always knew you were a masochist, but this is ridiculous. Matron of an old people's home. You're off your head.'

He was driving too fast as usual. He made her nervous.

'They needed someone and I'd had enough of the hospital. Besides, after my father died, it did at least give me somewhere to put my mother. She can't manage on her own, and this way I can keep an eye on her without having her to live with me.' She still thought it sounded bad, but it was the truth. 'I couldn't stand that.'

'Oh, I suppose there's method in your madness.'

He sounded so unconcerned that she said sharply, 'You might have come to the funeral.'

'Yes, I might. But we weren't exactly close.'

'Do you never do anything you don't want to do?'

He laughed. 'It's against my religion.'

At the grave they had what was becoming their usual familiar conversation, only each time it was a little more sharp-edged.

'It looks very tidy. D'you come here all the time?'

'Once a week. It's all I can manage.'

'Shame on you. I thought at least you'd come every day.'

That was so near the truth that she felt herself starting to blush. She finished doing the flowers and knelt down to say a quick prayer. He always managed to make her feel uncomfortable when he watched her praying.

'What's that going to do for him, poor little sod?'

'Jamie, I don't want to quarrel with you, but you try my patience –'

'I know, but think about the living for a change. It's too late for Duncan, and that old woman in the nursing home is a real pain, she'd be better off dead –'

She got up. 'Now look here –' It struck her that there was a pattern to their meeings: she looked forward to seeing him and then he riled her. It was sad.

'However, there is something you could do for my father.'

She looked at him, catching a new, triumphant, even sinister tone of voice.

'Hold his hand when he finds out his new daughter is really his grandchild. Oh, and yours too, of course.'

The silence went on much too long. Eventually he had break it himself.

'Well, aren't you going to congratulate me? I'm not joking.'

She said faintly, 'No. I can see that.' Suddenly it all made sense. Terrible sense.

He perched on a gravestone and said briskly, 'I'm going to take Lisa away pretty soon and I think Dad might be lonely. Diana's brat seems to be growing up fast. Now if you just happened to turn up at the right moment, you'd be in with a chance.'

She was suddenly very angry. What right had he to do these dreadful things and then come up here and try to destroy all her hard-won tranquillity? 'What makes you think I want to be?'

'Well, you're not doing yourself much good up here, are you? Have you got a man?'

She was silent.

'No, I didn't think you had. Dad and the Catholic Church have just about ruined your life between them. But fear not. Jamie is here to put it all right.'

She gathered up her things. Could he really shatter her fragile peace so easily? She felt sick: she was frightened. She had made sacrifices and endured. Didn't he realize what it had cost her?

She said, 'I'm ashamed of you, Jamie. You've done a wicked thing and I'd rather you hadn't told me.'

'But you're tempted, all the same.' He sounded smug; he stared at her. 'Well – aren't you?'

After that, she tried to keep very calm. When he had gone, she sat alone, telling herself that none of it mattered, it made no difference. It was Jamie's sin and his responsibility. Perhaps Lisa would not go with him. She had always seemed very decent. Perhaps it was not even true.

438

But if it was, what a terrible cross for Robbie to bear. What an awful retribution. In all these years, Jamie had never forgiven. It shocked her deeply that anyone, especially her own son, could be so implacable. What a cruel revenge.

Robbie would need comfort, if it were true. But no, that was not the way to think. It probably wasn't true, and if it were, it was no longer anything to do with her.

November the fifth also happened to be the birthday of Robbie's mother, and Jean paid her customary visit. They had a pleasant enough evening discussing Marie and Ella and Margaret, and the various grandchildren. Annie was of the opinion that losing his money would do Robbie nothing but good. She had met Lisa once or twice, and liked her well enough, but Jean had the impression that she had never really connected with her as Robbie's wife. It was as if she had exhausted her role as mother-in-law with Jean and Diana, and could not really tune in to anyone else. Or else she felt Robbie's behaviour had finally exceeded all reasonable bounds. She did not seem to concentrate on him as she once had: it was as if he were out of focus for her. She did not appear unduly excited about the new baby, either, but rather more interested in Andy's retirement. Jean felt more like an old friend than a former daughter-in-law on these visits.

When she got back to the nursing home it was after midnight. She was tired, but soothed and refreshed, as always by Annie's company, and ready for bed. She made the routine check of her desk for messages and found one to ring Jamie urgently. She was alarmed. She had not heard from him for some weeks and hoped that meant the whole business of Lisa and the child had died down. Now what?

She had trouble getting through: at first the phone was engaged and then it misrouted and she got a very surprised and bad-tempered stranger. When she finally reached Jamie, he was hysterical. He had told his father everything and they had had the most dreadful fight, as if they wanted to kill each other. In the middle of this there had been a phone call about Diana, who had apparently taken an overdose. Robbie had rushed from the house and set off for London in the car. He had crashed.

'It's all my fault,' Jamie kept repeating, sobbing down the phone. 'It's all my fault.'

Within a few hours they knew that Robbie would live. Within a few days they also knew that his injuries would keep him in hospital for several weeks. There would then have to be a prolonged convalescence at home. He had multiple fractures of the pelvis and both legs, and would have to learn to walk again, like a child.

Jean debated what she should do. She sent flowers and messages of sympathy to the hospital and to Lisa, but that did not seem to be enough. Yet she was scared of intruding. She longed to see him; she forgave him everything. To her own surprise she found herself thinking sympathetically of his grief for Diana. She thought it would be harder for him to bear the fact of her death than his own injuries. She thought of all the times she had wished Diana dead, with real passion, meaning it, not as something you say in a rage but with shaming sincerity, which she had forced herself to repent in the confessional and do penance for. And now Diana *was* dead. She felt no satisfaction at all. It was such a terrible thing, to take your own life. She had a Mass said for Diana's soul. Perhaps God would be merciful. Perhaps Diana had been sorry at the last moment. She had no religion, poor Diana: she couldn't have known what she was doing.

As Robbie began to recover, Jamie talked less about guilt and remorse and more about Lisa and the baby. He didn't believe that Robbie would accept the baby. He thought that Lisa would find nursing an invalid a considerable strain. He made it sound as if Robbie would be ill indefinitely. Jean was worried. She wanted to visit Robbie, but Jamie said Lisa would not welcome a visit. Not yet, he added, as if he knew something she didn't.

Jean tried to give cheerful bulletins to Robbie's mother, who saw the whole thing as a judgment on him and said as much. Jean was shocked by this stern attitude. She didn't understand how any mother could say that about her own son. It made a coolness between them.

At Christmas she could bear it no longer and rang the house. Lisa answered. It was five years since she had spoken to Lisa. She didn't know how to regard her: as Robbie's wife or Jamie's mistress. She didn't know how she ought to feel about her. Was Lisa a friend or an enemy? Would she go or stay?

'Hullo,' Lisa said.

'It's Jean. I hope you don't mind ...'

'Oh, hullo. No, of course I don't. Just a minute.'

Silence. Jean waited. Her heart began to thump. What was she doing? Then Robbie came on the line. It was five years since she had spoken to him, too.

'Hullo, Jean, how are you?'

He sounded just the same. It hurt her to picture him in a wheelchair. Tears came to her eyes.

'I'm fine,' she said. 'You must be glad to be home.'

'Aye, it's great.'

She swallowed hard. 'You've had a bad time. I'm sorry.'

'Och, the worst is over now. I'll be up and about in no time at all.'

'I hope so.' How determined and vigorous he sounded. As if he hadn't changed at all. 'I really do, Robbie.'

'Did you tell your mother I'd had an accident? That should give her a good laugh.'

'Trust you to think of that.' Tears ran down her face. 'Get better soon,' she said. 'I'm worried about you.' And I should be with you, she thought.

'There's nothing to worry about. I'm right as rain.'

'Happy Christmas, then.'

'The same to you. Take care of yourself, hen.'

He hung up. She put down the phone carefully, wiped her

eyes, poured herself a strong drink. After a while she felt calmer. Anything might happen: life was so unexpected. That much had already been proved. And he had sounded pleased to hear from her. Was it so wrong to hope?

More about Penguins
and Pelicans

For further information about books available from
Penguins please write to Dept EP, Penguin Books
Ltd, Harmondsworth, Middlesex UB7 0DA.

In the U.S.A.: For a complete list of books available
from Penguins in the United States write to Dept
CS, Penguin Books, 625 Madison Avenue, New
York, New York 10022.

In Canada: For a complete list of books available
from Penguins in Canada write to Penguin Books
Canada Ltd, 2801 John Street, Markham, Ontario
L3R 1B4.

In Australia: For a complete list of books available
from Penguins in Australia write to the Marketing
Department, Penguin Books Australia Ltd,
P.O. Box 257, Ringwood, Victoria, 3134.

Recently published in Penguins

BIRDY
William Wharton

One of the most extraordinary and affecting novels
to be published for decades, *Birdy* has electrified the
critics on both sides of the Atlantic. Out of a young
boy's need to escape and his consuming obsession
with birds and flight, William Wharton has spun a
story dazzlingly shot through with humour, wisdom,
tenderness, tragedy and longing.

'Wonderful' – Doris Lessing
'Wharton is exceptionally gifted' – John Fowles
'Will become a classic' – Patrick White

SCHULTZ
J. P. Donleavy

Schultz, Sigmund Franz, Impressario producer of
flops in London's West End. He's a walking or
sometimes chauffeur-driven and often boot-propelled
disaster area. Which disasters are often indulgently
plotted by his aristocratic partners, His Amazing
Grace Basil Nectarine and the languid Binky.
But more frequently caused by Schultz's desperate
need to seduce as many beautiful women as is
humanly possible – and then more.

THE 400
Stephen Sheppard

'Looking at the Bank of England that night, George
had become quiet and calm. His American voice
spoke softly – "We'll take her," he said.' So begins
an adventure so daring, a scheme so breathtakingly
elegant, a fraud so cheekily flamboyant that it defies
the imagination . . . Stephen Sheppard's international
bestseller, set in 1872 in London, Rio de Janeiro and
Europe, is as full of verve and dash as his characters
– four rascals you'll never forget.

'Could rival Forsyth' – *Now!*
'Blockbusting' – *Sunday Express*

Andrea Newman in Penguins

A BOUQUET OF BARBED WIRE

Peter Eliot Manson is in love – with his own
daughter. Confused, he hides behind a guilty affair
with his secretary. Within a few short summer
months a whole family is turned inside out.
A Bouquet of Barbed Wire gains the tense momentum
of a thriller as convoluted relationships lead to
tragedy.

ANOTHER BOUQUET . . .

Prue is dead, but Gavin and Manson cannot let her
go. Her presence lingers in the tangled relationships
of the people who knew her. And the shifting
aftermath of Prue's death takes a new, tragic course.

THREE INTO TWO WON'T GO

Andrea Newman turns the eternal triangle on its head.
The angles are not all equal, three into two won't
go – and somebody has to lose.

ALEXA

In answer to a call for help from her friend Christine,
Alexa arrives in the household, only to tangle with
the husband Paul . . .

Andrea Newman in Penguins

AN EVIL STREAK

Alexander Kyle, a sardonic and perverse academic, is engaged in the translation of Chaucer's *Troilus and Criseyde*. Whether his motives are evil or merely frivolous, his attempt to play Pandarus in masterminding and corrupting his niece's love life becomes an obsession.

'Its readability has an uncommon hold, and the narrative brings unexpected bends, dips and heights ... The book itself glows with inner balance. Buy it! – *The Times*

THE CAGE

Locked in a cage – in a flat, with a baby and husband. Was that what Val wanted from life? Was that what 'happily ever after' meant? Of course not. She had to escape, she could escape. The question was not how, but when?

A SHARE OF THE WORLD

Andrea Newman's first novel is a devastating account of student life in the early 'sixties.

'Makes a candid, sexy addition to the Robbins Report' – *Punch*

MIRAGE

Jane's marriage with Dino was a dream fulfilled. But like all dreams, this one turned to sand ... she had exchanged a perfect mirage for empty desert.

Recent books by women writers in Penguins

WOOLWORTH MADONNA

Elizabeth Troop

'She was very ordinary, a sort of Woolworth
madonna, there must be millions like her.' Elizabeth
Troop's heroine is more than that though. Faced with
the demolition of her house, the slow sliding of hopes
and dreams into middle age, the onset of high-rise
living and flabby flesh, she still remains a force to
be reckoned with – a force that is truly and
unbeatably feminine and unforgettable.

'A rare discovery' – *New Statesman*

ADJACENT LIVES

Ellen Schwamm

Tender, truthful, obsessional, the story of a love
affair that is different. Ellen Schwamm's magnificent
and poignant novel dissects the anatomy of sexual
love and moral scruple in a truly modern novel
that is humorous, wry, and tenderly affectionate.

'Exquisitely rendered' – *Guardian*

THE UNMADE BED

Françoise Sagan

'My novel, *The Unmade Bed*, is only the story of love
between a man and a woman. It has neither a sad
nor a happy end.' With sophisticated insight
Françoise Sagan plots the tempestuous course of an
affair between a young playwright and a ravishingly
beautiful actress.

'From the oldest story in the world, Sagan produces
a "big" novel full of irony and tenderness. It may be
her best book' – *Le Monde*